Driven to Distraction

"Barrett—we need to kiss!"

"Kiss what?" he asked. Stacy sure seemed to know how to fake a relationship on the spur of the moment.

"Each other, silly. On the lips."

Oh.

Stacy continued, "We have to kiss each other later at the canned-food party. Just one kiss ought to do it. But it has to be a good one. Nita's going to be the judge, but everyone'll know if we're just pretending."

Barrett was desperate for their scheme to succeed, so asked, "What is the criterion for a good kiss? Duration? Amount of movement?"

She looked exasperated. "You can't judge a kiss on those terms. What determines a good kiss is chemistry. It's how great you feel, how totally lost in the moment you are." She paused, searching for the right description. "It's...it's the swoon factor."

Now, Barrett had been a scientist for a long time, and he'd heard many theories on many subjects, and though the thought of kissing Stacy *was* heating his Bunsen burner, he couldn't help but ask, *"The swoon factor?"*

For more, turn to page 9

Winging It

"I was here first!" "No, you weren't, I was!"

The shrill female voices echoing down the hallway brought Mackenzie to a dead stop. "Now, ladies, let's be rational about this," a familiar voice pleaded. Mackenzie realized there was no way she could avoid the quarrelsome trio. She pretended to ignore them as she searched for her keys.

A buxom blonde was facing off with a leggy redhead, and blocking the doorway like a sentry on duty was Alec, his hair damp and his bare chest glistening from his interrupted shower. Mackenzie's eyes dropped to the towel he was clutching tightly around his waist, then back to the panicked look on his handsome face.

"Ladies," Alec lied confidently, "I really appreciate your thoughtfulness, but I already have a date tonight. Right, Mackenzie?"

Oh no, you don't, not this time, Mackenzie decided. "Gee, Alec, our date's for tomorrow, remember?" She sent him a sweet smile just as Alec lost his grip on the towel.

Mackenzie gasped and quickly scurried into her condo. She stood listening to the voices, and tried to convince herself the incredible specimen of manhood she had just seen hadn't affected her in the least.

For more, turn to page 197

HARLEQUIN DUETS

ISBN 0-373-44148-7

Copyright in the collection:
Copyright © 2002 by Harlequin Books S.A.

The publisher acknowledges the copyright holders
of the individual works as follows:

DRIVEN TO DISTRACTION
Copyright © 2002 by Tina Wainscott

WINGING IT
Copyright © 2002 by Candace Viers

This edition published by arrangement with Harlequin Books S.A.

® and TM are trademarks of the publisher. Trademarks indicated with ® are registered in the United States Patent and Trademark Office, the Canadian Trade Marks Office and in other countries.

Visit us at www.eHarlequin.com

Printed in U.S.A.

Driven to Distraction

Tina Wainscott

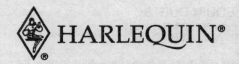

HARLEQUIN®

TORONTO • NEW YORK • LONDON
AMSTERDAM • PARIS • SYDNEY • HAMBURG
STOCKHOLM • ATHENS • TOKYO • MILAN • MADRID
PRAGUE • WARSAW • BUDAPEST • AUCKLAND

Dear Reader,

That's right...take one woman who's given up on
ever finding romance—she's going straight for the
baby. Take one guy who's a little too smart for his
own good—he thinks romance is a study in science.
And factor in a group of nosy busybodies who believe
they know best—they'll go to any length to make
things work their way. Add an ugly dog, a lovesick
maintenance guy, plenty of good intentions, and what
you have is a wacky story of plans gone totally awry.
Isn't it just right that when you think you've finally
figured out what you really want, life throws you a
curveball?

I hope you enjoy *Driven to Distraction!*

Tina Wainscott

Books by Tina Wainscott

HARLEQUIN DUETS
34—THE WRONG MR. RIGHT
54—DAN ALL OVER AGAIN

This book is dedicated to the gals (and guy)
of the Southwest Florida Romance Writers.
May we always celebrate with chocolate and whine....

It's also dedicated to my workout class
in my second home of North Carolina.
Despite "Moon River" and the battle hymns,
you all are the greatest.
Thanks for welcoming me in with open arms.

1

THE WOMAN NEXT DOOR was driving Barrett Wheeler to distraction, and he hadn't even seen her. This was not a good thing since he had exactly seven days, one hour and four minutes to complete his research study for a grant on the mating habits and preservation of tree snails for the University of Miami. The university would then take the data and approach the government with a plan to preserve these important inhabitants of the Everglades.

He'd trudged through the swamps of Everglades National Park for a year, sure that he had finally found what he'd been seeking the last twelve years—the life goal his father had been haranguing him about since he'd graduated high school when he was fifteen. He was sure biology was what he should have gotten into in the first place. That's where he belonged. But that's what he'd thought when he'd undertaken course work in physics and mathematics, too. Now, though, he had his PhD and was satisfied with that. He was. He only needed to figure out what field of biology interested him and stick to it. Instead, he kept choosing different kinds of projects, hoping to find the one field that grabbed his interest permanently.

He did care about the plight of the endangered tree snail, and he always gave his all to whatever project he was working on. He was proud to be part of the effort to preserve the dwindling tree snails. Even if his mind was already wandering to the endangered seahorses. Or maybe survival aspects of the big cats in Africa.

Maybe he just didn't know what he wanted. He was ashamed to admit it, even to himself. He started a project with all kinds of interest and lost some of that steam along the way.

It wasn't his mental meanderings that were hindering his progress on the tree snail study. First, there had been a mistake made on the due date of the study. Barrett had three weeks less than he'd planned on to complete his study. Then his sister, Kim, had shown up at his condominium with her husband and four kids needing a place to stay after the pipes in their house burst. That crisis was averted by a colleague's offer. Since his parents were going on a cruise, Barrett could stay at their house in Sunset City, a retirement community. It sounded perfect. He'd stick to himself and complete his study with nothing but the occasional call of "Bingo!" to disturb the quiet.

At least in theory.

Sunset City wasn't exactly what he'd envisioned. It was, in fact, a small city, with a grid layout lined with cozy homes and quaint yards. A large community center and pool were situated in the middle of the city, and toward the front entrance was a small store and gas station. Instead of being a quiet, restful place, it bustled with activity. When he'd pulled in evening before last, he was nearly run down by a pack of women wearing T-shirts with bright pink flamingos who were doing a remarkably good imitation of a power walk. Instead of rocking chairs on the porches of the small, neat homes, there were three-wheeled bicycles and even a Harley. A yoga class was doing their moves in the park, striking storklike poses to Chubby Checker tunes. Three men were dismantling a classic Mustang's engine under a covered driveway.

Well, the sign had said Older Persons Community, not a word about retirement. Still, no one should bother him here.

At least in theory.

Normally, his theories were sound. What he hadn't factored in was the woman next door. Yesterday, he took his files and laptop computer onto the back porch after his morning jog to enjoy the gorgeous fall weather. Maybe reward himself with a dip in the small pool in the backyard if he were particularly productive. The yard was small and private, surrounded by thick, tall hedges. He settled in to work, fingers poised above the keyboard.

That's when her voice had floated through the hedge that separated their yards. He couldn't see into her yard to verify, but she had to be an older person. Yet her voice had a young, provocative sound to it. He didn't know why it had caught his attention. He usually immersed himself in a project and didn't come up for hours. He was utterly embarrassed at the stirrings in his body. Come on, it was a *voice,* for Pete's sake!

He had tried to ignore her when she called to her husband. Then she crooned about how handsome he was despite the fact that he apparently drooled a bit. But Barrett got completely off track when she said, "Would you stop licking me, Frankie? I swear you've got the biggest tongue I've ever seen."

Mental images like that he did not need. He'd gone inside.

Early that evening he'd taken a break and eaten his TV dinner on the porch. Again, her voice floated through the hedge. "George, did you fart again? Holy stink bombs, honey, no more beef Stroganoff for you! I don't care how much you beg. And I know how much you love to beg."

George? Wasn't she with Frankie earlier? Was he staying next to a senior citizen floozy? For a moment, he actually felt a spark of curiosity, an urge to peek through that hole in the hedge and see who this woman was. But that kind of nosy curiosity was impractical, at least outside his research. It didn't serve much purpose in the real world.

Not that he could claim to be part of the real world in any sense. He'd been raised by his father, the man from whom he'd inherited his one-hundred-eighty-five IQ. His mother had gotten bored with her scientist husband and his scientist friends and even having a son who was smarter than she was by the time he was twelve. So she'd taken his sister, Kim, and moved to West Palm Beach. Barrett and his father moved onto the university campus and, at fifteen, Barrett entered University of Miami's program. Because he was years younger than his peers, he felt more comfortable hanging out with his father's contemporaries. Even now, professors and other research scientists were the people he related to best.

"Aw, do you love me? I love you, too," she crooned, and Barrett thought he heard an answering groan. "Give me some sugar." She'd giggled, a sound that sent a trill through his stomach. Then she'd squealed. "That tickles!"

He'd gone inside.

This morning she was with Buddy. He hadn't said much, but the woman was rambling on as though they were old friends. "You're one big boy. Oh, you want your butt scratched, do you?"

He'd almost gone inside then. The words, "Oh, you like that, don't you? Mmm," stopped him. He tried to put an older woman's face to the voice, but couldn't.

"Oh, goodie, sit on me, why don't you?" She made a grunting sound, as though trying to shove the guy off.

"Get off me, already! Geez, you weigh a ton!" After sounds of a struggle, she said, "Stop pawing me, you animal!"

It wasn't his curiosity that finally propelled him to that hole in the hedge. The lady obviously required some assistance. He could tell himself that, anyway.

The hole, unfortunately, wasn't as deep as it had looked. He had to bend down, stick his head into the gap and push branches aside before he could see into her yard.

The first thing he saw was pink spandex wrapped snuggly around a behind that wasn't anywhere near octogenarian. He took her in as he would any fascinating specimen—slowly, analyzing each part. White sneakers with pink balls at the ends of the laces, shapely calves, then the pink spandex—forget about the pink spandex— a white tank top and short, brown hair.

"Get off my foot!" she said as she shoved Buddy aside.

Buddy was a large, tan horse dog that was sitting squarely on the woman-who-wasn't-a-floozy's foot. And Buddy had no intention of moving...until he spotted something more interesting.

That something more interesting, unfortunately, was Barrett. Buddy stampeded toward the hedge, a string of drool hanging from his sagging lips.

Barrett was at Buddy's face level. He pulled back, but the hedge had other ideas. It pinned him in place with branches and one well-placed sharp edge against his neck. Buddy screeched to a halt in front of Barrett, some of the drool flying forward and just missing him. The dog was staring at him, its head tilted in utter fascination.

When the woman turned to see what had distracted the dog, she let out a warbled scream. "Oh, my goodness!"

"Get it away!" he said, still trying to extricate himself and wishing he could spontaneously combust.

Buddy had finally figured out how to investigate the head in the bushes, and he did so with a warm, wet tongue. Not to mention the drool, which caught Barrett on the chin. The more Barrett wriggled to free himself, the more entangled he got.

All in all, a fine way to meet the neighbor.

"Buddy, cut it out!" She tugged on the dog's leash, but he tugged back so hard, she nearly crashed into the bushes. She caught her balance and focused on the dog. "Sit! Sit, now!"

As she wrestled with the horse dog, all Barrett could see was flashes of neon pink that covered curves he shouldn't be noticing. And he really shouldn't be feeling some stirring in his body, since he was here to work on his study and nothing more. His body, he realized, was smarter than his brain was. It knew instinctively the voice belonged to an interesting woman. An interesting *young* woman, at that. He finally extricated himself from the bushes just as she got Buddy under control. He wiped his face with his sleeve, trying not to think about the kinds of bacteria that thrive in a dog's mouth.

"Sorry about that," she said, though he should have been the one apologizing and she should have been much less charitable toward the man who'd been peeking through her hedge. She ducked down to the level of the hole, and he forgot about everything but how cute her face looked framed in shiny green leaves. "You must be the supersmart scientist dude who's working on some important study on frogs. I'm Stacy Jenkins."

And even more amazingly, she slid her hand through the hole. It took him a moment to realize she wanted to shake his hand. He'd been too busy noticing the elegant lines of her fingers and the spots of bright pink on her short nails.

He took her hand in his and returned her firm handshake. Her hand was soft and warm, and a sensual feeling slithered through his body. What came out of his mouth was, "Tree snails."

"Pardon?"

"I'm tree snails." He blinked. *Get a handle on yourself, man. You've met attractive women before and had the wherewithal to introduce yourself properly.* "I mean, you said frogs, but I'm studying tree snails." The feel of her hand in his, plus the awkwardness of the whole situation, made him lose his train of thought. This never happened. "I'm Barrett Wheeler. I want to apologize for—"

"Peeking through the bushes at me?" she offered cheerily, extricating her hand and ducking to peer through the hole. "Gene does it all the time."

"He does?"

"Just to be neighborly, to say hi."

He couldn't help notice the hint of cleavage showing above a tank top that hugged small, firm breasts and thought, *Fat chance he was just being neighborly.* Since he wasn't exactly in a position to comment, however, he let it drop. "So Frankie and George were also dogs?"

She glanced at Buddy, who was whining but still holding his position. He had a fresh string of drool hanging from his lips. "Oh, sure. I work with the problem dogs at the Humane Society. We're a no-kill shelter, which means we work extra hard to fix the reasons the animals got put up for adoption. I bring them home for half a day or overnight sometimes and teach them manners." She tilted her head at him. "What did you think they were?" An expression of horror crossed her face. "George, Frankie, Buddy...you thought I was entertaining men, didn't

you?'' Just when he was hoping for spontaneous combustion again, she laughed. Not the demure, quiet kind of
laugh the women he socialized with had, either. Stacy's
laugh was an explosion of sound. In fact, she doubled over
and braced her palms on her thighs. "If you only knew
how preposterous that thought was!"

Barrett thought he felt a warm flush creep up his face,
though he was sure he was mistaken. He never blushed.
"Not that it's any of my business, of course, and my
intention wasn't to eavesdrop—"

That laugh of hers vibrated through him. "Too funny!"
But her laughter and the delightful smile that lit up her
whole face faded. "And too sad, when I think how long
it's been since—" Buddy nudged her behind, sending her
into the bushes. She caught her balance, and Barrett
caught a whiff of strawberry. "Well, I try to teach them
manners, anyway," she said.

How long since what, and why was the thought of her
entertaining men preposterous? There was that curiosity
again. He was probably better off not knowing. "Is that
what you do for a living? Teach manners to dogs?"

"Not for a living, no. I'm just volunteering at the shelter until I get a real job." She glanced at her watch. "In
fact, I'm waiting for a callback on a job any time now,
hopefully with good news."

"Aren't you a bit young to live in here?" he asked
through the hole.

"My granny raised me here. I was grandfathered in on
the sixty-five and older rule—well, grandmothered in, if
you want to be technical. When I graduated from high
school, I wanted to go to college, live on campus and
everything. But the more I talked about it, the weaker
Granny's heart got, so I didn't go. When she passed on
two years ago, I was going to sell the house and move,

but everyone asked me to stay. They're all like family to me, so I did. I'm a surrogate granddaughter to a lot of them. And no one else is brave enough to lead the workout classes at the community center."

"Workout class?"

"A combination of aerobics and light weight work." She gestured with her arms as though she were lifting weights. She had great biceps, just enough muscle to still look feminine. "Keeps the bones strong."

"So you stayed."

She lifted a shoulder. "Well, it's not like I had anyplace else to go."

He gave her a smile. She smiled back, and their gazes locked. His stomach started feeling rather odd, as though he'd forgotten to eat. He sometimes did that when he was immersed in his research, but he was fairly certain he'd eaten a bowl of Cap'n Crunch cereal that morning. Maybe if he ceased looking at those eyes of hers, the feeling would go away.

He shifted his gaze down a couple of inches. That's when he noticed what a great mouth she had, small but lush, coated in a clear pink color. The funny feeling wasn't going away, it was intensifying. He went back to her eyes, a rich brown color that reminded him of the chocolate syrup he mixed in his milk. None of this looking was helping the strange feeling in his stomach. Still, he couldn't seem to break away or find something, no matter how inane, to say.

Buddy helped by giving her another nudge, sending her forward again. She let out a yelp, and Barrett held out his hands even though he couldn't do much good on the other side of the hedge. He got another whiff of that fruity scent before she regained her balance and made Buddy sit again. That gave Barrett another glimpse of that pink spandex, and though he'd never been fond of the color pink, he was reconsidering.

Buddy approached the hedge again, and Barrett backed away.

"Are you afraid of dogs?" she asked.

"What makes you think that?"

"Just how you were asking me to get Buddy away from you in a desperate sort of way."

"Oh. Not afraid, more like…uncomfortable."

"Have you ever had a dog before?"

"No."

"That explains it. They're really great to have around." She nodded toward Buddy, sending a lock of brown hair to brush against her nose. She swiped it away. "You want one?"

"No." His quick answer took her aback, so he added, "Not today."

"Well, guess I'll let you get back to your work. Welcome to the neighborhood. If you need anything, just come on over."

"I will, thanks," he said, wondering what he might need and then deciding not to delve too far in that direction.

Still, they remained there for another moment or two, until she smiled and said, "See you."

"I see you, too."

"No, I mean, see you around."

"I knew that." He knew that. So why was this woman skewing his logic?

"Okay," she said with slightly widened eyes. "See you—I mean, goodbye."

And then she was gone, playing hide-and-seek around her orange and grapefruit trees with the horse dog. Okay, that was over. Now he could focus on his work and not be distracted by his next-door-neighbor who was not a floozy. Right?

Wrong. Twenty minutes later, he was still distracted by her. Still thinking about those pink shorts and her small but lush mouth. He didn't have to imagine her voice or her laugh. She was working with Buddy, pleading, cajoling, praising.

"Sit! Good boy." This in a honey-coated voice that sent that strange feeling spiraling through his insides again. "Down. Good boy! Smile. All right!"

Smile? Before he could ponder how a dog could smile, his thinking process came to a halt. She couldn't be distracting him. Women didn't fit into the equation of his life. He couldn't quantify them, for one thing. There wasn't one rule that delineated them, one formula that they fit into. They consisted of way too many variables.

In the scientific world, everything added up. He loved the predictability, the formulas, knowing it would always make sense. A plus B equaled C every time. Science was a beautiful thing.

Relationships were something else altogether.

His parents were a prime example of two different people who should have never married. His mother was a free spirit who followed her whims and didn't have a clue as to what her life goal was—or a care about finding out. After the divorce, she followed her whims into and out of several different jobs. Now she was a blackjack dealer on a cruise ship.

His father—well, he was still professor and chairperson of the Department of Biology at the University of Miami and always would be. After watching his parents' marriage disintegrate, Barrett wasn't inclined to date women who didn't have his interests. He'd dated women in his peer group and been intellectually stimulated. He'd met women outside his peer group who'd physically stimulated him. But never had a woman done both.

So he'd accepted that a woman wasn't going to comprise one of the elements that made up his life. He was fine with that. He derived all the satisfaction he needed in life from his work. As soon as he figured out what field interested him, anyway. Then there wouldn't be any vague sense of something missing. And that something wasn't a woman. After all, the shortest distance between points A and B was a straight line...and women were all curves.

2

STACY TRIED to forget about that hole in the hedge and the handsome face that had been framed there a few minutes before and especially the flutter in her chest whenever she did think about that handsome face. She knew about the smart scientist-type guy working there—everybody knew everything in Sunset City—but she'd never imagined he'd be so young and yummy. Well, at least as much as she could see of him with the hedge in the way. Vivid blue eyes with a warm tilt to them, almost shaggy blond hair. Dimples! Who would have figured?

She wondered what the rest of him looked like.

Forget it. He's way too smart for you. What guy's going to be interested in a skinny chick who lives in a retirement community and has no career? A bit of a tomboy who can't grow her wispy locks into anything even resembling a sexy mane of hair?

Not that she hadn't been working on a career. She'd gotten roped into continuing Granny's T-shirt business out of the garage. Every time she told her customers—mostly the residents of Sunset City—that she was going to sell the equipment and get a real job, T-shirt orders came in like mad.

Last year she stopped letting the orders keep her from looking for a job where she could find purpose in her life and meet people her own age.

"Down." She pushed Buddy on his haunches to give

him the idea. When he complied, she gave him a dog snack. "Good boy!" He pulled his lips back in a dog smile. "Smile," she encouraged so he'd eventually do it on command. "All right!"

The problem was, she rarely got a chance to meet eligible men. Well, men who were under sixty-five, anyway. On the rare occasion when she did, as soon as he came to Sunset City, he suddenly developed a condition or life situation that kept him from seeing her again. She wasn't sure if she was a thirty-one-year-old has-been or never-been.

On her last birthday, she was about to once again push back her having-a-baby deadline. At twenty, it had been twenty-five. When she'd approached twenty-four with no prospects, she bumped it to twenty-eight. Then to thirty. Then thirty-two.

She refused to bump it again. Thirty-two was it. She was taking the situation into her own hands.

When she sneezed, she was gratified to hear Barrett say "gesundheit" through the hedge. "Thanks!"

Then the phone rang.

It was Ernie across the street. "God bless you."

"Thanks," she said sweetly. "Now turn that sonic ear thing off and stop eavesdropping on people, you nosy old fart!" Ever since he'd gotten that listening device, no one had any privacy.

He chuckled. "I was born to spy. Back in the war, they used to call me—"

"The Black Weasel, I know."

"Gopher, not weasel! You don't know nothing 'bout spying."

"I know I don't like being spied on."

"Sorry, Stacy. I won't do it no more."

He always sounded so darn sincere, and she always believed him. Until the next time.

"It's all right. It's not as if I ever do anything that interesting." She thought of the interesting science dude and then stopped thinking about him.

"Ain't that the truth," Ernie muttered, and he had the nerve to sound disappointed in her!

"You still need help with finding that old book you're after on the Internet?"

"Sure do. Been looking for the *Tall Book of Tall Tales* for years now. Appreciate you coming over and helping me climb the Web."

"Surf the Web, Ernie."

"How can you surf a Web, now tell me that? I'm climbing it."

"Fine, climb it," she said with a laugh. "I'll be over tomorrow—oh, got another call coming in. Bye!" She pressed the talk button twice and said, "Hello? This is Stacy Jenkins."

"This is Bob over at Mary's Grooming. You applied for the grooming position?"

Her heart started thumping. She was a shoe-in! She helped Arlene with her poodles and Betty with her miniature schnauzer. They would give her glowing references, along with her boss over at the shelter. "Yes, yes, I did."

Finally, a job. A real job with a regular paycheck and benefits. Direction.

"I'm afraid we hired someone else. Now, it's nothing personal, you've got to believe that. We chose someone more qualified, that's all. Good luck with…finding something else. Just remember that we were real nice about it."

She dropped the phone on the grass, feeling as deflated as the beach ball Buddy had popped with his teeth earlier.

She'd failed again. Not that she necessarily needed the money. Granny's house was paid off, and her expenses were minimal. The folks at Sunset City always paid her for her help, even though she always refused. What she wanted was purpose and a college fund for the baby.

What she had was a drooling dog staring at her with the phone in his mouth. "Give that to me!"

Buddy took off, ready for the chase. After she finally retrieved the phone and dried it off, she loaded Buddy into her old pink boat of a convertible and headed to the Humane Society. His ears flopped in the wind, but he didn't seem to mind much. As usual, she got caught up in visiting the other animals at the shelter before she was able to head home. She started the engine and sank into a Celine Dion song while her car idled. A mushy love song, of course. She'd think that love was overrated, except she'd never been in love and couldn't say for sure.

Then, miracle of miracles, a handsome man had entered her world—and he was all wrong for her. Too smart, too handsome, too temporary. Bummer. That was all right. She'd gotten used to the reality of not finding a soul mate. Well, mostly. And she had three successful men vying to give her what she really wanted—a baby. A software engineer, five foot eleven with blond hair and blue eyes. An artist who painted landscapes and portraits, six feet with brown hair and blue eyes. Or a model, six foot one with brown hair and eyes.

The fact that she didn't know their names or what they looked like hardly mattered. No, not at all. Oh, there was a fourth candidate, and she did know his name—Ricky Schumaker, the maintenance engineer at Sunset City. He'd seen the three profiles of the sperm donors taped to her dresser mirror when he was fixing a leak in her bathroom. He'd been bugging her ever since to be the father of her child.

When ferrets flew.

For some reason, that face in the hedge popped into her mind as Celine crooned about everlasting love. No, he wasn't going to be an everlasting love. He'd be a nice distraction for a while, nothing more. The best thing to do would be to forget he was there. Yeah, that's what she'd do, put him right out of her mind. Not another thought.

She put the car in gear. He probably wasn't much of a cook. Maybe he was too busy to worry about food. All right, she'd be a good neighbor and bring him dinner. No harm in that. And after that, not another thought.

Decision made, she pulled out onto the highway, images of homemade biscuits, ham and cheese soufflé and apple pie in her head. Unfortunately, she wasn't much of a cook, so she pulled into a fast-food chicken joint and ordered a bucket of extra crispy.

AFTER NAVIGATING the ten speed bumps leading to her street—some of the residents liked to race down the main drag—Stacy pulled into her driveway. Balancing the bucket and the side containers, she headed next door.

The first sign of trouble was the golf cart parked in the driveway. It, like most of the golf carts and cars in Sunset City, had a poofy flower atop the antenna. That thanks to Granny, who had given one to all her friends one Christmas. Because the flower was blue, she knew it belonged to Arlene of the blue poodles. Said poodles—their silvery-blue fur tinted the exact shade of Arlene's hair—were sitting in the golf cart in a car baby seat. Arlene also had a niece with a curvy figure. A *single* niece she'd been trying to find a husband for, because her only offspring had become a priest and wasn't likely to produce any grandchildren for her. That left Tanya as her only hope for sort-of grandchildren.

Hugging the warm bucket to her belly, Stacy advanced up a walkway lined with pink flamingos—they lit up at night. Arlene was standing at the doorway talking to Barrett.

"It's called Pissin' in the Snow, one of my specialty dishes. See, it's coconut gelatin, that's the snow part, and the lemon drops spell out your name." The white mold jiggled obscenely. "Where I was born in the Appalachian mountains, that was a compliment, spelling out someone's name in the snow. It was trickier for the gals, of course, but we managed." Arlene chuckled. That was an image Stacy didn't particularly need. "I guessed at the spelling. My niece, Tanya, now she's a whiz with names. Did I tell you about her? Beautiful, single, has a great job. Did I mention she's a mechanic? How handy is that? You probably know how hard it is to find a good mechanic." She glanced at the black Saab sitting in the driveway. "Are you having any car trouble at all? Any knocks or pings? I could have her come out and take a peek under your hood."

Barrett's mouth was slightly open, as though he wasn't sure what part of that to address.

"Hi, Arlene, Barrett," Stacy said, taking some delight in the relief that passed over his face when he took her in. Of course, he could have been eyeing her bucket of chicken.

"Tell him how beautiful Tanya is," Arlene said, beaming as proud as a mother. "And didn't she get the knock out of your engine just last month?"

Something bugged her about Arlene's question, but

Stacy couldn't figure out what it was. "She did get the knock out," she agreed, but let the beautiful part go.

"Exactly!" She turned to Barrett. "I'll bring her over sometime. Tonight, maybe."

"I'm not looking—" Barrett tried.

"Everybody says that," Arlene said with a wave. "I mean, who admits they're looking, only desperate people if you ask me. And it sure would be nice to have a doctor in the family. Do you know how much it cost me to have my corns removed? Let me tell you, it wasn't cheap."

Stacy stepped in for him since he was still obviously trying to get his mind around the corn removal. "He's not that kind of doctor, Arlene. He does frogs."

"Tree snails," he said.

Arlene's mouth dropped open. "You're a doctor for tree snails? Good grief, they just have doctors for everything nowadays, don't they? Maybe you can get a discount when the babies come. That'll help with the expenses."

Barrett's expression bordered on horrified. Sort of like the one he'd had when Buddy had been eying him, only worse. "Babies?"

"Tanya's a healthy woman in the prime of her life. She'll give you lots of babies."

"I...don't do babies."

Arlene's optimistic smile faded. "What do you mean, you don't *do* babies?"

He waved his hand as though refusing a pushy cookie salesperson. "All those noises, and the crying, and they can't tell you what they need or what's wrong. There's no rhyme or reason to them. I just don't do babies."

Stacy narrowed her eyes. "Are you afraid of babies?"

He took in both their puzzled expressions. "Not in a

Godzilla or unknown-bacterial-virus way. It's more of an extreme-discomfort thing.''

Arlene dismissed that. ''You just haven't been around babies enough, is all.''

''Oh, yes, I have. My sister's had four of them. In fact, there are two in my condominium right now. She tried to acclimate me, but it hasn't worked. She'll take me by surprise, put it in my lap when I'm not paying attention. There it sits, looking up at me wanting something, and then it starts bawling.'' He shuddered. ''It's better to keep my distance.''

Arlene was clearly at a loss for words for a moment, a rare thing. Then it dawned on Stacy. Barrett was even smarter than she gave him credit for. Afraid of babies, indeed.

Arlene shook her head and turned to Stacy. ''You still working on those T-shirts for my sweetie pies?''

''I'm having trouble finding a size small enough for your poodles, but I'm working on it.''

''That's going to be so cute, blue shirts with their names on them—Blue, Suede and Shoes.'' She winked at Barrett. ''I'm a big Elvis fan, long live the king. So, Stacy, heard about that job at the dog salon?''

She felt her shoulders sag and perked them up again. ''Not yet. Did they even call you for a reference?''

''Sure did, and I just went on and on about you, how you get the exact right shade of blue and everything, using natural ingredients even. I can't believe they haven't called you. Maybe soon, hon.'' She patted Stacy's head, then touched Barrett's arm. ''You enjoy my gelatin, now. Bet you've never had anything like that before, course you haven't. It's my own creation. I'll just let you go back to your work, and we'll be by to see you soon.''

Arlene greeted her three poodles with kisses on their

noses when she got in her cart. She tooted her horn and backed out of the driveway.

"That was good, about being afraid of babies. And your expressions! Nice touch. Maybe that'll detour her matchmaking."

He gave her a sheepish look.

"It's true, isn't it? Just like with dogs, you're afraid of babies."

"Not afraid. Uncomfortable."

Her gaze scanned him. He was surprisingly yummy for a scientific kind of guy—broad shoulders and an unbuttoned white cotton shirt hanging loose over jeans. Bare feet. Now, Stacy had never considered herself a foot person, but his bare feet with the faded jeans tripped her heartbeat big time. She was, however, a flat-stomach kind of gal, and his ridges of muscles sure didn't hurt. She was so distracted by his stomach that she almost didn't notice his shirt was inside out.

When she realized she was close to gawking, she snapped to and saw he'd been doing the same thing, making her realize she looked ten degrees off appropriate for a dinnertime visit. She still wore the pink shorts, though she'd thrown a long T-shirt over her tank top. The fact that the shirt read Don't Treat Me Any Differently Than You Would The Queen probably didn't lend much appropriateness to it. She should have picked out a more genteel one, but it wasn't like she was trying to impress him or anything. Supersmart, afraid of dogs and babies...he couldn't be farther from her type. She redirected her gawking to the sunset. "Wow, look at that sky, will you? It's almost heavenly."

"Heavenly?"

She let out a breathy sigh. "Yeah."

"I don't understand people's fascination with the setting sun, like it's some phenomenon."

When she turned to him, he was looking at her. He shifted his gaze to the sky. "The colors are just a by-product of—"

"Stop! If you're going to tell me the science behind a sunset, I don't want to know. How can you think about science when you look at those gorgeous colors?"

"Quite easily," he said, barely giving the splashes of orange, purple and red a glance.

"No, take a good look." She waited until he did. Stretched across the horizon was cloud stubble gilded in sunlight. Below that were her favorite kinds of clouds. "See that bunch of clouds over there?"

"Those cumulus—"

"Yeah, those. Doesn't that one over there look like an angel? Look at the wings. And beside it, a barking dog." She loved the dog clouds best of all. "And over there is a dragon. Uh-oh, it's about to eat the dog. Run, pup, run!" When she looked at him, he was watching her with a speculative grin. "What?"

"They're clouds. Nothing is eating anything."

"I bet when you look at a starry night, you see burning suns and not magical twinkling lights. I bet you don't even make wishes on falling stars."

"Technically, the whole star isn't falling—"

"I *know* that. But it's just kind of magical to think of it as a falling star…and to make a wish."

Of course, her big wish—meeting her soul mate—hadn't come true. Since Barrett was still regarding her with that amused smile, she lifted the bucket. "Eaten yet?"

He eyed her offering. "Ah, food I can actually relate to. Join me for dinner?"

She shouldn't. Let the guy get back to work, don't spend too much time with him. "I'd love to."

She followed him inside. Gene and Judy's place looked like what King Kong would regurgitate if he ate Florida—flowery prints, pink—yes, pink—carpet with green throw rugs in the shape of lily pads, and a three-foot-high neon flamingo. Barrett walked into the kitchen, which had the same fanatical I-love-Florida decor, complete with magnets on the fridge attesting to every attraction they'd ever visited.

"I haven't had a chance to put these away yet. I guess you can set the bucket between the Spam-and-pea casserole and something called a pretzel salad." He looked at the orange dish questioningly.

"Scary, isn't it? That's Frieda's speciality. A layer of crushed pretzels, a mushy layer that I think is cream cheese and strawberry gelatin on top, then a layer of grated cheese. I've always been afraid to try it." She eyed the counter full of homemade offerings. "Uh-oh."

First, they made her fast food look pitiful. Second, all these dishes meant Barrett had been thoroughly checked out by the local populace who had female relations to pawn off. They'd obviously been perusing the gelatin recipe book they'd compiled a few years back.

"It's a very friendly community," he commented, taking the Pissin' in the Snow casserole to the refrigerator. He eyed it as though he expected it to wiggle right off the plate under its own power. "I've never lived anywhere where people bring you food."

Poor guy didn't have a clue. Or a chance. He bent to slide the gelatin into the fridge, and his jeans molded a very fine behind. It was a very good thing she wasn't interested in him, because she could have some very fine fantasies about that very fine behind. And, she thought with a sigh as he turned to grab another dish, that very fine face with a mouth that could turn a bad day into ten degrees from Heaven.

"Here, let me help," she said, setting down her bag and bucket and handing him the remaining three dishes. They sure hadn't wasted any time, that was for sure.

"Guess I won't need all these," he said, opening the freezer door to show her stacks of gourmet TV dinners. "At least for a few days anyway."

"You'll be set your whole stay, believe me."

He must have picked up on the ominous tone in her voice. "You make it sound like that's a bad thing."

"That food, my friend, comes with strings attached." At his blank look, she added, "Obligations. Let me put it this way. You're going to meet a lot of single women in the next week. Think parade."

He still didn't get it, not by his questioning look as he took out two plates from the cabinet.

"Parade of women," she clarified.

"Women? But why?"

"You're single. Judy, the owner of this house, considered it her social duty to tell everybody. These women have nieces, daughters, granddaughters…you name it, they've got at least one woman in their family who, in their opinion, needs marrying off. And you are the target."

Ah, the smart guy finally figured it out. His voice cracked when he said, "They're going to bring women here for me?"

"'Fraid so." She took the plates from him since her warning had sidetracked him.

"But I've got to finish my study in—" he glanced at his watch "—six days, fifteen hours and two minutes or the snails might not get their land. And I'm never late.

Parades of women would be worse than having my sister and her four kids cavorting around.'' Then he obviously thought of the babies and added, ''Maybe not.''

''Well, for one thing, everyone knows about your sister raiding your place. The fact that you let her family stay makes you one swell guy. Any guy who treats his sister so nice is on the A-list right off the bat. You're smart, another plus. You have a job.'' She started to set the plates on the table, but it was covered in papers and books on snails. On half of the table sat an aquarium filled with branches. The bottom was covered in moss. She redirected herself to the vacant counter. ''And you're a hottie, another downfall for you, I'm afraid.''

He lifted his eyebrows. ''A hottie?''

''Yeah, you know...you don't know. Hot. Good-looking.''

He set two cans of lemonade on the counter. ''You think I'm good-looking?''

She blinked, holding back the words, *Well, duh.* He wasn't kidding, wasn't fishing for a compliment. She also held back the words, *Would telling you I'd love to jump your bones make it any clearer? Nah, probably not.* ''You're not so bad.''

He took her in, not with a leer like Ricky the maintenance dude did, but casual curiosity. Still, she felt all twitchy knowing his gaze was on her. ''You're not bad, either.'' Merely a scientific observation, that. ''Why isn't anyone trying to pawn *you* off on me?''

''I, uh...well, I don't have any relations to pawn since Granny passed on.'' Wait a minute. Why *wasn't* anyone trying to match her up with the yummy snail doctor? These people were like her family, right? That's what had bugged her about Arlene's question. She wasn't even considering Stacy a contender. ''Let's eat, shall we?''

"I'm sorry about your grandmother."

She slid onto the stool next to him. "Yeah, me, too. I miss her like the dickens." She opened the containers and spooned out coleslaw and mashed potatoes. When she spotted a tree snail slithering up a branch, she walked over to investigate.

The swirled shell was banded in yellow, white and brown. The snail itself wasn't so pretty, gray and slimy-looking, but it looked kind of cute in a snailish sort of way. Little eyeballs were perched on the ends of two long tentacles. Two smaller ones felt along the branch like a blind man using a cane.

"That's *cingulatus,* one of the forms of *liggus fasciatus.*" He was standing so close behind her that his breath tickled her neck.

When she turned to ask him, "Huh?" they bumped noses.

"All tree snails are *liggus fasciatus.* The one you're looking at is *cingulatus.* That's the name of its color form. There are fifty-two different color forms. See the white one in the back with the faint green and beige bands? That's *septentrionalis.* The one moving across the rock with the multicolored bands is *vonpaulseni.*"

Her knees were going weak. It was partly because he was close and because he smelled really nice. But part of it was those snail names. Or more precisely, him saying those snail names. "Wow," she said at the realization of how strange that was.

"They're called the gems of the Everglades," he said, obviously mistaking her reverence. "Their populations have been decimated by collectors and by development of their habitats, primarily hammocks. The purpose of the study I'm working on is to obtain more land for protected environments."

"So why do you have some here?" The first snail she'd spotted, cingu-something-or-another, had transferred to the glass. She could see its tiny T-shaped mouth searching for food.

"These are from a collection a botanist raises in his yard to help propagate the species. They're here to keep me in the mind frame."

Except he was looking at her. His hands were braced on the table beside hers. She caught herself inhaling his aftershave and covered by saying, "They're kind of cute. They look like some creature you'd see in a Star Wars movie."

He regarded the snail. "Cute. Never thought of them that way."

"You probably never noticed how beautiful they were, either."

"Er...no, I suppose not. I think they're an essential link in the food chain and should be preserved."

She gave him an admonishing look. "You need to stop and smell the snails, fella."

"Smell...?"

"It's an expression. Well, sort of. Like stop to smell the roses. Stop to admire the snails. Notice what's around you!"

He was, only it was her he seemed to be noticing.

She pointed to one of the snails. "What was the name of that one again?"

"*Cingulatus.*"

"Mm—I mean, mm. As in interesting, mm." Not as in, *I love the sound of your masculine voice saying that foreign-sounding word, especially right next to my ear.*

She abruptly stood and returned to her task of spooning out food. Forget about the way his voice sounded around those words, how his breath felt against her neck. "How smart are you, anyway? I mean, what's your IQ? Or is that one of those improper questions, like how much do you make or do you wear briefs or boxers?''

"I…" He glanced down. "My IQ is one eighty-five. And why would anyone want to know whether I wear briefs or boxers?''

He really didn't have a clue, which made him so cute, she wanted to crawl into his lap and kiss him silly. *Get hold of yourself. You're not looking, remember? Only desperate women look.* Sure, she wanted romance, wanted a man in her life who would cherish and appreciate her, but she'd passed desperate so long ago, she was in a whole new state—acceptance.

"It's a…woman thing, I guess. Probably like the way men try to figure out if a woman wears a T-back or regular panties." She waved the image away and grabbed a chicken leg. Tried not to picture him in briefs or boxers. Tried not to picture herself sitting on his lap kissing him silly. Not doing a good job of either.

"Briefs," he said with a nod. "In case you were wondering." He bit into a chicken thigh as innocently as if he hadn't set her imagination off on a Barrett-in-white-briefs tangent.

"I wasn't," she blurted. "Wondering, that is." She stuck a big spoonful of mashed potatoes in her mouth so no other dumb words could come out. It had been so long since she'd seen either on a man, other than at the men's underwear section of the department store. But she'd never admit to detouring through the section just to ogle the models on the packages.

Gawd, she was pitiful. She did draw the line at stopping to look, however. She had standards of conduct, after all. It was only a fly-by gawking.

"What's a T-back?" he asked.

She nearly choked on her spuds. "You know, a thong. A panty that has more material in the front than in the back." She took a sip of her lemonade and hoped that would be the end of that particular conversation.

"What about you?" Again, he looked totally innocent. "Thong or regular?"

She choked on her drink this time, a mere degree from spewing liquid. Could she really be discussing underwear with a guy she'd only just met? Well, heck, they were moving faster than any date she'd been on in the last four years.

"Thong." She pushed the word out at last, since he actually looked interested in knowing. She wiggled her fingers to the bucket of chicken. "Eat up, go on."

"What are the advantages and disadvantages of regular versus thong? Has anyone ever undertaken a study?"

"Uh...huh?"

He shrugged. "It's what I do, study and research. I'm afraid I look at everything with an eye to analyzing it."

"I thought you were a snail scientist."

"I'm a research scientist at the biology department at the University of Miami. The Liggus project—tree snails," he added at her blank look, "is a one-year grant project on the survival and propagation of tree snails in the Everglades. I have to analyze population changes over the past year, species propagation, variant temperatures of the water...I'm boring you, aren't I?" He gestured to her face. "The blank stare and open mouth are always a give-away."

"I wasn't bored, just absorbing."

He took another bite and changed the subject. "So, are there strings attached to your meal?" he asked. "Obligations?"

You could give me a long, wet kiss in gratitude. She

blinked and hoped those words had only been in her head. What was wrong with her? "No strings. Just being nice."

"Nice like making T-shirts for Arlene's dogs and leading the workout classes?"

"Yeah, just like that."

Totally, unselfishly nice. No ulterior motives at all. He was way out of her intellectual galaxy, for one thing. And he had an important project to finish, for another thing. It would be unfair to expect him to fall madly in love with her when he was under deadline.

He was looking at her mouth. Not in a sensual way, exactly, but a curious way. Oh, geez, there wasn't a piece of chicken sticking to her face, was there? How gross would that be? She grabbed up a napkin and rubbed it vigorously across her face. What if she had something between her teeth? Even more gross! She kept her lips together and smiled, since he was still looking at her. Meanwhile, her tongue searched her front teeth for lodged food particles.

Oh, no. What if he wasn't looking at her mouth at all, but at her nose! That would be even worse, the grossest thing in the whole, wide world. She rubbed her napkin over her nose, trying to be discreet. He continued eating, but his gaze remained on her. He didn't look grossed out, though, just…curious.

"All right, I give up. Why are you looking at me like that?" she asked at last.

"I was thinking that the grease made your mouth look all shiny and interesting. After that, I was wondering why you were rubbing it all over your face."

She looked at her rumpled napkin covered in grease and crumbs. "Would you please excuse me while I go stick my head under the faucet?"

This was undoubtedly why no one was trying to pawn

her off on the eligible newcomer, she thought as she raced to the bathroom. She took in her shiny face with specks of batter and thought it was a darn good thing she wasn't interested in snagging the man for herself.

3

THE FOLLOWING MORNING Barrett was scientifically sure that his distraction over the woman next door was finished. She had suffered some fit of embarrassment over the chicken crumb issue the night before and fled the scene shortly thereafter. So the aberrant curiosity was done, and now he could get to work. He spread out his paperwork on the patio table and dove into a year's worth of data on water levels.

"You are so ugly, you're cute," a feminine voice announced from the other side of the hedge.

He looked around to see if she was talking to him. Apparently Stacy was working with another dog. Instantly that image of the pink spandex filled his mind instead of the tree snails and comparative numbers. Then the T-shirt about being a queen that overwhelmed two small but interesting-just-the-same breasts came into mental view. He'd only noticed them because the words *any differently* were scrolled across them in big, loopy letters. The snails were long out of his mind by the time he remembered her legs and the cute white sneakers she wore.

Uh-oh. She was distracting him again. Time to go in.

He started gathering up his papers when she yelled, "Don't you run off on me!"

He froze. A rustling in the bushes caught his attention. For a moment, he hoped it was Stacy and then realized that as small as she was, even she couldn't be pushing her way through the hedge.

One of the ugliest dogs he'd ever seen emerged, shook itself and pranced over to him. It looked at him the same way Barrett was looking at it, as though thinking, *What the heck is that thing?*

The dog was possibly a Chihuahua, with tufts of beige hair sprouting from its ears and tail. Otherwise, it looked nearly bald. Its brown buglike eyes never left him.

"Elmo! Where'd you go? I didn't mean it, honest! You're not so ugly. Just a little...beauty-challenged."

When Elmo turned toward Stacy's voice, Barrett took the opportunity to scoop him up and walk over to the hole in the hedge, the dog held out at a distance. Then he took a full minute to watch her look beneath her chaise longue and in a children's pool that was situated under a palm tree. She was wearing blue spandex shorts today, and another T-shirt with words on it that he couldn't read. Totally unbidden came the image of the thong underwear she said she wore.

Elmo started wriggling in his arms, and he realized he'd gotten off track again. He pushed the dog into the hole. "Over here, Stacy."

She lifted her head and traced his voice to the hedge. "Oh, my God, Elmo, you can talk!"

"Uh, no, it's me, Barrett." He angled his face next to Elmo's as she neared the hedge. "I've got your underwear over here." He blinked, realizing what he'd said. "Dog, I mean."

"Did you say underwear?"

"No, I didn't say underwear."

She gave him a speculative glance and headed over. "I knew the dog wasn't talking, by the way. And speaking of, what are you doing with my dog? I thought you didn't like them.''

''It came over to visit. I'm sure it would like to go back now. And it's not that I dislike them.''

Their hands tangled as they exchanged the dog, who was wriggling like bacteria under a slide. She hoisted him under her arm and peered down. ''I know, you're afraid of them.''

''Uncomfortable.''

''And babies.''

''Pardon?''

''And you're afraid of babies.''

''I'm slightly more uncomfortable around babies than I am dogs.''

She let out a quick little sigh. ''Thanks for returning Elmo.''

They stood there for thirteen seconds before they cleared their throats and said simultaneously, ''Well, I'd better get back to work.''

Another five seconds passed until she said, ''See you.''

''I see you, too.'' He rolled his eyes. Why did this woman have him tongue-tied?

Then she was gone, and that was a good thing, because he really had to get back to work. Before he'd even reached the table, Elmo had returned. It was looking at him in an odd way, with its head tilted. What did it want? Why was it back? Then it jumped up on his lap and continued looking at him with those bug eyes. With a frog-quick tongue, it licked Barrett's chin.

''Stacy,'' he called, avoiding another assault. ''Get it off me, please.''

''Coming.'' She appeared around the corner of the house with a leash in hand. Today her yellow T-shirt said Madness Takes Its Toll. Please Have Exact Change.

"He's not an it." She tilted her head and studied Elmo, who was lapping at the air Barrett exhaled. "I'll be darned. I think he likes you."

He handed the dog to her. "But he doesn't even know me."

She laughed at that, just a quick giggle actually. Still, making her laugh, though he had no idea how he'd done it, sent a flood of warmth through him.

"Don't you believe in love at first sight?" she asked, rubbing her cheek against the top of Elmo's head.

"The sensation of falling in love, or romance in all its various forms, can be explained scientifically. I did a report on it in college. Feelings of euphoria are produced by natural stimulants in the brain—dopamine and norepinephrine. It's all hormone driven, all geared for the sole intent of propagating our species. The euphoric feeling of falling in love is simply a chemical reaction that can be broken down into—"

"Forget it!" She lifted her hand as though to physically stop the words from leaving his mouth. "I don't want the magic of falling in love to be ruined by technicalities. Wait a minute." She narrowed her eyes. "You're not afraid of romance, are you?"

"Of course not."

"Uncomfortable with it?"

A loud horn honked three times out front before he could respond. The challenge faded from her face. "Tanya," she said. "The parade has started."

"Arlene's niece?"

"The one and only." Stacy clipped the leash on Elmo and set him on the ground. The scrawny dog tried to get to Barrett, its little legs flailing when it hit the end of the leash. "She always honks her horn when she comes into Sunset City. This time she's honking for you."

"Be still my heart."

That got an interesting look from Stacy—and a smile. They headed around the side of the house and met up with a pretty woman in jeans so tight, if she sneezed, they'd probably disintegrate. Her thick blond hair was tied back with what looked like a belt that belonged in a car engine. Her blue shirt was smeared with grease.

"Hey, Stacy. You must be Barrett." She took a moment to survey him, and her voice shifted an octave lower. "Aunt Arlene said you might need a thrust angle alignment. Want to show me where your shimmy is?"

"I need a what?" Barrett said.

"His shimmy is just fine," Stacy said. "I mean, he doesn't need to put his car in your garage...if you know what I mean." She lowered her chin and stared at Tanya meaningfully.

"Oh, I get what you mean. You already have a garage in mind."

"Exactly."

Tanya's eyes narrowed. "Nita's bagged him, hasn't she? Dang, she's fast." She handed Barrett her business card, letting her fingers linger against his. "If you want me to lube your ball bearings, give me a call sometime."

Barrett cleared his throat. "My ball bearings will keep that in mind."

"Cute." She winked, clucked her tongue and hopped in her tow truck.

"She called me cute. After you called the snails cute, I don't think that's much of a compliment. And what did she mean, Nita's bagged me?" he asked. "Who's Nita?"

"Oh, you'll meet her soon enough." Those words came out from between gritted teeth. "And never mind the bagging. Look, I suggest you lock your doors for the rest of the day. Don't answer the phone or doorbell.'' She tugged on Elmo's leash. "Come on, boy.''

STACY STALKED back to her house and tried to continue working with the recalcitrant Elmo. For some reason, the little weasel was completely enamored with Barrett. He kept glancing longingly toward the hedges and whimpering. "He doesn't do dogs," she said in a low voice. "Or babies. Or even romance!" Perfectly good reasons not to be interested, if she needed more than the disparate intelligence factor. So that swirling feeling inside her at the thought of him must be the ovulation countdown. She had a deadline for her project, too.

It was hard to actually imagine herself as a mother. Particularly a single mother.

Forget that part. Just think about the baby part.

She hadn't started converting the second bedroom into a nursery yet. She didn't want to alert the neighbors. But she knew exactly what it was going to look like—bright yellow, the flowers-with-faces theme she'd seen at the department store.

Elmo made the dash to the hedge once again, yanking her out of baby daydreams. She tried to grab the end of the trailing leash, but weasel boy was gone before she could reach it. Then she heard a soft *oof* from the other side, and then, "You again, huh?"

He probably thought the same thing whenever he saw her. With resignation, she walked around the hedge to the backyard where Barrett sat at the table with all his notes, charts and his laptop computer...and Elmo sitting on his lap, his insanely long tongue flicking toward Barrett's chin. Barrett was shrunk back as far as the chair would allow.

"I'm officially renaming him Weasel Boy," she said.

"He does look a bit like a weasel, doesn't he? You know, I haven't seen that dog take to anyone in the whole time he's been at the Humane Society."

Weasel Boy gave up on the licking and curled up on Barrett's lap, an enviable position to say the least. She only let herself dwell on that particular fantasy for a moment before she realized he'd said something. "What?"

"How long has he been at the shelter?"

"Five months. The problem is, when people come in looking for a dog, they want pretty or cute. Weasel Boy is the cute kind of ugly that baby birds are. And snails. He won't come to anyone, hardly eats, whines all the time, looks lost..." She tilted her head. "Well, until now."

Barrett studied the dog. "Why is he in there?"

"God supposedly told his owner to join the Peace Corps. Weasel Boy had been with him since he was a puppy. He took it hard, naturally. Dogs bond with their pack leader, their owner. He does seem to adore you for some odd reason. Not that you're unadorable, because you're not. Are. Not that I think you're adorable. Or that you're not." If only she had some mashed potatoes she could stuff into her mouth. "Anyway, that dog obviously adores you."

After trying to make sense of her senseless barrage of words, Barrett tilted his head at Weasel Boy. "I've never been adored before." He picked him up and handed him to her. "Nevertheless, I must relinquish him to your custody."

"You've never been adored?" she asked.

"Well, in third grade there was a girl who called me adorable all the time. Then again, I was a couple years younger, the smallest kid in class. She stopped adoring me when I got an A and she got a C, so I don't think that counts."

She took Weasel Boy from him. He'd never been adored, not really. How sad, how…wait a minute. She'd never been adored, either. Better not to dwell on how sad and pitiful it was.

"So what other kinds of things do you research? All kinds of critters?"

"I've only been studying—" he smiled "—critters since I got my PhD in biology a couple of years ago. My father is professor and chairperson of the department of biology at the University of Miami. I thought that field might be interesting."

"So you went and got a PhD in it, just for something to do?"

He missed the sarcastic tilt to her voice. "Right."

"What about before that?"

Too bad he wasn't geeky-looking. A man that smart shouldn't be gorgeous, shouldn't look so good in blue jeans and a wrinkled blue cotton shirt that set off his eyes. A man who looked like that should be dumber than a box of hair. It just wasn't right.

"I got a BS in mathematics and studied time."

"Time? How does one study time, exactly?"

"I worked with a team on leading-edge research on an optical time standard that relies on laser light and a single atom of ytterbium." He was really getting into it, using his hands and everything. "We needed to find something with a regular motion, like the pendulum on a clock. What we used was the movement of the laser's light wave. The trick was, of course, to make sure the light was oscillating at a precise frequency. Enter the ytterbium atom, which worked wonders by absorbing the light of a defined frequency. Now that was *magic*. Once we…" He took in her expression. "I'm boring you again, aren't I?"

"Sorry. You're talking to three-point-oh grade average, no college here. You lost me after the first ytterbium."

Barrett leaned forward, and she caught a scent of woodsy aftershave. "Don't apologize."

"So you studied time for…a time, and then what?"

"Then I got bored with physics and got a degree in botany."

She would have disliked him on principle except there wasn't a trace of pretentiousness in his voice. As though that's what everyone did.

"So, botany's your thing."

"I lost interest in that and switched to biology."

"Ah…I see." Not. "So biology is your chosen field then. Tree snails for now."

"I work on various short-term projects. Keeps things interesting."

"Sounds like you get bored easily."

"I just haven't found what I'm looking for yet."

"I used to feel that way, too."

He looked genuinely interested. "What did you do to remedy it?"

She almost wanted to tell him about her plans, but with his baby fears, he wouldn't understand. "I changed what I wanted." Or at least she thought she had, but looking into those eyes of his, she realized she hadn't convinced all of herself that she didn't want a man in her life. She pushed herself to her feet. "Come on, Weasel Boy, let's leave the scientist dude to his work. See you."

He smiled. "I see you, too."

She smiled back and started to carry Weasel Boy around the hedge to her yard.

"Howdy, Stacy." Jack Nelson walked around the side of the house. "No wonder no one was answering the door. Just wanted to introduce myself to our temporary resident." He aimed his perfect white smile at Barrett. "I'm Jack Nelson, king of Sunset City."

Barrett dutifully walked from the table and accepted Jack's outstretched hand. "King?"

"No need for formalities. I stopped requiring people to curtsy years ago. Hear you're a frog doctor. Pretty interesting. I used to wrassle alligators myself."

Between being a fighter pilot and a professional surfer, Stacy thought, but held the words. Let him indulge in his harmless fantasies. At least his were more harmless than hers.

"Tree snails," Barrett said.

"Mighty fine eating, them. Well, gotta go. Duty calls, as you'd imagine it does with someone in my position. Stacy, remember, taxes are due beginning of the month."

"Yes, your majesty."

"Sorry you didn't get that job. Seems like you got enough going on here to keep you busy, though. Heck, don't know what we'd do without you. Well, I've gotta go have a talking with Nita. Seems she's been playing her bunny music too loud again."

"Bunny music?" Barrett asked.

"Hip-hop," Stacy clarified.

Jack nodded to Barrett. "Glad you got to meet me." And then he was off, humming a jaunty tune as he walked away.

"He said you didn't get the job."

Word traveled fast, as always. She waved that away, as though it didn't matter. "That job I applied for at the dog grooming salon…"

"You're not disappointed then?"

"No…well, a little. Mostly in that it's the fifteenth job I've applied for over the last year, and not one of them has panned out. But, like Jack said, I've got a lot here to keep me busy."

"Jack, the king of Sunset City who collects taxes."

"Yeah, I know. It's his little fantasy. We indulge him. He only collects a quarter a month. In January he throws a big Christmas party with the money."

"January?"

"All the Christmas stuff is on sale then."

Barrett seemed to contemplate all this. "Are the people here considered…normal?"

"Define normal."

"Conforming to the standard type. Usual. Not abnormal—"

"I didn't mean for you to actually define…oh, never mind. Normal is relative. If I were hanging around with your supersmart scientific friends, I'd probably consider them abnormal. See what I mean?"

He was considering her in that speculative way. "I understand. Interesting, this relativity. My only real gauge as to what people are like outside my own circle is my sister. She's a housewife with four children. The things she's concerned with are beyond my level of understanding. Entering sweepstakes with insurmountable odds of winning. Spending hours clipping coupons and consulting sale fliers to spend the saved money on gas driving all over town. Do you know, she'll spend an hour on her hair to make it look like it did when she woke up?"

Stacy laughed, even though she'd done all of that. "Is your sister normal? I mean, not supersmart like you?"

"She's of average intelligence, like my mother."

"So, you get along with your sister then?" *Watch it, Stacy. You're getting your hopes up.*

"Get along…I suppose we do. We don't have much to talk about, though. I bore her with my latest research, and she bores me with talk of every detail about her offspring. It's amazing what amazes her. Every tooth lost, every word spoken. The first time they use the pottie is a big celebration. That is, after all, the normal progression of a human being.''

Oh, boy. Well, it wasn't like she cared, right? ''You've obviously never had to change a diaper.'' His horrified look gave her her answer. ''Where's your mother?''

''She's doing a stint on a cruise ship as a blackjack dealer. We get a postcard from her every week.''

Postcards reminded her of Florida tourists, which reminded her of pink flamingos, which reminded her of something else. She glanced at her watch. ''Oh, shoot! I didn't realize how late it is. I've got a workout class to teach in ten minutes.'' She looked at the dog. ''Which means I don't have time to take you back. Guess you're staying the night.'' She caught herself mid-sigh. ''Well, guess I'll see you around.'' Better not to see him at all. He didn't get why a mother would celebrate every achievement her child made, something Stacy hoped to be doing on a regular basis soon.

Barrett asked, ''Would you like to come over for dinner? I've got plenty of food.''

Say no, you're busy, you're not hungry, you gave up food! ''Sure.'' Maybe he just wanted to ditch some of that awful food. ''Why not?''

Why not, indeed. She could think of a few reasons off-hand. Let's see, gorgeous guy who was out of her league brainwise. Didn't have a clue about committing to a direction in life. Afraid—no, uncomfortable around dogs and babies. Got bored easily, and when he did, he just went right out and got himself another degree.

She trudged through the too-high grass and knew she was a bigger dummy than she'd ever suspected because she still couldn't wait to see him again.

4

"HE'S A HOT MAMA," Nita said as the class did a second set of bicep curls.

"A man can't be a hot mama," Frieda said. "It's against the laws of nature."

Nita chuckled. "*I'm* against the laws of nature. And I'll be personally checking that man out tonight." The petite woman looked at odds with herself, a lascivious grin coupled with her graceful movements.

Ernie, the only male in class, grinned. "I won't even have to use my sonic ear to hear what'll be going on."

Nita rolled her eyes. "You're such a dirty old man."

His grin widened, nary a trace of shame on his face. "Yes, indeedy."

Sunlight poured through the rows of windows along the wall and glinted off the water in the community pool.

Arlene said, "He's got an eight-pack, too."

Nita said, "It's a six-pack, goofball."

Arlene sniffed. "I'd think an eight-pack would be better than a six-pack."

"And here we thought he was going to be a dork," Maureen said. "Boy, were we wrong!"

Stacy cleared her throat. "Ladies—and Ernie—can we please focus on our arms?" This was the fourth time she'd had to steer the conversation away from Barrett.

"Moon River" played in the background. She'd tried to introduce them to Janet Jackson, Billy Ocean and

'NSYNC. The whole class had been *out* of sync, bumping into each other, kicking each other...it was back to Barry Manilow, Barbra Streisand and "Moon River." And every now and then Maureen insisted on playing battle hymns. Which were better, she supposed, than working out to the hymns Annette sometimes brought in.

Even Weasel Boy looked like he was trying to cover his ears. His face was snuggled between his front paws.

"Oh, come on, he's the most exciting thing that's happened here in Snooze City for a long time," Betty said. "We've all got someone we'd like to fix him up with."

Nita chuckled again. "I sure do."

"He's afraid of babies. Isn't that right, Arlene? She heard him say it," Annette said.

Arlene waved her hand. "Ah, all men are afraid of the little buggers. Until they hold their own in their arms, that is. Then it all changes."

Stacy let out a sound of exasperation, and not because everyone had halted in their movements, all thinking and planning and conniving. "Maybe he doesn't want to be fixed up with a woman. Did you all think of that?"

All eyes swiveled toward her at the front of the community center's rec room. "What, is he gay?" several of them asked simultaneously.

Okay, it was tempting—very tempting—to tell them he was flaming gay. She even opened her mouth to say yes. But she couldn't do it, not when those broad shoulders and that very fine behind came to mind. "I doubt it."

A wave of relief swept over the group of women in their pink, purple and, in Nita's case, slut red—Nita's words—leotards.

"It's a darn shame when a good-looking man is gay," Frieda said.

"A real waste," Nita said.

"Except if you're a gay man," Betty said with a lift of her shoulders.

"All right, class, are we ready to proceed?" Stacy lifted her weights to ear level. "One-two-three, two-two-three…"

Arlene wasn't even pretending to work out. "We need to approach Barrett logically, since he is, after all, a logical man."

"There's a perfect woman among us for him."

"Someone we're all overlooking."

That got Stacy's attention. And since no one else was working out, she dropped her weights to the floor.

"Down to earth, that's what she needs to be," Arlene said. "No woman on a permanent flight of fancy."

"Definitely. But she should have a sense of humor."

"And she should be compassionate," another woman added. "The kind of woman who puts others before herself."

Nita said, "But who knows how to have a good time."

They all agreed on that one. Stacy was beginning to get a warm feeling inside.

"She should be cute," someone else said. "Not gorgeous, not a woman who gets caught up in her appearance. A scientific man isn't going to understand why she'd spend an hour making up her face."

Stacy glanced in the mirror. Well, that was her, cute, definitely not gorgeous and not a woman who spent a lot of time in front of a mirror. That was evident. Granny taught her the practical things in life—using Spam to polish the furniture, using the bathroom before leaving the house and carrying a sweater just in case it was chilly where you were going. Makeup, hairstyling…Granny had been too simple to care about that kind of thing.

"And a woman who needs a man in her life. Someone

who's aching with loneliness, who needs affection and love..."

Stacy cleared her throat. "What about me?"

"Good one, Stacy! Like you'd be interested in some smarty-pants like that," Nita said.

"Can you imagine the two of them?" Arlene said, shaking her head.

They must have imagined, because they all giggled. Stacy glanced at the mirror again to see if she'd missed something. Warts on her nose, for instance. A hunched back. Nope, just the cute-but-not-gorgeous gal that always looked back at her.

Arlene said, "Stacy, you have us."

Betty said, "You've got a full life, just like your granny did. She didn't need a man."

Nita said, "You can babble on all you want, but the right woman for that man is here in this room." She smiled. "Me."

"Or the right woman for Ricky," Betty said, nodding toward the wall of windows where Ricky the maintenance dude made his usual obvious attempt at not appearing as though he were watching them work out. That strip of decking between the windows and the pool was the cleanest few feet of concrete in the whole community. Stacy couldn't understand why with his beefy, blond good looks he was so annoyingly desperate.

He wiggled his eyebrows at Stacy and patted his stomach. She shook her head and hoped no one had seen it. No way did she want these folks to know what she was up to until the deal was done. Till it was too late for them to tell her what a selfish, un-Granny-like thing that was to do.

"Too young," Nita said with a dismissing wave. "No

staying power. He's like a small town—blink and you'll miss it.''

A rousing polka filled the room after the laughter subsided. Still, no one moved. Pink and purple dumbbells had been forgotten on the carpet.

"What we need is a game plan," Arlene said.

Frieda said, "Gene's son Marty has worked with Barrett on a couple of projects. Says he's a real good guy. Honest. Hardworking. Got his smarts from his father. Barrett's mom has average intelligence, and that's why the marriage didn't work out. No connection, no communication. They got bored with each other."

"Ah, so he needs a smart woman," Betty said. "Good thing my Denise is smart. She was in all those advanced classes in high school, you know."

"We know," Arlene said with a roll of her eyes.

"Why don't you just leave the poor man alone?" Stacy said, picking up her weights in a lame attempt to jumpstart the workout session. "He has an important project he's got to finish in less than a week."

"That's all the time he has?" Arlene asked.

Finally, some understanding. "Yes, he's down to the wire and he's never late. He needs some peace and quiet, not a date."

"We're running out of time, girls," Betty said, clapping her hands. "We have mere days to snare him."

"What about that game plan?"

"Arlene, you've already sent your niece over," Nita said, glancing at her reflection in the mirror and fluffing her Lucille Ball red hair. "It's my turn next."

Arlene accused, "Tanya said you'd already bagged him, which isn't true at all, is it?"

Betty raised her hand. "I was the second one to bring him a casserole, so Denise is next!"

Frieda made a snorting sound. "I brought him the first casserole, so I get next dibs on him."

"But Breanna's already married!" Betty objected.

"So? He's a loser. Do you know what the man does for a living?"

In unison, they all answered, "Nothing."

"And he beats her all the time," Frieda added.

"At poker!" Stacy interjected. "That's different."

Frieda sniffed. "Is not. She's into hock to him for thousands. He keeps a tab going."

"Well, I guess we're not going to agree on who the best woman is for this man," Nita said. "So it's going to be a free-for-all."

As they all stormed toward the door, Stacy yelled, "He's gay! Really, he's gay!"

The only person who heard her was Ricky, who was standing in the doorway with a perplexed look on his face.

"YOU HAVE a big problem," Stacy announced when Barrett opened the door.

As if in response, a hank of his blond hair fell over his forehead. He pushed it back and stepped aside to let her in. "I do?" She was wearing white leggings and a red tank top that revealed an interesting slice of flesh at abdomen level.

Weasel Boy walked in with her and strained at his leash to get to Barrett. After he made some choking sounds, Stacy let go of the leash. He made a beeline to Barrett.

Her nose wrinkled. "What is that *smell?*"

He referenced the index card with heating instructions on it. "The Tater Tot casserole."

"I remember it. Ground beef, cream of mushroom soup, onion-flavored Tater Tots, all thrown in a dish and topped with cheese. Grossville. It was a good side benefit of the canned-food party, no casseroles.''

Barrett realized he was paying way too much attention to her mouth and shifted his gaze to her eyes. Chocolate syrup eyes. He loved chocolate syrup. ''Canned-food party?''

Stacy sauntered into the kitchen and opened the oven door. She quickly closed it with a grimace. ''We're having one this Saturday at lunch. Granny started the monthly potluck parties to foster community spirit. So, do you want to know why you're in trouble or not?''

He could think of a few reasons, like his preoccupation with her mouth and her spandex. ''Maybe you'd better tell me.''

''The women around here seem to think you need a lady in your life.''

He surveyed her, from the way the tip of her ear peeked out of her brown hair down the skintight workout outfit and her sneakers with the little red balls at the ends of the laces. ''Tree snails,'' he said. ''I mean, I have to study the tree snails.''

''Do you have a girlfriend?''

''Definitely not.''

She was tracing her finger along the edge of a plate, following the curves of the flowers. ''Is the reason you're afraid—don't feel comfortable with romance because of your parents?''

His eyebrows furrowed. ''How did you know about—''

''There are no secrets in Sunset City.''

''That's right, you did mention that. That's not the singular reason, though it was painful to watch them try to communicate. I just haven't met a woman who makes me want to understand…well, women. And relationships. I've come to the conclusion that I never will. The women I work with share my interests but don't inspire me. Whenever I'm physically attracted to a woman outside my peer group, I tend to send her into sporadic boredom when I talk about my work. I have, in fact, sent you into a near comatose state twice already.''

She waved that away. ''But only for a few seconds. Otherwise, I've been quite aroused—aware—I haven't been bored,'' she finished quickly.

He found himself smiling at the news that he hadn't bored her. ''I'm glad I've aroused you.''

She started coughing, then cleared her throat. ''So, any moment now a flock of women is going to descend on you. They think you need a woman in your life. And they also think they know best. We need a game plan, a defensive position.''

He cleared enough of the paperwork off the table to set down plates. ''Defensive?''

''Football speak. Go Miami Dolphins! I don't suppose you...'' She shook her head. ''Nah, you don't look like much of a football fan.''

''I've seen fans in hotel lounges before, groaning and yelling at the players on the television. It seems like a lot of energy to expend on something you can't influence.''

''But it's fun.''

''They seem to be in agony.''

''Well, yeah, but we're also in ecstasy. When a running back sweeps around the end, breaking beastly tackles along the way to the end zone. When a wide receiver catches a pass while he's sprinting down the sidelines and beats the last tackle, he's going for the touchdown, he's going for the touchdown...and score!'' She blinked. ''Sorry, it's been a while since I've seen a good pass. Ah, so, anyway, we need a defensive position. What you need is a girlfriend.''

''But I thought the whole point was that I don't need a girlfriend.''

''Ah, but the point is you need a fake girlfriend. If they think you're otherwise engaged, they'll leave you alone so you can get your project done. I'm willing to step in and help you out.''

''You'd do that for me?''

''Sure.''

''That's awfully nice of you.''

''I'm a nice person. And I know how important your project is.''

The prospect had him smiling for some reason. It must be because he'd get some peace and quiet. ''Thank you.''

The oven timer dinged, and he took out the steaming casserole dish and set it on a hot pad on the counter. She poured two glasses of water. Then she spooned a bit of the casserole onto a smaller plate and set it on the floor.

''Here you go, Weasel Boy.''

''So he's staying the night with you?'' he asked as he scooped the aromatic food onto their plates.

She batted her eyelashes at him. ''Unless you'd like to keep him.''

''Er, no.''

She pointed to the dog, who had already slurped up the food and was sitting next to Barrett's bare feet. ''You can't tell me you're afraid of that?''

''I'm not afraid.''

''All right, you can't tell me you're uncomfortable with that harmless little thing.''

''A dog isn't an option. I'm off on research trips, sometimes for a year or more at a time. My next project is working with the Wildlife Conservation Society in the Madidi National Park in Bolivia for two years.''

Elmo laid his chin on Barrett's foot but never moved his buggy-eyed gaze from him. He let out a throaty sigh.

"He's small. He could go with you. Having a dog is a lot easier than having a girlfriend,'' she said. "Even a smart girlfriend.''

"That's another thing. I've never had an actual girlfriend before. Observing it has always been enough for me. 'I'm fine,' she says, but sounds angry. He accepts this as fact, and then she blows. Or she gets mad because he's forgotten the anniversary of their first kiss. We won't have to do any of that, will we?''

"Uh, no.''

"Good. Tell me what's involved.''

Her forkful of Tater Tots paused midway to her mouth. "The truth is…I haven't really had a boyfriend before, either. I mean, I've dated guys, of course, but no one long enough to be legally considered a boyfriend.'' She ate the casserole and washed it down with water.

"I'd think you would have had a lot of boyfriends.''

"Really?''

"You have nice attributes.''

She blinked. "Thanks. I think.''

"So why don't you have a boyfriend?''

She speared a Tater Tot covered in cream gravy and studied it. "I don't get to meet a lot of men my age here in Sunset City, as you can imagine. Some of the men I meet, well, they're not comfortable with where I live. One guy had a phobia about older people. He wouldn't even drive into the community to pick me up. He made me walk to the entrance. And the others…well, maybe they all had phobias about older people. As soon as I brought them here, they disappeared. Poof.''

"Spontaneous combustion?"

"No, nothing as exciting as that." She gave a sigh that sounded a bit like Elmo's, only not so throaty. "It was usually preempted by some lame excuse."

Before he could contemplate that, the doorbell rang.

"Uh-oh. The offense is moving in." She shoved away her plate and smoothed her hair. "We're on."

"Wait a minute. What am I supposed to do?"

She glanced at Weasel Boy. "See how he looks at you in that adoring I-can't-live-without-you way? Take his lead."

5

BARRETT TILTED his head and looked at Stacy. "How is this?"

His blue eyes looking at her with something sort of close to adoration was a bit too much to handle, even if it wasn't real. Just the fact that this hunky, broad-shouldered man was trying to look adoring sent a tickle right through her belly.

"Why don't we hold hands?" she said, reaching to take his hand in hers.

"Why?"

The doorbell rang again, but she could only stare at Barrett, who was totally serious. And then she realized she didn't know how to answer his simple question. "Because that's what people do when they're dating."

She expected a soft handhold, considering he hadn't a clue, but when he grasped her hand, it was firm and solid and felt all kinds of good.

The corner of his mouth lifted. "Oh, right. I knew that."

She tugged him toward the door. "Couples hold hands because it feels good. It connects them. It's romantic." She gave him a wry smile. "But you knew that."

He was looking at their linked hands as she opened the door to find Nita standing there wearing a tank top and a pair of tight-fitting jeans. Her red hair was teased wanton-woman style. Her blue eyes smoldered with a come-hither look. For a retired woman, Nita was one hot mama. But she was in no way the right hot mama for Barrett.

Nita's smile faded when she saw Stacy. It crumpled completely when she spotted their linked hands. "You?"

Stacy nodded, wishing for one slightly—okay, really—insane moment it was true.

Barrett was still staring at their linked hands, a look of wonder on his face. He'd clearly taken the adoration thing a bit too far. Stacy squeezed his hand, and he finally looked at Nita.

"Hello," he said with a genuine smile.

Nita looked again at their hands, as though she still couldn't believe what she was seeing, and said, "I...just wanted to see how you liked my Tater Tot casserole."

"We're eating it right now," he said. "It's interesting."

"Glad you're enjoying it," she said in a distracted tone, still taking the two of them in. "Well, guess I'll cruise and leave you two to it. I..."

The buzzing sound coming from down the street drew their attention. Barrett leaned out the door and scoped out the otherwise peaceful community.

"It's the Power Squadron," Stacy explained.

They came into view, a group of women power walking—Stacy would never tell them they looked like ducks—and power talking—the buzzing sound. They wore matching pink T-shirts—made by Stacy, of course—with flamingos in bomber gear. Arlene, as usual, was pushing a triplet's baby stroller filled with her blue poodles. The group all glanced at the house at different times, and each stopped when they saw Stacy and Barrett standing in the doorway holding hands. To cover their blundering and stumbling, they waved, said hello in too-high voices and pushed onward.

Nita gave a long-suffering sigh. "Might as well join 'em, since there doesn't seem to be any other interesting ways to increase my heart rate tonight."

The buzzing grew louder when Nita joined the squadron. They couldn't believe Stacy had snagged the smart guy. Well, phooey on them. It was okay if *she* didn't believe she could snag a guy like Barrett, but they didn't have to look so darned surprised.

"That ought to hold them," she said, noticing he hadn't released her hand yet, enjoying the feel of smooth palms and pencil calluses and hoping he'd hold it for a while longer.

He was studying their hands again. "This holding hands thing is interesting."

She tried not to sound too horrified when she said, "Interesting like Nita's Tater Tot casserole?"

He turned their hands at an angle. "Interesting in a different way." He met her gaze and said, "Arousing."

"Arousing," she repeated in an airy voice, not sure if she was agreeing or clarifying that he'd actually used that word.

He rubbed his thumb over her skin, back and forth. He had hands more suitable for a carpenter than a research scientist. They were strong, with long fingers and neatly trimmed nails. The kind of hand that would look really good sliding across her stomach or down her thigh, for instance.

She was standing in the pink foyer surrounded by the flowery couch and palm tree prints and she wasn't grossed out by the Florida decor because she was totally, completely *aroused* by the feel of his thumb moving across her skin and his fingers tightening over the back of her hand. The fact that he was aroused, too, even if he didn't actually mean the sensual meaning of the word, made it more arousing yet. She didn't even think about how tragic it was that she was getting off on the most innocent of touches because it had been so long since she'd had any kind of touch.

He met her eyes after another few moments. "Definitely more interesting than the Tater Tot casserole."

When she heard the whining sound, she had the horrible suspicion it was coming from her. She was relieved to trace it to Weasel Boy, who was staring at Barrett with desperation in his brown, bulging eyes. Barrett let go of her hand. "Guess he's feeling left out."

She gave Weasel Boy the evil eye for interrupting. "Guess so."

They returned to their half-eaten plates of the casserole, looked at each other, then at the plates.

"I have cereal," he said with a shrug.

"Sounds good to me." She scooped the casserole down the garbage disposal. Even if he ate bran flakes, it would be better than...she turned to find him pouring kid's cereal into two bowls.

"I used to love this stuff!" She slid into the seat and poured in milk.

"Used to?"

"Well, I got out of the habit of eating sugar-coated, peanut-butter-flavored cereals. When you grow up with an older lady, you eat a lot of bran cereals. Granny thought fiber was God's greatest creation, right next to prunes and chocolate."

Nothing could look more out of sync than Barrett holding a box adorned with a cartoon pirate. They sat down to eat.

"What kind of kid were you?" she asked. "I'll bet you were way ahead of all the kids your age, huh?"

"Intellectually, maybe, but not in any other way. I was

terrible at sports and games. I was the first kid to get out during dodgeball and the last kid to get picked for a team. It didn't help that I was always the smallest kid in the class.''

''I'll bet PE was the only class you didn't ace.''

He gave her a crooked grin. ''I even failed recess. And I was accused of being every teacher's pet. I couldn't help that I related to them better than the other kids in class. I had always related to adults better. I was unpopular even back in kindergarten.''

''But you were only a little kid then.'' She was beginning to see how tough it was to be supersmart.

''Unfortunately, I was the first person to tell them Santa Claus and the Easter Bunny couldn't exist. I laid it out logically until they saw the truth. I thought I was doing them a favor, dispelling a myth that had no purpose. Three mothers called my parents to complain. Nobody liked me after that.''

''And here I thought you'd had it easy. I always wanted to be smart.''

''And I always wanted to be like everyone else.''

Wow. She never thought she'd feel sorry for someone as smart as Barrett. ''But it got better in college, right?''

''When I started attending college, I was barely fifteen. I was surrounded by students who didn't seem to have time to do much else but party and think about sex. I had friends, only they were the professors and research scientists my father socialized with. I managed.'' He nodded toward her bowl. ''How is your cereal?''

''Better than the Tater Tot casserole.'' She wanted to ask him more about his childhood, but he was apparently finished talking about what must have been a painful time of his life. Could they have been more different? She'd had to struggle with every test, particularly math and the

sciences. But she hadn't been very popular, either, growing up in a retirement community, raised by her grandmother. She'd been way low on the cool scale.

She shifted her gaze to the aquarium in case she gave
away her sympathy. All of the snails were gliding along
their branches. If she asked him about the study, maybe
she could spend the whole evening with him. Maybe they
could practice holding hands. Maybe…

She stopped those selfish thoughts. He had work to do.
The only reason she had offered to be his girlfriend was
to be nice, right? To help him out. Not because she
thought she had any chance of making Barrett fall in love
with her. Certainly not because she was falling for him.

That would never do. He'd become bored with her in
no time even if he were interested to begin with, which
was probably ninety degrees away from reality. And she
wanted a baby. Barrett was eyeing Weasel Boy with concern. He'd be way out of his league with a baby.

She tilted the bowl and drained the remaining milk into
her mouth. "I'd better let you work," she said, pushing
her chair back and taking her bowl to the kitchen. "Come
on, Weasel Boy. Let's leave the scientist dude in peace."

Weasel Boy wasn't budging. He followed Barrett into
the kitchen when he put the bowls in the dishwasher, then
to the foyer where Stacy was waiting. But he was firmly
at Barrett's heel.

"You must really like dogs," he said at the same moment she made a grab for the dog and landed face first
on the floor.

"I love dogs," she muttered as she made another futile
grab.

Barrett was watching as she played tag with Weasel
Boy all around his legs. "Then why don't you have one?"

"Granny was allergic to animals, so growing up, I

couldn't have any pets." Another lunge, another miss. "We compromised when I started bringing the problem dogs home from the Humane Society. I kept them outside, of course. It worked out pretty good."

"But you could have a dog now."

"Yes—" her hands slid over the dog's slippery body "—but the problem is I want *all* the dogs at the shelter. I can't look at those faces and pick just one to adopt. I wish I had acres and acres of dogs, cats, rabbits...everything. So I've continued to bring them home and spread my love out to a lot of them."

He scooped up Weasel Boy and handed him to her. "Because you're a nice person."

"Yeah, real nice," she said breathlessly. When she met his gaze, he looked almost...disappointed. Nah, she must be misreading him. "I got it from Granny. She was a saint." Weasel Boy started wriggling in her arms. "Well, I'd better go." She wanted to stay. Bad. But she reminded herself about his deadline and opened the door.

"What about your being my girlfriend?"

She stopped mid-movement and turned. "What?"

"What are we supposed to do? To convince the neighbors?"

Her shoulders deflated. Boy, he really was afraid of those women. More precisely, afraid they'd interrupt his work. "Oh, that. We'll make a few appearances. That should do it. Nothing that'll distract you from your work." She gave him a wave. "See you."

He grinned. "I see you, too."

NITA JOINED the women at the corner just out of sight of Stacy's house. "She's pretending they're dating, I just know it."

"Wait, here comes Ernie."

He was putting a lot of effort into appearing casual as he strolled down the sidewalk. Occasionally he glanced behind him, then around. As soon as he turned the corner, he sped up.

"Well? Are they?" they all asked.

"I never give up my secrets to the enemy," he said with a lift of his chin. "Not even if you torture me."

"You're spying for us, you dingy!" Betty said.

He took them in with narrowed eyes. "But how can I be sure of that? Maybe you're all just pretending to be on my side. Maybe you're double agents. I'm good at ferreting out the bad guys. That's why they made me a spy in the war, you know."

"We know, we know already," Nita said. "Out with it."

"They called me the Black Gopher. That was my code name."

"All right, Black Gopher, out with it!"

He lifted his chin. "I never cracked under the interrogation. No matter what they did to me, I held my secrets. I...ah!"

"Give it up!" Nita said, a firm grip on his earlobe.

"All right, all right! You're dislodging my sonic ear, woman!" He pushed it back in. "I pretended to be watering my plants when they was by the door talking. They didn't have a clue I was listening. They used to call me the Black Gopher, you know."

"We know! Are they or aren't they?"

He nodded, pride gleaming on his face. "It's a charade, all right, just like you said."

"Like *I* said," Nita said, releasing her hold. "That's just the kind of thing she'd do to protect that man from us."

Betty said, "But I think it's more than that. She really likes him. She's got a glow about her."

Annette gave it some thought. "Yeah, now that you mention it, she does."

"So what's our game plan? The usual?" Arlene asked.

"No, it's different this time. Barrett's different," Frieda said.

Ernie nodded. "He does seem like a good guy. Gene's son says so."

"Not like some of those other guys she's brought around." A chorus of agreeing murmurs went up. Ernie said, "It took a lot of convincing until that last guy believed Stacy was part of a Mafia family. I should have used the line I used the time before that with the dinner theater actor."

"But it's so mean to make up stories about Stacy's mental health," Frieda said.

"Maybe we've finally found the guy she deserves."

"And she's everything we said Barrett needs in a woman."

"She looked so dang disappointed that we didn't see it at workout earlier," Arlene said with a slow shake of her head. "I feel just terrible about it."

"We were only thinking about ourselves. Game plan, game plan. Well, they're already pretending to be dating, that's a start."

"But you know our Stacy. She'll be diligent about not distracting him from his important project."

They all nodded in agreement. Then Nita got a glimmer in her eyes. "So we force their hand. Call their bluff. She's protective of Barrett getting his project done, right? If we keep bluffing about trying to set him up with our offspring, she'll have to spend more time protecting him. More time with him."

Betty rubbed her hands together. "Ah, and what if we come right out and tell her we don't believe her? Tell her we want proof?"

They all put their hands in the center of their circle, cheered, "Power Squadron, unite!" and pulled their hands away with a flourish.

"Oh, by the way, Arlene, good work nixing that grooming job for Stacy. It wasn't the right thing for her. What line did you use this time?"

"The one about her escaping the loony bin. It seems to do the trick."

Betty smiled. "We'll find her the right man, and then the right job. Hopefully the assistant director's position at the Humane Society will open up soon. That's where she belongs, not grooming dogs."

"Or working at a pet store."

Ernie had a glint in his eyes. "Maybe we can give that assistant director a little nudge...."

"WHAT DO YOU MEAN, I can't bring Elmo back in?" Stacy stared at the phone and imagined RJ's lean face and military-style haircut on the other end. She'd called to tell him she was keeping Elmo for the night.

The director of the shelter cleared his throat. "Naomi took in some boarders. Five of them."

"We only had four cages available."

"That would be the problem with bringing Elmo back. Look, I'm not pleased about it, either, but the woman with the dogs gave us a very generous donation. She had to fly out of town to attend a funeral, and she had no one to watch her dogs. I can't put Elmo in a cage with any of the other dogs, because he's so small, and the woman said all the dogs had to be kept separate. Sorry, Stacy, but you're going to have to keep him for a few days. I didn't think it would be a problem.''

She glanced at Weasel Boy, who was staring at the front door and whining. Yeah, he was going to be real grateful, wasn't he? "You're right, it's not a problem. He's fallen in love with the guy next door."

"Good for you, Stacy. It's about time."

"Not me! The dog!" But even as she denied it, her heart gave a funny dance inside her at the thought.

"Maybe you can convince him to take the little guy, then."

"Forget it. He doesn't believe in romance. I mean, he's not comfortable around dogs."

"I've gotta run. Thanks for helping us out. You're the best."

When she walked into her bedroom, she was drawn to those pieces of paper taped to her dresser mirror. She couldn't walk in here without looking at them. Which was good because then she didn't notice the clean clothes in a stack on the floor waiting to be put away or the unmade bed. Granny would be ashamed of her. What would she think about this unorthodox way to start a family?

She looked at the sperm donor profiles. Which one, which one? These were her top picks. Smart, talented, healthy. "Eeny, meeny, miny..." Her finger dropped to her side. She just couldn't decide. Why? Every time she thought she'd made a choice, she changed her mind. The calendar reminded her she had mere days before ovulation. She fell back on the bed and pulled the gingham comforter over her head. Why couldn't she commit?

FOR HALF THAT NIGHT, Barrett watched the snails and made diligent notes. Unfortunately, they were about Stacy. He couldn't figure her out, and more important, couldn't figure out why he couldn't get her out of his mind. When she left, he felt strangely empty. He'd never felt that way before. He knew it had something to do with her, or more precisely, her absence. So he sat down at the computer and started charting what he knew about her.

She was nice. In fact, everything he knew about her was involved with her doing things for others, things she didn't necessarily want to do. Now she was doing something for him just to be nice.

Then there was the hand holding. Now that was something. He'd never admit this to anyone, but he felt a little out of touch with the world. Like when he saw groups of people socializing and laughing at things he didn't get at all. Or couples strolling arm in arm. He'd never once seen his parents hold hands or nuzzle each other or perform any mating rituals.

He'd always figured he wasn't inclined to that kind of affection.

But when he'd held Stacy's hand…he'd connected with her. For the first time, he'd felt emotionally connected to another person. To Stacy.

He shot out of his chair, ready to walk next door. He sank into his chair as reality set in. He was sure his parents had felt some degree of desire, enough to marry, at least. Look how that had ended.

Here he was feeling, well, aroused, and she was just posing as his girlfriend to be nice. He grimaced at that. He didn't want her to be nice to him. He wanted her. To want him.

Go back to the first part, he reminded himself. And don't forget that you'll soon be in another country studying the rain forest. He tried to remember how excited he'd been at the prospect. He glanced at the snails. She thought they were cute. She saw angels and dogs and dragons in clouds. She wished on falling stars.

He tried not to see the dreamy sparkle in her eyes.

He was leaving the country for two years.

With a sigh, he closed her file and went back to work.

6

DESPITE THE LATE NIGHT, Barrett was up early. He ran the perimeter of the neighborhood, took a shower and started working on the snails. He made four charts for each season, with graphs for water levels, temperatures and snail activity. At sunrise, he moved to the back deck. Normally he wouldn't have noticed the dappled sunlight on the white concrete deck or the scent of jasmine from the bush in the corner of the yard. Or the waves of light as the sun reflected off the small pool. He wouldn't have been aware of the back door opening next door, of Stacy's voice calling, "Weasel Boy, stay in the yard!" He would have been so wrapped up in his work that he wouldn't have put the picture of Stacy's face with her voice. Or thought of her spandex-covered bottom.

But he would have probably noticed the mutant dog that stared at him with a happy yipping sound. And that same dog leaping into his lap. Normally he would have minded the interruption to a nice, quiet morning. But that interruption was coupled with Stacy's smile as she walked around the side of the house, so he could hardly mind too much.

"Sorry about that. I'm telling you, that dog loves you."

Barrett patted the dog's nearly bald head, finding it wasn't bald, but covered with fine, silky hair. "I guess he has to go back to the shelter today."

She scrunched up her face. "Well, no. The assistant

director boarded five dogs yesterday, which means Weasel Boy's cage is now occupied, and he's too small to be put in with any of the other dogs. Which means I'm stuck with him until they find a home for another dog and free up a cage. And I wouldn't mind so much being stuck with him, except—'' she glanced at the dog on Barrett's lap ''—it means you're stuck with him, too.''

Elmo tilted his head and gave a melodic whine. Something about that plea twanged a chord in his chest. He shrugged. ''I suppose he can hang around here for the day.''

''Really? That'd be great. Otherwise I'd have to leave him in the house, and he'd whine up a storm. That's what he did last night, whine and whimper for you. Kept staring at the door. I even let him sleep with me, just so he'd feel better.''

Barrett glanced at the dog again, because looking at Stacy while she was talking about whining and whimpering for him was doing strange things to his body. Then he actually envied the dog for snuggling up with Stacy all night, and that had him looking at her again. Sunshine slanted down over her, glinting off her brown hair and making her purple spandex leggings look nearly fluorescent. Her calves were muscular and shiny from what he guessed was suntan oil. Her arms were set off by the white tank top she wore. She was squinting, and then she shaded her eyes with the flat of her hand against her forehead.

''I have something for you,'' she said, coming closer. He could smell the light coconut scent that obliterated the fruity scent she usually wore. And since when did he notice scents?

''I made it for you last night. What do you think?''

She shook out a white T-shirt and smiled as he read

the words in serious script. Alcohol and Calculus Don't Mix. Never Drink and Derive. "Cute, huh?"

He smiled. "Yeah...cute."

She walked closer and handed it to him. "You don't have to wear it if you don't want to. You're probably not even a T-shirt kind of guy. It was just for fun."

He held it up, wondering how long she'd worked on it, and what she'd thought about when she'd made it. "Thank you."

She shrugged. "It was nothing. I'll leave you alone so you can get your work done. Let me know if Weasel Boy bugs you, and I'll come get him."

He liked watching her walk. There was a bounce to her step, and of course there were the curves of her behind to consider, too. Elmo whined, and Barrett reluctantly drew his gaze to the dog. Happy with just that moment's worth of attention, Elmo curled up in his lap with his dog sigh. No way was Barrett going to tell Stacy the dog was bothering him. He set the T-shirt over Elmo like a blanket and settled in to work.

Thirty minutes later, a persistent noise penetrated his consciousness. It was time to get a glass of chocolate milk anyway, and perhaps a bowl for Elmo, too. And to find out what that high-pitched buzzing noise was.

The noise, it turned out, was Stacy up on her flat roof with some loud contraption blowing leaves out of the gutter. Since she hadn't noticed him yet, he figured it was all right to watch her for a minute or two. As she wrestled with the blower, it blew her hair into wild disarray. She wore sunglasses that occasionally caught the sun in a blinding flash. She moved around on the roof with ease, stepping toward the gutter where she aimed the nozzle and blew pine needles and debris over the edge.

In fact, she seemed to be...dancing. That's when he

noticed the headphones. She wiggled her hips and pursed her lips, mouthing the words to a song. Then she twirled with the blower close to her. It blew her hair straight up until she swung it out again.

She was dancing with the leaf blower. And while he should find that preposterous, he found himself smiling.

He forced himself to go into the house before she caught him staring. A woman like Stacy could make him believe things could work between a man used to his comfortable world of research and grants and a woman who wanted romance and worked with dogs. The only thing she lacked to make her perfectly wrong for him was a baby.

He and Elmo enjoyed their chocolate milk out on the lanai, and then Barrett went back to work. He wanted to glance toward Stacy's place, but he congratulated himself on keeping his focus.

Elmo wandered away only long enough to attend to his canine business before returning to his place in Barrett's lap. He did the strange air-licking thing for a few minutes and then settled down. Barrett laid out the pertinent field notes he had made over the last year as he'd trekked through Everglades National Park logging tree snail data. He glanced at the calendar and calculated the remaining time he had left. He had virtually no time between this project and the next. He knew his father was disappointed that he hadn't remained working on Everglades projects for the university. But that wasn't what called to him. Would he ever find the one thing that kept his interest indefinitely?

The blower noise had grown louder since he'd been in the house, though he couldn't see Stacy on her roof anymore. Focus on the tree snails, he told himself. If he kept his focus, he could probably complete his project on time.

The papers were laid out so he could gather the data he needed from each sheet in order. He got into a rhythm for a while.

Elmo's head came up a second before the papers on the table spiraled into the air and drifted gently down around and into the pool. The noise stopped abruptly, and he turned and looked up to see Stacy on his roof with her hand over her mouth.

"I'm so sorry!" She set the blower down, stood too fast and lost her balance.

He scrambled to position himself beneath her. She tumbled over the edge of the roof but hung onto the gutter. Without thinking, he wrapped his arms around her to help ease her to the ground. Only he didn't want to let her go.

She was warm and soft and firm all at the same time, and she smelled delicious, coconuty and sun-warmed. His arms were anchored around her stomach, and his hands brushed her bare waist. A catchy tune pounded from the headphones that were dangling around her neck. He thought about dancing with her, but that would be sillier than…than holding her for much longer than was strictly necessary.

"Okay, I've got it," she said.

For someone who had studied time, who knew the measurement of time remained constant and absolute, those moments felt longer than usual. She turned to look at him. "Barrett, we've got to get your notes out of the pool!"

The notes. Of course, how could he have forgotten? She slid down his body to her feet, tossed the radio headphones on the table and pivoted toward the pool. Twenty or more pages floated at the surface, the ink dissolving before their eyes. Stacy slid into the pool and started retrieving them.

"I'm so sorry. You must think I'm a klutz."

He grabbed the papers he could reach from the edge. "What were you doing up there, anyway?"

"Gene asked me to do their gutters the next time I did mine. I wasn't going to do the gutter above you, because I was afraid this would happen." She was plucking papers as she spoke. "I glanced down to see where you were, you know, to make sure I didn't bother you, and...lost my balance. I never lose my balance. Granny said I had the balance of a monkey."

The word monkey came out all garbled. The water was up to her mouth as she walked toward the deep end where most of the papers ended up. She wasn't going to be able to reach them. So he did something impulsive, maybe for the first time he could remember. He got into the pool with her.

The water was cool as it enveloped him. "Here, I'll get these."

"You didn't have to come in here. I'm the one who scattered them into the pool." She sounded breathless as she treaded water.

He wrapped his arm around her waist and held her up, facing him. "It's..." He forgot about the cold water, the papers and whatever he'd been about to say. Like when he'd held her as she'd hung from the roof, his body awakened as her body brushed against his. Her skin was cool beneath his hands.

"It's what?" she asked in a breathless voice.

"Hmm?"

"You said, 'It's.' You never...finished."

Their faces were inches apart as he pulled her flush against him. Beads of water dotted the pink lip gloss she wore. Why did he have the insane urge to lick them off? He wanted to kiss her, wanted it with every molecule in his body. He felt an intense desire to take her mouth and see if it tasted as good as it looked.

Her brown eyes were large as she watched him. Her breath was coming in short puffs, soft and barely audible. If he didn't consult his logic here, he was going to be in big trouble.

Logic.

"Tree snails," he said, and moved her toward the edge of the pool.

She grabbed onto the edge when he abruptly moved to retrieve the rest of the papers. "Pardon?"

He started reciting snail names with each piece of paper he snatched out of the water. *"Delicatus. Elegans. Floridanus. Lucidovarius."* He had exactly four days, four hours and twenty-nine minutes to complete this project. All right, he was focused again, his mind firmly on deadlines and Stacy's bottom as she pulled herself out of the pool... *"Septentrionalis."* He took a deep breath when he grabbed the last piece of paper and turned around. "Nipples."

At first he wasn't aware of what he'd said, only that she was sitting on the edge of the pool, and her white tank top was close to transparent. She glanced down and jerked her arms across her chest. Only then did he realize exactly what had come out of his mouth.

Not a snail name.

Not even close.

She jumped to her feet and set the wet papers on the edge of the table. "I'd better go before I die of embarrassment altogether," she said, her arms still fastened to her chest.

"I'm sorry—"

"No, *I'm* sorry. I'm an idiot. I'm going now."

Barrett had reached the side of the pool, where Elmo

was waiting for him. They both watched her stalk around the hedge and heard her door slam shut.

He was completely baffled. First that she'd affected him in such a profound way. And second that she'd blamed herself for his faux pas. It made no sense.

It made even less sense than his having gone in the pool fully clothed, shoes and all.

STACY LOOKED at herself in the bathroom mirror. Yep, there they were, showing right through the white material like brown beacons. No wonder the word had slipped out of his mouth! Gawd, could she be more embarrassed? Probably not. First sending his notes afloat and then this. He must think she was something else. He probably had some technical word for her, some fifty-cent word she wouldn't understand.

The only redeeming factor in the whole pool incident was when he was reciting those snail names. She had to be the only person in the world to be turned on by snail names. That probably made her a disturbed woman, but she could handle that. Of course, it more than likely had something to do with the fact that Barrett was reciting them, though why he'd been doing it just then was a mystery.

She peeled off the tank top and tossed it in the hamper. Okay, the other redeeming factor was when he'd held her against him in the pool. The water sure wasn't cold anymore after that. No, sirree. And if she'd been in her right mind, she wouldn't have thought for a minute that he was going to kiss her. She wouldn't have imagined the hunger she saw in his eyes. He was only holding her up in deep water, being nice. What he was probably thinking was that he'd like to throttle her for distracting him from his project yet again, and worse, for waterlogging his notes.

That's what she'd really seen, annoyance, not hunger. He'd probably been reciting those snail names to keep his temper at bay like other people counted to ten.

She stripped out of her leggings and left them in a wet pile on the bathroom floor. A glimpse of her boyish figure reinforced her misunderstanding. No way could this body entice that man.

She threw on shorts and a T-shirt and wandered into the living room. If Gene and Judy's home was regurgitated Florida, her home was granny style. The sturdy furniture was made to last more than a lifetime. Granny had had it since her early days of marriage. The colonial style would never be outdated. Brown sculptured carpet hid the stains and wear. Beiges and browns were neutral. For some reason Stacy had never quite understood, Granny liked mushrooms for a decor accent. The kitchen clock was shaped like a mushroom, and if that weren't bad enough, there were tiny mushrooms at the ends of the minute and hour hands. A mushroom statue sat on the coffee table. Though she wasn't enamored of the fungus, she couldn't bear to part with anything Granny loved.

When the doorbell rang, she found Nita standing on the front step.

"Hey, Nita. Nice shirt."

Nita wore one of Granny's classics: Coffee, Chocolate, Men—Some Things Are Just Better Rich. "I want a word with you, young lady."

"Uh-oh. Maybe you'd better come in."

Nita made herself comfortable on the afghan-covered couch while Stacy searched her mind for whatever favor or task she'd forgotten to do. Nothing came to mind as she sank into the brown chair Granny thought looked like an upside-down mushroom. "Okay, what's up?"

"I know you're lying. Out with it."

"Lying? About what?" At first she wondered if Ricky had spilled about the donor insemination. But technically she hadn't lied about that, just omitted information. Then it must be about—

"You know exactly what I'm talking about—your so-called romance with Barrett. I think you're pretending to be in love with him to throw us off his trail."

Well, that had been the idea. Unfortunately, it was becoming truer every time she saw him. And as hard as it was to lie to someone who was like family to her, she had to think about the mess she'd made of Barrett's notes. She owed him. "We're not pretending."

"Then how come he was jogging all by himself this morning? If you were really keeping company with that man, you'd be jogging with him. I know you. You wouldn't let him go out there alone with all these women just waiting to send their daughters and granddaughters out jogging with him, if you know what I mean. That's how I know you're lying."

Stacy swallowed hard. She hated jogging. It made her breasts feel like overused tennis balls.

"I was going to jog with him this morning, as a matter of fact. But he went earlier than we'd planned, and he was nice enough not to wake me up. Who's planning on ambushing him?"

Nita just lifted her shoulder. "Couldn't say for sure. But I've heard talk. Plans," she added in a low voice. "I'd be keeping a close eye on him, that's all I'm saying."

Oh, boy.

7

STACY STOOD at Barrett's door early that evening looking very serious in blue jeans and a pink short-sleeved sweater. "Barrett, we have a problem."

"Does it have something to do with the can of dog food you're holding?"

She lifted the can. "This is dinner."

At his horrified expression, she followed his gaze to the hand she held up. "This is for Elmo!" She lifted the bag in her other hand. "This is our dinner. Subs from the deli. Not a hint of processed ham or cream of mushroom soup anywhere."

She smelled fruity again, and he forgot about her declaration of impending doom. He followed her into the kitchen where she found a bowl and scooped something foul-smelling into it. It reminded him of the Tater Tot casserole.

"How's it going between you two?" she asked, nodding toward the dog.

"We have an understanding. I let him sit on my lap, and he doesn't whine."

She set the bowl on the floor and gestured to Elmo.

He didn't budge.

"Come on, it's your favorite. Savory salmon."

Elmo looked at Barrett.

"Go on," he said, and Elmo dashed forward and consumed it.

Stacy placed a plastic lid on the can. "How does it feel to be adored like that?"

"I'm growing to like it."

She looked at him, and he felt that strange tickle in his stomach.

"I'll bet you are." Her gaze shifted downward to his shirt. "You're misbuttoned."

She was right. "After my shower, I was deep in thought...about the tree snails," he lied. "Sometimes I don't pay attention to what I'm doing when I'm immersed in thought."

She started unbuttoning his shirt. "We have a problem that might affect your uninterrupted time. You see, they don't believe we're attracted to one another." She stopped when she finished undoing the buttons and was staring at his chest. She made a funny sound deep in her throat and quickly started buttoning the shirt. "Jogging. We have to go jogging together. That'll be easy. And we should probably hold hands a couple more times, just to show them. Why am I buttoning your shirt for you? I don't know." She took a step back.

"Because you're nice?" he offered, though he hoped it was more than that.

"Yes, that's it. I wasn't even thinking..." She glanced toward his chest again and then shook her head. "What I was thinking was we could go for a stroll together and eat dinner in the park. You, Weasel Boy and me. Holding hands. Think you can handle that?"

"Sure."

She studied him for a moment. "You don't seem very bothered by it. I thought, because it's going to cut into your work schedule, you'd be annoyed."

He shrugged. "I can work all night if I need to." Besides, he'd become immersed in a side project, and that was what he'd been thinking about when he'd put on his shirt. He'd pulled up his study on romance and found it dry and lacking in actual fieldwork. He'd gone over his notes on his subjects, the feelings they'd talked about having—tickle in the stomach, distracted, fantasizing—all things he'd been experiencing since meeting Stacy. He'd decided that even with all his interviews, he hadn't come away understanding romance at all. To be accurate, he needed to do hands-on research. Posing as a couple was perfect fieldwork.

Her expression lightened. "Well, okay then. I'll try not to let this interfere too much with your work." Her face crinkled with worry again. "Were you able to decipher those notes I ruined?"

"I just reprinted them. Really, it's not a problem," he assured her when the worried look didn't go away.

"All right. Good. Let's go then."

She snapped the leash onto Elmo's collar and they walked to the front door. She took a deep breath and shored up her shoulders. "Okay, here's the game plan," she said, using that sporting term again. "I'll hold Weasel Boy's leash, and you'll hold my hand. Like this."

She slid her hand against his, and their fingers entwined automatically. Which was strange since his reaction shouldn't be automatic at all. Before he could analyze that, though, he was overcome by that elating sense of connection. And an odd sense of anticipation.

"Ready?" she asked.

"Very."

They stepped out into the cool evening air. They had only reached the end of the walkway lined with the glowing pink flamingos when it became evident that he should be the one holding the leash. Elmo kept crossing in front of them to get to Barrett, tripping Stacy in the process. She carried the bag with the sandwiches.

The sun had just set, casting an orange glow across the western horizon. The rest of the sky was a brilliant indigo blue. Instead of thinking about how the colors were created, he took in the scene like Stacy obviously did. He'd never noticed the way the colors melted together before. Now he noticed not only that, but the way the light cast a glow across Stacy's face and made her look beautiful. The way her hand felt in his also cast a warm glow over him, though he knew that was scientifically impossible.

Several of the Sunset City residents smiled and waved, then turned and whispered to each other.

"This should go a long way toward convincing them we're madly in love," she said. "We can walk around to the lake, sit on a bench and pretend to enjoy each other's company."

Pretend? Perhaps she was pretending, but he was definitely enjoying her company. He didn't like the thought of her pretending.

"I appreciate you going to all this trouble for me," he said.

"It's no trouble."

Okay, that was better.

"You're sure?"

"Positive," she said, a content look on her face. She met his gaze. "Is it hard on you?"

To his surprise, he wanted to say yes. It was hard to look at her mouth and not kiss it, hard to understand why he wanted to kiss her when they were only pretending and the last thing he needed was someone like her in his life.

She was waiting for his answer, as though it mattered to her.

"No, not at all."

When they reached the small park area, he released Elmo to explore. The dog sniffed the ground as he traveled in circles, though he never took his gaze off Barrett for more than five seconds. If that was adoration, well, he did like it. He glanced at Stacy, who quickly shifted her gaze to Elmo, as well.

"Have you ever been adored?" he asked, making her snap her gaze toward him again.

"Me?"

"Yes, you."

For some reason, she tried to pull her hand free of his. He held on tighter, not ready to relinquish the charade.

She looked at their linked hands. "I…well, Granny adored me, though I'm not sure it counts when it's family. Not that they have to adore you or anything, but…" Her gaze lifted to his. "No," she finished with a soft sigh. "Not even by a dog. I'm sure my time will come."

He led her toward the bench that faced the lake. The surface reflected the sky and the palm trees that swayed in the breeze. Only the occasional ripple marred the mirror image. It amazed him how something so simple could be so beautiful. He looked at Stacy, who looked beautiful, too, even if she looked a little sad.

They ate, the wrappers making makeshift plates in their laps. Stacy kept dabbing her face, reminding him of the chicken crumb episode. At one point, she left a smear of mustard by her mouth, which she licked off with a swipe of her tongue. He heard himself make a small sound between a choke and a groan.

"Did you say something?" she asked.

He crumpled his sandwich wrapper. "Not me."

She stuffed the rest of her sandwich in the bag.

"Should we…" He gestured, then took her hand. "Tell me about hand holding."

"What?"

"What other uses does it have? Besides just being romantic."

He set their linked hands on his thigh and traced his thumb over her skin. Her breath hitched as she stared at their hands.

"Didn't your parents hold hands?" she asked.

"No. I've seen my sister, Kim, and her husband, Dave, hold hands. I was just wondering if it served some practical purpose."

"Why do you want to know?"

"If we're going to be a couple, I should be aware of all the nuances, right?"

"Well...it's a friendly gesture. But it doesn't last very long in that context." She demonstrated, loosening their hands, giving his hand a squeeze, then retracting her hand again. "It's a gesture of support, too. If you were going through something sad or trying, I might hold your hand for a while." She took his hand again. "I might even place my other hand on top of yours, just to give you extra support."

He was supposed to be cataloging all this for research purposes, but the feel of her hands enveloping his was making it hard for the information to register.

"What about this? I've seen men kiss a woman's hands before." He turned her hand over and kissed her moist palm.

She shivered. "You kiss the back of the hand...in greeting." She took his hand and planted a kiss on the back of it. "Like that. Only women never do it to men. It's a romantic gesture. Sometimes it's a classy greeting. I think the French do it."

A trace of moisture remained on the back of his hand from her kiss, skewing his thoughts. He'd never had trouble focusing before he met Stacy. "Have men kissed your hand before?"

"No. It's not an everyday sort of thing."

He kissed the back of her hand. She didn't react the way she had when he'd kissed her palm. "You didn't like it when I kissed your palm?"

"Well, actually…I did. No one's ever kissed my palm before. It was…interesting."

"Tater Tot casserole interesting?"

She laughed, and a warm, satisfied feeling flooded through him.

"Definitely more interesting than that." She took a quick breath. "It was arousing. Like this."

She took his hand, faced it palm up and kissed the center of it. Her mouth lingered there, hot and moist against his skin. She was right—it was arousing. And not just the legal definition of inciting to action, awakening… No, this was arousing in a different way. More than physical.

But very, very physical. His body was awakening, rising. If she asked if this charade was hard on him, he couldn't honestly answer no this time. Heat flushed through him. Was it dopamine or norepinephrine? All he knew was that it was *way* more interesting than Tater Tot casserole interesting.

She abruptly stopped pressing her mouth against his palm and sat up. "We'd better stop."

"But we're doing so well. I'm aroused. Aren't you?"

"Yes, but we're only supposed to *pretend* to be…aroused."

"Oh…right." That pretending thing again.

"Geez, look. No, don't look. There's Nita and Jack. And Arlene. Look at them, they're like vultures, moving in for the kill. No, don't look!"

He was getting dizzy with the looking and not looking. "The people we're supposed to be fooling," he whispered.

"Exactly."

"So, if I did this—" he kissed her palm again, very slowly, the way she'd kissed his "—it would help our defense position. Right?"

Her eyes rolled back in her head, and she whispered, "Exactly."

He'd never had this effect on a woman before, at least not that he'd noticed. He was noticing now, cataloging every action versus reaction. When he flicked his tongue against her skin, she inhaled sharply. When he traced his tongue across the lines of her palm, her breathing increased threefold. Out of the corner of his eye, he saw Elmo watching them with interest. When Barrett's tongue dipped into the crevice between her fingers, he didn't care what Elmo was doing anymore. She let out a long, low moan.

Her eyes snapped open, and she pulled her hand back. "Okay, that's good. I think we've got them fooled now, yes, indeedy." Her voice sounded shaky.

He was surprised to hear a quiver in his voice when he said, "Are you sure?" He leaned closer to her face. Her lips glistened after she licked them. He wanted to kiss her—just for show, of course. Mostly for show, anyway. All right, forget the show. "Maybe we should—"

"Go home. Yes, that's what we should do," she said in a breathless rush of words. "Our mission here is done."

Done, Barrett thought. But not over. He was a research scientist, after all. And he had a lot more research to do on Stacy.

THIS ENTIRE SITUATION was unfair, Stacy thought as she readied herself for a jog at six-thirty in the morning—six-thirty! After which, she had to teach her workout class. If she'd slept well, that would have helped. She couldn't even blame Weasel Boy. Barrett had kindly offered to keep him so she wouldn't have to abide his whining all night.

It was her own whining that had kept her up. Not actual whining. Except that one time when she caught herself staring out the window at the light burning next door and a strange sound had come out. But that was a fluke. Most of it had been internal whining.

She jerked her leggings up one leg, then the other, then realized she had them on backward and tugged them off again. One of them had taken this charade too far last evening, and she was mortified to admit it was her. She'd melted—*melted!*—when he'd kissed her palm. She'd been nearly orgasmic when he'd run his tongue over her skin, and when he'd dipped into the spaces between her fingers…forget about it! Even now, tremors of lust shimmered through her body. During their walk back, she'd convinced herself it was only because it had been so darn long, too long to even count how long, since a man had touched her. She'd been okay with that explanation.

Late into the night, though, it had fallen apart. She'd been around a man after a long absence before, and a simple thing like that hadn't turned her insides to gelatin. Hadn't kept her up all night uncomfortably aware of those long-neglected places on her body. Hadn't made her chest ache with wanting.

After wrestling with her yellow leggings so they were outside-in again, she tugged them on the right way this time. So it happened with a man she couldn't possibly find something in common with. A man she was only pretending to be attracted to. Because she was nice.

She made a face at her reflection in the dresser mirror. "Buy that, and I've got a mountain cabin to sell you on Miami Beach."

She'd also resorted to talking to herself, a sad state of affairs in itself. She donned her sports bra and a T-shirt that read, First Things First, But Not Necessarily In That Order, and tried not to think about affairs. The baby was what she wanted. That's what would satisfy her. She'd given up on the romantic part of the equation.

At least jogging didn't involve hand holding, which had become quite the erotic thing. Or even much talking. All in all, it was pretty safe. And that was something she didn't think she'd have to worry about with Barrett. He was a research scientist, for Pete's sake! A dull, geeky, sexy-as-hell, broad-shouldered man with a tongue that— a dull, geeky scientist who didn't have a clue about romance.

She looked at the hand she hadn't washed since the tongue event. Okay, he had a clue, he just didn't know he had a clue. It was better to keep it that way. Armed with a clue, that man could be dangerous.

Danger rang the doorbell. She glanced in the mirror, though goodness knew why. She was going jogging with a man she was only pretending to be attracted to.

"Good morning," he said when she opened the door. "I wasn't sure you'd actually be awake."

"Me, either. I...wow." She let her gaze scan his body. Blue tank top, nice arms, lean torso and shorts that showed off spectacular legs. He was only one degree off gorgeous. "I mean, wow, you're going to be cold, aren't you? You're hardly wearing any clothes."

She ran her hands over the goose bumps on her arms. They weren't from the coolish morning air.

"I'll heat up as soon as we start."

"Me, too." She snapped her mouth shut. "Shall we start then?"

"I usually stretch for a few minutes first. Don't you?"

She knew about stretching. She was nearly an expert on it. But everything fled from her mind as he bent over. If she hadn't been so preoccupied with his very fine behind, she would have noticed how nice his calves were. And maybe she wouldn't have been standing there staring when he looked up and said, "Aren't you going to stretch?"

"Oh, sure. I was just watching your technique, that's all."

She surreptitiously glanced his way as he continued to stretch to see if he was watching her watch him. But he was completely focused on what he was doing, so it was not for her benefit.

"Where's Weasel Boy?" she asked.

"I didn't want to accidentally step on him, so I took him for a walk earlier."

"You two are getting along pretty good, aren't you?"

He shrugged. "It's kind of nice having someone in bed with me all night."

Oh, and like she was supposed to breathe after that! "Don't you think you might want to commit? To Weasel Boy, I mean? Adopt him, I mean?"

"I can't." He glanced at his watch. "In thirteen days, eight hours and twelve minutes I start on my next research project for the National Science Foundation. It's a two-year study in the Madidi, a new national park in Bolivia. Four point seven million acres, some never before explored. I'll be working with various environmental agencies to determine the impact of opening the park to tourists. Part of it will be studying the dynamic demography of ant- and bird-dispersed seeds—divergent responses to tropical forest gap-phase regeneration. It's an important program to help regrowth in decimated forests. Uh-oh, I'm boring you again.''

"No, not at all." She'd just gotten lost after the two-year part.

Far away. In another country even. For two years. She forced a smile. "Sounds exciting."

"It is. Probably the most important project I've been involved in yet."

He didn't sound excited, but then again, men didn't often show their emotions.

"And after that project?" she asked.

"Maybe this will be the area I'll settle into for a while."

"Still sounds to me like you get bored easily."

"Not bored. I just haven't found where my passion lies."

Instantly her mind went to his tongue bathing her palm. Forget that. Remember gone for two years. Gets bored easily. Too smart.

As they started their jog, she was amazed at how many of the female residents were up at that ungodly hour. Since she was never up this early, she couldn't say for sure how many rose this early anyway. It was the clusters of women that gave it away. They were all seated on front porches with their coffees…waiting. Oh, yes, the anticipation was clear on their faces. They were waiting for Barrett to jog by.

"Good morning, Barrett," they crooned. "Stacy," they added as an afterthought. She was surprised they'd even noticed her.

Twenty minutes into the jog, the burning in her chest and legs won out over pride, and she slowed to a stop. Barrett, focused as always, kept right on running. She braced her hands against her thighs and huffed and puffed to catch her breath. She wasn't a jogger. If she was going to have to endure this for the remainder of the week, she wasn't going to make it.

"Are you all right?" Barrett asked.

She only had a moment to feel good about his returning for her—for noticing she wasn't beside him at all—because of her annoyance that he was running in place and not even breathing hard.

"I'd like to see you try a stint in my workout class. On second thought, that probably wouldn't be a good idea." Twenty or so women and Barrett...no, not a good idea at all.

"Do you want to take a break?" he asked.

She pushed herself upright. "No, I'm fine. Let's go." Maybe if they could continue to jog, that would be enough to convince the women in Sunset City to leave Barrett to his project. Certainly this kind of effort should count for something. After all, only a woman in love would subject herself to this kind of torture *and* get up early to do it.

"THAT HAND-KISSING THING was a pretty good show," Nita said during workout class.

"And the jogging's a nice touch, too," Betty said.

"But we ain't seen you kiss yet. On the lips," Nita finished, pursing bright red lips.

"Mouth-to-mouth resuscitation, if you know what I mean," Ernie said with a lascivious chuckle.

"Making suck face," Arlene added.

"Doing the wild thing with your tongues," Frieda added.

"Okay, already! Eight-two-three, nine-two-three. We almost kissed. Does that count?" She got distracted remembering that almost kiss that probably wasn't an almost kiss at all. When Barrett had moved so close to her and looked at her mouth and was about to suggest something and she just couldn't stand it anymore.

''No!'' A chorus rang out.

Stacy's legs already felt like overcooked spaghetti, but she pushed through the leg lifts. ''Thirteen-two-three. Our first kiss should be private.''

''Nothing's private in Sunset City,'' Ernie said.

''A kiss'll prove it to us,'' Betty said.

''But only a really good kiss,'' Nita added.

''Otherwise, we just can't be sure.''

''If we think you're trying to fool us…''

''We'll have to launch an all-out assault.''

They were all talking at once, and so fast she wasn't sure who was saying what. It didn't matter when the bottom line was, they still didn't believe she and Barrett were in love.

And that meant, if she was going to pull off this charade, she was going to have to kiss him. Maybe he'd only gotten lucky on the palm-kissing thing. He was probably a lousy kisser. He'd be dry, too clinical. Heck, he probably wouldn't understand the purpose of kissing!

She'd be safe then. There'd be none of that heart fluttering and stomach clenching she'd felt over the hand kissing.

''All right, I'll kiss him.''

''When?'' several people asked at once.

''When we're ready already!''

''You've got to have a deadline,'' Nita said as she pumped her red-sheathed leg in the air. ''By the canned-food party.''

''You don't have to do it right in front of us, but we

want to see you two smooching in the distance," Arlene said.

"Smooching really good," Nita added in a threatening tone. "Or we move in."

Oh, boy.

8

STACY WAITED until long after the dinner hour before talking to Barrett about their problem. Eating dinner with him was getting to be a habit, and it was a bad habit that would be ending soon.

She'd been in her backyard when she'd heard Weasel Boy whining. Or was that her? No, it was the dog. Maybe Barrett had forgotten to take him inside. Shadows filled the corners of her yard and made the tall green hedge look like a solid wall. The moon wasn't big and romantic. It was only a sliver. Not enough to steal moonlit kisses, for instance.

Pain reverberated through her body with every step she took. The jogging, followed by the workout class, had taken its toll. With what breath she'd had left, she'd made Barrett promise not to jog the last two days he was there.

She walked around the hedge and followed the whining sound to his backyard. The soft splash of water drew her attention to the small pool lit up like an aquamarine. And swimming in that pool was Barrett. Weasel Boy was at the edge trying to figure out how to be near his master without getting wet. The dog gave her a cursory glance before returning that adoring gaze to Barrett.

It was too bad Barrett didn't want a pet. That poor dog was going to be lost without him. Unlike her, who would go on as before because that's what she always did. And, she reminded herself, she would finally choose the man to father her child. She'd adopt Weasel Boy, but with a baby in her near future, she could hardly give the dog the attention he needed. Plus, he didn't seem to want her attention, anyway.

She walked to the edge of the pool and watched Barrett swim underwater from end to end. He came up for a breath, plunged beneath the surface and pushed off from the wall again. Ripples of watery light played over his body and made it look a lot like he was naked. Because she wanted to make absolutely sure no one would be embarrassed, she checked. He was wearing those aforementioned briefs. She no longer had to imagine what he'd look like in them.

Not that she spent much time doing that, of course.

She waited for him to finish his laps, but he was a man possessed, back and forth, back and forth. She walked closer to the pool. When he surfaced briefly, she touched his shoulder. He jerked his head out of the water, his breath coming heavily.

She smiled. "I see you."

He smiled back. "I see you, too." He ran his hand over his face squeegee style. Drops of water spiked his lashes. Blond hair was plastered against his forehead. "Did you come over for dinner?"

"Dinner? It's eight-thirty. Way past dinner time."

"I didn't realize how late it was. Sometimes I lose track of time when I'm working on a project." He pulled himself out of the water and looked around. "I also sometimes forget to get a towel. But at least I remembered to take off my clothes this time." As he gestured down his body, he seemed to realize he was in his underwear. She, on the other hand, was too busy staring to point that out.

"I hadn't planned on taking a swim," he said as he walked to where he'd tossed his pants. "I was having trouble working out some analyses, and the pool looked good.''

Beads of water dotted his shoulders and ran down his arms. The hairs on his chest were curled tight in an interesting array of swirls. His white briefs were molded to his body. Not that she was looking *there,* mind you. She pulled her gaze from his briefs and said, ''Looked like laps of frustration to me.''

He slid into his pants, still dripping wet. ''That would probably be a correct analysis. I'm having trouble with some of my calculations on mating habits and courtship rituals. I don't have enough data to make a correct analysis.'' He ran his fingers through his hair, leaving trails behind. ''And time is running out.''

''I didn't realize tree snails could be so perplexing.''

His expression went blank for a moment. ''Oh, right, the tree snails. Yes, very perplexing.'' He sat in one of the wrought-iron chairs near the table and did indeed look perplexed.

She took the seat nearest him. ''How do they mate?'' Maybe she could get him to recite snail names again.

''They engage in a long courtship of caressing. They rest, then caress, rest, then caress. This goes on for hours, even as long as a day.''

''Mmm.'' Oops, she'd gotten off track. She had been picturing two individuals lying about in bed all day. ''Snail romance. Who would have figured? And they go on all day, you say?''

''That's just the courtship ritual. The actual mating can go on for another day.''

''Wow, a whole day of foreplay? Now that's romantic. Then what?''

''Snails are bisexual, so they switch roles and repeat the ritual.''

"Oh." That popped the balloon on her romantic snail image. Well, she wasn't here to discuss snail mating habits, anyway. Or romance. She crossed her legs and angled herself sideways in the chair, pleased to see Barrett's gaze drift down her bare legs. Though it was mid-seventies, she'd thrown on a summery dress. "Are you cold?"

He looked poured into the chair, legs outstretched and arms relaxed on its arms. He didn't look the least bit cold, though his nipples were hard and puckered. Sort of the way hers had looked, she thought, and then didn't want to think about it after all.

"I'm quite warm, actually. You?"

"Warm," she said. "Look, the reason I came over, and you know I'm trying not to bother you so you can get your work done, but we have a problem."

"Does it involve jogging?"

"No."

"Holding your hand? I didn't mind doing that. Especially the part when I—"

"No, no, it's not that. We still haven't convinced the folks here that we're...involved. They're giving me until tomorrow to give them more proof before the parade of women starts again."

She had to admit that for a man on a deadline, he didn't look terribly upset. He did glance at his laptop computer, but that was the only indication that he was even thinking of his deadline.

"We need to be more aroused?"

"I...uh, yes. We need to kiss."

"Kiss what?"

A warped laugh escaped her, but she held it back before it became an all-out gale. "Each other," she said in the calmest voice she could manage. "On the lips."

"I knew that. I did," he added at her questioning look.

He struck a classic thinker's pose, his hand on his chin, his fingers stroking his mouth.

"You do know what kissing is, don't you?" she asked. Oh, boy, he *was* going to be a lousy kisser.

"I know what kissing is."

"Human kissing. Not snail kissing."

"Snails don't kiss. They caress."

"For hours, I know."

"I've kissed a few women. It was nice."

She forced a smile. "Nice. Oh, goody." But isn't that what she wanted, for him to be a crummy kisser? Yes, it was. No more of that eyes-rolling-back-in-her-head reaction. No more jelly knees.

She pushed herself to her feet. "We have to kiss each other at the canned-food party tomorrow. Just one kiss ought to do it." She paused. "But it has to be a good one. Nita's going to be the judge. She'll know if we're just pretending. She'll know if it's not a good kiss."

He stood, too. "What is the criterion for a good kiss? Duration? Amount of movement?"

"You can't judge a kiss on those terms. A short kiss, a long kiss, standing, sitting, moving, not moving...none of that matters. What determines a good kiss is chemistry. It's how high you feel, how totally lost in the moment you are. It's..." She tried to remember what a really good kiss felt like. She was sure she'd had one or two, but nothing came to mind. "It's the swoon factor."

"Swoon factor?" he repeated as though she'd uttered a foreign phrase.

"That's the total sum of a good kiss, how much each party swooned. And they should both swoon equally if it's a really good kiss."

He shook his head. "There's got to be a formula. A plus B equals C...or swoon, in this case. A successful kiss, like anything else, has to be broken down into various components that, when combined, invariably equal the desired result. We can factor in such variables as action versus reaction, environment, lip-to-lip ratios and...uh-oh. I'm boring you again, aren't I?''

She forced a smile. ''I have to say that I'm amazed anyone could make a kiss sound boring. But you've done it.''

He gave her a lopsided smile. ''This is why I avoid the whole romance thing. You can understand why it's easier that way.''

''Definitely.'' If she could just have his body and turn off his mind... She felt a grumble emanate from within. But no, that never worked. The swoon factor involved body plus mind plus soul. ''Well, maybe if we kiss a good distance from everyone, they won't notice.''

Then she had a horrible realization. He might think she was a lousy kisser, too. Maybe it was true. After all, that was about as far as she usually got with men. It was a sad moment in self-esteem land.

''Is something wrong?'' he asked.

She'd been worried about boring someone smart like Barrett. But the truth was probably that she bored all the men she met. ''I'm fine.''

''Uh-oh, this is the kind of thing my parents did all the time. I don't think that's what fine sounds like.''

It would be a disservice to him if she tried to pawn off her wan *fine* as fine. Not when he was trying to understand her. ''When someone says *fine* like that, it means they're not fine, but they don't want to talk about it, okay?''

''Why not just say that, then? It would be much clearer.''

She found herself laughing. ''You're right. But that would be too easy. We wouldn't need all those men-women books. Makes it much more interesting this way.'' She headed toward the hedge. ''I'm going to make a fruit salad to bring to the party.''

''What should I bring?''

''You don't have to bring anything. The salad covers both of us, since we're a couple and all.''

How strangely wonderful those words sounded, even though they weren't true.

''A couple of what? Oh, a couple. I got it.''

She rolled her eyes. ''I'll see you tomorrow!''

LATER THAT NIGHT, when the doorbell rang, Stacy told herself she wasn't feeling that jump in her pulse because she thought Barrett was at the door.

''Hey, there, sweet thing. You made up your mind yet on who's going to be the father of your yet-to-be-conceived child?''

Ricky leaned in the doorway, one arm raised against the doorframe. A large damp spot was evident on the armpit of his silky blue shirt. A yellow toothpick jutted out of his mouth and bobbed as he spoke.

''Ricky, be quiet!'' She glanced around to see if any of the neighbors, especially Ernie, were around. Then she stepped back. ''Come in, but you're not getting fed, sex or a beer.''

He sauntered in, looking suitably insulted. ''I don't come here just for...all right, sometimes I do. But you never give me any of the above, so you gotta know that's not why I'm here now.''

''And you can't be the father of my child, either.''

''Why not?'' he asked. ''I'm just as good as any of those guys on your mirror. Even better, 'cause I'm here. And I'm free. You don't have to pay me or anything. And we can have fun doing it.''

"Okay, you can go now."

"I just got here. I wanna help you, that's all. I may never have a kid otherwise."

"I thought all these women wanted you. You're always talking about this one and that one."

"They only want my body." He looked around the room, but his gaze swung back to her. "Okay, there aren't that many women. Only a few." He flopped down on the couch and pulled the afghan over his lap. "All right already, there was one in the last month. Year."

"Nita."

"How'd you know?"

Stacy slid into the chair kitty-corner to the couch and sank into the brown mushroomlike cushion. She wasn't about to repeat Nita's small-town analogy. "Just a rumor."

"See, that's how a guy's reputation gets besmirched. People'll think I'm easy or something."

"It hasn't helped, has it?"

"Nah, darn it." He seemed to deliberate for a moment before dropping to the floor in front of her on one knee. "It's been driving me crazy, thinking about you going down to that sterile place and having some guy's sperm injected into you. I want a little Ricky or Rickette crawling around. I want to be the one." He really meant it, too. His hooded eyes begged her to give in.

"I can't. The whole thing about going to the sperm bank is that the guy never knows about his child."

His voice became stern, and he made a waving gesture. "And how cold is that? He doesn't care. He doesn't want to be involved. What kind of man does that?"

"A man who needs money, I suppose. Or wants to contribute to the gene pool without the responsibility."

"And that's another thing. Those places aren't cheap. I could save you lots of money."

It was taking a small chunk of her savings to do the procedure, that was true. "Ricky, I appreciate your offer, I do. Sort of. But I don't want complications. If I can't have the whole shebang—the romance, the marriage—I only want the baby. Besides, if you're the father, you'd have to support the baby. You'd be responsible."

He scooted closer to her chair and grabbed hold of her bare feet. "I can do the whole shebang. The romance, marriage... I can do all that." He was giving her the pout.

She wriggled free of his hold and tucked her feet beneath her. "Why do you want this so bad?"

He shifted his gaze left and right before finally looking at her. "I don't want to end up all alone. My biological clock is ticking, ticking, ticking." He hugged her knees. "I want someone to love me, and you're my last chance."

"Oh, Ricky." She put her hands on his shoulders. Then his last words sunk past the pitiful plea. "What do you mean, I'm your last chance?"

He sniffed and sat up. "I'm a failure at love, you're a failure at love... seems like we're the only people on earth who haven't hooked up with someone yet. Hey, why are you looking all mad like that?"

"You're saying I'm your last-ditch effort. The last woman on earth who would have you. I'm not sure I can handle the flattery. Plus, you called me a failure!"

"But only in the nicest way. Ah, come on, you know what I meant. We're both desperate. We're made for each other."

"Out! And don't bug me again about being the father of my child. It's not going to happen. In two days, I'll be inseminated. And not a word to anyone about this, you hear me?"

Ricky shuffled to the front door. "I'll try to keep it a secret. But you know you can't hide things from the people around here. Everybody knows everything."

"If you tell them, I'll make sure you never procreate, if you know what I mean." She slammed the door. Two days. She had two days to choose the father of her child, about three days until ovulation according to her ovulation predictor test. Ricky was right. Everyone knew everything in Sunset City. And with his big mouth holding her secret, she knew time was running out. It had to happen Monday.

9

STACY SNAPPED the lid on the fruit salad bowl and set it in the refrigerator. That was another good thing about the canned-food party—no cooking required. She glanced at the mushroom clock on the kitchen wall. Ten-fifteen. Since she was somehow deemed queen of the canned-food party, she was responsible for organizing things.

She'd get the tables and chairs set up, then come back and get the fruit and Barrett. At the thought of him, she glanced at her reflection in the dining room mirror. That reaction wasn't a good sign. He was only her *pretend* boyfriend. She shouldn't be worried about how she looked for him. The really bad sign, though, was the fact that she'd put on foundation—*foundation!*—for the canned-food party. And pink lipstick. She'd rationalized the eye shadow, justified the hint of blush but hadn't quite fooled herself on the cute pink-and-white-polka-dot jumpsuit.

She changed into her more standard T-shirt—You're Just Jealous Because the Voices Only Talk To Me—and leggings and toned down the makeup. It wasn't as though she were trying to impress Barrett or anything. Right?

Right.

He probably wouldn't have noticed anyway. Scientific guys didn't notice stuff like that, she was pretty sure. Heck, he'd never even enjoyed a sunset!

An hour later, the tables and chairs were set up near the lake. A handful of folks always helped her set up and break down. A light breeze fanned the palm trees and ruffled the surface of the water. The sun coated everything in a layer of bright warmth. A perfect day for a perfect kiss. A kiss that everyone was going to be watching, judging.

A kiss that couldn't possibly live up to everyone's expectations.

The tightening of her stomach as she imagined that kiss was because of the pressure, not anything close to anticipation. Probably it was dread.

People starting filtering into the park carrying their assorted casserole dishes filled with canned goodies. Dogs scampered on the grass, chasing butterflies and each other. Some of those dogs had come from her shelter. A couple of the regulars weren't there, though, including Killer the Chihuahua and Teeny the Saint Bernard. She pinned down the corners of the yellow tablecloth so they wouldn't fly up in her face.

"Hello, Stacy." The Swensons greeted her in a long, drawn-out way. "Lovely day, isn't it?"

"Good afternoon, Stacy," Nita said as she set her pickled lima beans on the table. She smiled, just stood there and smiled.

"Ah, there's our Stacy," Ernie said. Frieda set their jelled cranberry can-shaped mold next to the Swensons' mandarin oranges with maraschino cherries. "You're looking quite cute, isn't she, Frieda?"

"She's got a glow about her, doesn't she?" Frieda said.

"Yep, definitely a glow."

What they were all saying, in not so many words, was, *We're looking forward to seeing that kiss.* They were making up the part about the glow.

Stacy gave them a forced smile. "Thank you." She focused on Arlene. "Where are Blue, Suede and Shoes?"

"Shoes has a cold, and you know how they hate to be separated."

"Where's your fellow?" Ernie asked.

"He'll be here any minute. He was in the shower when I knocked on the door. I left him a message to meet me here."

"Ah," he said with a long nod.

She felt a little guilty fooling them like this. Barrett would leave, and she would start a new life with her baby. How would they take it? She'd just tell them that she and Barrett weren't compatible. He was afraid of babies. Telling them she had chosen to have a baby by herself was going to be the hardest part. But she couldn't think about that. She didn't want anything to deter her.

Ricky sauntered into the park area and headed straight over. He winked at her, clucked his tongue and said, "Hi, there, little mama," in a low voice just like he always did. "You're looking particularly fine today."

She glanced around to make sure no one heard him. "Gee, thanks, Ricky. Nice of you to notice."

"I always notice."

She waved him away. "Yeah, yeah, set your dish down and scoot. And shush," she added.

Once she'd had a fever of one hundred and five, a red, runny nose and every other symptom of the flu, and he'd complimented her.

She held out her hand, and he handed over his plastic dish. He always brought the same thing, sardines, and he was the only one who ate them. She wrinkled her nose as she set them at the very end of the line of dishes.

She wasn't sure what made her look up. Barrett was walking across the lawn toward her. Wow, what was that *pow!* feeling in her chest all about, anyway? The breeze ruffled his damp hair, and he brushed it from his face. He was wearing her Don't Drink and Derive T-shirt across a broad expanse of chest and baggy blue shorts that showed off his legs. The sun lit the hairs on his legs and arms and made them look like spun gold. Oh, boy. Had she ever noticed the hair on a guy's legs before?

He nodded to a few people who greeted him, but his track never wavered. Weasel Boy's tiny legs were a blur as he kept up with Barrett's strides.

She held out her T-shirt and nodded toward his when he neared her. "Very couplelike, don't you think?"

His gaze lingered a little too long on her shirt. "Very."

She was fast falling for those dimples—only the dimples, you understand. Not his smile, or the way a hank of his hair sometimes fell over his forehead, or the way he said exactly what was on his mind. Or the way he focused on her as though she were the only important thing in the whole wide world.

"Can I help with anything?" he asked, taking in the long table of dishes.

"I've got it under control, thanks. As soon as the king arrives, we'll eat."

"Aren't you two cute?" Arlene said, touching Barrett's shoulder as she took in both their shirts. "Our Stacy is just the best at finding these cute expressions. Oh, wait a minute. She's not our Stacy anymore. She's *your* Stacy now."

Stacy laughed to cover how that made her feel. To be someone's Stacy. "I'm my own Stacy, Arlene."

Jack, the king, was always the last resident of Sunset City to arrive at the canned-food party. "Good to see me," he said to each person who inclined their head as he made his way to the table. "Glad I could make it." He scanned the offerings, made his usual scowl at Ricky's sardines and handed Stacy his usual dish of bread-and-butter pickles.

Nita poured him a cup of iced tea, and he led everyone to lift their cups in a toast. "Here's to Mae. May she be baking her lemon curd tarts and scones in Heaven."

"She's the reason we have these wonderful get-togethers. We can't ever forget that," Frieda said.

"I wonder if they have canned food in Heaven," Ernie asked.

Everyone formed lines on either side of the long table.

"So your granny started this, and then you took over when she passed on?" Barrett asked, following Stacy down the line and repeating everything she did.

"Someone had to do it." She dumped a spoonful of canned chili on her plate with two taps of the spoon and then tossed a few corn chips on top.

He did the same thing, though he wasn't paying attention to what he was doing. "But why you?"

"Because…" She dumped a spoonful of mashed pumpkin onto her plate. "You ask too many questions, you know that?"

He shrugged. "It's what I do. I'm just trying to understand who Stacy Jenkins is. How much of your personality is made up of doing things for others." He glanced at the orange mushy stuff and passed.

When their plates were full, they found an empty table. "Don't try to study me. I'm not a tree snail, you know."

Of course, Ernie and Frieda walked by just as she said the last of that. They glanced at her and went to another table. "He thinks she's a tree snail," Ernie whispered.

"You fascinate me," Barrett said.

"I do?" Before her heart could warm too much, she remembered how he became fascinated, then bored, with many things.

"Didn't I say you had nice attributes?" He tossed a green bean to Weasel Boy, who surprised her by eating it.

"Yes, you did." She dropped a cracker next to the dog's nose. He sniffed at it, then looked at Barrett. She tossed a green bean the dog's way. He still didn't eat it.

Now that was the ultimate low point—rejected by a dog.

AFTER LUNCH, Stacy helped to clear the mess and stack everyone's containers in some kind of order. Barrett looked as though he were trying to stumble through a conversation with Ernie and Frieda, Lord knew about what. She heard the words Black Gopher and rolled her eyes. But when Barrett glanced at her, she felt a strange thrill of excitement shiver through her. Not excitement, dread. *Keep reminding yourself of that. You're not looking forward to kissing Barrett. Lousy kisser, remember? And all that pressure!*

He rubbed his hand over his mouth, and instead of remembering the lousy kiss, she remembered the way that mouth felt on her palm. So vividly, in fact, that she found herself rubbing her palm against her thigh. It was just a fluke.

Nita floated by with the words, "We're still waiting. Better make it a good one."

"If it's not, I take total responsibility. I...I'm not sure I'm a good kisser. I'm probably lousy."

"Oh, pooh. If it's meant to be, it'll just come together...like magic." Nita snapped her fingers. "And if it's not meant to be, he's fair game."

Great. Barrett didn't believe in magic, didn't believe in things coming together without a formula or scientific reason. "We'll give it our best shot."

''And I want to see some tongue action,'' Nita said as she sauntered away.

''No tongues on the first kiss!''

Let's get this over with, Stacy thought, walking to Barrett. She looped her arm around his. ''Shall we take a walk around the lake, sweetheart?''

He looked at her as though she'd given him the formula for cold fusion. ''You called me sweetheart.''

She squeezed his arm tighter before realizing how that action pressed his arm against her breast. Under Ernie and Frieda's watchful eye, she didn't dare move away. ''Yes, I did, dear.''

His smile grew wider. ''I like that.''

''Me, too,'' she said aloud when she'd only meant to think it. Except for the dogs, she'd never called anyone sweetheart.

''What should I call you?'' he asked as they strolled toward the lake like a real, honest-to-goodness couple. ''Dearest?''

''Er, no.''

''Snookums?''

She sputtered. ''Definitely not.''

''I heard Ernie call Frieda that, though I'm not sure what it means.''

''I think it's a...well, it might be a... Actually, I'm not sure what it means, either.''

They shared a laugh, and she noticed how his eyes sparkled like the ocean on a sunny day.

''Would it offend you if I called you babe?''

She tightened her hold on his arm.

''Uh-oh, that means it would offend you.''

She pulled him in front of her. ''I like babe.''

''Okay...babe.'' He didn't quite have the hang of it,

and yet it still shimmered through her and left a trail of what felt like champagne bubbles going through her veins.

"Kiss me," she said, sounding a little more urgent than she'd intended.

He glanced at the dozens of people all watching. "Now?"

"Now's as good a time as any."

"Well, all right then."

He leaned down, and she lifted up on her tiptoes. She slid her arms around his neck. After a moment of deliberation, he put his arms around her waist. This was it, the big kiss. They needed to look passionate...in love. She tried not to think about the tongues part.

"Should I move my head to the right or left?" he asked.

"Don't think about it. Just let it happen." Magic.

"Oh, right."

They both moved forward—and bumped noses. They adjusted, tilted their heads the other way—and bumped noses.

"You stay that way, I'll move," she said.

She tilted her head a fraction. With a narrowed eye, he measured the angle. He tilted a little more, a little less. Then he nodded a ready-to-go, which put him out of angle again. Finally, they were lined up and ready to have this all-out passionate kiss. They moved in, but at different rates of speed. Their mouths banged together, and they both instinctively backed up.

"I forgot to calculate rate of acceleration. I'm usually good at that, like those riddles, if two trains are traveling at ninety miles per hour..."

She raised her hand, and his words drifted off. "Forget trains. Forget the kiss. It's not going to work."

"No kiss?" He actually looked disappointed.

Some part of her felt the same way. As much as she'd been dreading it, she'd obviously been looking forward to it, too. "I guess we're kind of committed at this point. But first, we have to forget all those people watching us."

"What people?" He was doing that focusing thing again, and she realized that he had already forgotten about their audience.

"No more overanalyzing. I know. Tell me snail names."

"Snail names?"

"Trust me on this."

And he did. *"Delicatus, elegans, floridanus, fuscoflammellus, lucidovarius, nebulosus, osmenti, roseatus, septentrionalis, vonpaulseni—"*

She let that delicious rush overwhelm her as his voice caressed those exotic names. She leaned forward and kissed him. Direct contact, no hesitation, no aiming—connection! Magic. They lingered there for a moment before backing away. She wondered if she looked as shell-shocked as he did.

"That was...nice," he said.

"Yeah, nice."

Then he leaned forward and kissed her again. Their mouths brushed against each other in a slow, back-and-forth motion. His movements were light and feathery, his mouth deliciously soft. Her breath hitched. She sneaked a peek at him, gratified to find his eyes closed. He was totally focused on his task. Her eyes drifted shut, and she sank into those deliberate, almost experimental caresses. Maybe this was what the snails did.

They finished the kiss and stepped back again.

"Really nice," he said. His eyes were a darker blue than usual as he took her in.

"Yeah...really nice."

This time they both stepped forward at the same time. His arms slid around her shoulders, her arms went around his waist, and their mouths connected perfectly again. Tingles skittered along her nerve endings as the heat from his body enveloped her. His fingers were slowly massaging the back of her neck. His mouth gently grasped her lower lip, tasting it, nibbling ever so slightly. She could taste the tang of the mandarin oranges he'd had for dessert and the sweetness of the cherry. She was almost dizzy from this more-than-nice kiss.

This time when they parted, he blinked and said, "Wow."

"Yeah...wow."

Okay, so she wasn't saying anything profound. That was because she was feeling profound. That one fairly innocent kiss had moved her more than any tongue kiss ever had.

Stacy had that light-headed feeling she got when she'd just come out of a movie that had totally enraptured her. Especially when it was a matinee. She blinked in the light and wondered where the rest of the world had been lately.

A sound at the level of her knees brought her attention to a toddler in a puffy pink outfit. Barrett took one look and stumbled back—right into the lake. Luckily he didn't fall in. He splashed like an ungainly duck and gained his balance before taking the long way back to the bank.

Stacy ignored him and knelt down to the toddler's level. "Hi, there, Lynsey!"

"Sorry about that," Eric said as he headed toward them. He was Betty's son and Lynsey's father.

"That's okay. She knows her aunt Stacy, yes, she does."

Stacy sometimes baby-sat Lynsey, who gurgled in

delight. "And that's...that man *way* over there is Barrett."

He was shaking water from his pants, but he managed a nod.

She picked up Lynsey and kissed her sticky cheek. "Hi, there, sweetie." She felt the ache in her chest at wanting one of her own. Boy or girl, it didn't matter. Having those arms wrapped around her neck, the pure love that only a baby can bestow, made her even more resolved to go through with her plan.

Barrett was by the picnic tables, pouring water out of his shoes. She sat beside him and held out Lynsey. "You can't really be afraid of this sweet little... Barrett, come back here."

"I know they're sweet and little and harmless, but I just can't relate to them. They make no sense to me. They..." His gaze took her in, Lynsey in her arms. For a moment that stiff expression softened. Just as quickly, he grabbed a couple of chairs. "I'll start taking these inside the rec center."

Arlene watched him make a hasty retreat. "I'll be darned. He really is afraid of babies. I figured he was making it up, you know, to throw me off."

Stacy was watching him, too. "He's not that calculating." She kissed Lynsey's cheek and handed her to her uncle Joey, Eric's twin brother. "Just a little hopeless."

Stacy noticed Barrett looking at her, obviously checking to see whether she still had the baby in her arms before he made his way back to her.

Nita said, "Now that you're a couple, you must come dance tonight."

"I don't ballroom dance, you guys know that."

"Dance?" Barrett looked horrified at the prospect, and he hadn't even seen her dance yet.

Nita answered Barrett's question. "Ernie and Frieda teach ballroom dancing at the rec center on Monday evenings, and every Saturday night we have a dance. Stacy doesn't take lessons because she doesn't have anyone to dance with."

"Once in a while I fill in for someone," Stacy said.

Frieda gave her a sympathetic pat on the shoulder. "Yes, she does, bless her heart. Bless all of our hearts."

"But I don't know how to dance," Barrett said.

"It's like that kiss," Frieda said. "Well, the second one. And the third one. It'll come together just fine."

"All right, we'll be there." Stacy turned to Barrett. "Won't we, sweetheart?"

"We'll give it our best shot, babe."

It didn't sound quite natural, and yet it had that same effect on her. Part possession, part endearment.

"It's salsa night!" Nita called as they walked toward the table, giving a demonstration of a crazy hip swing type of movement.

They were hanging onto their charade by their fingernails. Tonight they'd bumble through the rumba and the tango, probably do permanent damage to each other's toes.

Barrett helped her load chairs and boxes of plastic silverware and napkins into the rec center. They tied Weasel Boy's leash to the door handle so he wouldn't get stepped on.

She preceded Barrett into the large, dark closet, set down her boxes and turned right into him. He braced her arms automatically, and she glanced at those strong hands.

"Sorry," they both said, and it took him another several moments before he realized his hands were still on her. He released her, but remained there.

"About that kiss," he said.

She said, "We shouldn't talk about the kiss."

"I didn't actually want to talk about it." He leaned closer, his gaze on her mouth.

He was going to kiss her again, and oh, she wanted him to, but it was such a bad idea because…well, precisely because she wanted that kiss. "Good, then let's not talk about it," she said briskly and headed out.

She caught him glancing at the calendar as they walked out of the closet and wondered if she'd misinterpreted the whole thing. Maybe he hadn't been about to kiss her at all. "Look, I'll leave you alone for the rest of the afternoon so you can get your work done. I'll bring a pizza over for dinner at seven, and then we'll head to the community room. We'll only stay for a while, just to show up. Then you can go back to work."

"All right, but I'll get the pizza." He grabbed the last stack of chairs and carried them into the closet. She grabbed the folded tablecloth and followed him in. Again they ended up face to face in the dark closet, which smelled faintly of mothballs. He took the tablecloth from her and ended up grabbing her hands, too.

And not even accidentally. He had the same serious expression on his face that he'd had when he might have, but probably didn't, want to kiss her in the pool.

"Stacy, have you ever done something just for yourself? Because you enjoyed doing it?"

She shook her head even as her mind accused her of participating in the charade for less than unselfish reasons. "I mean, I enjoy working with the dogs. And organizing the canned-food party. And leading the workout class."

He increased the pressure on her hands. "What about pretending to be my girlfriend?"

"That's nice, too," she said on a whisper. She cleared

her throat. "But it's only a charade. Don't worry, I understand that."

"So the charade is only to help me out."

"Of course. Why else would I be doing it?" She sounded guilty and hoped he didn't pick up on it. "And speaking of work, we'd better get you home. You're running out of time."

He glanced at the calendar again, but his expression didn't change from the tense one of before. "Yes, I am."

10

THE LIE was haunting Stacy long after Barrett returned to work while she tried to motivate herself with some rigorous housecleaning. Maybe it was the effect of all the reminders of Granny around the house that was doing it to her. Granny who never lied, who never did self-serving things. The afghans, the quilts, all the small, loving touches that marked the life of an upstanding, honest woman.

Stacy had done her best to follow in Granny's footsteps. Didn't she owe it to Granny to make her proud, even though she wasn't around to see it? After all, Granny had given up her relaxing retirement years to raise a little girl who'd suddenly become orphaned. Stacy stopped in front of an old picture of her and Granny soon after she'd come to live with her. Granny's husband had recently passed on, and she was faced with the reality of not knowing how to do anything on her own. They'd learned together, two orphans and a family of Sunset City residents who were always there when they needed them. Granny had sacrificed, she'd worked to support them, and she'd fought to raise her granddaughter in Sunset City.

Granny had been a saint. From those early days when Stacy had picked weeds in Ernie's garden, baked cookies for Valentine's Day and spent her Christmas money on presents for others, she'd tried to be a saint, too.

She was failing miserably. Not only was she lying to

the people she considered family, but she was lying to herself and now to Barrett. She'd tried to think of one thing she did just for herself when he'd asked. One selfish thing besides having the baby. The only other thing that kept coming to mind was this charade. It had started as selfless, though, hadn't it?

She remembered the first time they'd met, his handsome face in the hedge. Already her feminine interest had been piqued. But surely her offer to act as his girlfriend had been completely—okay, mostly—unselfish, right?

The doorbell kept her from completing that thought. It was probably better not to examine her motives too closely. Wanting Barrett and having him were two totally different things. He'd be off to save the rain forest, and then he'd be off to the next thing that piqued his interest, and then the next.

She made sure there was no evidence of baby books or the profiles lying about before opening the door. Arlene and Betty smiled from the front stoop.

"Hi, Stacy. Thought we'd come over and see how things were going," Arlene said sweetly, walking right in.

"He's not here. He's working."

Both ladies raised an eyebrow. Betty's went so high, it nearly disappeared into her hairline.

"He's got an important project, remember?" Stacy said. "We can't be together every minute, you know."

Stacy noticed that Arlene was carrying a large tote bag. "Pooh, real romance knows no project deadlines."

"Wow, it's just like it was when Mae was around," Betty said as she took in the living room.

"Yeah, well, every time I think of redecorating, I can hear Granny's voice saying, 'Why throw out perfectly good stuff to spend money on the same thing?'"

"Practical woman, she was."

Betty honed in on the quasi-knitted booties still attached to the skein by an umbilical cord of yarn. "Are these for the Hansons' grandson?"

"That's the intent, though he'll probably be a teenager by the time I get them right."

Another way she'd failed Granny. No domestic skills. She'd be turning over in her grave when Stacy had a baby on her own.

"All ready for the dance tonight?" Arlene asked.

They scanned her outfit. "Is that what you're wearing?" Betty asked.

Stacy glanced at her ankle-length dress with tiny flowers and shrugged. "I don't own many dresses." No reason to.

Arlene narrowed her eyes. "That's one of Mae's dresses, isn't it?"

"No, it's mine." Stacy tried not to sound too insulted.

Betty said, "You sure don't look like a girl set to sweep a man off his feet."

"She sure doesn't," Arlene added with the appropriate tsking sounds.

"I don't want to be obvious," Stacy protested.

Arlene said, "It's a good thing we just happened by. See, we're going down to the dance studio. Their little dress shop is having a big sale. You'll just come along with us and pick something out for tonight."

Betty took one arm, Arlene took the other, and Stacy didn't have a chance to protest as they dragged her to the car.

Etta's Dance Studio was a stand-alone building adorned with glittering musical notes and dancing feet. The wood floors gleamed under the bright lights. A lively polka flowed from the speakers even though there wasn't a class going on. Etta clattered across the floor in spiked heels and greeted them.

"We're here for the sale," Arlene said. "And to find something for Stacy."

Etta sized up Stacy with a narrowed eye. "Size two?"

"Seven."

"Come this way, child. I think we've got just the thing for you. It's even more on sale than the rest because it's been sitting here forever." In a conspiratorial voice, she added, "Not many size sevens waltzing these days."

"We want something sexy," Betty said. "Maybe even see-through."

"See-through?" Stacy couldn't help but think of her nipples showing through her tank top.

"At the top and over the arms," Betty clarified.

Etta rustled through the collection of the gaudiest-colored dresses Stacy had ever seen and several minutes later pulled one from the rack. "Tah dah! It's a bright one."

That it was, a splashy mixture of reds, purples and yellows. Large crinoline ruffles that matched the hues in the dress adorned the sleeves and the hem. "It's, uh, kind of low-cut."

"Well, you shoulda seen what Nita was going to send over," Arlene said. "She thought we ought to loan you one of our outfits, but we thought you should own one for yourself."

Stacy held it up. "Yeah, but it's really low-cut."

"We want you to look seductive."

"Enticing," Betty added.

"Yummy."

"I think you pushed it a bit too far, Arlene," Betty said out of the corner of her mouth.

Stacy wondered what Barrett would think about it.

``It has built-in booby boosters,'' Arlene said, pushing her own breasts together to demonstrate.

Stacy glanced down at her chest. ``Yeah, well, you gotta have something to boost.'' But she could hardly protest when they shoved the dress in her hands and ordered her to put it on.

``It reminds me of the dress I wore years ago in a ballroom dancing competition when I was married to Harry. Before he left me for the instructor,'' Arlene said, walking into the large dressing room with Stacy.

``Too bad it was a man,'' Betty said, genuinely dismayed, as she followed them in and closed the door behind them.

``Go on, put the dress on. And it was a woman who liked to dress like a man.''

``I thought it was a man who liked to dress like a woman.''

Arlene waved that away. ``Whatever.''

``Good news!'' Etta called from the other side of the door. ``I've got a matching shirt for the gentleman.''

Stacy's mouth quirked. ``Oh, he'll love that.'' She was tempted to try to get him out of wearing it, but then figured, if she had to endure the costume, so did he. She was doing this for him, after all. Well, mostly.

``What do you have to go with the dress shoe-wise?'' Arlene asked as she helped Stacy strip out of her clothes.

``Basic black pumps, low heels. They'll go good with this dress.''

``Just like your granny,'' Betty said, shaking her head. ``Practical.''

Stacy said, ``You say that like it's a bad thing.''

``A woman's got to have some unpractical clothes, too. Seductive clothes. I'll bet your underwear is practical, too.''

"Well, in case you haven't noticed, I'm not the kind of girl who does seductive well."

"We noticed," they said in unison.

So that *was* why the men hightailed it out of her life.

"That's better." Betty pointed to Stacy's pink thong underwear. "Ooh, la la."

"No panty lines," Stacy said, wondering why she felt the need to justify or make them seem practical. She slid into the dress and decided she did feel more exciting in it than in her other dress.

"Very nice," Arlene said, surveying her.

"Can you zip up the back please?" Stacy turned her back toward Betty.

"It is zipped."

She groped around the back and felt skin. Lots of it. The dress made whispery sounds as she walked out of the dressing room and over to the three-way mirror. The back plunged to just about her panty level. "What did Nita's dress look like?"

"Like that in the front." Arlene popped the clasp on her bra. "Can't wear that. But it's got those boosters, so you won't need it."

She barely needed it anyway, but she didn't point that out. She maneuvered out of the bra and looked at the front of the dress. The front did some dipping, too, and amazingly enough, it did give her cleavage.

"Betty, you want hair or makeup?"

"I'll take makeup."

"You can't do anything with my hair," Stacy said. "It's wispy."

"We'll just see about that."

The women were all business when they steered Stacy into the rest room. The front part of the room was a large dressing room. The walls were red-and-black-flocked velvet. A long counter stretched along the wall, and three ornate, red velvet chairs were tucked beneath it.

Arlene pointed to one of the chairs. ``Sit.'' She pulled a curling iron out of her bag and plugged it in.

Betty dug through her purse. ``I have some makeup in here, since you don't own any.''

``I do, too!''

Betty narrowed her eyes at Stacy's face. ``Who taught you how to fix your face, anyway?''

``Well...no one.''

``I guess Mae wasn't much into making herself up, was she? A simple woman, your granny.''

``Practical all the way,'' Arlene agreed as she clamped the curling iron around a lock of Stacy's hair. Stacy tried not to blink at the tickle of the eyeliner or when Betty swiped mascara on her lashes. Had she ever worn mascara? Had anyone ever put makeup on her like this? It made her feel all warm and gushy inside that they were doing this. But it did raise the question. ``Why are you two doing this? I thought you wanted Barrett for Denise and Tanya.''

Both women paused. ``Well—'' Betty met Arlene's gaze ``—if you're interested in Barrett for yourself, we want to help give you the best chance for it.''

``But only if you really are interested and not pretending.''

``I'm not pretending.'' Wow, she sounded convincing.

``Well, then, you haven't got a thing to worry about.''

``There.'' Arlene leaned back and surveyed their work. ``Beautiful.''

Beautiful? No way. She turned to the mirror. Her straight, wispy hair waved in soft curls. Spiky lashes accented brown eyes that looked enormous. ``Wow.''

``Is that all you can say, wow?''

Stacy nodded. "I think so." She turned to the side, getting a glimpse of the open back and all the ruffles. Some emotion bloomed in her chest as she saw the sexy woman looking back at her from the mirror. She was sure she'd never been anything close to sexy before. This was close. Real close.

"Get ready to rumba!" Arlene said.

BARRETT HAD CALLED Stacy to tell her he'd ordered the pizza, and she'd told him not to put a shirt on. That had him perplexed, but he didn't dwell on it. He was too distracted by the kiss they'd shared that afternoon. He had kissed women before, of course, and there wasn't anything particularly different about the kiss with Stacy. Not in the technical sense, anyway. But in every other sense, it was largely different. He'd lingered, for one thing, really enjoying the feel of her mouth against his. Totally immersed, yet not thinking or analyzing. It made no sense.

No more sense than feeling all the things he'd written about in his paper on romance—the rush, the charge of adrenaline and all the physical signs of arousal. There was yet another element he couldn't put his finger on, and it certainly hadn't been in any of the literature he'd read. He'd felt...lost, as if he were spinning out of control, throwing caution to the wind, bordering on crazy. When he'd started to feel it, he wanted to analyze it. That was another strange thing—he couldn't. It flew out of his mind before he could even try to get his thoughts around it. He would have snagged another kiss in the closet if she hadn't been so closed to the possibility.

Stacy arrived at Barrett's two minutes after the pizza did. When he opened the door, they both stood there taking in each other. She looked like Stacy, only more vivid. She radiated like the phosphorescence of the seashore. Her mouth glistened red, but her eyes captivated him. They were full of fire. All manner of thought fled his mind, and all he could do was stare at her.

"What's wrong?" she asked at last.

"You're beautiful."

"Really? I mean...thanks."

"And you're bright." He stepped aside to let her in.

"*You're* half-naked," she said.

"You told me not to put a shirt on."

"Oh, that's right." She knelt down and patted Elmo's head. "Hi, fella."

She made a rustling sound as she walked into the kitchen with a bag. She held up a bottle of wine. "For rhythm. Or courage, whatever's needed first." Then she pulled out a long-sleeved shirt with ruffles on the sleeves that matched her dress. "And this is for you, courtesy of Arlene."

"It's...bright."

"Yes, it is." She handed it to him, then opened the cabinet and took down two wineglasses.

He'd set the table. All the papers that he hadn't worked on this afternoon sat in a pile on the counter, along with his laptop.

He put on the shirt. It only buttoned halfway up his chest. "Some of the buttons are missing."

"It's supposed to be like that." She patted him on the chest. "Sexy."

He glanced at her hand. His chest hair curled over her fingers, and a hot feeling curled inside him.

She quickly removed her hand. "We'd better get it on. I mean—" she cleared her throat "—get going."

Stacy seemed interested in the tree snails as they ate. In fact, she was so interested, she asked what their names were again. When he listed them off, she let out a little sigh similar to the sound Elmo made whenever he curled up on Barrett's lap.

Could it be that she liked tree snails? She did have a rather dreamy expression on her face, and he wondered what it would be like to have that dreamy expression aimed at him. Then he realized that *he* was watching *her* with a dreamy expression.

After they ate and cleaned up, she said, "Don't worry about getting the dances right. We'll dance for a while, sit and watch the rest of them dance for a while, and then we're out of there. Got it?"

"Got it. Are we going to be kissing again?"

She stopped mid-movement. "Probably not."

"Are you sure? Do you think there were any doubts left by our kiss this afternoon? They're awfully skeptical. Maybe we'd better make sure."

"Oh, I doubt there were any doubts. We did a good job out there."

He caught himself grinning like a hormone-driven teenager until she said, "Such a good job, I don't think we need to do it again."

He ran his finger across his mouth. "Too bad. I was looking forward to it."

"I, uh…you were?" She was staring at his mouth. She blinked and cleared her throat.

"Weren't you?"

Her shoulders sagged. "Yes, but it's more complicated than that. That kiss today was a little *too* good, you see. We're supposed to be convincing *them* we're involved, not each other. It might be easy—for me, at least—to forget that. And then you're leaving to disperse your seed in the rain forest for two years—"

"Not *my* seed."

"You'll be gone for two years and…we'd better not, okay?"

"I suppose you're right." Though he wasn't so sure.

"You bet I am," she said too quickly and with a forced smile.

He reviewed their plan. "No kissing, a little dancing, a little not dancing…I believe I have it. But one question. What exactly is salsa night?"

11

THE DANCE was under way when Stacy and Barrett stepped through the gate that encircled the pool. Streamers spiraled from the ceiling of the community center and muffled music penetrated the glass windows to encompass them in seductive Latin rhythms. The pool looked like a fluorescent gem with the faintest ripple across the surface of the water. The moon was still a sliver, but bright nonetheless. It was a bit like a fairyland, and that feeling was enhanced when Barrett took hold of her hand. They turned and looked at each other, and his fingers tightened. He'd called her beautiful, and she tried to forget her dumb response. As his gaze scanned her face, she knew he was thinking it again. He'd said he wanted to kiss her again. The way he was looking at her, he wanted to kiss her now.

The wavering blue light from the pool danced across his face. The way he looked at her with total focus sent warmth washing clear through her body. His mouth was slightly open, relaxed. Very kissable. She sighed.

"You are so beautiful," he said in a soft voice.

Her instinct was to negate that. She wasn't beautiful, after all. Okay, maybe she was pretty if she worked at it, like tonight. But not beautiful, not by any stretch of the imagination. It was the lights, the music, his gratitude because she was helping him out. She felt her eyes well up, and in a thick voice, she said, "Thank you."

"Did I say something wrong?"

She laughed, though it came out all choked. "No, you definitely did not. It's just that...no one's ever told me that before. It made me feel really good."

His head tilted. "But you're crying."

"I'm not crying exactly. I'm...don't even try to understand it, okay?"

The perplexed expression never left his face. "You won't start bawling if I tell you that you smell nice, too, will you?"

She laughed. "No, I won't. It's Euphoria."

He inhaled softly and smiled. "Just about."

"That's the name of the lotion I use. Euphoria."

"Oh. Sure, I knew that."

Their gazes met, and a tickle bubbled through her veins. His blond hair was glossy under the wavering lights. She felt an overwhelming urge to see if it felt as silky as it looked. She found herself hoping he would kiss her palm again. And hoping he wouldn't, since that would be way too romantic for people who were only pretending.

"Do you..." She tried to clear the flutters from her throat. "Do you remember when we were in the closet this afternoon?"

"Oh, yes."

She did, too, the tension crackling between them, the way— She focused her thoughts. "When you asked if I'd ever done anything just for me?"

He nodded, giving her his entire attention.

"There is something I'm going to do that's just for me. I'm going to have a baby."

His fingers tightened on her hand, and he glanced at her stomach. "Right now?"

She laughed, though it came out a bit strained. Why was she telling him this? Maybe to put an end to any hope that she and Barrett could make a go of it. She pulled free of his handhold. "I'm not pregnant now. But soon. I decided that I wasn't going to have a man in my life, and I can live with that. But I can't live without having a child. That's what my life has been missing. I'm almost thirty-two, and I can't wait around forever."

He looked shell-shocked. Hair had fallen over his eyes, and he hadn't even pushed it back. "Who's the father?" His voice sounded quivery.

"It's no one I know," she admitted, even though she'd been trying hard to convince herself that she did sort of know the guys those profiles represented.

"You don't know the future father of your baby?"

If it weren't such a serious moment, she might have laughed at the perplexity on his face. "I'm using a sperm bank and artificial insemination."

"Oh." Relief surged through his expression. "But why artificially? It seems to me that a woman could go out and find a man to impregnate her."

"I suppose I could, but it's easier this way. I can see a man's attributes up front, the sperm is free from disease, and there won't be any custody issues."

She was touched by the concern on his face.

"You're going to do it alone?"

"Sure, why not? A lot of women do. I mean, I wanted the whole shebang, but I'm not going to get that. So I've adjusted my life goal. I axed the husband and went right for the baby. I'm not sure I can do romantic relationships, but I'm good at taking care of things."

His mouth was open, but nothing was coming out. She'd really knocked him for a loop. It didn't matter. In another day he'd be leaving Sunset City, and in less than two weeks, he'd be off on another expedition and she wouldn't see him for at least two years. Probably forever.

She felt a pang in her chest at that thought. No, more like a yawning chasm of loneliness waiting for her to slip and fall in.

Uh-oh. She'd gotten more attached to him than she'd realized. And with him being so darned cute and sexy, and with his straightforwardness and honesty... Good thing she'd popped the bubble.

"Looks like they're having a serious discussion."

Those words hung in the air for a moment, suspended in the music she hadn't realized had grown louder. Since she hadn't said it, and Barrett hadn't said it, that must mean... She turned. Faces were pressed to every window, so close their noses were smashed. The door was slightly ajar, and both Nita and Jack were squeezed into the small opening.

"You two coming in to dance?" Nita asked as though they weren't all invading her privacy. In fact, no one made even the slightest move to not look like they were all spying.

"Uh, sure," Stacy said off key and headed toward the door.

It wasn't until they stepped through the open doorway that everyone resumed their dance positions as though they'd been doing that all along.

"Ah, here's the happy couple," Betty said, waving them inside.

"Come in, come in," Frieda said, pulling them into the melee of dancers. "Punch and cookies are over there. But first, you must dance!"

The rhythm pulsated through Stacy as she faced Barrett. "Shall we?"

Frieda tapped their shoulders. "Don't worry about following the form. Just let the rhythm move you. And Stacy, dear, try not to crush his toes."

"I know, I know."

Frieda sauntered toward Nita and Jack and in a sing-song voice said, "Arms, Nita. Untidy feet, Arlene!"

"How do we do this exactly?" Barrett glanced at the other couples and positioned his hands accordingly.

"Remember how we kissed? Like that. Don't think about it, don't analyze. We'll do just fine."

Amazingly, neither stepped on anyone's toes. Magic. Almost as though they were meant to be together.

Which they weren't, she reminded herself as they moved to the beat. With Barrett's arms holding tight to her waist and her dress swishing pleasantly with each movement, it was getting harder to convince herself. It was just the moment, the music...Barrett.

Oh, boy.

Betty and Mary danced by—they were both widowed—and gave them a thumbs-up. Frieda and Ernie winked as they went by. Even Nita gave a nod of approval.

"I think we've finally convinced them," Stacy said.

"We're finally aroused enough, huh?"

She sputtered a laugh at that one. "Oh, yes, I believe so."

Even though they laughed and twirled around the edge of the dance floor, something had changed between them. She could feel it in the way he looked at her. It wasn't horror, thank goodness, though the disbelief lingered. He who was afraid of babies was probably glad he was on his way out of her life before any of that business could begin.

"What do the people here think of...your plans?" he asked during a slower dance.

"I'm not telling them until I'm pregnant. I know they'd talk me out of it, tell me I was crazy to do it alone. But I'm not alone, not really. I have them, and...well, them.

Once they get over the shock, they'll support my decision, I'm sure.''

His fingers tightened on her waist. ''I'm the only one who knows?''

''Well, you and Ricky, but that was an accident. He saw the profiles of the donors on my dresser mirror, the nose bag.''

''He was in your bedroom?''

''He was fixing a leak. Anyway, he's been sworn to secrecy, though I'm not sure how long he'll hold out. But it doesn't matter since I'm having it done in two days.''

''Two days?'' He nearly yelled, causing a couple of people to turn and look.

She whispered, ''Let's not talk about this anymore.''

''Why not?''

''Because it doesn't really concern us, and you're giving me funny looks now. I liked it better when you thought I was beautiful. Now you're looking at me as though I'm one degree off crazy.''

He purposely looked away. ''I don't think you're crazy. I think I understand why you're doing it. And I'm...glad for you. Really, I am,'' he added at her skeptical look. ''At least you know what your life goal is. That's important.''

She leaned forward and kissed him lightly on the mouth. ''Here's to life goals. A baby for me, rain forest regrowth for you. May we find happiness therein.''

ONLY BARRETT wasn't happy. It was two in the morning, he was trying to put some touches on the conclusion of the tree snail environmental study, and he was having a hell of a time concentrating on anything but Stacy. Papers cluttered the dining room table, and his computer hummed gently, reminding him of the work to be done. And reminding him that he was never, ever late. But here he was, running late, and still not focusing on the project at hand.

He glanced at Elmo, who was asleep in his lap. Content. Satisfied. Mere days ago, the thought of a dog lying in his lap would have given him hives. Now...well, now it gave him a warm feeling in his stomach. That warm feeling evaporated when he realized he was going to leave this place, Elmo...Stacy. He was committed to two years in a Bolivian rain forest. He tried to remember how excited he'd been when he'd been awarded the financially rich grant. It would pay his bills while he immersed himself in the kind of study that fulfilled him. Maybe even his life goal.

Stacy's news had completely thrown him off. He envied her that she knew what her life goal was and that she was flexible enough to change it. But to have a baby by herself? He'd been looking at her as this fun, cute, unselfish person, and here she was a whole different person inside—a woman who yearned for love and family.

A woman.

He'd changed out of the frilly shirt and put on a cotton button-down shirt. The frilly shirt was lying on the chair next to him. He rearranged it until it resembled a nest and carefully set Elmo in the center of it. The dog stirred slightly before settling back to sleep.

Barrett walked outside, hoping the cool night air would knock some sense into him. After all, most sane people were asleep. Stacy, for instance, would be snuggled in her bed having baby dreams.

Then why was her living room light on? That didn't mean she was awake. It didn't mean he should go over and knock on her door.

Or maybe it did, he thought as he did just that. As though he'd lost his will.

It only took a minute for the door to open. She was wearing pajamas with sheep and clouds floating against a sky blue background. She'd only buttoned the center two buttons, which left a bit of her collarbone and stomach showing.

"Barrett? What's wrong?"

Leave it to Stacy to instantly think something was wrong and want to help him rather than chastise him for knocking on her door at this late hour.

"Can I come in?"

"Of course." She stepped aside, running her fingers through her hair as she walked into the living room. The television was on, but the sound was turned down. Lucille Ball was shoving a conveyor belt's worth of chocolate candies into her mouth.

"I didn't wake you, did I?"

"No, I couldn't get to sleep." She glanced at him. "Why is your shirt on inside out?"

"Oh, I—" She was right. No wonder he couldn't get the buttons to button right. He'd given up, so not only was his shirt inside out, it was unbuttoned. "Sorry, I just threw it on." She was waiting for him to explain himself, and not even impatiently. Darn it, she was such a good person. A caring person. Someone who would make a good mother. "I couldn't stop thinking about what you told me earlier."

She ruffled the hair she'd just finger combed. "I shouldn't have told you. I hadn't meant to, and then it was coming out of my mouth. Just forget about it, okay?"

"I figured you didn't want to talk about it when you said you wanted to turn in as soon as we returned from the dance. But I can't forget about it, Stacy. That's not the kind of thing a man can forget. I can't rewind the tape and erase the words.''

She dropped down onto the couch, which he noticed also held her pillow and a blanket. An empty mug sat on the coffee table with marshmallow fluff sticking to the insides. Gooey chocolate puddled on the bottom.

``But it doesn't concern you, Barrett. You'll be tromping through the forest long before I even start showing.'' She met his gaze. ``That is what you want to do, right? Your life goal?''

He sat on the coffee table in front of her. ``I think so. But I have to go through with the project regardless. I'm committed, and I've never backed out of anything in my life.''

She smiled, though it wasn't a happy smile. ``And you're never late.'' She hugged the pillow to her stomach. ``This has nothing to do with you. I'm the crazy one who's going to be doing this. I have a lot of people around me to help out.''

``Will they let you stay here after the baby is born? It is an older persons' community, after all.''

She shrugged. ``Probably. If they don't, I'll move. No biggie.''

``But where will you go?''

``I'll figure something out. Even if I can't stay here, the folks will still help me. They're like family.'' She laughed softly. ``Barrett, don't worry about me. I'll be fine. You…are worried about me, right? That's what this is about?''

``Yes, I'm worried about you.'' He didn't like the idea of her moving into a strange neighborhood without her friends close by. ``But how will I know what's happened to you?''

``I can send you letters, pictures even. We can get together when you come back.''

``Two years is a long time.''

``I know.'' The words came out like a soft sigh. ``Everything will be different then. We'll be different, and the baby will be Lynsey's age, if it takes the first time. There'll be toys all over, *The Little Mermaid* playing on the television for the hundredth time, laughter, crying and dirty diapers. I'll be crooning over every little thing the baby does. It'll be chaos, a perfectly wrong place for a research scientist to concentrate on a proj—'' Her eyes widened. ``Let's not pretend we'll get together then. Let's not even go there.'' She narrowed her eyes. ``You didn't come here to talk me out of it, I hope. I wouldn't have told you if I thought you were going to do that.''

He ran his hand over his mouth, reminding him of their kiss, which was something he definitely shouldn't be thinking of at that moment. ``I would never try to dissuade you from your life goal. I don't know why I came over. I couldn't stop thinking about it.''

She leaned forward and took his hands in hers. ``I'll be fine, really. This is what I want, right here in my heart.'' She removed one hand to rub her heart.

He nodded. ``I'm happy for you, Stacy. You'll make a good mother.''

She beamed at that, and he couldn't help notice a gleam in her eyes. ``Thanks.''

``I didn't make you cry again, did I?''

She shook her head, but her voice was thick when she said, ``It was just nice to hear. Sometimes I feel like such a failure. But this is something I'm going to excel at. I can tell already.''

He gave her hands a squeeze. ``Me, too.''

``Do you think it's selfish of me, though, to bring a

baby into the world without a father? I wonder about that sometimes…all the time, actually. Is it fair to the child?''

''You deserve to do something selfish. As long as you have your friends here, you'll manage. Look at all that you do now. And I'll bet you have enough love to make up for a lack of father.''

''Oh, my yes.'' She gave him a sweet smile. ''Thanks for saying that.''

It was a good time to leave. Two in the morning, a nice end to their conversation, and the project to finish at his place. Instead, he caught himself saying, ''Can I see the profiles? I'd like to see the men who might father your baby.''

''Actually, you're sitting on them.''

He jumped up and saw the three sheets of paper on the coffee table. ''Sorry about that.''

''They didn't feel a thing, I promise.'' Her smile warmed him deep inside. ''You really want to see them?''

''Yes.''

''Well, okay, I guess.''

They both leaned forward over the profiles he set on his legs. Their hair mingled in a light, tickling sort of way, and their knees pressed together.

''I've narrowed it down to three men, but I've been having a hard time figuring out which one I want. Maybe you seeing them isn't such a bad idea. You can give me a new perspective.''

''How long have you been deciding?''

''Two months. I know, a long time, but it's an important decision, and I can't seem to nail it down. If I could combine them into one person, they'd be perfect. I can't put it off any longer. I'm making the decision tonight, and Monday I go in. This guy is the leading candidate, I think,'' she said, pulling out the bottom sheet of paper.

``One-one-six-seven-two-five. He's smart, has his own software company, good entrepreneurial genes—''

``He's not so smart.''

``What?''

``His IQ isn't impressive.''

``Nobody can beat your IQ, Mr. Smarty-pants. The only thing that kind of worries me is that he has twins in his family. I'm not ready for two at once.''

Barrett flung the paper over his shoulder. ``Forget him. Who's next?''

She watched the paper float to the floor behind him but didn't put up too much of a fight. ``This guy is an artist. I like that he's got creative talent, which would be a good match for my practicality. My daughter, or son, could be a famous—''

``Poor, struggling artist selling paintings on the sidewalk for five bucks a pop.''

``Or she could be a commercial graphic artist and design award-winning ads—''

``Travel with a carnival doing caricatures in charcoal.''

She narrowed her eyes at him. ``My kid's going to be successful. But you know, it doesn't matter what she or he decides to do with their talent. As long as it's what they want, I'm good with that.''

``There isn't even an IQ on the profile. How can you choose a guy without knowing how smart he is—or isn't?''

``That's how most people do it. They don't require an IQ test before you get married or have a baby. I doubt most people even know their IQ.''

``Don't know their IQ? That's preposterous!'' Most of the people he associated with knew their IQ the same way they knew their social security number.

``I don't know mine.''

This was the real world, he reminded himself, not his closed circle of associates. Stacy, Nita, Arlene, Ernie…they were real. They didn't live and die by their IQs.

"All right, let's not discount him because of the lack of IQ information. We'll set him aside for future consideration." He tossed the profile over his shoulder, and she watched it float to the floor with the first one. "Who's next?"

"You're not going to like this one either. One-zero-three-four-two-one is a model. I know looks aren't the most important thing, but with me looking plain, I figured my kid should get the best chance she can have. They've done studies, you know. Good-looking people get more breaks."

"You're not plain."

"Yes, I am. I'm okay with that, believe me. I've gotten used to it. I just want better for my child."

She believed that she was plain. Even with that mouth and the way her hair wisped around her face, and those chocolate-syrup brown eyes. He catalogued all that for future dissemination and focused on 103421.

"No IQ again."

"I knew you weren't going to like that. But look, he's French. Some exotic genes, and maybe my child will learn French easier."

"French is easy to learn, especially when you're young."

"Easy for you to say."

"No, it's true. There have been studies on it. Young minds can easily learn more than one language. Our brains get more rigid as we age."

"You know French?"

"And Spanish and Italian and German."

She wrenched her gaze to the profile he was holding.

"He went to college and got an associate's degree. That counts for something. But he was making so much money modeling, he decided to do that for a while before returning to his studies."

"But he doesn't know what he wants to do with his life."

"Neither do you."

She had him there. He scanned the sheet. "He has your coloring."

"Yeah, I thought that was neat. We'll almost be guaranteed to produce a baby that looks like me."

He couldn't argue with that point, if that's what she wanted. Then he found the fatal flaw. "Look at his blood type. It's less common, harder to find blood in the event of a transfusion situation. Forget him." He tossed the paper over his shoulder with the rest.

She let out a sound of exasperation. "Then what kind of man do you think should be the father of my baby?"

He hadn't meant to say it, but the word came out just the same. "Me."

12

"VERY FUNNY, BARRETT." Stacy started to get up, because even just his saying the word had her insides jumping around.

He grabbed her hands and said, "I'm not being funny."

"You can't be serious."

"I am." He looked serious, earnest even.

She took a breath, never taking her eyes off him. "Is this why you came over tonight?"

He ducked his head and ran his hand through his hair. "No. Maybe. What I mean is, I didn't know that's why I was coming over. But I suspect some part of me knew. Ever since you told me what you wanted to do, I couldn't stop thinking about it. Something wasn't right, you getting sperm from some guy you've never even seen. I don't have any diseases, my family background is healthy, and I won't ask for custody. I can't do much about our disparate hair and eye coloring, but I understand brown eyes are often dominant. What do you say?"

He had her hands in his again, waiting for her answer. It was lodged in her throat right next to her heart. "You *are* serious."

"If you're going to do this, I want to be the father. I don't know that I'll ever get married and have a family, and I like the thought of having a child out there. With you."

She took another long breath, trying to allay the quivering in her body. She already knew the answer, and she pushed out the word. "Yes."

He hugged her, crushing her to his chest. "Thank you."

When they parted, she said, "*You're* thanking *me?*"

He let his hands remain on her shoulders where they felt warm and comforting. "For letting me be the one. I didn't realize how important it was until you didn't say yes right away."

She glanced at the discarded profiles on the floor. "None of those guys felt right. Now I know why."

"I feel right?"

"Oh, yes."

He smiled. "What do we need to do?"

Make wild and crazy love right here on this couch. She cleared her throat, pushing away those thoughts altogether. Making love with Barrett would be a bad idea. It would make it so much harder to let him go.

"We go to the clinic Monday. I think they'll give you some dirty magazines, a cup and some privacy."

"Oh. Oh," he said with a nod as it came together. "I guess I'll manage."

She didn't even want to start with those mental pictures, so she stood. "Maybe we'd better sleep on this for what's left of the night. In case of any second thoughts."

"You think you might change your mind?" He looked so worried, she almost laughed.

"No, but you might. This is a big step. You'd better give it some thought. I'm just giving you that option, that's all." *Please don't change your mind, please, please.* She loved the idea of Barrett fathering her child. Probably she loved it too much.

He stood, too, squeezing them into the small space between the coffee table and the couch. They maneuvered around each other, bodies, legs and arms brushing. They stopped, his pelvis pressed to her stomach and his hands on her shoulders. The contact sent a rush of warmth through her. He was looking at her with a serious expression on his face. *Forget the clinic and the cup! Strip him naked and lose yourself in him, skin against skin, mouth against mouth, mouth on other parts of her body, his body.* She wasn't even going to try to convince herself he would be a lousy lover, not when he was a great kisser, not when they came together so naturally. Magic.

So have fun, keep it casual, make a baby...and fall in love.

It would be way easy, looking into those vivid blue eyes while he was inside her.

The cup. It has to be the cup.

She backed around the coffee table and walked him to the door, becoming more and more afraid that this was some bizarre dream. She shouldn't have finished that pint of chocolate-chunk peanut-butter ice cream. At this very moment, she was probably sleeping on the couch.

"I'm not going to change my mind," he said, reinforcing her suspicion that it was a dream. "If that's what you're worried about."

She realized she was frowning. "More or less. I think I'll believe it better in the morning. Let's have lunch. We can talk more then. Or do you need to work on your project? I know you're running out of time."

"I'm fine." His gaze wandered over her face. "Should we shake on the deal?"

"Sure." She tried not to laugh at the absurdity of shaking hands and held out her hand. He kissed her instead.

It started out as the tender kind of kiss they'd shared that afternoon. The kiss for the benefit of Sunset City because she was nice. He massaged her neck as his mouth moved across hers, back and forth in that sensual movement she once thought impossible for a scientific kind of guy.

She felt his tongue slide across her lower lip, leaving behind a warm, moist feeling. Her fingers tightened against his back as her insides were rocked off their foundation. She let out a soft sound between a whimper and a groan, something she'd never heard from herself before. Her lips parted, and he dipped into her mouth with the tip of his tongue. She felt an electrical charge when their tongues touched. It wasn't that it had been a long time since she'd kissed anyone. She had never been kissed like this, never felt this soul-bending, melding connection with anyone else. When she heard him make a sound deep in his throat, she nearly melted.

He stepped closer so that their bodies nearly touched and deepened the kiss. She could feel the full length of his tongue sliding against hers now. She was so caught up in all the sensations, she realized she hadn't been moving her tongue. She played, skipping across his teeth, tickling the roof of his mouth and teasing the tip of his tongue. She could tell it worked by the sound in his throat again.

When they parted for breath, she said, "You are a fantastic kisser." Wow, when was the last time she'd sounded so breathless, so satisfied?

"I followed your advice, just go with it, let it happen."

She nuzzled closer to him. "Can we let it happen again?"

He answered with his kiss, covering her mouth, doing the lip slide before moving in to make it ten degrees past erotic. He was cradling her face now, thumbs brushing across her cheeks as they made slow love with their mouths. When she sucked on his tongue, taking it all in and running her mouth along the length of it, he really let out a strangled sound. His kiss became even more fervent than before.

"You taste good," he said between kisses, "and you feel good, and I'd probably better leave before I want to do a lot more than kiss you."

She pulled on his shirt before he could back away. "You're not going anywhere, not after kissing me like that."

After another one of those soul-deep groans, he kissed her again. She pulled him toward the couch, not breaking the kiss for a second, pulled him around the chair and the coffee table and down onto the spongy couch. They had barely touched down before Barrett, who was on top, was kissing her again.

Where had this passion come from? Was it the same passion that eventually petered out?

No, don't think about that. It doesn't matter. This is what you want, making love with him now, having his baby, saying goodbye...

She pushed his shirt over his shoulders, and he shrugged out of it. Her hands skimmed down his back and then up through his hair as he kissed down her neck, over her collarbone to the V of her pajama top. He unbuttoned the two buttons and pushed the shirt open.

"You are definitely not plain," he said, caressing the curve of her breasts.

She didn't feel the least bit plain as his gaze took her in with hungry desire. He pulled her to her knees and slid off her pajama top. He hugged her close, skin against skin, and seemed to relish the feel of holding her. She held him tight, pressing her cheek against his chest and listening to his heartbeat race beneath her ear. One of his hands traced across her back in affectionate circles while the other rubbed her neck in the way she was beginning to love.

The same way she was beginning to love him, she realized. Despite all her warnings to herself, she'd fallen for him. That's why it felt so right to have his baby. Some deep part of her needed to conceive in love. She could never be clinical, could never think of her child's father as 1234567. She pressed closer to Barrett, feeling all that love wash over her, wanting it to spill over onto him. He was giving her this precious gift—not just the baby, but also the most tender yet passionate lovemaking she'd ever experienced. And most importantly, love.

When they parted, he tilted her chin up. He traced the curves of her face with his finger so softly it tickled, so tenderly, it nearly made her weep. He swallowed hard, then leaned down and kissed her just as tenderly. What was he doing to her? She was dying inside. It was bad enough that she loved him. Would he make her fear that she couldn't live without him, too? A fat lot of good that would do her as he trudged through rain forests in pursuit of a life goal that changed with the seasons.

"Is something wrong?" he asked, and she realized she'd been so lost in the agony of her thoughts, she hadn't kissed him back.

"How did you learn to make love like this?"

"Why do you ask?" he asked.

"It's just that…well, you're a scientific guy, and what you're doing is definitely not scientific or clinical. It's wonderful. It's better than anything I've ever experienced. You astound me."

He took in her words, smiling at her last pronouncement. "It's like the kissing, Stacy. I'm not analyzing, not working toward the end result, not thinking at all. I'm letting the moment move me."

She climbed off the couch and held out her hand to him. "Seems wrong making our baby on a couch."

She led him into her small bedroom, turning on the night-light and nothing else. The bed was unmade, as it always was. Everything looked the same, and yet it looked dramatically different. Barrett had changed it the same way he'd changed her. She reached for the waistband of his pants, but he pulled her close before she could unbutton them.

''There's one more factor in the way I'm making love to you—you.'' He kissed her again, a deep, languid kiss that shook her down to her toes and made them curl. If he were anyone else, she'd suspect those eloquent lines. But it was Barrett, who took everything at face value.

She unzipped his pants and pushed them to the floor. His briefs followed. Her fingers grazed his legs as she pushed the pants down, and she reveled in the brush of his leg hairs and the hard muscles beneath. He stepped out of the pants and kicked them to the side. His body was gilded by the small light, every muscle defined by shadow and light.

He hooked his finger over the top of her waistband and pulled her close, kissing her as though he couldn't get enough of her. She was so lost in that kiss she almost didn't realize he was sliding her pajama bottoms down her legs. He used his toe to push them the rest of the way down so he didn't have to interrupt the kiss.

She pulled him onto the bed. The jumble of pink gingham comforter was cool against her skin. He explored her body with his hands the same way a man explores a fragile and precious object. The reverence was clear on his face as he watched his hand glide over her skin, over each curve, down her legs and between her toes. Every part of her body seemed to deserve his full attention, even the curve of the bottom of her foot and the bone of her ankle. She closed her eyes and sank into the sensations that curled all through her body, no matter where he was touching. He slid his hands up the backs of her calves, lingering on the backs of her knees and sending her straight to ecstasy.

"I could do this all night," he said in a soft voice.

"Okay," she whispered.

He chuckled, but continued to caress her with soft, smooth strokes. She was floating, soaking everything in and...not giving anything back. Her eyes popped open, and she started to get up.

"Your turn."

He gently pushed her down. "No, it's your turn. Maybe you should get used to being selfish once in a while."

"But you're giving me a baby! I want to do something for you."

His hand planted on her chest kept her from getting up. "I thought giving you a baby was totally unselfish, and I liked the idea of doing something unselfish. But it's not, really."

"It's not?" Did he want to be involved in the baby's life?

"Not when I think about how it feels to know you're having my child. It kind of takes away the unselfish factor. So I can do this."

He took one of her nipples in his mouth and teased it with his tongue. Her toes went into instant curl-up mode. He wanted to do something just for her. She tried to hold onto the thought as he traced the undersides of her breasts before assaulting her other nipple. She ached with the wonder of Barrett doing this—all of this—for her. And wanting nothing in return.

"You always smell so good," he whispered.

"Euphoria," she said on a sigh as his mouth went lower, leaving a wet trail down her stomach, nestling in her intimate hair before teasing a whole new area of her body.

He touch was so exquisite, she was sure she was going to die. No one had ever done this to her before, and she was sure no one could do it better.

It didn't take long to move to the edge of euphoria, and she wasn't talking about her body lotion. He knew exactly what to do, when to back off and when to come back, how fast to flick his tongue and when to do a full stroke. And he knew when she'd had enough, when her fingers were wound around the folds of the comforter and her breath was coming in heavy puffs. She uttered his name once, and he let her fall over the edge.

And just when she'd gotten her bearings, he sent her over the edge again. All with a few flicks of his tongue in the right place.

He kissed his way to her neck and her ears, then whispered, ``You taste so good,'' and she nearly lost it again.

``You *felt* so good.''

She wrapped her legs around his hips and reached for him. He was fully aroused, hard and ready to go. She guided him inside her. He inched in slowly, backed up, then slid in again. He filled her more than physically. Her fingers dug into his shoulders as he moved in a slow rhythm inside her. She caught her breath, meeting him thrust for thrust. His skin was slick, his hair damp as he kept up the stride for longer than she would have imagined he could. The tight feeling in the pit of her stomach intensified until she thought she was going to explode from the inside out. And then she did.

She shuddered, and he pulled her close. With a quick thrust and a groan next to her ear, he let go. His whole body trembled as he crushed her against him. He was breathing hard, sweeping her along with his rhythm. It was several long minutes before he rolled them onto their sides, still joined intimately. His face was flushed, his body glistening with sweat. He reached up and touched her cheek, running his thumb across her lips.

"I suppose..." She cleared the mugginess from her throat. "I suppose you could explain all that scientifically? Endorphines, whatever. Just physical actions and reactions?"

He nuzzled her neck, sending chills down her heated body. "There's only one way I'd explain it—euphoria."

WHEN SHE WOKE at ten that morning, she relished that prewakening feeling of reliving the night before. Until she realized she was alone. She sat up, feeling sweetly exhausted but vaguely abandoned. She listened for sounds in the house. Nothing. Maybe he couldn't handle the awkward morning-after stuff. But why should he feel awkward? They'd made no promises, no commitments. Just the opposite. He'd be gone soon—too soon—completely out of touch with her and the legacy he'd left behind.

She pulled herself out of bed and jumped in a hot shower. She could still feel him all over her. She smelled like him. It was almost like he was there. But he wasn't, and no matter what, she couldn't justify the empty feeling that created.

"Would you like some company?"

She turned to the frosty door, her heart doubling its speed. Weasel Boy peered through the opaque glass, held aloft by the man who had rocked her world the night before. Or technically, earlier that morning.

"If that company is the dog, no. If that company is you, yes."

He set the dog on the tile floor and stepped in. He was already naked, she noticed. Weasel Boy started to whine as soon as the door closed, but the running water drowned him out.

She lathered up the washcloth and ran it across his chest. ``Is that why you left this morning? To get the dog?''

``I figured he'd be wanting to go out and he was probably getting hungry.''

Gawd, she hadn't even thought about the dog. Perhaps she'd taken this selfish thing too far. She slid the cloth down one of his arms. ``I thought you'd hightailed it out of here.''

``Why would I do that?'' He really couldn't comprehend it.

``I figured you didn't feel comfortable with the morning-after thing.''

He took the washcloth from her and lathered it again. ``It's not that I'm opposed to sleeping over. I've just never wanted to.'' He carefully washed her breasts, lavishing a lot of attention on them. He continued to slide the soapy cloth down her back and over the curves of her butt. She let out a soft sigh and arched slightly. He was kneeling, washing her legs with the utmost care and precision. The cloth grazed her femininity and made her shudder. He kissed her pubic bone and nuzzled her.

She placed a finger under his chin and guided him up. ``Do you remember how you did everything for me this morning? How you let me be selfish?''

She took the washcloth and let it drop to the puddle of water at their feet. As she left a trail of kisses across his collarbone and down his stomach, she said, ``Now it's your turn....''

13

SUNDAY PASSED in a languid blur of lovemaking, lounging about and even some productivity. Barrett made French toast. After an impromptu romp on the couch, he brought over his computer and notes and put together the first draft of his study. Stacy dragged out Granny's recipe box and cooked a meat loaf for dinner.

As he adjusted the last of his numbers and calculations, he watched her in the kitchen. During his sister Kim's four pregnancies, his mother had talked about the way she'd glowed. Barrett hadn't noticed it, really. He hadn't noticed a lot of things, like the colors of a sunset and dogs in the clouds. Stacy glowed. In fact, he spent more time watching her than he did putting those final touches on his study.

He'd also made some notes on their lovemaking. She astounded him, too. He'd let himself go and gotten lost. It wasn't clinical, wasn't a mental checklist of action versus reaction. It was beyond analysis. It transcended any of the scientific studies he'd done on romantic attraction.

In the space of a week, Stacy had become a part of him. Tomorrow Gene and Judy would return from their cruise, and Barrett would return to his condominium to prepare for his two-year trip and perhaps find his life goal at last. The timing was perfect—the repairs on Kim and Dave's home would be done tomorrow.

The timing was rotten. He wanted more time with Stacy to explore these feelings he'd never had before.

He felt a curious ache deep inside. It wasn't hunger. Lack of sleep wouldn't produce pain. Even glancing down at Elmo, who was curled up in his lap, didn't help the pain go away. In fact, it got worse.

He who didn't like dogs was going to miss this little critter, too. He'd tried to talk Kim into taking him. After she got up from the floor upon hearing her brother was around a dog, much less concerned for its welfare, she listened to his argument.

"Barrett, I have four kids, two in diapers yet. When do you think I'd have time to take care of a dog?"

"Dave could help. And the two older kids."

"Uh-uh. It would fall to me. I'm sorry, but I can't. They don't put the animals down at that shelter, so you don't have to worry about that. He'll find a home."

As though Elmo sensed Barrett was thinking about him, he glanced up in a sleepy way. Then he yawned, showing his full complement of tiny teeth, and tucked his nose under his paws. Elmo probably wouldn't be happy in a house full of kids anyway. He liked peace and quiet.

Barrett looked at Stacy and caught her with her hand over her stomach. "Are you all right?"

She gave him a sheepish smile. "I've heard women say they could feel the moment they got pregnant. I thought it was a bunch of hogwash, to be honest with you. But I can feel it, Barrett. I really can."

He stood up so fast, he almost forgot about Elmo. He caught the dog just in time and set him on the chair. "You're pregnant?"

"I...I don't know. Maybe."

He walked into the kitchen and put his hand over hers. "Wow."

She laughed. ``Yeah, wow. It's really happening. It's been a dream for so long.'' She met his gaze. ``You'll have to give me your address so I can send you pictures and updates. If you want them, that is.''

``Of course I want them. I've already typed out all the information. My mail will be forwarded to me on a regular basis, though I want to find out how you can get hold of me if you need me immediately. I'll keep in touch.''

``I hope so.'' Her voice sounded soft and just a little sad.

Two years away from her. Two years not watching her belly enlarge, not being with her when she had the baby, not watching the baby grow.

But he was afraid of babies, some distant part of his mind reminded him. And Stacy had already decided she wanted to do this on her own. She didn't look like she wanted to do it alone at the moment, though. In fact, she looked scared.

She took a deep breath and shored up her shoulders. ``Don't worry, I know you're going to be busy and out of touch for a long time. Then you'll probably have another project, or maybe you'll decide to get another PhD. I don't expect anything from you. That was our deal, after all. If you'd like to be part of our lives when you're in town, you can. Just remember that I hadn't planned to have the baby's father around at all. I don't want you to feel obligated, is what I'm trying to say.''

She turned and checked on the meat loaf again.

``I'd like to be part of your lives.''

He thought he could be a peripheral part of their lives when he'd made the offer. Like an Uncle Barrett. See them once in a while, help out monetarily. That's what he was comfortable with. But the thought of it wasn't settling well in his belly. It was making that ache even larger.

"As much as I can," he added as those two years in a remote jungle loomed like a decade.

She smiled, though it wasn't a real smile. "That'd be nice. Well, I think we're ready to eat."

Elmo slurped up his portion of the meat loaf, then after some vigorous air licking, settled onto Barrett's lap. Stacy didn't eat much of her own dinner. She was watching Elmo.

"He sure is going to miss you."

"I'm actually going to miss him, too. I've tried to figure out how I could keep him, or at the least find him a home. There doesn't seem to be any way to work it out."

She propped her chin on her upturned hand and sighed. "I know." She was looking at Barrett, but quickly averted her gaze to the dog. "I've thought about keeping him myself, but with the baby coming, and the fact that he doesn't even seem to like me...well, it just doesn't make sense. Sometimes what you want out of life doesn't make sense."

"Are you going to be all right?"

"Me?" She let out a hoarse-sounding laugh. "I'll be fine. Great, even. I got exactly what I wanted—a baby. Or at least I think I did. If I'm not pregnant, I can still go the sperm donor route."

"We could try again."

She stood and took her plate into the kitchen. "You'll be gone for two years. I can't wait that long. I appreciate your trying to help, but..."

"Let me know. Get a message to me. We'll work it out."

He liked the idea of her getting impregnated by one of those guys on the profile sheets even less than he had before. *He* wanted to do this. Only him. The sharp jab of possession surprised him. He'd never felt possessive of anything.

He'd never had anything that mattered.

"You should probably go on home," she said in a soft voice. "I know you've got that report to finish, and it's due tomorrow. Remember, you're never late."

"Are you asking me to leave?"

She paused. "Yeah. Less complicated that way, don't you think? Besides, I don't know about your stamina level, but making love all night, and all day, is catching up to me. I'm fried."

He nodded, set his plate in the dishwasher and headed to the table. "I could come back later."

"And ruin my reputation in this community?" She forced a smile. "I don't think so. I'll see you in the morning, before you leave. I've got to take Elmo to the shelter tomorrow. If he's going to stay with you tonight—and please say he is, otherwise he'll whine all night—I've got to come get him anyway. We can say goodbye then."

"I could come over tomorrow evening. I've got some time before I leave." He didn't even calculate the exact time. Didn't care to.

"It's tempting, believe me. But like I said, it's less complicated if we stop this thing here."

"This thing?"

"Us."

There was an us, he realized. Tomorrow there wouldn't be. The pang returned full force. "Less complicated. I understand." Then why did it feel even more complicated as he packed up his computer and notes? The prospect of saying goodbye to Stacy was even more complex. Leaving had never been this hard before. He'd never left anyone behind who meant that much to him. "All right then. Good night."

He kissed her, keeping it simple and quick. Still, he heard her intake of breath. Before he could think of coming back for another kiss, she took a step back and said, "Good night."

AS TIRED AS SHE WAS, Stacy got little sleep that night. Twenty times she'd wanted to go next door and throw her less-complicated baloney to the wind. It was really better this way. Just the one night in his arms made her feel lonelier than she'd ever felt in her life. Worse, the bed smelled like him. She wallowed in the sheets and dreamed of being with him for the rest of her life.

Then she woke in the morning to reality. He wasn't the family kind of man. He got bored quickly, which guaranteed he'd get bored with her real fast. He liked to travel to far, exotic places to study things that might one day help the planet. There wasn't much room for her dreams in that formula.

She resigned herself to washing the sheets and then felt bad that she couldn't smell Barrett on them anymore. She couldn't keep them indefinitely, after all. Granny wouldn't have done anything like that. Of course, Granny wouldn't have slept with a guy she had no future with either. She wouldn't be having a baby on her own.

With a weary sigh, Stacy took in the disarray in the bedroom. She'd let Granny down, for sure. She'd be disappointed that Stacy hadn't turned out like her.

Wait a minute. Had Granny ever said she wanted Stacy to be like her? No, she hadn't. Stacy surveyed Granny's decor. Some things had sentimental value, like the afghans and needlepoint. Some did not, like the mushroom clock and couch. Who had planted the directive in her head that she had to live up to Granny's standards?

She had. Only her. Just because Granny had been a saint didn't mean Stacy had to be one, too. She smiled. Then laughed. The sense of freedom was positively thrilling. She raced around the house gathering up all the ugly stuff she didn't want around anymore. So what if she was throwing away one clock and therefore having to buy another one? Who cared about practicality, anyway? She was going to set a good example for her child—being the right combination of selfish and giving. And having the baby by herself, that was a good thing, too.

What would Barrett think about these changes, she wondered. Would he like them? Or would... She stopped her thoughts there. He wouldn't be around to notice them. Her energy drained, and she tossed the last mushroom item onto the pile by the door and sighed. Forget about him. These changes were just for her.

An hour later, she started over to Barrett's place to get Elmo and say goodbye. Her chest was tight, and her eyes felt prickly. It was ridiculous to be in love with a man she'd known for a week, but there it was. She'd dated guys for longer than that—okay, for maybe two weeks— and never felt anywhere near this way about them. She adored him. There it was. And there wasn't a darn thing she could do about it.

Barrett was carrying a pile of clothing to his Saab. He tossed the neat pile into the passenger seat when he saw her and headed over, Weasel Boy at his heels.

"Good morning."

She shielded her eyes from the bright morning sun. "Morning."

"How'd you sleep?"

"Fine. You?"

"Terrible."

He was too darn honest. Lying was much simpler. Better not to say *I was thinking about you all night long and wondering how I could tie you up so you'd miss your flight and not bore you after a month or two.* She looked at Weasel Boy. "Ready to go back?"

As though he knew exactly what she was saying, he stepped behind Barrett's legs like a shy child. She crouched and said, "Sorry, fella, but sometimes we don't get what we want."

"But you got what you wanted, right?"

She stood and wrapped her arms around her waist. "Sure, I did."

Could he see the lie in her eyes? She tried not to think about how his blue eyes made her feel all jittery and sad and happy at the same time. And adored. There it was, the same way it had been when they'd made love, and she hadn't even recognized it. Because she'd never seen it aimed at her before.

"If you'll wait a few minutes, I'm going to close up the house and I'll follow you to the shelter," he said.

"Oh. Sure, that'd be great."

"Later this morning a woman will be coming by to clean the place. She takes care of my condominium, and I asked her to come over so it'll be ready for Gene and Judy's return this afternoon."

Why was he rubbing it in how thoughtful he was? It would be better if he'd left the place a wreck, broken a plate or two and clogged up the toilet. Gene and Judy would be disgusted with him, and soon everyone in Sunset City would think he was a terrible person and not wonder why Stacy couldn't keep him around.

A few minutes later, Barrett and Weasel Boy followed her out of Sunset City. Some of the female residents were sitting on their front porches, and she wondered if Barrett had given them one last glimpse of his spectacular legs early this morning. They waved, sad smiles on their faces. Were they going to miss those legs, and were they wondering if Stacy was going to manage to let another one get away? A good one, this time.

Ten minutes later they pulled into the shelter's parking lot. Well, this was it. The big goodbye. And, she realized, the final test. He'd grown fond of the dog, even Barrett had admitted that. If he could truly leave the dog there, he could leave her behind, too.

One of her favorite volunteers, Coreen Ernest, was manning the front desk. The feisty short brunette was on the phone. "Are you serious? Why would you consider moving into a no-pets apartment building when you have a dog? Did you even think about how your dog was going to feel when you dumped him here? Did you try to look for a pets-allowed apartment? That's what I thought. Here, I'm going to give you a list of them in this area. Your dog is going to love you for this. Ready?" She winked at Stacy, took in Barrett and winked at Stacy again.

RJ waved at her from behind the glass window of his office. He was on the phone, too. She'd already verified that morning that the woman had picked up her five dogs and that Weasel Boy's cage was free. She and Barrett walked into the building where the dogs resided and down the corridor of cages, sending the animals into a barking frenzy. Bright pink Adopted! signs adorned Buddy's and Frankie's cages. She gave them a thumbs-up as she passed them by, feeling happily choked up like she always did when one of her guys got adopted.

Weasel Boy's pillow bed was situated in the corner, bowls filled with fresh water and food. Barrett had probably fed him Cap'n Crunch for breakfast. "Home, sweet home," she said, unlatching the gate.

Barrett looked torn as he took in the concrete floor and forlorn bed. The dogs hadn't abated in their barking yet, and Weasel Boy cringed at the noise. Stacy understood Barrett's dilemma, and also why he couldn't take the dog. Dogs, babies and families didn't fit his lifestyle. But she had to admit she was hoping he'd give in to the dog. Because if he did, it might mean he'd give in on the babies and family, too.

"Thanks for trying to find him a home. Someone will take him soon, I'm sure of it." She took the dog and set him on his bed. "See you later, Elmo."

Elmo stood at the gate and watched them with those sad, buggy eyes.

She nudged Barrett toward the entrance. "We'd better go." *Before I start crying,* she didn't say. It was so loud, he probably wouldn't have heard her anyway. She led him to the front entrance and out into the sunshine. "I'm going to stick around for a bit, make sure Weas—Elmo's okay."

"Can I sponsor his adoption fee? Offer a bonus if someone takes him?"

"Afraid not. The shelter wants to make sure that whoever adopts an animal can afford to keep him."

He let out a long breath, lifting his face into the sun for a moment before looking at her again. "Keep me updated on everything, okay? Even Elmo."

"Sure."

"Thanks for all your help with the folks at Sunset City. You know, pretending to be my girlfriend and all."

"I have a confession to make. It wasn't a totally unselfish act. I thought you were pretty cute, and I wanted to get to know you better. I'm glad I did."

"Me, too."

"And thank you for—"

He put his finger over her mouth. "Don't even say it. I wanted to do it. Maybe I wanted to be close to you, too."

She threw herself into his arms, and he held her tight. "I'm going to miss you," he said in a strained voice. Probably she was holding onto him too tight.

"Me, too."

"I wish I didn't have this project—"

This time she put her finger over his mouth. "Don't even say it. I know you have to follow through, because that's who you are. I wish you luck in finding your life goal. Maybe you'll find it in the rain forest."

"Maybe." He didn't sound convinced.

He gave her a kiss like the one last night, sweet and tender and much too quick. Which was a good thing. A goodbye kiss should be quick, not long and lingering. Not arousing.

He never took his eyes off her as he walked to his car. And because she knew this, she realized she'd done the same. He sat in the car for a moment, started it, then sat there for another minute. She didn't let herself think he'd changed his mind. He couldn't. He had an obligation, two years' worth. And after that...who knew? A lot could happen in two years. And if they'd been successful, a lot *would* happen in two years.

When he finally pulled out of the parking lot, she felt a bone-deep ache. "Bummer," she said, hoping to feel as casual as the word. It didn't work, so she went inside. She worked with a couple of the dogs she'd taken home before and tried not to think about the life growing inside her womb and the emptiness growing inside her heart. But after hearing Elmo crying for thirty minutes straight, she knew this wasn't the place to be, either.

"Coreen, tell RJ I couldn't stay today. I'll be in tomorrow, though."

"Who was the cutie?" Coreen asked with a lifted eyebrow.

Stacy couldn't help putting her hand over her stomach. "Just a friend."

14

BARRETT COULD HEAR the noise emanating from his apartment as he neared the door. Inside, the place was chaos. The two older boys were chasing each other around the furniture. The carpet wasn't wholly white anymore.

Kim's voice carried like a bullhorn. "Tim, Paul, slow down!" She was sitting on the couch with her youngest on her lap. She looked up and saw Barrett at the door. "Hi. We're going to be out of your hair in thirty minutes, I promise. Dave's picking up the van now, and he'll be here to load everything up. I'm sorry we kicked you out of your own place. I hope you got your project done in time."

"Sure did."

"That's great."

He shrugged. It was great, wasn't it? He'd managed to put the final touches on it last night, since he couldn't sleep anyway.

"When do you head off to Bolivia?"

"Next Friday."

"You've got to be excited about that."

"Yeah. Sure."

She tilted her head. "You sound different. And you look like poopie. You all right?"

He smiled at her use of the kid's word. Would Stacy be talking like that in a year? "I'm fine." But he didn't sound fine, and he didn't feel fine, either. Even worse, he wasn't the least bit excited about the upcoming project. And he suspected he knew why.

Kim noticed her toddler rambling right toward Barrett. ``Ronnie, come back, honey! Come to mama. Uncle Barrett's not a baby person.''

A knock on the door was followed by Barrett's father's entrance. He was wearing his standard plaid shirt and striped pants with a tweed jacket. ``Well, let me see it. You've got the study done, right? Of course you do, a nonsensical question.''

Of course he did. He was never late, and he never backed out of something he'd committed to. ``It's in here. I haven't put a cover and binding on it yet.'' He cleared away the stacks of diapers and opened his briefcase. His father dropped into the seat and started leafing through the thick study.

Kim said, ``Hey, Dad, it's nice to see you, too.''

Their father made a grunting noise, lifting his head briefly but not meeting his daughter's eyes. Barrett had never noticed that before, how his father focused only on what mattered to him. Not on his two offspring or even his grandchildren who, Barrett noticed, had settled down since their grandfather's arrival. They moved away from him and continued their playing at a quieter level.

His father was oblivious to it all. He perused the report, happy in his own little world. A world that excluded love and companionship. Barrett could remember his father being like that with him and Kim, though it hadn't seemed unusual then. The only way to get his attention was to talk to him about what interested him. Luckily, Barrett could manage that. Kim couldn't. Barrett couldn't remember his father ever holding him or giving him a hug. *He* obviously didn't feel comfortable around young children, even his own.

Barrett watched his father's eyes widen in excitement at the report in a way they never widened for anything else. He didn't want to be like that. The realization hit him like a wrecking ball tearing through a building. He didn't want to be like that…but he was. Not because he was born that way but because he'd become that way.

The moment Barrett felt something touch his ankle, Kim's voice shouted, "Tim, get your little sister! She's going to freak out her uncle."

The girl was similar in age to the Lynsey toddler from the canned-food party. He didn't feel the fear. Discomfort, yes, but not enough to keep him from picking up the baby. He held her out for a moment, and she showed a couple of teeth in a drippy smile. He remembered the way Stacy had held Lynsey against her waist, so naturally. He did the same, though probably not as naturally.

"Barrett…" Kim was watching with her mouth open.

"It's okay. This is my niece. I should be able to hold her, right?"

She smelled sweet. She picked at a button on his shirt, totally enthralled by it. She felt warm and real in his arms. He was going to have one of these. He was going to be a father. Suddenly his motives were more selfish than ever.

Even the two boys were watching their uncle with shocked expressions. When he looked at his sister, it was his mouth that hung open. She was breast-feeding her youngest. A blanket was covering the baby's head, making the act discreet.

It was incredibly easy to imagine Stacy doing the same

thing. He wanted to be part of it. He turned to his father, who was oblivious to the scene.

``Dad? Dad?''

Finally his father looked up but didn't notice Ronnie in Barrett's arms. ``What?''

Barrett walked over and set the toddler in his lap. ``Have you ever held your granddaughter?''

His father looked at a loss, staring at the toddler, who found his glasses enthralling. ``No. Why would I?''

``Why don't you hold her for a while and figure it out. By the way, I've finally figured out my life goal.''

``Liggus fasciatus? That's wonderful! I knew you'd take to them. They're the gems of the Everglades, you know.''

``No, it has nothing to do with snails. In fact, all this time, I've been looking at the life goal as being something professional. Scientific.''

``What else would it be?''

He stared at his father for a moment. That's what it was all about to him. Luckily Barrett had seen the light. ``It might be about sunsets, and seeing dogs and dragons in the clouds. It might be about the pleasure of having a little dog curled up on your lap. It's definitely about the woman who taught me to see all of that. And if she doesn't think I'm too dumb, I'm going to convince her to let me adore her for the rest of her life.''

STACY DROVE AROUND for a long time, just thinking. The sun was bright and hot, though the breeze, especially in the convertible, was enough to keep her comfortable. She drove into the area where Barrett's condominium was, though she didn't let herself pinpoint which of the tall buildings overlooking the water was his. She had his phone number with her, but it was too soon to be calling him. If she hadn't heard from him by the day before he left for Bolivia, she'd give him a call to wish him well. She would probably have an idea whether she was pregnant or not by then.

When Stacy pulled into her driveway, she already had the sense that something was wrong. Maybe it was the residents who were conspicuously lurking, or the fact that some of the Power Squadron was taking their walk hours early and just happened to be rounding the far corner as she turned down her street. She could have sworn, too, that they'd jumped to action as soon as they'd seen her car.

``Why, hey there, Stacy,'' Ernie called.

``Hello, sweet pea,'' Frieda said as they both strolled over.

Jack dinged the bell on his purple bike as he rolled by. Then he turned and came back. ``Morning,'' he called to the folks who were gathering around. ``Good to see you, Stacy.''

``Good to see *me?*'' It was always good to see *him*.

Arlene pulled in behind Stacy's car with her golf cart. The blue flower bobbed on the end of her antenna as she came to an abrupt stop. She released the poodles into the yard and walked over. ``Morning, Stacy. Mighty fine day, isn't it?''

Mighty suspicious, she thought. Then she felt a jolt of panic. Ricky had told them about her insemination plans! She wasn't ready to tell them about the baby yet. First, she had to make sure there was a baby. She'd already decided to stick with the sperm donor story and keep Barrett out of it. She didn't want the folks here to think he was a cad for deserting her in her time of need when it wasn't like that at all.

"What's up?" she asked once everyone was in attendance, all trying to look casual as though they'd happened to end up there by accident.

"We saw Barrett leave this morning," Betty said.

Stacy allowed herself a small breath of relief. This wasn't about sperm. "Yes, he left. He finished his study despite all of you, and in case you'd forgotten, Gene and Judy are returning this afternoon."

"So when's he coming back?" Arlene asked.

A jab of pain shot into her chest. "He's got a two-year study he's embarking on in the rain forest of Bolivia next week. At least that long. Maybe never."

A murmur of outrage rippled through the crowd. "You mean there's no commitment?"

"No pronouncement of undying love?" Frieda cried.

Stacy leaned against her car and crossed her arms. "I suppose I should fess up now and tell you it was a charade. Our romance, I mean. So you'd all keep your matchmaking grubs off him." If only that had remained true, at least on her end.

"A charade?" Arlene stamped her foot.

"Well, I never!" Betty said.

"Knock it off, girls," Nita said. "We should fess up, too. At first, yeah, we did want to set up our offspring—" she cleared her throat "—and possibly myself with him. But when we saw that spark between you, we realized you'd finally found a guy worthy of your big heart."

"Spark?" They'd seen a spark?

"We knew about the charade. Ernie's sonic ear," she said at Stacy's shocked expression. "But we knew, you being so nice and all, that you wouldn't want to bother

Barrett with his study, even though you had to pretend to be his girlfriend. So we forced your hand a little.''

Stacy's mouth dropped open as she took all of them in. They were nodding, some not even having the decency to look a little sheepish. ``You mean the deadline, the demand for us to kiss and prove it—all part of your plan?'' She remembered when Nita had said they were making plans.

``Yep,'' Nita said. ``But it didn't work!''

``Where did we go wrong?'' Betty lamented.

Ernie said, ``The first guy we don't run off, and he leaves on his own!''

Amid all the whining, that one comment perked Stacy's ears. ``Wait a minute! What do you mean, the first guy you don't run off?''

Everyone went silent. Nita looked around. ``Who said that? No one said that.''

``I did,'' Ernie admitted, his shoulders hunched nearly to his ears as though he were trying to pull his head in like a turtle.

``And Nita, you said a guy finally worthy of me.''

``Well, sure. Didn't you get a good look at those losers you brought here over the years?''

Frieda started listing names by her long, spindly fingers. ``Bob had been married four times and he'd lied about it. Ted had once been convicted of fraud and embezzlement. Cal didn't have a lucrative job at an insurance company like he told you. He didn't have a job at all.''

``And Rupert not only had been married before, but he still was!'' Ernie said.

Stacy felt a curious pressure in her chest as she took in her family. ``How did you know all this?''

Ernie lifted his chin, pride on his face. ``They used to

call me the Black Gopher, you know. I have ways of finding things out.''

''And then we simply, er, discouraged them from coming back around,'' Arlene said.

''We only did it because we love you, m'dear,'' Betty said.

''We want you to be happy, but it's got to be the right guy. Someone who won't hurt you or take advantage of your good nature,'' Jack said.

The pressure was turning into a big warm spot in her chest at their protectiveness.

''Just like with the jobs,'' Ernie said with a nod. When everyone went silent again, he realized he'd revealed another secret he shouldn't have.

''You don't know squat about keeping secrets!'' Nita yelled among the groans.

Stacy could barely speak the words. ''You sabotaged my job possibilities, too?''

''We know what's best for you, hon,'' Frieda said. ''Trust us, those jobs were all wrong for you.''

''I was beginning to think I was a failure.''

''We felt kinda bad about that part,'' Jack said. ''But when you get that assistant director's job at the shelter, it'll all be worth it.''

''The *what* job?'' This was too much to take in!

''That woman couldn't care less about animals. I don't think she'll be there much longer,'' Betty said.

That was probably true, and Stacy had been known to complain about it to them from time to time. Betty had seen Naomi's callousness firsthand when she'd adopted her second cat from the shelter.

Frieda said, ''What I don't understand is how you let Barrett get away. That man was clearly in love with you.''

"Clearly?" Stacy asked, ignoring the part about letting him get away.

Nita took that part up. "If he has commitments, there isn't anything he could do about it. He's an honorable man who keeps his promises. You can't blame him for that. They can write, keep in touch."

"Pooh, those things never work out," Frieda said.

Ernie said, "We kept in touch when I was in the war. It worked for us."

"We were married! You had a legal obligation to come back!"

Arlene had gathered Blue—or was it Suede?—in her arms. "But I don't understand how he could have walked away from our sweet Stacy. When you have something that special..."

"Good love is so hard to find," Betty said on a sigh.

Nita sighed, too. "A good man is so hard to find. And a hard man is so good to find, too, but that's a whole other can of beans."

Stacy couldn't keep Barrett here. Mental images of her grabbing onto his shirt as he tried to board the plane danced through her mind. Then they changed to images of everyone here pinning him down, and she shoved those away. Maybe there was something she could do, a way to remember Barrett and to give love to someone who once had it and had lost it along with her.

"I've got to go."

"She's going to stop him!" Frieda said, clapping her hands.

"No, I can't do that. It wouldn't be right. Barrett's not the kind of guy to back out of a commitment."

"She's too nice," Nita grumbled to the others.

"But I'm going to go rescue Elmo from the shelter.

It'll be like having a little bit of Barrett with me.'' She might possibly have more of Barrett with her than they'd ever guess, but she wouldn't talk about that just yet.

She took in the beloved faces around her and wondered whether she should chastise them or hug them. Maybe if she played it cool, they'd cut her some slack when she told them she was having a baby on her own.

"I love all you guys," she said, getting into her car. "Now scoot!"

Thoughts and feelings careened through her mind during the short drive to the shelter. They had been directing her life behind the scenes, but for the right reasons. Loving reasons. They'd saved her from heartbreak, checking up on those men and discouraging them from showing up again. She wasn't sure she wanted to know exactly how they'd accomplished that. Probably not.

It was both endearing and annoying as all get out.

Adopting Elmo—she'd have to call him that now—wasn't the impulsive decision it seemed to be. She'd been thinking about it, pondering it. All the while, hoping Barrett would adopt him and show her that he could get over his dog and baby fears and make a commitment. The two-year study was the big obstacle. How could she convince him he couldn't live without her and Elmo if he wasn't around?

She couldn't, she decided with a heavy heart as she pulled into the shelter's parking lot. Having a baby on her own had seemed like a much better idea before she'd gone and fallen for Barrett.

As soon as she walked in, RJ waved her into his office. "Hey, I'm glad you came back. Coreen said you'd gone for the day."

"I thought I had. What's up?"

"I fired Naomi this morning."

Stacy sank into the chair in front of his desk. "Why?"

"You know she hasn't been doing a great job, but she had been better since I had a talk with her. The incident with the woman's dogs this weekend was the final factor."

"It wasn't very nice of her to rent out Elmo's cage just so the shelter could get a donation."

"There's more to it than that. According to the woman who boarded the dogs, Naomi got a little payoff herself. And that's what I can't tolerate. She admitted it after I accused her of taking the money. So...would you like the job? I can't think of a better person for it."

It was a good thing she was already sitting. "I'd...love it."

"Great." He glanced at the window behind her. "My fund-raiser is here for an appointment, so we'll talk money and benefits tomorrow morning, okay?" He shook her hand. "I'd like to officially welcome you to the staff."

Stacy was in a daze as she walked toward the door. A sense of foreboding made her turn and ask, "What was the lady's name who boarded the dogs? Just so I know what to expect if she ever comes back."

"Elvira Presley, can you believe it? And get this—she had three poodles named Blue, Suede and Shoes. And they were blue!"

Stacy forced a laugh before pushing herself to the lobby. Arlene had boarded her dogs, something she said she'd never do, to get rid of Naomi. Considering the way she adored those dogs, it was a big, big sacrifice. Arlene must have borrowed Killer and Teeny, two of the other residents' dogs, as well. They were meddlesome, well-intentioned as they were. She'd have to take that up with

RJ tomorrow when they had their meeting. Still, she couldn't help the warm glow that flowed through her at the trouble they'd gone to. They adored her, she thought with a sigh.

Coreen was busy helping a woman fill out the paperwork to adopt a cat, so Stacy went to the dog area to get Elmo. Wouldn't Coreen be surprised to see her adopting a dog? And it was about time, really. She could give Elmo a home and still spread her love to the other animals. She'd buy him a new bed first thing, and a bunch of toys, and—

The cage was empty.

She checked the name on the gate. It still read Elmo, but all his paperwork was gone. Whoever had adopted him had taken him right away. The pink Adopted! sign wasn't even in place yet. She was happy he'd gotten a home so suddenly. Wasn't she? Sure she was. If she had a baby coming, she'd be busy enough.

She said hello to each of the dogs before heading to the lobby, where Coreen was verifying that someone's apartment allowed them to have a cat. RJ was in his meeting. She waved to Coreen and RJ and headed into the sunshine, wishing she could feel as cheery as the day felt.

That's when she saw Barrett sitting in the passenger seat of her car. It was a mirage, of course, a manifestation of her overwhelming desire to see him there. She walked to her car and opened the door. The mirage remained, and in fact it added Elmo sitting in Barrett's lap.

"Hi, Stacy."

It even spoke! Visual and audio. Her imagination was more vivid than she'd ever given it credit for. When she slid into the driver's seat, she could smell his aftershave.

The breeze rustled through his blond hair, washing a bit of it over his forehead.

She held onto the steering wheel, took a deep breath and turned to him. "If you're a figment of my imagination, stop teasing me and disappear already."

"I'm not a figment."

She touched his arm. He was real, all warm from the sun. She laughed. "I had to make sure. It's just that I've been thinking about you a lot, and I thought I might have imagined you or something."

"I've been thinking about you, too," he said, leaning against the seat and resting his cheek against his hand.

She looked at Elmo, who was looking at her from Barrett's lap. "You adopted him?"

"Yep." He reached out and pushed a lock of her hair behind her ear. "I readjusted my life goal, too. You set a good example."

Her heart jumped into overdrive, and she could hardly speak, "I did?"

"Yeah, except that *you* axed the husband part of your goal. *I* added a wife and family."

"You did?" It came out as a squeak. "What about spreading your seed in the rain forest?"

He winced. "I wasn't going to spread *my* seed—ah, never mind. It's not important. I'm working on getting someone to take over the project. I might have to head down for a week or two to get things going, but I've already got some calls in. It's a lucrative project. I won't have any trouble finding someone to take it over." He took her hand in his. "Will I have any trouble convincing the lady I'm in love with to re-readjust her life goal? Uhoh. I'm not boring you, am I? You've got that glazed look with your mouth hanging open—"

She rushed forward and kissed him. Elmo scooted out of the way just in time for her to land in Barrett's lap. When she had thoroughly kissed him, she said, "Does that answer your question?"

"I believe so."

At that moment, RJ and the fund-raiser walked out. RJ stopped when he saw her. Then he steered the woman away, muttering, "I'm going to have to have a talk with my new assistant director about showing gratitude toward people who adopt a pet from us."

She and Barrett laughed, and he held her tight against him. She looked at him. "Did you say you were in love with me?"

"Well, I'm no expert on romance, you understand, but I believe so. In fact, there's a ninety-nine percent chance that I adore you. I'm undoubtedly going to have to do more research—a lot more research—to be sure."

Her voice sounded quivery when she said, "Would that include graphs and charts?"

He touched her lower lip. "No, that'd be boring. I'm talking fieldwork here—kissing, touching, holding hands, that kind of thing."

"I'm pretty sure that I adore you, too. Shall we compare notes?"

"Good idea. When I'm around you, my heartbeat increases at least thirty percent. This phenomenon even happens when I'm just thinking about you."

"Me, too. And I *love* kissing you. I could do that all day long."

"Me, too. I notice a definite increase in dopamine and norepinephrine levels in my brain."

She rolled her eyes. "Does that mean that when we're

together, you feel kind of high and dizzy and even a little bit giddy?''

''Exactly.'' He shifted beneath her. ''And then there's the arousal factor.''

She could feel hard evidence of that. ''Oh, yes, there's definitely an arousal factor.''

''I think we should do a study on this.'' At her raised eyebrow he added, ''Just the two of us, working side by side, exploring all the various levels and feelings of arousal, romance.'' He took her hand and turned her palm up. Then he ran the tip of his tongue across the surface. ''I'm scientifically sure we'll be experts in, say, about nine or so months.''

''Dr. Barrett Wheeler, I'm inclined to agree.''

Epilogue

One year later

AS IT TURNED OUT, they had a few extra months to get that study done. Stacy hadn't gotten pregnant during that wild and crazy weekend. It was, in fact, on their wedding night three months later that they conceived. Two days ago she delivered a healthy baby girl, and today Barrett's ladies had both come home.

Stacy was snuggled into the various pillows he had propped on the couch. Megan lay in the crook of his arms, sound asleep, her tiny hand clutching his finger. Elmo lay in Stacy's lap, glad to have his mistress home again. The dog's loyalties had shifted big-time when Stacy became pregnant. As though the dog knew she was in a special state, he had become her biggest fan.

"Looks just like her mother," Barrett's sister, Kim, said, gazing at the baby.

Nita shook her head. "No, I think she looks like Barrett. Look at her hair, thick and blond."

Ernie said, "I think she looks like a prune."

"Ernie!" several of the women in the living room said, but only gave the man a second's worth of attention before turning back to the baby.

Stacy looked tired, but never more beautiful. Barrett wanted all these people out of there so he could spend some quiet time alone with his wife and daughter. It was a brief, selfish thought that vanished as quickly as it had come. After all, these people were his family. He'd have her to himself soon enough. Well, not quite soon enough, but soon.

She took in her husband and her baby and gave him a glowing smile, renewing that selfish thought. "I think she looks like both of us."

He had arranged for a month off between the projects he was working on at the University of Miami. Interesting that, since falling in love with Stacy, he didn't feel the restlessness or the need to keep going from project to project. He was happy staying right there in Sunset City. Happy working in one place. Very, very happy with Stacy.

Oh, they'd talked about moving to his condominium— no yard for the kid—or buying another place, but the Sunset folks wouldn't hear of it. Since they liked to take credit for their part in getting Stacy and Barrett together, by golly, they wanted to be close by so they could gloat. So they'd stayed in the condominium while renovating Stacy's house by adding a second floor for their bedroom, the nursery and a playroom. The baby and the house had been nearly done at the same time.

Megan shifted, yawned and settled back into sleep. Her tiny pink mouth was puckered like a cupid's bow. Maybe he didn't see angels in clouds, but he sure saw an angel in his daughter.

"I want one," Ricky whined, leaning over to stroke the baby's arm.

"Your time will come," Arlene said, patting his arm. "You and Tanya seem to be getting along just fine."

Ricky smiled. "Yeah, we are. Thanks for the intro."

"Just behave yourself, you hear me?"

``Yes, ma'am.''

Ricky sounded so contrite, everyone laughed. Barrett was grateful that Ricky had never parted with Stacy's intention to get a sperm donor. Turned out he wasn't such a bad guy after all.

``Good thing you got over your fear of babies,'' Arlene said to Barrett with a nod. ``That'd be darn inconvenient, wouldn't you think?''

Stacy said, ``He's been practicing with his sister's babies.''

Gene and Judy scooted close to them. ``All this because we took that cruise, Gene,'' she said. ``Best cruise we ever took.''

Barrett couldn't imagine them not taking that cruise, not letting him use their place next door, him not meeting Stacy. ``I'm going to send you two on another one in thanks.''

Kim said, ``Hey, I want a cruise, too! If our pipes hadn't burst, you wouldn't have stayed here.''

``Okay, I'll send your pipes on a cruise,'' Barrett said.

Kim made a shocked sound. ``Barrett made a funny. Oh, my, gosh, I can't believe it.''

Barrett winced. ``I'll send you on a cruise if you'll stop teasing me.''

``That's a deal.''

She sat next to Stacy. ``Maybe in a couple of years, we can all go on one together. If we could only find baby-sitters…''

``Me!''

``I'll do it!''

``We can do it!'' A chorus of offers filled the room.

Barrett pulled Stacy toward him and started rubbing her neck. What she had done, delivering his baby girl, still filled him with such awe, he couldn't even put it into words. But he'd work on that. For now, he couldn't stop touching Stacy, couldn't keep his eyes off her.

Kim said, "Barrett, I don't think you knew this, but Dad came by the hospital this morning. He was looking at Megan through the nursery window, just looking at her. He didn't stay long. But you know, he actually said hello to me when I walked up to him. I said, 'Congratulations, Grandpop.'"

"What did he say?"

"He smiled. Maybe he's coming around. He even said a whole sentence worth of words to Mom before she left. I think she's going to settle in Miami for a while. Said she missed us, missed her grandkids. She seems happy at her new job at the restaurant. Barrett, remember how she and Dad danced together at your wedding? Maybe there's hope for them, too."

Arlene whispered, "Look, Stacy's asleep. Let's leave the little family alone for a bit, shall we?"

Barrett sighed in relief, but thanked everyone for coming by. They all filed out silently, but he didn't even see the last of them leave. He was watching his wife sleep, her head tucked against his chest. He was content to sit there for the rest of the night and watch her. Or maybe he'd carry her upstairs to the renovated bedroom and connected nursery. He could put Megan in her bassinet, lay Stacy on the bed and watch her there.

Except she wasn't asleep. She opened one eye, then the other. "Are they gone?"

"You faked?"

She nodded, a wicked grin on her face. "I just wanted to be alone with my hubby. Can you blame me?"

"No way."

She looked at the baby, sound asleep and not even near to faking it. "We could put her to bed and do some interesting things to your body. You've been kind of neglected these past couple of months.''

He gathered Megan and stood, then helped Stacy to her feet. ``Interesting like Tater Tot casserole interesting?''

``Oh, much more interesting than that.''

Winging It

Candy Halliday

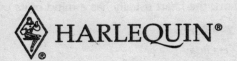

HARLEQUIN®

TORONTO • NEW YORK • LONDON
AMSTERDAM • PARIS • SYDNEY • HAMBURG
STOCKHOLM • ATHENS • TOKYO • MILAN • MADRID
PRAGUE • WARSAW • BUDAPEST • AUCKLAND

Dear Reader,

I've often thought of love as a wild roller-coaster ride. It can have you flying high one minute, only to plunge you downward when you hit the first curve. It can make you laugh and scream and sick to your stomach all at the same time. Love can also make a liar out of you. I should know—it made one of me. I vowed I'd never get involved with a man like my father, who traveled for a living. The man for me would be a man who wanted to put down roots, who wanted a normal life and the standard thirty-year mortgage. Yet what did I do? I married a man with the same wanderlust my father had, who has kept me on the move for most of our married life.

In *Winging It,* my heroine, Mackenzie Malone, makes a similar vow about the type of man she'll never get involved with. A man like her father. Sound familiar? A man who is too handsome for his own good and who has women falling at his feet from every direction. I feel rather guilty for not warning Mackenzie that the word *never* just loves to sneak up behind you and bite you directly on the hiney. Of course, she soon learns that lesson for herself when Alec Southerland, a handsome pilot with a faithful troop of female admirers, moves directly across the hall from Mackenzie and enlightens her to the fact that despite your best laid plans, the heart usually has a mind of its own.

Hope you enjoy,

Candy Halliday

Books by Candy Halliday

HARLEQUIN DUETS
58—LADY AND THE SCAMP

I give special thanks to my talented agent, Jenny Bent, for being my guardian angel, and to my gifted editor, Susan Pezzack, for bringing out the best in me.

This book is for Blue,
my real-life hero in every sense of the word.

"SEX ON THE BEACH?"

Mackenzie Malone looked down at the mysterious drink her best friend and business partner, Angie Crane, placed before her. "I hope you're referring to this blue concoction with the paper umbrella."

"Or what about skip and go naked?" Angie asked, holding out drink number two.

Mackenzie looked from one drink to the other, then back at Angie who flopped down in the chair beside her at their small table in the bar. "My, what original choices," Mackenzie mused. "I can either skip and go naked or try sex on the beach."

"Sounds like a great idea to me."

"If you're looking for a one-night stand, maybe," Mackenzie threw in. "Which I'm *not*."

"I had a one-night Stan once," Angie said, staring off for a second in fond remembrance. "He was wonderful."

Mackenzie laughed. "I said *stand* and you know it."

"All I *know*," Angie argued, "is that you've been complaining about not having a decent date in months. Not to mention that professional bridesmaid role you've been playing lately. How many weddings have you already attended this year? Three?"

"Four to date," Mackenzie admitted with a groan. "And my mother just called last night to rub it in that cousin Julie, whom I've always despised by the way, just landed the absolute catch of the century.''

''And what disgusting color will you have to wear this time?'' Angie wanted to know.

''Thank God Julie doesn't care for me, either,'' Mackenzie said. ''I'm off the hook this time.''

''Oh no, you're not,'' Angie corrected. ''We came here so we could possibly meet someone new tonight, and we just happen to be two of the hottest looking chicks in the room. Now, take one of these drinks and try to look available.''

Mackenzie opted for a sex on the beach, then let her gaze drift slowly around the singles bar. Faces, according to Angie, was Charleston, South Carolina's most popular place to be. If you were looking to rub elbows with the brightest and most successful young professionals in the city, that is.

The bar was filled to capacity with other singles who had stopped at the trendy gathering place after work for happy hour, and possibly to make a love connection for the upcoming weekend. A weekend Mackenzie would probably spend the way she'd been spending most weekends over the last few months, with a stack of movies from Blockbuster and enough popcorn and ice cream to feed a small army.

When she noticed an extremely pretty redhead moving in on an unsuspecting victim, Mackenzie wasn't sure if she and Angie were two of the hottest looking women in the bar, but they could at least lay claim to the successful part. It had been a difficult uphill climb, but after six long years their interior design business had finally become one of the most sought-after design firms in the city. Mainly, Mackenzie knew, because she and Angie made perfect business partners.

She glanced at her best friend again and mentally smiled. A true Southern belle in every sense of the word, Scarlett O'Hara would have found a kindred spirit in Miss Angie Crane. Angie could charm the pants off every man she met when it suited her. Yet, like Miss Scarlett, Angie didn't hesitate to be a bit ruthless in order to get her way.

Mackenzie, on the other hand, felt totally comfortable in her role as the peacemaker. To date, their good-cop, bad-cop routine had worked like a charm in a business world that was mainly controlled by men like the architects, the builders and the developers they were forced to deal with on a daily basis.

"Look over there," Angie said, inclining her head toward a group of suits and ties gathered at the bar. "The tall one. Standing at the end of the bar. He's one of the most successful stockbrokers in Charleston. What do you think?"

"I was trying to imagine him with a full head of hair."

Angie shrugged, then tossed her own shoulder-length blond hair for effect. "Sorry, kiddo, but a receding hairline is just a fact of life when you're hovering around thirty like we are. At least he's not trying to disguise the inevitable with one of those disgusting comb-overs. Besides, I think he's rather sexy."

"Him? Or his *portfolio?*" Mackenzie challenged.

Angie ignored the question, letting her dark eyes skip around the room. "Then take a look at bachelor number two," she whispered behind her hand. "Third table on your left. He sells pharmaceuticals. Has his own beach house not far from mine. Drives a Porsche."

"Needs a good orthodontist," Mackenzie mused.

Angie made a face. "Since when have *you* started paying attention to physical appearances? You? Jaded by the age of ten because your mother convinced you after your parents divorced that attractive men were the equivalent of the dreaded Ebola virus?''

Mackenzie frowned. ''Well, I certainly haven't had any success going for those strictly cerebral types, now have I?''

''Well, hallelujah!'' Angie exclaimed. ''What finally made you see the light?''

Mackenzie twirled the paper umbrella sticking out of her drink several times, thinking about her most recent ex. Who would have ever believed a devoted microbiologist with an impressive PhD would dump a reasonably intellectual businesswoman like herself for his flighty lab assistant with surgery-enhanced boobs?

''I guess my ego's still a little bruised after Doctor Germ-buster lost his head over a fake set of ta-tas,'' Mackenzie admitted and took her first taste of sex on the beach.

Angie's face softened for a moment before she said, ''I'm sorry, Mackie, but I never could imagine you and that geek in bed together anyway. All I could picture was him begging you to slide your butt under the microscope so he could inspect you for any signs of a new amoeba strain.''

Mackenzie and Angie both laughed so hard Mackenzie finally took the napkin from beneath her glass and dabbed at the corners of her eyes. ''I hate to admit it, but we never got as far as the bedroom,'' Mackenzie said with another laugh. ''The poor guy was so terrified I'd contaminate him, I could have been standing before him completely nude and he would have been looking around for a spray can of disinfectant.''

Another fit of laughter overtook them before Angie gasped, ''I guess his lab assistant had an advantage with those big double-D hooters of hers. She probably shoved one in each eye and refused to let the poor man see what kind of nasty stuff she was planning to do to him.''

When they finally stopped laughing, Mackenzie let out a long sigh and said, ''Well, at least I wasn't serious about him.''

Angie raised a perfectly shaped eyebrow. ''Like you've ever been *serious* about anyone you've dated?''

Mackenzie opened her mouth to protest, but Angie cut her off. ''Take that mathematics professor, for instance, whose glasses were so thick he actually needed a seeing-eye dog but couldn't have one because the poor guy was allergic to animals? Or that computer nerd you stopped seeing when he asked you to engage in a little cybersex? Or….''

''Okay, okay,'' Mackenzie interrupted. ''So I don't have a long list of perfect men in my past like you do.''

''Which is exactly why I brought you here tonight,'' Angie reminded her, then reached across the table and grabbed Mackenzie's hand. ''Another potential candidate just walked through the door.''

Mackenzie turned and looked across the room. ''Get serious, Angie, he barely comes up to my shoulder.'' And it was true. Mackenzie stood five-feet-eight in her stocking feet. She'd had a problem since puberty finding a date she didn't tower over like an Amazon at a pigmy convention.

''So?'' Angie grumbled. ''I admit he's a bit vertically challenged, Mackie, but he's also a very prominent podiatrist.''

Mackenzie laughed. ''Great. That's just what I need. A midget with a foot fetish.''

Angie shook her head disgustedly, then leaned back in her chair and folded her arms stubbornly across her chest. ''You know what I think is really wrong with you?''

"I'm afraid to ask."

"You'd never admit it, but I think you secretly have the hots for that new neighbor of yours."

"Alec Southerland? Ha!" Mackenzie said, but her protest sounded phony even to herself.

Maybe because in her best friend type of wisdom, Angie had hit the proverbial nail directly on the head. There was certainly no one in the bar who could measure up to the raven-haired hunk who lived across the hall in her singles complex. But would she ever allow herself to stand in line with the constant stream of women who were already competing for the handsome pilot's attention?

Not a chance.

Alec Southerland was exactly the type of man her mother had warned her about from the moment her father walked out on them. And though her father had remained devoted to Mackenzie in spite of his philandering ways, Mackenzie preferred skinny-dipping in a vat of acid to having her heart broken by a man who attracted women as easily as a black wool blazer attracted lint.

"You can forget about the pilot. You're way off base on that one," Mackenzie lied.

"Am I?" Angie challenged.

"Yes!" Mackenzie insisted. "We're talking about the same guy I allowed to hide in my living room last week until one of his sex-starved vultures finally gave up and stopped circling our building. Remember?"

"But you said you really liked the guy."

"Sure, I *like* him," Mackenzie admitted. "What woman wouldn't? He's gorgeous. He's funny. And he's so blasted charming I'd have to be in a coma not to be attracted to him."

"And the problem is?"

Mackenzie shook her head in disbelief. "Exactly what part did you *not* understand?"

"Your implication that *you* couldn't possibly be enough woman to hold him, maybe?"

"Hold him? Me?" Mackenzie croaked in disbelief.

"Yes, you," Angie said. "I admire your innocent quality of not realizing you're drop-dead gorgeous yourself, Mackie, but I'm tired of sitting by silently while you cut yourself down. You're smart. You have a great sense of humor. And it doesn't hurt that you could pass for Demi Moore's twin sister. In fact, if I didn't love you like a sister, I wouldn't hang around with you at all. I personally don't like the competition of being seen with another woman as attractive as I am."

Mackenzie didn't have a comeback for that statement. She loved Angie like a sister as well, but like Miss Scarlett, modesty had never been one of Angie's strong points.

"Do yourself a favor," Angie insisted. "If you're truly mentally scarred over your parents' divorce, get yourself a good therapist. But if you're not, take a short walk across your hallway and knock on that guy's front door. You'd be crazy if you didn't."

No, I'd be crazy if I did, Mackenzie thought, yet just thinking about such an exciting, yet frightening proposition, prompted Mackenzie to toss the paper umbrella aside and drain the last drop of sex on the beach from her glass.

MACKENZIE ARRIVED HOME that Friday evening alone. She had politely bowed out when Angie captured the attention of a good-looking attorney who was practically drooling all over the table after a single look from her friend. The guy had hurriedly brought over his buddy for Mackenzie, and though she liked attorney number two well enough, Mackenzie declined the invitation when An-

gie invited both attorneys and a few other people from
the club to head off to her beach house for the remainder
of the evening.

Mackenzie had attended enough of Angie's spontaneous beach parties to know they could run nonstop
throughout the entire weekend. Which was the main reason Mackenzie had vetoed the idea of buying a beach
house in Angie's section of Charleston herself. She preferred instead a quieter, less social, and much more relaxed type of atmosphere. And the condo Mackenzie pur-
chased at a singles complex known as Colony by the
Shore had given her just that.

Located on Charleston's famous Battery, Colony by the
Shore was also oceanfront, but it was located in an older,
more reserved section of the city. At the Colony you could
always find a party if you wanted one, but you also didn't
feel pressured to participate if you really weren't in the
mood.

And tonight, after an exhausting week and finally landing the contract for a multistory office building she'd been
working on for days, Mackenzie definitely *wasn't* in the
mood for an all-night party.

Pulling into the driveway of her building, Mackenzie
drove around to the back and parked her Mercedes in her
reserved parking space. A new jade-green Jaguar convertible sat in the space next to hers. For a moment, Mackenzie remained sitting behind the wheel, staring at the
classy car. She tried to imagine herself sailing down the
highway with the very man she and Angie had argued
about earlier in the evening. She pictured the wind whip-
ping through her short dark hair, her carefree laughter
echoing through the still night air, a full moon looming
above them, casting a silvery glow on...*the herd of*

women running right behind the car, quickly gaining ground.

Sobered by her own reality check, Mackenzie promptly stuck her tongue out at the snazzy Jag, left her much more sedate sedan, then trudged toward the building with her friendly Blockbuster bag clutched tightly in her hand. The second she opened the back door to her building, however, shrill voices echoing down the hallway brought her to a dead stop.

"I was here first."

"No, you weren't. We arrived at the same time."

"Well, at least I'm prepared to *cook* tonight."

"I brought food."

"Take-out can't compete with a home-cooked meal."

"What I have in mind for *dessert* certainly will!"

"Now, ladies, let's be rational about this," a familiar voice pleaded, leaving Mackenzie no doubt who was at the center of all the confusion.

Irritated that she'd spent even one second fantasizing about a man who obviously needed a personal bodyguard for his own protection, Mackenzie reluctantly started up the hallway, knowing there was no way, short of sleeping in her car, to avoid the quarrelsome trio. The door to her own condo was, after all, directly across the hall from *his*. And though Mackenzie pretended to ignore them when she arrived at her own door, she did manage a quick peek at the potential ménage à trois as she dug through her purse searching for her keys.

A buxom blonde with a surly look on her face was standing in the hallway holding a grocery sack that had a large loaf of French bread protruding from the top. Facing the blonde with a scowl of her own, was a leggy redhead with a death-grip hold on what appeared to be a container of Chinese takeout. And blocking the entry to his condo like a sentry on duty, stood Mr. Wonderful himself, his hair damp and disheveled, and his magnificent bare chest still glistening with droplets of water from his interrupted shower.

Mackenzie's eyes dropped to the towel he was clutching tightly around his narrow waist, then back to the panicked look on his too-handsome face. She was only one second away from making her escape when he called out her name.

"Girls, girls," he said with confidence when Mackenzie turned back around to face him. "I really appreciate your thoughtfulness, but I already have a date tonight. In fact, she just got home this very minute, didn't you Mackenzie?"

The blonde and the redhead immediately turned and glared in Mackenzie's direction.

Oh, no you don't! Not this time, Mackenzie decided on the spot. *You can get* yourself *out of this mess.*

Purposely sending him a mirror image of his own glowing smile, Mackenzie said in the sweetest voice she could muster, "Gee, Alec, I hope you haven't been waiting on me. Our date's for tomorrow. Remember?"

He groaned in desperation, but he never had the chance to argue with her statement. The blonde tried to sneak past him, but the redhead grabbed the blonde's arm and pulled her back into the hallway.

"Now, cut that out, you two," Alec warned and reached out to push the two enraged lovelies apart before they ended up in a wrestling match in front of his door.

Unfortunately, the second he let go of the towel, Mackenzie knew it was the wrong thing to do. The towel instantly crumpled to the floor. And then, there it was! In the flesh, so to speak, displayed like a prize-winning trophy before three startled women who were all now staring openly at his crotch.

Had he not looked so helpless, Mackenzie would have laughed.

She never got the chance.

Instead of scrambling for the towel to cover himself, Alec kicked the towel aside and then he slammed his front door with such force Mackenzie jumped in spite of herself.

"Now see what you've done?" the blonde accused.

"Me?" the redhead wailed. "You're the one who almost knocked him down trying to get through the door."

"Because I was here first!" the blonde insisted.

"And this is where I came in," Mackenzie mumbled to herself, then turned her key in the lock and stepped quietly into the safety of her own condo.

She stood there for a moment, listening to the angry voices as they faded down the hallway, and trying to convince herself the incredible specimen of manhood she had just seen stark naked hadn't affected her in the least.

It didn't work.

Even in her wildest fantasy, he had looked ten times better than she ever imagined.

She let out a wistful sigh, then dumped her purse and the bag of videos on the table by the door, thinking that even the leading men she *had* brought home with her that evening paled in comparison with the bronzed god who was currently living directly across the hall. In fact, had Brad Pitt and Russell Crowe both walked up beside her only a few seconds earlier, Mackenzie would have knocked their heads together and tossed them both aside just to get a better look at her neighbor.

And who could blame her?

Alec Southerland was every woman's version of tall,

dark and handsome multiplied by about ten billion. No, make that twenty billion, Mackenzie decided, judging from the number of women who had been parading up and down the hallway of their complex from the moment he'd moved in.

She should have been pleased with herself for not allowing him to drag her into his ongoing saga with his groupies again, but instead, Mackenzie felt a bit guilty about not playing along as his alibi. Though she personally had a hard time seeing Alec as a victim in the situation, there *had* been a lot of truth in the statement he'd made on the night he'd taken refuge in her living room. Many women today *were* bold and aggressive. Just like the blonde and the redhead, who apparently had no qualms about pursuing a man to the point they were willing to slug it out in the hall.

Alec's problem, of course, which he'd also admitted, was that he just hadn't figured out how to graciously say *no* to his growing entourage without hurting someone's feelings.

And didn't that sound familiar?

Mackenzie had watched her own father struggle with the very same problem. Big Dave Malone *still* hadn't figured out how to say no to a pretty face. As a result, his marriage had failed, and at fifty-two, he was still no closer to settling down with just one woman than he had been when Mackenzie was ten years old.

"But don't you worry," Mackenzie told the large orange and white cat who appeared from nowhere to rub against her legs. "I'd never get involved with a man who's a carbon copy of your grandpa."

Marmalade, whom Mackenzie's mother called her *grandcat* as another barbed reference to Mackenzie's single status, mewed in agreement, then darted off ahead of Mackenzie in anticipation of her nightly meal.

"But I did meet a really nice guy tonight when Auntie Angie dragged me to a new hot spot where they serve pornographic drinks," Mackenzie told the cat in confidence when she walked into the kitchen where a not-so-patient Marmalade was already twitching her tail.

Taking a can from the overhead cabinet, Mackenzie filled Marmalade's bowl with a cat's version of caviar, judging from the price Mackenzie paid to satisfy her beloved pet's finicky appetite, and placed Marmalade's bowl back on the floor.

"And tomorrow, while you snooze the day away as usual, I just might head out to Auntie Angie's beach house and see if this prominent young attorney liked me as much as I think I liked him."

The haughty feline looked up for a moment as if to challenge Mackenzie's wisdom in that comment, then again buried her head over what was supposed to be a moist and tender tuna fillet.

"And don't give me that look," Mackenzie said with a frown. "I know what you're thinking, but this guy isn't anything like the other morons I've been dating. Of course, he's not to die for like Mr. GQ across the hall, either," she added absently, "but he's cute enough."

Marmalade's tail twitched again, showing her annoyance at being disturbed during dinner, so Mackenzie added out of spite, "And by the way. I think this new guy has a dog. Possibly a pit bull."

Unfortunately, enough was enough, even for Marmalade.

In her customary I'm-a-cat-and-you-bore-me style, Mackenzie's cohabitant suddenly turned her nose up at the remainder of her dinner, lifted her tail straight in the air, then strolled politely out of the kitchen without looking back.

WHILE MACKENZIE SPENT time arguing with her cat, Alec was getting ready for his turn-around flight to New York City that would put him back in Charleston during the wee hours of the morning. He was also still stewing over the fact that he had exposed himself to two pushy flight attendants who *never* would have received an invitation to see him naked, and his comely neighbor who would have thrown such an invitation right back in his face.

Or not?

She certainly hadn't covered her eyes, that was a fact, but Alec had also seen her struggling to keep from bursting out laughing right there on the spot.

"Well, I'm glad someone thought my accidental exhibition was funny, because I sure didn't," Alex told his reflection in the mirror.

He wiped what was left of the shaving cream from his face, knowing that he really couldn't blame his neighbor for refusing to play along with another one of his silly charades. After all, he'd already taken advantage of her kindness once before when he'd found himself in a similar jam, compliments of another eager co-worker determined to make contact with the new, single pilot who had just arrived in town.

However, complaining about his current popularity with the ladies had resulted in Alec receiving nothing but scorn from his buddies.

"Are you nuts, Alec?" his copilot had jeered when Alec recently complained that his impromptu visitors were driving him crazy. "I'd give my left arm to have your kind of troubles."

And Alec supposed his copilot had a point. Only an idiot would be griping because women found him attractive. Telling himself his current popularity would surely die down after a few more weeks, Alec slapped a few dabs of Calvin Klein aftershave on his cheeks, ran a comb through his hair, then strolled out of his bathroom in the pair of boxer shorts he *should* have grabbed instead of that damn towel, when his two surprise visitors took out their frustration on his front door bell.

It had been that urgent buzzing that sent him scampering to the door in a panic in the first place.

Half expecting a five-alarm fire, Alec had been astonished to find not *one* but *two* of United Airlines' finest and fittest standing in his hallway arguing nose-to-nose like two spoiled second-graders in a playground squabble.

And then, to make things even worse, *she* had to come home and witness the entire ordeal.

"Damn embarrassing is what it was," Alec said aloud as he lifted up both shoes for inspection, then grabbed a dirty sock that was lying on the floor to polish the toe of his left shoe.

He should have found it rather refreshing that unlike the meals-on-wheels brigade, his pretty neighbor was apparently immune to his charms. But he didn't. After all, the dark-haired beauty was by far the most attractive woman he'd seen since he arrived in Charleston.

On the day he moved in, he'd almost tripped over his own feet when she sauntered up the hall in a pair of short-shorts that left his mouth dry, and a half T-shirt that left him staring directly at her belly button. An inny, by the way.

Unfortunately, within two minutes into their conversation her body language let him know real quick that he wouldn't have to worry about Mackenzie Malone attaching herself to him like a strip of Velcro.

Oh, sure, she'd been friendly enough in that detached I-can-take-you-or-leave-you sort of way. She'd even been gracious the other night when he hid out at her place telling him to let her know if he needed any help decorating his new condo and handing over her business card.

Thinking of her business card now, Alec headed for the nightstand beside his bed. He picked up the card that had *Design Specialties* written across the top in gold letters. Her home number was there, but as he reached for the phone to call and apologize for the misguided melodrama she had just witnessed in the hallway, Alec suddenly had a much better idea.

Smiling to himself, he dropped the card back on the nightstand and turned his attention to his closet instead. After removing the dry-cleaning bag, he took out a freshly pressed flight uniform, thinking how great she'd looked in that short little black dress she'd been wearing tonight.

And those legs. Jeez, they went on forever.

Yes, her legs were definitely her best feature, and he'd always been a leg man himself.

Of course, those huge brown eyes of hers were enough to leave him feeling like he'd been sucker punched in the stomach. Even her short, sassy haircut got his motor running. That dark ebony hair of hers all soft and wispy, and cut in one of those slightly tousled styles that gave the impression she'd just tumbled out of bed. Oh, yeah. She turned him on, all right.

Especially the fact that she didn't seem the least bit attracted to him.

It had been a long time since a woman represented any type of challenge to Alec. Possibly all the way back to his senior year in high school, when he thought about it. He had only been eighteen then and he'd spent his entire senior year trying to woo a skinny girl named Anne who never did give him the time of day. He'd soon be thirty-six, but Alec still remembered the excitement he felt during his quest to win over the lovely Anne.

Just like the excitement he was feeling now, wondering what it would take to make his classy neighbor have a change of heart.

Of course, he'd have to be careful and not go overboard just to risk a little flirt with danger, Alec realized as he carefully removed his pants from the hanger and stepped into them. Because as far as he was concerned, there were two kinds of women in a confirmed bachelor's life; the kind you could date without any chance of getting involved, and the kind who immediately sent alarm bells ringing in your head.

Mackenzie Malone definitely belonged to the second group, but the lovely Miss Malone had added a slight twist to the situation. Alec was definitely attracted to her, but she wasn't the least bit interested in him.

So what harm could come from one simple date?

He kept asking himself that same question as he buttoned his shirt and slipped on his shoes, telling himself that all he was really interested in was one measly date. Partly, so he could prove to himself that he really wasn't the toad she seemed to think he was. But mainly so *she* would realize that he really was a nice guy after all.

"And I am a nice guy," Alec said aloud with conviction.

He then picked up his coat and his captain's cap with the gold leaf brocade running across the brim, grabbed his keys and walked through his condo that was still too cluttered with unpacked boxes to comfortably feel like home. He opened his front door and stepped cautiously into the hallway, looking up and down the corridor for any signs of another ambush. Satisfied that the coast was clear, Alec closed his door and locked it, then stood for a moment staring across the hall at door A-2.

Was it possible? he wondered, as a chilly feeling of déjà vu overtook him. That like the skinny girl Anne, the lovely lady in A-2 might never give him more than just a passing glance?

Shoving his cap firmly on his head, Alec decided maybe it was time to find out.

2

THE NEXT MORNING, Mackenzie flew through her house-work like a merry maid on steroids, trying to get out the door and on her way to Angie's. She spent thirty minutes looking for her sunglasses, then took a final look in the mirror, pleased that the new hot-pink shorts she was wearing showed off her dark tan to perfection. She then spent another ten minutes making sure Marmalade had food, water and the multitude of cat toys she kept hiding and Mackenzie kept having to find and put back in her pampered pet's three-tier play tower.

After one last look around her now tidy abode, she grabbed up her beach bag and opened the door to find herself face-to-face with Alec Southerland, who was standing in the hallway with his index finger poised just above her door.

"Well, this is a surprise," Mackenzie said with a smirk. "Not only are you clothed, but you're also *alone* today."

"And totally pumped for our big date," Alec countered right back, wiping the smirk completely from her face.

"Very funny," Mackenzie said as he leaned against the doorjamb, blocking her path.

She stepped back a bit, out of range of the imaginary magnet that seemed to be drawing her closer to him than they were already standing. Of course, having seen him stark naked less than twenty-four hours earlier didn't help matters either. Mackenzie was struggling to block the image of his vivid tan line from returning to her memory when he reached down to pluck the bottom part of her skimpy bikini out of the corner of her beach bag.

Holding it up for inspection, Alec smiled and said, "Looks like my gut instinct to dress casual this morning was on target. Just let me run back in and get my swim trunks and we'll be ready to hit the beach."

Mackenzie snatched her bikini bottoms from his hand in one easy swoop. "Sorry, but *we* aren't going anywhere," she was quick to point out. "*I'm* going to a party at my business partner's beach house. Just as soon as you move your delusional self out of my way, that is."

He clutched his chest with both hands, implying he was stricken with grief. "Say it isn't so," he teased. "I distinctly remember you saying our date was today."

"And I distinctly remember you saying our date was last night, but that didn't make it so, now did it?"

"It could have. If you'd been willing to play along."

He maintained the same hangdog expression, and even went as far as looking at the floor while he kicked at the carpet with the toe of a well-worn Birkenstock sandal. In fact, he looked so much like a disappointed little boy, Mackenzie almost wanted to hug him, until he looked up and hit her with one of those devastating grins of his.

"You could always let me go to the party with you," he said in a voice a step beyond pleading. "And I promise I wouldn't get in your way. I mean, I'm sure you're already meeting someone there. Right?"

Mackenzie lifted her chin a bit. "Yes. I am meeting someone there, as a matter of fact."

"A steady beau?"

Mackenzie hesitated. "Not that it's any of your business, but it's someone I recently met." *As recent as last night, if you must know the truth,* Mackenzie thought, but she certainly didn't say it.

"Then, see? You have your own plans, so you wouldn't have to put up with me at all. I'd be as inconspicuous as a fly on the wall. Promise."

Mackenzie laughed. "Oh, sure. You. Inconspicuous. That's certainly the joke of the century."

"Let me prove it," he challenged. "Be a good neighbor. I'm new in town, remember? And it's hard to meet people when you're new in town."

Mackenzie's mouth dropped open. "I can't believe you said that, Alec! I've been expecting to get a notice any day now that our condo association fees are going to being raised in order to expand the parking lot just to accommodate your visitors."

Alec shook his head in adamant disagreement. "I'm not talking about my co-workers. They're giving me nightmares right now and you know it. I'm talking about people *outside* the workplace. And I've always hated the singles bar scene, haven't you?"

Mackenzie blushed. She'd never cared for the singles bar scene, either, yet how else *did* one meet new people outside the workplace?

"Just give me two seconds to run back in and get my trunks," he said when Mackenzie didn't immediately say no.

"Whatever," Mackenzie finally said with a sigh, but she was also mentally kicking the crap out of herself for being such a pushover. "But you'll have to follow me in your own car, Alec," she called out as he headed back across the hallway. "I probably won't come back tonight."

"I thought you said you'd only met this guy recently," he tossed back over his shoulder as he unlocked his door.

Mackenzie glared at the back of his head. "I didn't say *he* would be spending the night. I meant *I* would probably stay rather than drive back home tonight."

"Hey, you don't owe me any explanation," he called out as he disappeared into his condo.

Then why did you ask for one! Mackenzie wanted to scream.

He was back in a flash, trunks in hand and another stop-your-heart smile on his face. "Lead the way," he said, linking his arm through hers as he ushered her down the hallway.

And like the gentleman that he was, he held the door open for her when they reached the exit door of their building.

"You know, something tells me this is going to be a really fun day," he said, literally beaming as they walked across the parking lot.

And something tells me I might as well be dancing toward the gates of hell with the devil himself skipping right along beside me, Mackenzie thought, but as usual, she didn't say it.

IT WAS ABOUT A FORTY-FIVE minute drive from the Battery to the Isle of Palms, a secluded stretch of beach where the inhabitants could not only afford, but also didn't mind, paying the exorbitant prices for their own slice of beachfront property. Mackenzie had talked to Angie earlier that morning and learned that the two attorneys they'd met the previous night at Faces planned to return for Angie's regular Saturday afternoon beach bash. The fact that she was now bringing Alec along wouldn't bother Angie one bit. Angie's standard motto had always been the more the merrier, and it would be hard to guess how many other stragglers would wander up on Angie's deck before the weekend ended.

Glancing in her rearview mirror, Mackenzie saw Alec's Jag pass a car that had gotten between them, then fall back into the right lane behind her Mercedes. How any guy dressed in a faded pair of cut-offs and a simple red polo shirt could look that damn good was a mystery to her. But he did. He was every mother's nightmare, all right, sailing down the interstate with the top down on his flashy car and a deadly come-hither look that even his expensive pair of Ray•Ban sunglasses couldn't quite hide.

One French fry short of a happy meal. Yeah, that's me, Mackenzie decided, glancing in her rearview mirror again.

Even her blasted horoscope had been waving a red flag under her nose with those cautious words: *Don't tempt fate today.*

And what had she done?

She'd totally ignored the fact that her second moon was somewhere behind the fifth planet of the eighth star, or whatever the heck it had said, and not only had she *tempted* fate, she'd even invited Mr. Destiny to politely tag along!

Maybe I do need a good therapist, Mackenzie decided, then made a left turn that took them on a winding driveway out through the sand dunes.

But I can handle this, she kept telling herself. And it really shouldn't be a problem, should it? She would do her thing. He could do this. And that would be that.

Plain and simple.

Right?

Slowing down, Mackenzie looked ahead to the large cedar and glass beach house that had the reputation for being the best party place on the south side of Charleston. And she wasn't surprised that Angie's parking area looked like a who's-who car lot. Every type of automobile imaginable was stacked end-to-end, from a yellow Corvette parked near the deck, to a popular oversized SUV that took up more than its fair share of room. She finally saw a plausible parking space that was more sand than driveway and eased into it, then held her breath when Alec did the same and came to a stop only inches from her bumper.

As if by magic, he was standing by her car door before she even had time to turn off the ignition.

"Great house," he said, looking around the place.

"Glad you think so," she told him and accepted his hand when he opened the door to help her from the car.

Music blaring from the front of the house and the din of robust conversation left no doubt where they needed to go. Mackenzie started up the steps of Angie's back deck first, but she stopped when Alec suddenly reached out and grabbed her hand.

For a second, Mackenzie thought he had one of those gag-type buzzers in the palm of his hand. At least that's how it felt when a strong vibration suddenly pulsed through her body.

"Thanks," he said, seemingly unaware of the effect he was having on her. "For letting me tag along, I mean. I owe you one."

"No problem," Mackenzie lied, easing her hand out of his grip and wondering exactly how long her hand would stay paralyzed merely from his touch.

"You just stick to your promise," she added as she started back up the steps on rather shaky legs. "Inconspicuous, remember? Just like a fly on the wall."

"Just like a fly on the wall," Alec repeated, but when Mackenzie looked back over her shoulder, the twinkle in his dark blue eyes reminded her exactly what a pesky little insect a fly could actually be.

They walked along the side portion of Angie's wrap-around deck to the front of the house that faced the ocean. The front deck was one of those multilevel types that meandered out onto the sand, expanding Angie's outdoor entertainment space. A group of at least forty people were scattered here and there, some in pairs, some in small groups, some just standing off by themselves staring at the white-capped waves or canvassing the crowd. Mackenzie scanned the crowd herself, and it only took a second to find the attorney she had come there to meet. He was taller than average, blond, broad shoulders, nice build, straight teeth. Extremely attractive, actually, she decided. His face broke out in a wide grin when he looked up and saw her. Mackenzie smiled back.

"Shoo fly," Mackenzie told Alec, who was still hovering at her elbow. "Go mingle. Go take a swim. Just go!"

Alec followed her gaze toward the attorney who had started walking in their direction, but he didn't move an inch. Suddenly, Alec's hand shot forward. "John Stanley!"

"Well, Alec Southerland, you old dog," John said, pumping Alec's hand. "What are you doing here in Charleston? The last I heard you were out in Los Angeles."

Mackenzie looked from one man to the other as Alec grinned back. "Oh, you know me, John. I never let too much grass grow under my feet. When United made me an attractive offer, I just couldn't turn it down."

"Well, I bet moving back to the sunny South sure made your folks happy," John said, then turned to Mackenzie. "Alec and I both grew up in Savannah, Georgia, and went to high school together," he offered in the way of an explanation. "How do the two of you know each other?"

"We're neighbors," Alec piped in before Mackenzie had a chance to say a word. "In fact, Mackenzie has seen quite a lot of me lately, haven't you Mackenzie?"

The double meaning of his statement made Mackenzie blush. She reserved her drop-dead look for Alec, then smiled sweetly up at John and said, "I assure you, John, what I've seen of Alec lately is *nothing* worth mentioning."

Take that, mister! she thought triumphantly, but Alec never missed a beat when he asked, "And what about the two of you? How do you and Mackenzie know each other, John?"

John opened his mouth to comment, but Mackenzie jumped in first this time. "I personally like to think that Fate brought us together, don't you, John?" she asked sweetly, then gave John her most dazzling smile before she purposely took his arm and began leading him away from the fly who was going to be *splattered* against the wall if he didn't leave her alone.

"Enjoy yourself, Alec," Mackenzie called back over her shoulder as she and John headed to the far side of the deck. "Your hostess is playing bartender. Go introduce yourself."

ALEC WATCHED THE HAPPY couple walk away, hoping it didn't show that he was seething inside. But he was. He still couldn't believe it, but of all the people in the world to find himself up against, it would have to be his old high school rival, John Stanley.

The same guy, by the way, who had been Alec's competition for his teenage crush, Anne.

It had been eons since he and John had matched wits for the hand of sweet Anne, but it didn't matter. Just like it didn't matter that Anne had only been a silly high school infatuation. He was being childish, and Alec knew it, but that didn't matter either. Because there is always one person in everybody's life who manages to get under your skin just enough to be annoying.

And John Stanley had always been that person for Alec.

He watched Mackenzie laugh at something John was saying, trying to be rational about the situation. So maybe it was ridiculous to let that old jock versus geek mentality from his high school days haunt him now. But he and John Stanley had had a long, drawn-out school boy rivalry. In junior high Alec had been captain of the junior varsity football team while John was president of the student council. Then in high school, Alec had been voted all-American halfback and John Mr. Most Likely To Succeed. After college Alec had gone straight into the air force to earn his wings while John was off to Harvard to earn his law degree.

And now it looked like Alec wasn't going to get a second look while Fate stepped in and happily brought John and Mackenzie together.

Like hell! Alec decided at about the same time someone yelled out from the crowd, "Hey, Angie. What's this mystery drink you're serving called?"

Alec glanced at the attractive blonde who was happily serving drinks at a makeshift bar set up on the far corner of the deck. She had a dynamite figure, he would give her that, and a perfect tan that was concealed only by two tiny swatches of purple material that barely covered her most private parts.

"What you're drinking now is skip and go naked," his hostess yelled back. "And when you're through with that, come on over here and try a little sex on the beach."

Everybody laughed.

Except Alec.

Instead, he glanced again at his old pal John, wondering how Mackenzie could possibly look so interested in anything the bore had to say.

She wants interesting? Fine. I'll show her interesting, Alec decided, then yelled across the deck, "Hey, I could use a little sex on the beach."

"Then come on up here and see me, big boy," his hostess teased back, doing a better than average Mae West impersonation.

Everybody laughed.

Except Mackenzie, Alec noticed with satisfaction.

Watch this, he thought to himself, then walked directly toward the bar and the blonde with his best let-me-rock-your-world smile plastered on his face.

"IT'S REALLY A VERY interesting case," John had just finished saying when Alec made his bold announcement to the crowd about his current frame of mind.

Give me a flyswatter. Now! Mackenzie thought when Alec strolled right past her.

"Yes, I hate to say it, but corporate America has really gotten out of hand these days," John continued, oblivious to the fact that Mackenzie really wasn't paying attention. "Take my client, for instance. This guy had worked for the same company for twenty-two years. He always received top marks at his annual review. He even made his sales quota during extremely difficult times when the economy was down and most of the guys half his age didn't even come close."

"Uh-huh," Mackenzie said, trying to concentrate on what John was saying and keep tabs on Alec at the same time.

"And how does his company reward him for twenty-two years of faithful service?"

Mackenzie missed the question when she noticed Angie's eyes widen in full appreciation the second Alec stepped up to the bar. *Down,* she mentally told the green-eyed monster as it reared its ugly head, but she could almost smell the smoke blazing from its dragonlike mouth when Angie tossed her hair playfully and said something, probably lewd, that made Alec throw back his head and laugh.

"I'll tell you how they rewarded him," John said when Mackenzie failed to answer. "They flew him all the way to their corporate offices in Boston to inform him that he had to accept an early retirement package so they could give his territory to a younger, less qualified man. Can you believe that?"

"No. No, I can't," Mackenzie managed, but her eyes wandered back to her best friend and her neighbor who had suddenly left the deck and stepped inside the house.

So? What do I care if they disappear together? Mackenzie asked herself as visions danced through her mind of them ripping off their clothing so they could have wanton sex on that fluffy, white faux-fur rug stretched out in front of Angie's fireplace, the one Angie insisted was worth every cent of the four thousand dollars she paid for it.

Delete that thought! Mackenzie leaned up against the banister of the deck to steady herself.

Or maybe they'd go to Angie's kitchen, pushing everything off the counter to make room for the lust they simply couldn't deny. Glasses would explode as they crashed to the floor. Pots and pans would clang and clatter as they bounced across the room....

Delete! Delete! Delete!

"So, by the time the guy finally wanders into my office,

the poor man is a virtual basket case,'' John said, shaking his head sadly.

Exactly like I am now, Mackenzie thought, but her sanity was thankfully restored when Alec suddenly appeared back on the deck.

He'd been gone no longer than five minutes tops, Mackenzie decided, allowing herself to breathe a silent sigh of relief. After all, even the fabulous Alec Southerland would surely need more than five minutes to perform either of those sexual fantasies that had driven her close to madness.

BACK OUT ON THE DECK, Alec glanced around the crowd, pretending not to notice the cozy couple at the far end of the deck and reminding himself that his current agitation was his own fault. Didn't Mackenzie tell him up front that she already had a date for this party? Yep, she definitely did. Alec just hadn't expected to be up against such a formidable opponent.

And John Stanley *was* a fierce competitor, Alec would give him that much. John was also an overall nice guy, though Alec found no comfort in admitting it. Especially since he suspected Mackenzie had already come to the same conclusion herself.

Of course, he could always take advantage of his past association with John and saunter over to bust up their intimate little conversation. Talking over old times with John would be good for at least thirty minutes, possibly even an hour if he pushed it. If he wanted to play dirty, that is, which Alec didn't. No, Mackenzie was sure to see right through that ploy. Not to mention the fact that it would only make him look like the jerk his lovely neighbor obviously already thought he was.

No, if he wanted to get Mackenzie's attention in a positive way, Alec knew he would simply have to tough it out and....

"Hey, look alive, partner," a rather fit-looking dude with a military haircut suddenly called out to John. He sprinted down the steps to the volleyball net that was strung out directly below Angie's deck. "Let's show these sissies a thing or two," he said, tossing a volleyball above his head, then catching it. "In fact, right here, right now, the law firm of Stanley and Jameson is willing to purchase an individual case of the beer for every man on the first team able to beat us at our own game."

Alec immediately looked at John.

John looked back with a level stare.

"What about it, Southerland?" John challenged before Alec had the chance. "I've kept in shape since our high school days. How about you?"

Mackenzie's tense look from one man to the other made Alec smile.

Some things never change, Alec thought with glee, and trying to conceal the fire in his eye he quickly called back, "Sounds like a worthy challenge to me, Stanley. Just remember you asked for it."

His old rival quickly pushed off from the banister he'd been leaning against, then handed Mackenzie what was left of his drink. "This shouldn't take long," Alec heard him say with confidence.

You're right about that, Alec thought with a grin. *They'll be calling the rescue squad to carry your fuzzy butt out of here in about another thirty minutes.*

Like magic, a group of guys lined up behind Alec on one side of the net. Another group fell in behind John and his overconfident partner. John took the ball from his partner and purposely tossed it over the net to Alec.

"Ladies first," John teased, getting a good laugh from

the crowd that had gathered on the deck to watch the game.

"Let the games begin," someone yelled from the deck up above and Alec threw the ball into the air for the serve, then smacked it with such force it almost took his old buddy's head off as it whizzed over the net.

"Does the firm of Stanley and Jameson want to make that *two* cases of beer?" Alec called out, getting a good laugh of his own from the eager spectators on the deck.

Everyone except Mackenzie, that is.

Alec could see her out of the corner of his eye. She was standing where John had left her, glaring in his direction. Alec could definitely feel the weight of her stare as he threw the ball into the air for serve number two. Like the first one, Alec left too much spin on the ball for anyone to successfully return it. This time, he purposely sent Mackenzie a wink that only made her roll her eyes, but God, how he did love the thrill of a good game.

The remainder of his serves were just as effective as the first two, but by the time Alec turned the ball over to one of his teammates he had already worked up a pretty good sweat. Grabbing the collar of his polo shirt, he pulled it up and over his head, then tossed it aside, prompting several appreciative female onlookers to clap and cheer.

Mackenzie, of course, wasn't one of them.

He even got a few whistles when he flexed his muscles a bit, trying to loosen himself up for the battle at hand.

And yes, maybe he was showing off a bit.

But so what?

Despite Mackenzie's pithy little remark about having seen him naked being nothing worthy mentioning, John had been responsible for unleashing that old Neanderthal type of reasoning when he challenged Alec to the game.

Alec's need to prove himself had him by the throat now, and it wasn't about to let go anytime soon. At least, not until someone won the game and was crowned the victor.

Of course, Alec intended for that someone to be him.

And then?

Well, for starters, he would have earned the privilege of strutting back up to the deck the winner, right? And like those ancient caveman cousins who had passed down a man's occasional need to prove his own brute strength, the outcome should be fairly simple.

Right?

Me man. You woman. I won. Now, come home with me.

"HOW MUCH LONGER CAN THIS game go on?"

Mackenzie glanced at Angie who had suddenly appeared at her elbow. "Not long, I hope. Poor John looks like he's about to have a stroke."

"He probably will if Alec doesn't kill him first," Angie said. As if on cue, several people gasped as one of Alec's deadly serves grazed John's left ear.

"It never ceases to amaze me that something as simple as a game can turn grown men into a group of competitive schoolboys," Mackenzie grumbled, then toyed with the ice in her cup for a moment before she added, "Of course, letting Alec talk me into bringing him here was my first mistake. Not that the two of you didn't hit it off from the get-go."

Angie jerked her head around at her best friend's chilly tone. "And what's that supposed to mean?"

"Oh, please," Mackenzie scoffed. "People five miles down the beach could have heard him laughing. What did you say to him, anyway?"

Angie grinned. "Well, when he walked over and introduced himself, I told him we weren't as liberated as you guys were at the Colony. I told him he'd have to wear his trunks if he decided to take a swim here."

Mackenzie almost choked on the ice she'd been chomping. "Angie! Can't you ever keep a secret? The last thing I wanted was for Alec to know I'd even repeated what happened last night."

Angie shrugged. "So sue me. Besides, it's obvious you two have the major hots for each other. You practically need a chainsaw to cut through the tension between you."

"Bull," Mackenzie argued, shaking her head in protest. "I came out here today to see John. Remember?"

"And?" Angie probed.

Mackenzie sighed, then moved her hand back and forth in a so-so motion. She then stared down at Alec who had just made another spectacular save that had the whole deck cheering again.

"Well," Angie said as she watched the last seconds of the heated game. "Maybe it's better you aren't exactly smitten with your attorney."

"And why do you say that?"

"Because it looks like your pilot just killed off the competition."

"That's what *he* thinks," Mackenzie vowed, then walked over and grabbed her towel from her beach bag and hurried down the steps.

Purposely looking *past* Alec who was walking in her direction with the rest of his team, Mackenzie waited for John, then promptly handed over her towel.

"Thanks," John said, wiping the perspiration from his face.

"You guys played a great game," Mackenzie said loud enough for prying ears to hear. "I've always been a sucker for the *loser,* myself."

"Well, we certainly fit that bill," John said and handed back her towel.

John then slung his arm casually around her shoulder, and though Mackenzie was startled by his sudden familiarity, she didn't pull away. Partly because she was afraid John actually needed her help getting up the steps. But mainly because her little fly was currently less than two feet away and watching every move she made.

"Good game, John," Alec said, holding out his hand when they reached Alec's side.

John shook Alec's hand, but Alec looked directly at Mackenzie when he smiled and said, "And thanks for being so thoughtful and bringing us a towel, Mackenzie. We appreciate it, don't we, John?"

Mackenzie's look spoke volumes. She held firmly to her towel, forcing Alec to practically tear it from her grasp. And she didn't find it the least bit amusing when he did more than just blot the sweat from his face.

Purposely turning her back when Alec made a big production of toweling off that magnificent broad chest of his, Mackenzie said to John, "Why don't you cool off first, and then we'll take that long stroll on the beach you mentioned earlier?"

"Sounds great," John said at the same time Mackenzie felt the towel hit the back of her head.

"Oops! Sorry, Mackenzie!" Alec said with a grin, then made matters worse when he reached out and tried to smooth down her slightly ruffled hair.

Mackenzie slapped his hand away and held the towel out by the corner as if it were now dripping with poison. Draping it nonchalantly over the banister leading up to the deck, she smiled at John and said, "I don't know about you, but I could use something to drink."

"I was just about to suggest the same thing myself,"

Alec piped in as he threw one arm around John's shoulder
and the other arm around Mackenzie. "How about some
sex on the beach, guys? I promise, it's killer."

No, I'm going to be the killer, Mackenzie thought as
Alec pulled them with him up the stairs to Angie's top
deck. But the minute they reached the bar, John's partner
called him aside and Angie prissed up to hand Alec a
notepad and a pen.

"I'm going to take you up on your offer to make those
fabulous burgers you were telling me about earlier, Alec,"
she said with a smile. "Would you take the orders? So
we'll know how everyone wants their burger cooked?"

"I'd love to," Alec assured his hostess, then looked
back at Mackenzie when Angie walked away. "What?"

Mackenzie's eyes narrowed to tiny slits. "Like you
don't already know!"

Alec shrugged, then held up his notepad and pen. "All
I know is that I'm supposed to take your order. Now, how
would you like your burger, Miss Malone?"

"Well, aren't you Mr. Versatility today," Mackenzie
said, her hands on her hips now. "First you're the volleyball champion of the world, and now you're the freaking Galloping Gourmet! What happened to being a fly on
the wall, Alec? Weren't you supposed to be so inconspicuous I wouldn't even know you were here?"

Alec blinked at her statement, pretending to be clueless.
"I don't know what you're talking about, Mackenzie. But
I do know I need to get your burger order," he added,
poising his pen back over his notepad again. "What's it
going to be? Rare? Medium rare? Well done?"

"Well done," Mackenzie said through clenched teeth.

"Ah," he said, raising an eyebrow. "I see you like
your burgers the same way you like your men."

When Mackenzie refused to rise to the bait, Alec added,

"Because old John was pretty well done before that game was over, wouldn't you say?"

"Why, you...you..."

Alec cut her off when he stepped so close his breath tickled her ear. "You really should thank me, Mackenzie," he whispered. "For going easy on the poor guy. Otherwise, you would have been *carrying* old John on that long walk you plan to take on the beach."

Mackenzie jerked her head away from the hot breath that was sending tingles up and down her spine. And even the warp-speed sample of the sensation she might feel if those fiery lips *did* make contact with her now screaming-to-be-nibbled earlobe wasn't enough to erase Alec's cocky comment. Reaching out, she snatched the notepad and pen from Alec's hand, scribbled only two words across the paper, then gladly handed pad and pen back to her still-grinning nemesis.

"Here's your own personal thank you note, Alec," Mackenzie said, then sent him a satisfied smile before she turned and walked away.

"Hey, Mackenzie," Alec yelled after her. "I didn't realize *thank* you started with an *F*."

Alec was still laughing when Mackenzie closed Angie's sliding glass door behind her.

3

ASSURING HERSELF THAT SHE was only down in the dumps because she'd always hated Mondays anyway, Mackenzie sat at her desk, trying to channel her creative energy toward the sketches that were spread out before her. Unfortunately, it wasn't working. Instead, she found herself struggling with her overactive imagination, and trying not to think about what Alec had been up to since he left Angie's party on Saturday night.

His car hadn't been in the space next to hers when she returned home late Sunday night after spending the rest of the weekend at Angie's. Nor had it been there when she left for the office early that morning. Not that it was any of her business *where* Alec had been, she kept reminding herself. Just as it was none of his business that she'd had a rather enjoyable day with John on Sunday when he'd dropped by Angie's and asked her to take a drive out to the marina with him to check on his sailboat.

Given a little time, she could possibly even grow rather fond of John. Possibly even...

"Your twelve o'clock appointment is here, Miss Malone."

Mackenzie sent a puzzled look at her appointment calendar, but before she could buzz her receptionist with the news that she didn't have any such an appointment, she looked up to find Alec grinning at her from the doorway of her private office.

"I told your receptionist a little white lie about the appointment," he said, sending her a devilish smile. "I just wanted to stop by and tell you I had a great time at the party Saturday."

"Glad to hear you had such a good time," Mackenzie lied, shoving her heart so far back in her chest for protection she thought she heard it clang against her rib cage. "I'm afraid I was too busy to notice myself. In fact, I never even noticed when you left."

You liar! the little voice inside her head yelled. *Too busy to notice? Ha! You would have thrown poison darts at those three girls from Hilton Head if you'd had any poison darts to throw. And what about that personal trainer? The one Alec did leave with later on in the evening? You were only two seconds away from pouring your drink over the poor woman's head when Angie saw that look in your eye and stepped between you and your unsuspecting victim.*

"You stayed the night?" he asked casually, still leaning against the door frame.

"The rest of the weekend, actually," Mackenzie said with a smile. "It was late Sunday night before I even got home." *And where have you been? Hilton Head? Or working out with your new personal trainer!*

"I had an early flight out Sunday morning and didn't get back until a few hours ago," he said, relieving Mackenzie's angst about his mysterious whereabouts until he added with a grin, "Of course, I'm ashamed to say I damn near missed that flight, if you know what I mean."

Mackenzie had to restrain herself from grabbing the stapler on her desk and hurling it in his direction.

"But since I'm here," he added, "why don't you let me take you to lunch? It's the least I can do since you were nice enough to invite me to Angie's party so I could meet some new friends.''

You invited yourself, you nitwit, and I'm not one bit interested in any *of your new friends,* Mackenzie wanted to scream, but she said instead, "Sorry, Alec, but I already have a date with John today if his court case doesn't run through lunch."

Her comment didn't phase him in the least. Instead, Alec strolled into her office uninvited and took a look around the room. "Great office," he said. "It suits you."

"Meaning?"

"Your decor is unique, just like you are. Your desk, for instance. Where did you find something like that?"

"It was one of my design projects in college," Mackenzie admitted.

"How clever," he said. "What made you think of using driftwood as a base for the desk?"

"My student budget. The driftwood was free."

Alec laughed. "And the top?"

"A little more expensive," Mackenzie said looking down at the large piece of oval smoked glass that served as her desktop.

"Well, for what it's worth, I think you're amazing, Miss Malone," he said and winked.

And I think you're full of.... She was about to say when he looked down at his watch, and said with a slow smile, "You know, it's already half past noon, Mackenzie, so it appears your boyfriend got tied up. I guess that means you can have lunch with me after all."

Mackenzie opened her mouth to disagree, but the intercom on her desk came to life again.

"John Stanley is on line one, Miss Malone. Shall I take a message?"

"No, that won't be necessary, Karen," Mackenzie said,

sending Alec a smug look. "I'll be happy to take John's call now."

Reaching for the phone on her desk, Mackenzie turned her swivel office chair around and deliberately turned her back on her phony client. Sending what she hoped was a sultry "hello" into the receiver, she then spent the next few minutes whispering into the phone. And when she finally ended the conversation with a supportive "I'm really glad you won your case, John," she fully expected to receive a thunderous round of applause for her Academy Award-winning performance.

Unfortunately, her satisfied smile was wasted when she turned back around and found Alec standing with *his* back to her, admiring the view of the ocean from her floor-to-ceiling window on the opposite side of the room.

"Oh, well, you can't win them all," Alec said with his back still to her. But when he turned back to face her, he raised his eyebrow suggestively. "Besides, a nice long dinner tonight would give us much more time to discuss what I want to do with my condo."

Mackenzie sent him a puzzled look. "What are you talking about, Alec? And who said anything about dinner tonight?"

Alec grinned. "Me. Just now. You told me to let you know if I needed any help decorating my condo, so I'm letting you know. Surely you have an occasional dinner with a client don't you, Mackenzie?"

So now he plans to become a personal client of mine, does he? Well, we'll just see about that!

Reaching across her desk, Mackenzie flipped the button for her intercom. "Karen? Could you please come in and show Mr. Southerland to Miss Crane's office?" Mackenzie asked before she glanced back at Alec and smiled. "Sorry, Alec, but I handle our *commercial* clients. Angie's the one you need to see. And you saw for yourself what wonderful things she did with her own place. I'm sure she can come up with exactly what you have in mind.''

His surprised look pleased her immensely, and delivering the second wallop of her one-two punch was Karen, who promptly arrived at her office door before Alec could protest. "Alec, this is Karen," Mackenzie said, then purposely glanced down at her watch. "And since I don't want to keep John waiting, I'm sure you won't object if I leave you in Angie's very capable hands.''

"And if I do object?" Alec called out as she hurried out the door with her purse under her arm.

Mackenzie never looked back.

She couldn't.

Whether she liked it or not, Alec was beginning to wear down her defenses with all of these surprise appearances he was making. And Mackenzie feared if she wasn't extremely careful, she'd soon find herself acting out some of the sexual scenarios she'd envisioned on Angie's deck, since they kept popping into her mind every time she found herself in the damn man's presence.

IN SPITE OF MACKENZIE'S miraculous escape, Alec smiled to himself as he followed the young receptionist down the hallway to another spacious business office. Yes, his lovely neighbor had managed to slip through his fingers again faster than sand sifting through a fishing net. And although it was upsetting, Alec knew the battle was far from being over yet.

Under different circumstances, Alec would have even been pleased to see the attractive blonde sitting behind the desk. But even a real looker like Angie Crane couldn't erase his interest in his foxy neighbor. Alec hated to admit it, but he was hooked whether he liked it or not. And the fact that he *was* hooked only led to his growing concern about Mackenzie's current relationship with John Stanley.

And boy, she'd certainly laid it on thick to John on the telephone, Alec would give her that much. So thick, in fact, Alec clenched his fists now, trying not to think about exactly what type of *luncheon* date the two them really had in mind.

"Alec! What a wonderful surprise," Angie said, snapping him back to reality. "What brings you to our office today? Business or pleasure?"

Alec smiled. Okay. It was obvious the lovely Miss Crane was toying with him. And though Alec should have been a little embarrassed that she could see through him so easily, he was actually relieved Angie was being direct and to the point.

"Well, let's just say I was testing the waters today, Miss Crane," Alec admitted, "and from my fishing expedition it looks like I'm here on *business* today."

Angie laughed. "Well, if it's any consolation, I promise you've come to the right place for your decorating needs."

Alec smiled. "You might want to reserve that statement until you take a look at all of my mismatched belongings."

"Nonsense," she said as he took a seat by her desk. "Mismatched anything is the rage these days, Alec. They call it shabby-chic, but when we get through with your condo it'll be much more chic than shabby. Is there anything in particular you had in mind?"

Alec hesitated, then glanced down at his watch. "Look, Angie, I didn't exactly have an appointment today, and I'm sure this is your lunch hour. Would you at least let me treat you to lunch? Maybe we could toss around a few ideas then.''

To his relief, Angie agreed, and the second she said yes, Alec mentally clicked Plan B into operation. This woman was, after all, Mackenzie Malone's best friend and business partner. Someone who would know Mackenzie inside and out. Someone who might, with a little careful persuasion, give Alec some insight into what was going on inside that glorious head of shiny dark hair.

''WELL?'' MACKENZIE ASKED the second she walked into Angie's office after lunch.

''Well, what?'' Angie wanted to know, looking up from the sketches that were spread across her desk.

''I'm not in the mood to play games, Angie,'' Mackenzie grumbled as she flopped down in one of the chairs that faced her partner's desk. ''Did you get rid of our phony client, or didn't you?''

Angie smiled. ''Absolutely not. Alec's really serious about decorating his condo. And he actually has some pretty good ideas.''

''Like what? Installing a revolving door at the entrance to his condo, maybe?''

Angie laughed and shook her head. ''I swear, it would save you both a lot of grief if you would just jump each other's bones and get it over with.''

''Yeah, right. Like I'd ever let *that* happen,'' Mackenzie snorted. ''I can just see me now,'' she added, ''lined up out in the hallway with the rest of Alec's fan club, clutching a number in my trembling hand, waiting patiently for Alec to poke his head out the door and yell 'next.' ''

''That's a gross exaggeration, and you know it.''

The irritation in Angie's voice caused Mackenzie to

glare in her best friend's direction. "Oh, really? Let me guess. Alec spoon fed you his I-just-don't-want-to-hurt-anyone's-feelings routine, now didn't he?"

Angie lifted her chin a bit. "Sounds plausible to me."

"Come a little closer, my dear, probably sounded plausible to Little Red Riding Hood, too," Mackenzie tossed back, "and we all know how that turned out, now don't we?"

Angie laughed in spite of herself. "Well, I'm sorry, but I don't view Alec as the big bad wolf like you do. In fact, he seems like a really nice guy to me. He was a perfect gentleman at lunch..."

"Lunch!" Mackenzie gasped, jerking herself upright in the chair. "He took you to lunch?"

Angie's lips pressed into a thin line. "Now listen, Mackie, you can't have it both ways. You can't dump him in my lap and then expect me not to talk to him."

Mackenzie slumped back in the chair and folded her arms across her chest. "So? Where did he take you?"

"Alec suggested Antonio's, and since we both love Italian..."

"How cozy."

"Would you just listen to yourself?" Angie said, exasperated. "You're sitting there seething because *I* went to lunch with a guy *you* insist you want nothing to do with! Exactly how long are you going to keep lying to yourself?"

Mackenzie's look was apologetic when she said, "I'm sorry. You're right. Alec makes me totally nuts. When I'm around him I can't remember if I'm the good twin or the evil one. The good twin keeps reminding me I should stick with a nice, safe, dependable guy like John. And the evil twin keeps telling me...well, I'm too embarrassed to even repeat what the evil twin keeps telling me to do."

"Conflict only enhances the attraction people feel for each other, Mackie," Angie said. "You don't want to get involved with Alec because you think he's like your father, and he wants to win you over because you're probably the first woman who's ever turned him down."

Mackenzie sighed. "And how long do you think I'd hold his interest if I *didn't* turn him down?"

Angie shrugged. "I guess the only way to answer that question is to try it and see."

"Sure, and risk making the biggest mistake of my life?"

"Maybe. But the one good thing about making mistakes is that if you ever repeat them, you already know when to cringe."

"Thank you, Doctor Ruth."

"You're welcome," Angie said with a grin. "Sarcasm is just one more service I like to offer my friends when I can."

Mackenzie stuck her tongue out at Angie at about the same time Karen walked through Angie's office door holding a gigantic vase filled with fresh daisies of every color imaginable.

"Well? Who have you charmed today?" Mackenzie asked Angie, but she was afraid she already knew the answer.

"No, these are for you, Mackenzie," Karen said. "Should I put them on your desk?"

Mackenzie jumped up and grabbed the card. Leaning forward, she smelled the flowers first, then said, "Yes, Karen, please put them on my desk if you don't mind."

"I bet they're from John," Angie said, but when Mackenzie kept staring at the unopened envelope in her hand, Angie left her desk and grabbed the card herself. "Here, if you won't read the blasted card, I will."

Ripping the envelope open, Angie slid the card out, then looked back at Mackenzie and smiled. "It says, 'Love me? Love me not? But you could still have dinner with me one night. Alec.'"

Mackenzie grabbed the card back.

"He's getting to you, Mackie, I can see it on your face," Angie said, prompting a stern look from Mackenzie. "Well, the least you could do is think about it," Angie insisted. "Besides, wouldn't it be better to find out, instead of wondering the rest of your life if things might have worked out if you'd given Alec a chance?"

"I'll think about it," Mackenzie mumbled but she thought, *Who am I kidding? That's all I have been thinking about!*

"Just don't forget to let me know what you decide," Angie called out when Mackenzie walked out of her office. "If you won't date Alec, maybe I will. You already know I'm a sucker for a romantic man."

MACKENZIE RETURNED to her office, trying to ignore Alec's daisies and trying to convince herself that dating a safe, down-to-earth, predictable man like John Stanley was the best decision she could possibly make. And John Stanley was definitely safe, down-to-earth and rather predictable.

With John, Mackenzie's tongue didn't stick to the roof of her mouth when she saw him, nor did her pulse race to the point she found herself clutching her sweaty palms in order to still her thumping heart. She didn't even jump as if she'd been poked with a high-voltage cattle prod when she and John accidentally bumped into one another. In fact, the one and only time John had actually kissed her, Mackenzie had been amazed to find she had the ability to stay perfectly cool and collected.

She also kept telling herself that she really preferred cool and collected to the pandemonium a single look from Alec could produce. And that she favored *safe* over *reckless* any day of the week. The only problem was that *boring* seemed to tag right along behind *safe* and *calm* every time the adjectives popped into Mackenzie's mind.

But boring was safe. Just like John. And since she didn't feel like a powder keg ready to explode when she and John were together, they could take things nice and slow. Get to know each other. Fall into a comfortable routine....

"The answer is still *no*," Mackenzie said to the knock at her door without even looking up. "The flowers were nice, but I haven't decided to jump in bed with Alec, yet."

"Well, I certainly hope not," a stern voice announced from Mackenzie's open doorway.

"Mother!" Mackenzie gasped and bolted from her chair.

"And who, pray tell is Alec?" her mother wanted to know. "What happened to that nice microbiologist you were dating? The one with the PhD?"

Mackenzie ignored the question, dumbfounded that her mother was actually standing in her office. It had been ten years since she'd moved away from home, and not once had the distinguished Dr. Barbara Malone dared to leave her collegiate surroundings at Purdue University. Mainly, Mackenzie knew, because her mother had never truly forgiven her for leaving Indiana, not to mention her choosing interior design over some scholarly degree that would have put Dr. Barbara Malone's daughter safely in the bosom of modern academia.

"I can't believe you're here," Mackenzie said, wondering why a woman who kept a schedule so rigid you could predict what she was doing at every moment during the day, would show up now, not only *uninvited* but also *unannounced.*

And then it hit her.

"What's wrong?" Mackenzie demanded as she hurried across the room, but a closer look proved to find her mother looking better than Mackenzie had seen her look in years.

Her stylish turquoise sweater and matching skirt was actually short enough to show off her still shapely legs. Her dark hair wasn't pulled back in that severe schoolmarm bun Mackenzie despised. The woman was even wearing a flattering amount of makeup.

Had another degree recently been added to the long list of initials that flowed behind her mother's name like an impressive banner, Mackenzie wondered. Because since her divorce nineteen years ago, furthering her education had been the only thing that seemed to turn her mother on.

"I mean it, Mother. Tell me what's going on."

Instead of answering Mackenzie's question, Barbara Malone sent a semiapproving look around Mackenzie's office and actually smiled. "I never thought I'd admit it, but I guess you did the right thing staying here in Charleston, after all. Of course, while you and Angie were still in college, I have to admit I had my doubts about your big idea of opening your own…"

"Stop stalling, Mother," Mackenzie said, giving her mother a warm kiss on the cheek.

"I'm not stalling, Mackenzie," Barbara said, returning the kiss affectionately. "Is there some written law that says a mother can't drop in and check on her daughter now and then?"

"I hardly call traveling seven hundred miles dropping in, Mother. Not to mention the fact that I've lived in

Charleston for almost a decade now and not once have you felt the need to come check on me.''

This time Barbara flinched. "If you're trying to make me feel guilty, Mackenzie, it's working. And I guess I don't blame you for being a little surprised that I'm here.''

"A little surprised?" Mackenzie wailed. "I think the term shocked out of my gourd would be more appropriate.''

Groaning at Mackenzie's choice of words, Barbara said, "Well, if you're shocked out of your gourd as you so crudely put it, I can't help it. But I *am* here now. And there's no point in denying that I wouldn't be here at all if we definitely didn't have something to talk about.''

"Then let's get out of here where we can have a little privacy," Mackenzie said, already wincing at the huge knot of concern that was quickly forming in the center her stomach.

Unfortunately, it was much later that evening before Mackenzie and her mother were finally seated in a quaint little restaurant in the heart of the city. And at that point Mackenzie was ready to scream. Not only had her mother insisted on taking a grand tour of Mackenzie's office facilities, she had also chatted rather amicably much longer than necessary with both Karen and Angie, and had even insisted on stopping to browse in the rare edition bookstore they'd passed on their walk to the restaurant.

Mackenzie, on the other hand, had spent hours agonizing over what could possibly be so important that her regimented mother had made an unscheduled trip to Charleston. Of course, envisioning her mother with every horrible disease known to modern man had certainly come to mind, which was why the instant Barbara finally made her choice from the menu selection, Mackenzie wasted no time cutting to the chase.

"Spit it out, Mother," Mackenzie said when the young waiter walked away from their table. "I'm going slightly crazy here."

Never one to be rushed into anything, Barbara took her time opening her linen napkin and placing it properly in her lap, then she took a leisurely sip from her chilled glass of wine. When her eyes finally met Mackenzie's, she took a deep breath and said, "I've been dating someone, Mackenzie."

"I beg your pardon?" Mackenzie said as the room started to spin around her.

"I've been dating someone," Barbara repeated.

It was all Mackenzie could do to keep from reaching across the table and shaking her mother's shoulders until her teeth rattled. "My God, Mother," Mackenzie gasped. "Don't you realize how scared I've been? Here I am thinking something horrible is wrong with you, and you came all this way just to tell me that you're *dating* someone?"

Barbara took another leisurely sip from her wine glass before she leveled the second blow. "It's your father," she said with a matter-of-fact little sigh.

Mackenzie laughed out loud until she realized her mother was serious. "You're dating my father?" Mackenzie said so loud everyone in the restaurant immediately turned and looked in their direction.

"Lower your voice," Barbara whispered, squirming slightly under the scrutiny of the people who surrounded them.

"You're joking, right?" Mackenzie insisted. "You and Daddy? Dating? The lofty professor and the woman-chasing, snake in the grass, cradle-robbing, lecherous, phi-landering, seducer of anything wearing a skirt..."

"Your father said you probably wouldn't take this very well," Barbara interrupted.

"Take this very well?" Mackenzie squeaked, then snapped the bread stick she was holding into two pieces and literally pounded the table until nothing was left but a dusty pile of crumbs.

Glancing anxiously around the room when Mackenzie's actions brought even more eyes to their table, Barbara reached across the table and grabbed Mackenzie's clenched fist. "You're going to get us thrown out of this place," Barbara warned, her face now flushed a pretty crimson.

"Well, excuse me, Mother, for having a slight nervous breakdown here," Mackenzie said, slumping back in her chair and folding her arms across her chest. "But if they do have to take me out of this restaurant in a straight-jacket, I hope you realize you and Daddy are the ones who will be responsible for it."

"Oh, don't be dramatic," Barbara accused. "You've always worshipped the ground your father walked on no matter how many ugly things I said about him. And I was wrong to say those things, I admit it. But you have no idea how hurt I was over our divorce. I never got over David, not really. Which is pretty obvious from what I'm telling you now."

Mackenzie still couldn't believe what she was hearing. "And now, after all this time, you're ready just to forgive and forget the last nineteen years you've spent making yourself and everyone else around you miserable?"

Seemingly unaffected by Mackenzie's accusation, Barbara said, "I think David and I are both at a different place in our lives now. And we're certainly mature enough to realize what we both want out of a relationship."

"And when the next pretty face comes along?" Mackenzie couldn't resist saying.

Barbara never took her eyes from Mackenzie's face. "I'll deal with that problem if it ever comes up again, Mackenzie. But your father isn't stupid. And at the risk of sounding conceited, I don't think David would take that chance with me again."

Mackenzie shook her head and sighed. "So? Just how long has this been going on between you and Daddy?"

Now that Mackenzie was asking for a little more detail, Barbara's face instantly brightened. "It was the strangest thing," she said with a smile. "David and I bumped into each other at a local fund-raiser, and a few days later he called and asked me to lunch."

Mackenzie forced back the urge to gag, then motioned impatiently for her mother to continue.

"Well, I started not to go, but David seemed so sincere, I decided it really couldn't hurt anything. I mean, it was only lunch, after all."

Mackenzie rolled her eyes.

"And then one thing led to another, and before I realized what was happening we started meeting for lunch almost every day."

"And where were giggling Gina and the nutty professor during all of these secret luncheons you and Daddy were having?" Mackenzie wanted to know, referring to her father's latest live-in with the hideous laugh, and her mother's companion for the last fifteen years whom Barbara claimed was only her *learned associate*.

Barbara blushed. "Well, Theodore was so angry with me after my first luncheon date with David, he still isn't speaking to me. And Gina was still living at your father's place when we first started meeting for lunch. But then when David stayed over one night with me, well…"

"Stop right there," Mackenzie said, holding up her hand. "You've already told me much more information than I needed to know."

It was Barbara's turn to roll her eyes, but they were both saved from a rather awkward moment when a wary-looking waiter risked returning to their table long enough to deliver the two dinner salads they had both ordered earlier.

"I know this has to be a shock for you," Barbara conceded as she sprinkled a few condiments on her salad. "And I understand how you might feel a bit confused about us getting back together after all this time."

Mackenzie almost choked on the lettuce she had just placed in her mouth. "Getting back together?" she asked with a cough. "What happened to dating? I thought you said you and Daddy were just dating?"

"Well, we have *been* dating," Barbara said, "but your father just received a big promotion. David's company wants him to transfer to California and open a new communications office in San Francisco."

"So? What does that have to do with anything?"

This time, Barbara sent Mackenzie a perturbed look. "Well, I would think it was obvious, Mackenzie."

"Oh, for heaven's sake, Mother," Mackenzie said with an amused laugh. "Don't you think I'm a little too old for you and Daddy to continue that silly game of tug-of-war for my attention? Are you really so afraid Daddy's going to ask me to move off to California with him, that you felt the need to rush down here and warn me not to go?"

Barbara's irritated expression quickly faded into a look of genuine concern. "I'm afraid you don't understand what I'm trying to tell you, Mackenzie," she said so softly Mackenzie found herself leaning across the table in order to hear what her mother was saying. "Your father wants *me* to go to California with him. And that's why I'm here. We plan to be married next month. And we want you to be with us when we say our vows."

"Married?" Mackenzie tried to say but the word came out as a croak.

Letting out a sigh, Barbara's perturbed look quickly returned. "Well, really, Mackenzie. I just don't understand why you're reacting like this. I thought you'd be happy about our news. After all, us getting back together is something you've always wanted."

"Maybe that's what I wanted when I was a bewildered ten-year-old, Mother, but not now," Mackenzie cried out in protest. "Not when it doesn't matter. And certainly not after I've spent my entire life walking a tightrope, trying to do a balancing act between you and Daddy. So please don't sit there and tell me it didn't cross your mind that your little reconciliation just might push me over the edge."

Barbara placed her fork down on the table. "Well, whether you realize it or not, you're contradicting yourself, Mackenzie. If our getting back together doesn't matter because you're an adult now, then why in the world are you making such a fuss?"

Knowing there was no hope of winning an argument with her mother, Mackenzie leaned forward and put head in her hands so she could massage her now throbbing temples. She was trying to be logical about the situation, but the problem with logic was that it sometimes didn't apply to the real world.

Like now.

Mackenzie had spent most of her life watching her parents go out of their way trying to annoy each other, yet now they'd decided they couldn't live without each other?

Did that seem logical? Hell, no! Was it logical that her mother would forgive her father after nineteen long years? Absolutely not. And what about her father? Was it logical to think it had taken him nineteen years to realize he really loved her mother? Or had the greener grass on the other side turned out to be nothing more than artificial turf?

Deciding there was nothing wrong with her life that a good miracle couldn't fix, Mackenzie finally looked up at her mother and said, "You're right, Mother." And she forced a smile she certainly didn't feel when she added, "I am making a big fuss and I'm sorry. Of course, I'll be there for your wedding. I love you and Daddy very much. I'm happy for both of you."

Barbara's eyes filled with tears when she reached across the table for Mackenzie's hand. "We love you, too, honey," she said sincerely, but before Mackenzie had time to enjoy such a warm bonding experience, Barbara squeezed Mackenzie's hand and said, "And I just can't wait for you to see the fabulous gown I've picked out for you to wear as my maid of honor. I know you've never been that fond of green, but this gown is more mint than it is lime, and…"

"Excuse me, Mother," Mackenzie interrupted and bolted from the table.

Unfortunately, by the time Mackenzie reached the rest room, her face was more of the lime green variety, instead of the mint color she would soon be wearing to her own parents' wedding.

4

By the time Mackenzie pulled into her parking space it was midnight. To say that life had performed a lively little tap dance on Mackenzie's last nerve was putting it mildly.

After her mother's shocking announcement, she had been forced to listen to every sordid detail of the *fifth* wedding she would be attending this year. Not to mention the fact that she was thoroughly convinced her parents' guests would surely be whispering behind their hands over a soon-to-turn-thirty woman having the nerve to call herself the *maid* of honor.

Mackenzie had then taken her mother to the airport where she spent every minute looking over her shoulder half-hoping, half-fearing Alec would make another of his surprise appearances. And then, when she was only seconds away from putting her mother safely on a plane back to Indianapolis, her mother must have read her mind, because she looked directly at Mackenzie and said, "So who is this Alec person you're not going to jump in bed with?"

"He lives across the hall in my building," Mackenzie volunteered with a sigh, praying her mother would just drop it.

She didn't.

"And? How long have you known him? What does he do?"

"He's only been in Charleston about six weeks. He's

a pilot for United Airlines,'' Mackenzie said, suddenly relieved that they were standing at a *Delta* boarding gate.

The way her luck had been running lately, it wouldn't have surprised Mackenzie if Alec had turned out to be the pilot on her mother's plane. Mackenzie could just picture it. Dr. Barbara Malone forcing her way into the cockpit. Interrogating Alec to the point he had to call the control tower and request permission for an emergency landing. CNN announcing on the evening news that an enraged professor from Purdue University had hijacked Flight 602, demanding that the pilot keep his grubby hands off her pitiful, still single daughter.

''My word, Mackenzie,'' her mother had said, snapping Mackenzie out of her nightmare. ''You might as well just douse yourself with gasoline and go up in flames now, because you'll surely get burned if you set your sights on a man who has a fleet of pretty flight attendants constantly at his disposal.''

''Fine,'' Mackenzie had said right back. ''I'll get a *five gallon* can of gasoline, Mother. In case you need some for yourself in a month or two.''

''Now, Mackenzie. I understand why you think I might be making a mistake...''

''At least you'll know when to cringe this time,'' Mackenzie had mumbled absently.

''What?''

''Nothing.''

''Well, you still haven't told me what happened to that nice microbiologist. The one with...''

''The PhD?'' Mackenzie had finished for her. ''Sorry, Mother, but he lost his head over a fake set of boobs.''

Her mother had frowned on that one. ''That's such a vulgar word, Mackenzie.''

''Apparently *he* didn't think so,'' Mackenzie had replied, and then she'd breathed a huge sigh of relief when a Delta ticket agent finally announced that her mother could board the plane.

"You forget about that pilot," had been her mother's last warning.

It was probably a blessing in disguise that her mother had shown up and totally erased Alec from her mind for a few hours. And at the moment, she was too mentally drained to even wonder where he was, much less overload her mind any further by trying to decide if she should or shouldn't show a little interest if he tried to get her attention again.

"Just because my mother has gone temporarily brain-dead, doesn't mean I have to follow in her footsteps," Mackenzie told the full moon staring down at her from its lofty perch above.

She then killed the motor, but switched the ignition to accessory so she wouldn't interrupt her favorite oldies radio station. While Elvis belted out "A Hunka, Hunka Burning Love," she reached into the paper sack sitting on the seat beside her and pulled out a bottle of beer from the carton holder she'd bought at a convenience store only two blocks from the airport. Twisting off the cap, she glanced idly at the vacant space where her own personal hunka burning love's car should have been sitting, and then she took a long, slow gulp from her bottle.

Unfortunately, the minute the gold liquid slid down her throat, Mackenzie remembered why she'd never liked beer.

So why had she chosen beer in the first place? Simple. She figured she could drink a couple of bottles to take the edge off her mounting hysteria, yet the task would keep her from drinking enough to leave her smashed. In fact, Mackenzie was just congratulating herself for being such a sensible, levelheaded and responsible woman when Alec's jade-green Jaguar slid silently into the parking space right beside her.

Mackenzie's first instinct was to duck like a car thief, but a toot from Alec's horn told her it was too late. She could always run, she decided, but at the moment she simply didn't have the strength. Instead, she remained sitting behind the wheel of her Mercedes, still looking straight ahead. She didn't even turn her head when his car door slammed.

He walked up to her car door and tapped on her window, prompting her to take another quick sip from the bottle. Still looking straight ahead, she reluctantly pushed the appropriate button allowing her only protection to magically slide out of sight.

"Are you okay?"

Mackenzie took another swig, still refusing to look at him. "Sure, I'm great. Why do you ask?"

He leaned down and rested his arms on her open window, much too close for comfort as far as Mackenzie was concerned, but she finally turned her head and looked at him. It was the wrong thing to do. Alec looked so good in his flight uniform, and with his captain's hat pulled down on his forehead just enough to look incredibly sexy, *Coffee, tea, or me?* immediately popped into Mackenzie's head.

"Why did I think something was wrong?" Alec asked, pushing his hat back a bit. "Well, let's see. It's after midnight. I come home to find you sitting out here in your car alone. Drinking. But yeah, you're right. Why would I suspect something might be wrong?"

Mackenzie shrugged, then took another short drink. "If you must know, I'm celebrating," she said, and then she burst out laughing in spite of herself.

Alec sent her a wary look. "Do I dare ask why?"

She reached into the sack and pulled out another bottle, then handed it to Alec. "Here. Why don't you celebrate with me?"

Does anyone have that can of gasoline ready? This chick's gonna need it! Mackenzie's psyche yelled out, but she ignored the warning, determined to throw caution to the wind the way her mother had apparently been doing while *she* had been sitting on her toadstool looking around for a frog instead of a prince like the one that was standing by her window now.

Alec took the beer, then walked around to the passenger's side of her Mercedes. He opened the door, moved the carton of beer to the floor, and slid into the seat beside her. "You know, we could probably find a more comfortable place to celebrate," he said, twisting off the cap of his bottle. "I just happen to know two people who live here."

Mackenzie ignored his pun, then held her bottle out and clinked it against his.

"And what are we celebrating?" he wanted to know.

"My parents are getting married," Mackenzie said with a laugh, but the laugh ultimately betrayed her and Mackenzie burst into tears instead.

ALEC WAS SPEECHLESS. He quickly uprighted the bottle she'd dropped when she covered her face with her hands, trying not to stare at the now-soaked jersey material of the clingy blue dress she was wearing.

God, I really am *a jerk,* Alec thought. *She's sitting here crying her eyes out and all I can think about is the way that wet material is clinging to those incredibly long legs of hers.*

But he wasn't such a jerk that he could watch her cry

without pulling her toward him so she could sob against his shoulder. "It's okay," he kept telling her, hoping for Mackenzie's sake that what he was saying was true.

Though Mackenzie didn't realize it, Alec already had a pretty good grasp of the situation that currently had her in tears. His luncheon date with Angie had proved much more enlightening than he'd hoped. Not one to beat around the bush, Angie had told him quite a lot, actually. She'd told him about Mackenzie's overbearing mother. About Mackenzie's father, whom Mackenzie adored in spite of the fact that he had a roving eye. About her parents' nasty divorce, and how hard Mackenzie had taken it.

About why Mackenzie would probably never give a guy like him the time of day.

"I'm sorry, Alec," she said into his shoulder, then pulled away from him and wiped her eyes with her fingertips. "I'm not drunk, I've only had half a beer. I'm just a little overwhelmed and feeling incredibly sorry for myself at the moment."

"Hey, you don't have to apologize to me," Alec said and sent her a sympathetic smile.

She sent him a slight smile back. "I'm sure you think I'm an idiot for slobbering like a two-year-old, but you'd just have to know my crazy parents and what they've put me through all these years."

"I assume your parents getting remarried is a bit of a shock for you?" Alec asked, forcing himself to play dumb.

"Shock?" Mackenzie repeated. "If someone had told me the Pope had resigned from the Vatican so he could devote his time to developing a new birth control pill, I would have believed *that*. But my parents getting married again? After nineteen years of putting each other, not to mention *me*, through pure hell?'' She shook her head disgustedly as another tear rolled across her magnificent high cheekbone. "Tell me, Alec. Where is the logic in that?"

When Alec only shrugged she added, "Just to give you an idea of what I'm talking about, take my college graduation. Here was my mother, trying to impress the dean by tossing around her own degrees like a juggler center ring at the circus, and my father walks up and says, 'Tell me, Dean Whitcomb, if a man is talking in the forest, and his ex-wife isn't there, would he still be wrong?'''

Alec laughed, but Mackenzie's sharp look made it a short one.

"And so my mother says, 'You'll have to excuse my ex-husband, Dean Whitcomb, as you can see David's intellectual pursuits make professional wrestling look like a think tank.'''

Alec grinned. "And what was your dad's comeback to that one?"

Mackenzie sighed. "He didn't need one. It turned out Dean Whitcomb was a huge professional wrestling fan himself. My mother stomped off when the dean and Daddy started discussing how Hulk Hogan was and always would be the greatest professional wrestler of all time."

She leaned her head against the steering wheel and let out another shaky sigh.

"And it's not that I'm *not* happy for them, because in a way I really am," she said, wiping at her nose. "I mean, I should really be ecstatic when I think about it," she added, still trying to talk herself through her anxiety. "At least, now I won't have to spend every holiday rushing around so I can spend the morning with Mother and the evening with Daddy."

Alec nodded.

She smiled. "Hey, I can even save money. From now on, I'll just buy them *one* Christmas present. Something for that blasted new house with the indoor swimming pool Daddy's supposed to be buying for them when they move out to San Francisco."

Alec nodded again.

"You know," she said, her face brightening a bit, "now that I *really* think about it, Christmas in California doesn't sound bad at all. And I've always hated cold weather. That's why I loved South Carolina so much when I came here to college. Now I'll never have to spend another cold Christmas in Indianapolis again."

"See, you can always find good in anything if you look hard enough," Alec said, taking hold of her hand for a gentle squeeze of support. To his surprise, she sent him a thoughtful look and squeezed back.

Focus on comforting *her, dammit, not* copulating *with her,* Alec kept telling himself, but when she rubbed the pad of her thumb up the full length of his index finger, Alec Jr. snapped to attention like a private coming face-to-face with a four-star general.

"So? What about you, Alec?" she asked, holding him captive with those big brown eyes of hers. "Are you close to your parents?"

Alec almost missed the question since most of the blood in his brain had now been diverted south. "Yeah, we're close," he finally managed, relieved yet also disappointed when she let go of his hand. "In fact, you could say I grew up in a perfect sitcom family myself."

"Lucky you."

Alec shook his head more in an effort to get the blood flowing in the right direction again than he did in disagreement with her statement. "I guess that depends on how you look at it, Mackenzie. You see, in your case, you have at least a 99.9 percent chance of having a better marriage than your parents had. But me? My parents have a *perfect* marriage. Now, how hard do you think it's going to be to live up to that standard?''

She thought about his comment for a second, then let out a long sigh and leaned her head back against the headrest, offering up her exquisite throat like a cool drink of water to someone dying of thirst.

Alec licked his own dry lips. He was only seconds away from dragging her to him to satisfy his own thirst. She suddenly shifted in her seat and met his greedy gaze. ''Well, when you put it like that, Alec, I guess we all have our own problems, don't we?''

He managed to say, ''Yes, I guess we do. But I wasn't kidding about there being more comfortable places than your car to solve all the world's problems. Why don't you stop by my place for a few minutes? At least until I'm sure you're going to be okay.''

And just when he expected Mackenzie to say, not a chance, buster, she sent him a rather beguiling look and said, ''Why don't you come home with me instead?''

Alec had to bite his tongue to keep from cheering. ''Are you serious? You're inviting *me* to come home with *you*?''

''Is that so hard to believe?''

''Well, yes…'' Alec began, but Mackenzie broke in and said, ''You said just for a minute, didn't you? And I would go to your place, but my poor cat is probably starving by now.''

''Cat?'' Alec echoed as they both left the car. He grabbed what was left of the six-pack and hurried after her.

''Yes, I have a cat,'' she called back over her shoulder. ''She's elusive when strangers are around,'' she added when Alec caught up with her. "That's probably why you didn't see her on the night—"

"What kind of cat is she?" Alec cut Mackenzie short this time. Hell, he wasn't going to let her dwell on the night he'd hid out in her living room. Not now. Not when he was finally making progress. And certainly not when *she'd* been the one to invite *him* to go home with her.

"Oh, she's just a cat, but you'd think she had pedigree to go along with that attitude of hers," Mackenzie said with a laugh. "She's very temperamental. Very independent. Sometimes she won't even look in my direction. And then the next day she's all over me, eager for my attention."

Sounds familiar, Alec thought as he held the back door of the building open for her, then followed Mackenzie up the hallway.

She had been treating him like he had a third eye in the middle of his forehead from the moment he met her. Yet now, what was she doing inviting him home when it was already past midnight? What in the hell could that mean? That she'd finally realized she shouldn't have listened to her bitter mother all these years?

Or did her motive have a much deeper meaning?

"You know, sometimes I think that cat treats me the way she does out of nothing more than pure spite," Mackenzie added when they finally stopped in front of her doorway.

"Spite, huh?" Alec repeated. *Yeah, that's exactly the word I was looking for myself.*

Mackenzie unlocked her door, then stepped inside and flipped on the light. Alec followed behind her and found a large orange and white cat stretched out across the back of Mackenzie's overstuffed rattan-frame sofa. The cat raised its head slowly, twitched its tail and hissed when Alec took a step in her direction.

"Behave yourself, Marmalade," Mackenzie warned.

The cat sent another feral look in Alec's direction, then pulled itself into a crouched, ready-to-pounce position. *Great*, Alec thought. *Mackenzie's suddenly willing to endure my company, but now her attack cat wants to scratch my eyes out.*

The African motif Mackenzie had chosen for her condo certainly enhanced the jungle cat image where the currently stalking feline was concerned. On the first night he'd been there, Alec had been amazed at the small piece of the dark continent Mackenzie had been able to recreate for herself.

Glancing around the room again, he took in the heavy rattan furniture with its overstuffed cushions splashed in brilliant pinks and greens. A huge zebra-print rug covered her polished wood floors. African carvings and artifacts of every description decorated the room. Wild animal prints covered the walls. The place was primitive, yet exotic. And the huge plants and ferns Mackenzie had scattered around the room managed to bring the jungle indoors.

Still thinking about the jungle, Alec glanced at the back of the sofa again and tensed. The cat had vanished. He kept waiting for the miniature tigress to jump out at him from behind one of Mackenzie's giant elephant-ear ferns. Instead he found the dear kitty politely devouring a bowl of cat food in Mackenzie's small kitchen.

He glanced up at Mackenzie, who was appraising him so openly, that Alec stopped worrying about the cat and turned his attention to his hostess instead. *Run* his gut instinct tried to tell him, but another look at those gorgeous long legs of hers intercepted the message.

Holding up the carton of beer he'd brought in from the car Alec smiled and said, "Guess these should go in the fridge."

She gave him a sultry look, then walked across the room and took the carton from his hand. She then placed it on the glass top of the small table in her kitchen, also rattan, Alec noticed as he tried *not* to notice the determined look in her eyes.

"It was really sweet of you to send me flowers today, Alec," she said, practically purring like her cat was now doing over the food in its bowl.

"And it was even sweeter of you to worry about me tonight," she continued, taking a step forward that barely left any space between them.

God, she smells good, Alec thought. "I am a sweet guy, Mackenzie. I'm glad you've finally realized that."

"So am I," she said, then reached up and removed the captain's hat from his head.

Heaven help me, Alec prayed when she immediately sent it sailing backward over her shoulder.

The hat slid across the floor, causing the cat to smack at the gold braid running across the brim. Alec brought his eyes back to meet hers and cleared his throat. "Exactly what do you think you're doing, Miss Malone?"

In answer to his question, she reached up and pushed his coat off his shoulders. "I'm doing exactly what I've *wanted* to do from the first time I saw you, Alec."

Alec swallowed hard when his coat hit the floor. "Well, you sure could have fooled me, Mackenzie," he said, ignoring those alarm bells that were now ringing in his head.

What you need to do, his mind kept yelling, *is march your ass right out of here. Now!*

He never had a chance.

She loosened his tie, then grabbed the front of his shirt and gave it a tug, popping buttons left and right and sending the cat scurrying out of the room to safety. She then slid her arms around his neck and pulled his head down for a kiss so soft and sweet Alec almost relaxed.

Unfortunately, the kiss that charged right in behind the first one made Alec's head spin faster than a windmill in a hurricane.

Totally out of control now, Alec slid his arms around Mackenzie's tiny waist and crushed her to him. His traitorous tongue immediately joined in a slow tango with hers, producing a groan of pleasure that erupted from somewhere deep in his throat. In an instant, the wildfire she was igniting in a much lower location picked up speed to the point that all Alec could think about was how he was going to put that fire out.

"Come with me," said the spider to the fly he had once promised to be.

Alec didn't object when she led him from kitchen holding to the tie still draped around his neck. Besides, how could he? He was still lost in a foggy stupor from that soul-stealing kiss she'd just given him seconds earlier.

Opening the door, she pulled him into her darkened bedroom. *Welcome to paradise,* Alec thought when she flipped on her bedside light and he found himself staring at a king-size bamboo canopy bed with gauzy mosquito netting draped around the high posters of all four corners.

However, his interest in the bed instantly evaporated when Mackenzie stepped out of her dress and stood before him wearing nothing but two pieces of skimpy black lace.

Mackenzie saw his eyes widen when her dress hit the floor. Her own heart was pounding so hard she thought it might jump out of her chest. But when Alec continued to do nothing but stand there, staring at her with a dumbstruck look on his face, she feared her heart might come to a complete stop. Was he disappointed? The lower half of his body sure wasn't sending out that signal. Or was he now having second thoughts, just like she had been having from the moment the invitation to come home with her slipped off her tongue?

Maybe she should just make a break for it while she still had the chance, Mackenzie decided. She could always make a dive under her bed. Of course, what she really *wanted* to do was act on the undeniable attraction between them and simply tackle the sexy hunk right where he stood before she lost her nerve.

She had just opted for a disappearing act under her bed when Alec finally said in a voice barely above a whisper, "Dear God, Mackenzie, you're so beautiful you take my breath away."

His response, though belated, helped Mackenzie make her final decision.

Parting the heavy netting around her bed, Mackenzie slipped behind the privacy it offered, then stretched out on the bed with her hand held out, beckoning Alec to follow.

He didn't hesitate.

Pulling off his tie and what was left of his already damaged shirt, Alec quickly stripped down to nothing but his boxer shorts, then parted the curtain and lowered himself onto the bed beside her.

"What took you so long?" she whispered, then rolled on top of him and kissed him so passionately his eyes crossed.

The passion raging between them was so primal it frightened Alec. It was primitive. Wild. Completely untamed. An unleashed force like nothing Alec had ever experienced before. And when the realization of what he felt when he held this woman in his arms finally got through to his muddled brain, it abruptly grabbed him by the scruff of the neck and jerked Alec straight back to reality.

Surfacing from the long kiss he'd been drowning in, Alec quickly reversed their positions and pinned his temptress beneath *him* instead. He then looked down at Mackenzie as if she were a total stranger, asking himself over and over again, *what in the hell have I been thinking?*

He'd been so caught up in his quest to win her over, it had never occurred to him until just now that his feelings for Mackenzie went much deeper than just some foolish ego match with John Stanley. For the lack of a better word, everything about Mackenzie felt *permanent.* Like she was *meant* to be a part of his life.

What in the hell does that mean? Alec wondered.

And he didn't like the answer his heart came back with.

No way! Alec told himself as Mackenzie's tongue did a little snake walk up the side of his neck. Hell, wasn't he the king of no commitments? The guy who had managed to sidestep beautiful women literally coast to coast? The type of man who would sooner take a bullet than hand over his freedom in exchange for wedding bells and baby booties?

However, when she pulled his head back down and began teasing his left ear with the tip of her tongue, Alec realized he couldn't be sure of anything at that moment except the huge dose of desire that was flaming out of control directly between his legs.

Go for it! his body kept screaming, and he was only one step away from taking what she was willing to give him when she looked up at him with such trust in those big brown eyes of hers and said, ''Make love to me, Alec. Make love to me now.''

And God, how he wanted to.

But dammit, he just couldn't do it. Even if he'd had protection, which he didn't, he still couldn't do it. Not now. Not like this. And especially not when he realized that the feelings he had for Mackenzie Malone were much too strong for a quick roll in the hay.

Looking down at Mackenzie again as if he *had* just seen her for the first time, Alec kissed her forehead tenderly, then he kissed her eyelids. He kissed both of her marvelous high cheekbones, and then he finally kissed the tip of her cute little turned-up nose. And with his heart filled with something so new Alec still couldn't define it, he then rolled on his side and ran his finger lightly across her passion-bruised lips when he said, "As much as I *do* want to make love to you, Mackenzie, I think we'd better stop this while we're ahead, don't you?"

STOP THIS? NOW? When they were both practically naked and panting for more? Was Alec crazy? Or was she? Maybe things had gotten out of hand because she wasn't exactly herself tonight. Or had she really invited him to her bedroom for nothing more than the simple reason that she really was in love with this man?

I am in love with him, Mackenzie finally admitted to herself.

Unfortunately at the moment she didn't know whether to thank him or *spank* him!

Pushing Alec away from her, Mackenzie forced herself into a cross-legged sitting position in the middle of her bed. Reaching for one of the zebra-print pillows behind her, she whacked Alec over the head when she said, "Dammit, Alec! What happened to your freaking 'I just don't know how to say no,' affliction?"

Alec gently took the pillow she was using for a weapon

from her hand, then pulled himself up and rested his back against the headboard. "And what happened to that 'I don't want to be a member of your fan club' attitude of *yours?*"

Mackenzie sent a pouting look in his direction, then grabbed another pillow, this time one that was spotted like a leopard. "Can't a girl change her mind?" she wanted to know as she hugged the pillow to her exposed midriff.

"Is that what you've done, Mackenzie? Changed your mind about me? Or is your sudden interest in me only because you're upset about your parents getting back together?"

Mackenzie blinked at his question. "Is that what you think? That I want to sleep with you as some sort of twisted revenge against my nutty parents?"

"I think that has something to do with it, yes."

Smart guy!

Okay, so maybe her parents getting back together *had* finally been the catalyst that prompted her to let her guard down and act on her feelings. But she did love the big dope. She just hadn't expected Alec to be so damn analytical about it. No, she'd expected him to grab one of the dozens of condoms he probably kept on his person at all times and satisfy her sudden need to throw caution to the wind. Of course, there was always that nagging possibility that…

Sending him a suspicious look, Mackenzie said, "What's really the problem here, Alec? Don't I measure up to the other women you've been with?"

He leveled a stern look in her direction. "That question isn't even worthy of an answer and you know it."

"What then?" she asked as relief washed over her. "Surely you have some protection."

Alec laughed. "Yeah, right, Mackenzie. I keep a dozen

condoms pinned to the waistband of my boxers at all times.''

Great. He can even read minds.

Tossing the pillow aside, Mackenzie flopped down on her side, using her elbow as a prop while her head rested against her hand. *Go ahead,* she thought. *Stare at my cleavage. Why do you think I chose this position? I hope you ogle until your eyes pop out.*

But out loud she said, "I guess I can't blame you for being confused, Alec."

"I'd say confused is a pretty adequate description of how I feel at the moment."

"I wasn't lying when I said I've been attracted to you from the very beginning," Mackenzie admitted.

"But?"

Mackenzie eased her hand out of his grasp and sat up to face him. "Truthfully?" she asked, stalling for time. When Alec nodded, Mackenzie took a deep breath and said, "I'm sorry, Alec, but I'd always be afraid you couldn't say 'no' to the next pretty face that came along."

Alec leaned forward and kissed her. "And it never crossed your mind that if I had you, then I *would* have a reason to say no?"

Mackenzie wanted to believe he was serious. "Don't play games with me, Alec," she warned. "I'm pretty fond of this heart I've been carrying around for twenty-nine years. I sure wouldn't want to see it broken."

"I'm pretty fond of my heart, too, Mackenzie, so let's make a deal," Alec said, getting up long enough to pull back her leopard print comforter. He patted the bed then, motioning for her to slide beneath the covers. When she did, he tucked her in properly and sat down on the bed beside her. "No more games, okay? Let's just take it slow, really get to know each other, and see where it leads us. Is it a deal?''

Mackenzie stared at that magnificent broad chest of his, trying not to let her eyes follow the dark line of hair that trickled down to...*what I'm not supposed to be thinking about now!* ''It's a deal,'' she finally agreed.

''Good,'' he said, then leaned over and kissed her again with one of those gentle, sweet, see-you-later kind of kisses. ''You've had a rough day,'' he said. ''You'd better get some rest. I'll call you tomorrow.''

''Okay,'' Mackenzie managed, suddenly struggling to hold back the tears at the thought of being left alone on this particular night.

''And just for the record,'' he added as he stood up and bent down to pick up his pants from the floor, ''what I feel for you is more than a mere attraction, too. So when we do make love, Mackenzie, I want it to be for all the *right* reasons. Understand?''

His statement caught her completely off guard. ''Who would have ever figured you for such a nice guy?''

He grinned. ''I am a nice guy. Now hush and get some sleep.''

Mackenzie blinked back the tears when he sat down on the side of the bed to put on his pants. ''Alec?'' she began, but when he turned back to look at her one tiny tear betrayed her and slid down her cheek.

Without her having to ask, Alec simply tossed his pants on the foot of the bed, then reached over and turned out her bedside light. When he slipped into bed beside her, Mackenzie rolled on her side and Alec pulled her close in the darkness.

''You only have to stay until I fall asleep,'' she whispered, as they snuggled into a perfect spooning position.

"We'll see," he whispered back, but something in the way he pulled her even closer, told Mackenzie she wouldn't have to get through the rest of this night alone after all.

5

ALEC AWOKE TO THE illusion that he was surrounded by a white, fluffy cloud like the ones he normally saw from the window of his cockpit. But when he remembered the netting around Mackenzie's high poster bed, he jerked his head to the left and found two yellow eyes staring back at him.

"Well, good morning," he said, only to be greeted by a hiss.

"Is my breath really that bad?" he asked, then reached out and scratched his self-appointed observer gently behind the ears.

Marmalade hesitated for a moment, then leaned into his hand and started to purr.

"Yeah, you're just like your mistress, all right," Alec said with a laugh. "You don't know whether to hiss me or kiss me."

When the big cat rolled over for a belly rub, Alec was glad to oblige his new buddy, but when he glanced at Mackenzie's bedside clock, he was surprised to see it was only six o'clock in the morning.

"And where did that temptress you live with run off to so early in the morning?" he asked his furry friend, and the sound of the front door closing in the distance gave him his answer.

Alec vaulted from the bed and made it to the peephole

in Mackenzie's front door in time to see her headed for the exit. Dressed in short running shorts and a midriff top that had the power to jerk him wide awake, she paused for a moment to do a few leg stretches, then disappeared out the back door of the building.

"I could use a good run myself this morning," Alec said aloud as he stretched and rubbed his stomach.

He then hurried back into her bedroom, snatched up his damaged shirt, his tie, his pants and his shoes from her bedroom floor, then winked at the cat who was now curled up in a comfortable ball in the middle of Mackenzie's big bamboo bed.

"Don't get too comfortable on that bed, Lady Marmalade," Alec said over his shoulder as he started out of the room. "I might have been a gentleman last night, but today happens to be a brand-new day."

MACKENZIE HEADED DOWN TO the beach, trying not to think about the man she'd left sleeping in her bed. It was impossible. Just as it had been impossible to move more than an inch away from Alec during the entire night. Each time she had tried to slip out from under that big, strong arm of his, he had managed to drag her back against him, molding her to that warm, rock-hard body that he was keeping to himself for all the right reasons.

And if that hadn't been sheer torture, Mackenzie didn't know what could be.

Of course, he had immediately captured her heart by being sensitive enough to realize that she really *was* too upset to jump into anything physical with him. But as for his statement about waiting for all the *right* reasons before they went any further, Mackenzie wasn't exactly sure what Alec had meant.

Love, maybe?

She let the word *love* rattle around in her brain for a moment and found the possibility that she and Alec were actually falling in love was powerful enough to send a warmth spreading through her body that was hotter than the new morning sun making its first peek over the horizon now.

But I'm not going to think about love or about Alec now, Mackenzie decided as she ran in place for a few seconds. No, her morning run was her own special form of therapy and the one thing that helped keep her sane. It was a time she treasured. A time when she could turn up her energy level, tune out the world, and simply let herself run.

Pacing herself accordingly, Mackenzie started down the beach, enjoying those first rays of the warm morning sun on her face and the sound of her own footsteps splashing along the edge of the water. Her heart sank slightly when someone else's footsteps pounded close behind her. But her heart soared right back into overdrive when Alec suddenly fell in beside her wearing nothing but his swim trunks and his usual devilish grin.

Before Mackenzie could even ask how he'd found her, Alec's "Race you to the pier," was all it took to launch her swiftly into action.

They sprinted down the beach, elbow to elbow, legs pumping, hearts pounding. And though the sight of so much raw, pulsing muscle left Mackenzie's mouth dryer than if she'd swallowed a gallon of the saltwater they were currently running through, she raced up the beach beside him, matching Alec step for step. In fact, she had just managed to pull slightly ahead of Alec when he bumped into her playfully, purposely disrupting her stride.

"Give it up, Malone," Alec teased but his attempt to slow her down only made Mackenzie pick up her speed.

Darting forward, Mackenzie had just pulled ahead of Alec again when a loud thud followed by a low moan forced her to an abrupt halt. Turning back around, Mackenzie continued to run in place while she eyed him suspiciously. Alec was now sprawled out on his back in the sand less than three feet away from her.

"What's the matter, Southerland?" Mackenzie called out. "Rather play dead than let a woman beat you?"

But the instant Mackenzie saw the blood, she closed the distance between them in one easy stride.

"Ahhhhhhh," Alec yelped when Mackenzie cradled his left foot to inspect the nasty gash along his instep.

"Are you in much pain?" Mackenzie asked, sending Alec a worried look.

"The pain I can stand," Alec told her through clenched teeth. "It's the blood I can't take."

"Well, you shouldn't have been running on the beach barefoot in the first place," Mackenzie scolded.

"If you don't mind, I'd rather not have a lecture while I'm bleeding to death," Alec told her, but the minute he sat up and looked at his foot, he turned pale even under his deep bronze tan.

"Don't look, if it bothers you, silly," Mackenzie chided, prompting Alec to fall backward in the sand again with another loud moan.

As luck would have it, on this particular morning there wasn't another soul in sight Mackenzie could send for help. Alarmed by the amount of blood Alec was already losing, Mackenzie knew she had to act fast. Yanking off her headband, she doused it several times in the salty water, then promptly wound it tightly around her patient's injured foot. She had just sat back on the heels of her Nikes to see if her makeshift bandage would stop the bleeding when Alec let out another agonizing groan.

"Damn, Mackenzie, what kind of a sadist are you?" he grimaced when the salt water seeped into the gash along his foot.

Sending him an annoyed look, Mackenzie lifted her chin defiantly. "That's the best I could do for a temporary bandage, Alec, but my headband certainly isn't sterile. I was hoping the saltwater might kill some of the bacteria."

"Well, thank you, Florence Nightingale," Alec groaned, but he didn't resist when Mackenzie extended her hand and helped pull him to his feet.

"Lean on me," Mackenzie instructed as she slid her arm around his waist.

She shivered slightly when he slung his powerful arm over her bare shoulder, and when he pulled her close enough to use her as a human crutch, Mackenzie knew the sudden rise in her body temperature had nothing to do with the new morning sun.

"Damn, this is embarrassing," Alec complained as they hobbled up the beach together.

"Oh, please," Mackenzie scoffed. "Like you haven't embarrassed me before."

"That's different," Alec argued. "You're adorable when you get embarrassed. I pass out."

Mackenzie laughed. "Well don't pass out on me now, big guy, because if you think I'm going to try to drag your heavy carcass all the way to the emergency room, you're crazy."

"Emergency room?" Alec protested in what sounded like a squeak.

"That cut is going to need stitches, Alec," Mackenzie

informed him determinedly. "And you'll definitely need a tetanus shot," she added, watching a wrinkle form in the center of his handsome brow.

"I'm not real fond of needles, either," Alec mumbled, causing Mackenzie to laugh again.

"What is it with you big, strong hero types, anyhow?" Mackenzie teased. "I'd think a little blood and the sight of a simple needle would be a walk in the park for a big, tough guy like you."

Alec tightened his grip on her shoulder, pulling Mackenzie much closer than was needed for their current journey through the sand. "Gee, Mackenzie," he said, moving his thumb suggestively over the sensitive skin of her collarbone. "I had no idea I was a hero in your eyes."

"You're impossible," Mackenzie told him. "But as soon as I throw something on over my jogging clothes, I *am* taking you straight to the emergency room, Alec Southerland. And I want my smiling face to be the last thing you see before they wheel you behind that big dark curtain and…"

"Okay, dammit, I get the picture," Alec groaned, causing Mackenzie to flash Alec one of *her* toothpaste commercial smiles.

MACKENZIE GLANCED AT THE clock on the waiting room wall, a little worried that a few minor stitches were taking so long.

She had teased Alec about being squeamish, but the fact that he hadn't pulled some macho it's-only-a-little-scratch routine had actually endeared him to her more.

If that were possible.

In fact, the more time spent with Alec, the more Mackenzie realized there was nothing put-on or phony about him at all. Alec was his own man. And the fact that he was masculine enough not to hide his emotions was a trait Mackenzie had to admire.

On the way to the hospital he had thanked her a dozen times for coming along, though for some reason Mackenzie got the impression Alec had something else on his mind that he wanted to tell her. Maybe it had only been the thoughtful way he kept looking at her, both in the car and in the waiting room before they took him away for treatment. And that intense stare of his had unnerved her immensely.

Like any look from that man doesn't turn you inside out, Mackenzie reminded herself, then left her seat and walked to the admitting desk. She was just about to demand some answers about Alec's condition when the matronly nurse who had wheeled Alec away for treatment suddenly appeared from behind a green curtain and started walking in her direction.

After handing Mackenzie a prescription and several samples of medication, she looked at Mackenzie and said, "The cut was much deeper than it looked, so I'm afraid he's been sedated pretty heavily."

"Sedated?" Mackenzie repeated.

The nurse rolled her eyes. "It never fails. These big strong guys come in here with a simple cut and you'd think they were facing amputation. And the fact that he's a pilot didn't help matters, either."

When Mackenzie gave the nurse a blank look, she added, "It doesn't take much medication to knock out a man who isn't used to taking drugs. Of course, I certainly don't blame the airlines for enforcing such a strict drug policy," she said and winked. "I sure wouldn't want to be cruising along at thirty thousand feet with a drugged-out pilot, would you?''

"Of course not," Mackenzie agreed, then followed behind the nurse as the woman led the way to the drugged-out pilot who, at least for the remainder of the day, *wasn't* going to be sailing along with his passengers at thirty thousand feet.

Mackenzie found Alec behind the curtain sitting in a wheelchair with a goofy grin on his face and his bandaged foot stretched out in front of him.

"All patched up," Alec announced proudly, trying to focus on the foot at the end of his leg.

Mackenzie turned back to the nurse when she handed Mackenzie another piece of paper. "The prescription I gave you is for the antibiotics he'll need to take for the next ten days, Mrs. Southerland, and this sheet gives you instructions on how to care for the wound."

Mackenzie started to explain that she was only Alec's neighbor, but the woman quickly cut her off. "I've already sent the orderly down to medical supply for some crutches, and you can take the wheelchair home on loan today and return it later. Just make sure he comes back in seven to ten days to have his stitches removed."

"And when will the sedative wear off?" Mackenzie asked, deciding details about her relationship to Alec wouldn't mean a hill of beans to a nurse with a waiting room full of patients to be seen.

The nurse and Mackenzie both turned and looked down at Alec who immediately rewarded them with a stupefied grin.

"It's hard to tell how long the sedative will last," the nurse said, but when Alec reached up and blew the woman a rather noisy kiss she added, "but I sure wouldn't give him any more pain medication unless I had to. It looks like he could be a real handful, if you know what I mean.''

"Oh, he's a real handful all right," Mackenzie agreed, and as if to prove it, Alec reached out and patted Mackenzie possessively on the bottom. "Keep that up, and you won't even get an aspirin later," Mackenzie warned as the nurse hurried on her way.

Shoving the papers and the free samples into her purse, she walked behind Alec to take control of his wheelchair. Alec grabbed one of her hands and immediately delivered a series of sloppy kisses up the full length of her arm.

"Behave yourself, Alec," Mackenzie scolded, wiping at her sticky arm.

"I wuz jus' tryin' to thank you," Alec slurred, and pulled her other hand down for another soggy kiss as a young male orderly with a deep tan and the spaced-out look of a serious surfer walked up and placed a pair of crutches across Alec's lap.

"Yep, you're my own sweet l'il nursy, Miz Malone," Alec said, running his hand up the length of her bare leg. "You got me all patched up and now you're gonna take me right home to that big canopy bed of yours and crawl on top of me like you did last night and…"

"I'm afraid he's having a drug-induced fantasy," Mackenzie lied, feeling the heat creep up her neck.

The orderly stepped back and openly appraised her from head to toe, then slapped Alec on the back. "I say go for it while you can, dude. Drug-induced fantasies are sometimes the best kind."

"Would you please not encourage him," Mackenzie told the orderly at about the same time Alec grabbed her from behind and forced her into his lap.

"Did you know how great you looked in that lacy little black thong?" he whispered in her ear loud enough for the entire emergency room to hear. "Man, you were killing me, Mackenzie. I knew it, you knew it and you knew I knew it."

"You're babbling, Alec," Mackenzie said, trying to pry his arms from around her waist.

When she finally did manage to pull herself out of his lap, he pooched out his bottom lip and said, "I'm not babblin'. I'm fallin' for you, Mackenzie. Don't you get it? I'm really, really, *really* fallin' for you!"

"Hey, he's falling *out* of his wheelchair," the orderly warned and Mackenzie and the orderly both rushed forward in time to keep Alec from hitting face-first in the floor.

While Mackenzie pushed Alec back into his chair, the orderly bent down and picked up Alec's wallet that had fallen from the pocket of the lightweight sweatshirt he'd grabbed before they left for the hospital. It was flipped open, showing Alec's driver's license. "Hey, that's me," Alec said with a silly grin when the orderly handed it back to him. "I'm gonna need this when I drive home, right?"

"Hey, dude," the orderly said, obviously disturbed by Alec's statement. "Anybody who thinks he looks like his own driver's license photo, really shouldn't get behind the wheel of a car."

"Don't worry, he isn't driving anywhere," Mackenzie said, glaring down at her unruly patient.

"Yeah, but it sure looks like you're gonna need some help getting him in the car."

"I'd really appreciate that," Mackenzie told the kid, and ten minutes later she and her now *snoring* patient were out of the emergency room parking lot and on their way home.

Unfortunately, Mackenzie soon found trying to hold Alec in his seat with one hand and drive with the other was an exhausting task. She was even relieved when Alec suddenly roused again and forced himself back into a sitting position. Her relief was short-lived, however, when Alec raised an eyebrow suggestively and sent her another moronic grin.

"Hey," he muttered, as if he were Sleeping Beauty and had just awakened him from a hundred year sleep. "You gonna let me go home with you and sleep in that big bed with the fancy curtains again?"

"We'll see," Mackenzie said, turning her attention instead to maneuvering through the early morning traffic as she picked up her cell phone. "Karen," she said when a voice answered. "Cancel my appointments. Something's come up. I'll call you later this afternoon."

"No, no, no," Alec said, shaking a finger in her direction. "My nursey can't leave me alone, alone, alone."

"I didn't say I was going to leave you alone, Alec," she told him and Alec grinned so wide Mackenzie saw a silver filling flash back at her from one of his molars. "Right now we're going to stop at the drive-through pharmacy window and have them fill your prescription."

He contemplated her words for a moment, then began fumbling through the pocket of his sweatshirt. He seemed rather pleased when he brought his hand out of the pocket and found he was actually holding on to his wallet.

"Take what you need," he said, his tongue still thick, then attempted to hand over the wallet but his groggy movement resulted in his hand ending up on Mackenzie's bare leg.

Even in his current condition, his touch was as potent as a bee sting.

Mackenzie quickly pried his fingers from around the wallet, then placed Alec's hand gently back in his own lap, almost thankful he'd dozed off again. She'd felt like strangling him back in the emergency room, but seeing him so defenseless was a completely different story. And she certainly wasn't going to leave him alone to fend for himself in his compromised condition.

Not for a minute.

Slipping a twenty from Alec's wallet, she paid the drive-through attendant, then headed back down the Battery, thankful they were now only a few blocks away from their complex. She was already ticking off in her mind how she was going to handle the situation. Alec had been right about it making more sense if he did stay with her. She could take care of him properly then and keep a close watch on his progress. After all, Alec *had* been barefoot. And God only knew what type of infection might set in with the kind of filth the ocean held these days. He might even develop a fever. He could possibly even wake up in the middle of the night and need her.

And besides, she decided with a smile, that sedative wasn't going to last forever, now was it? And if Alec *did* happen to turn to her in the middle of the night with a raging fever of a much different nature...well...

"What the...!" Mackenzie yelled and slammed on her brakes, stopping only inches away from a fancy little sports car that sat parked in her *reserved* parking space.

Instinctively, she had reached her arm out to keep her limber patient from sliding from his seat, but she hadn't been fast enough. Mackenzie was still trying to help a befuddled Alec adjust the seat belt that was threatening to choke him to death when the driver's side door of the sports car popped opened and the tall redhead Mackenzie remembered from the towel incident jumped from the car with a scowl on her face.

"Hey! You almost ran into me," the redhead shouted, but the minute she recognized Mackenzie's passenger she literally dashed to Alec's side of the Mercedes.

"Oh, Alec," she gasped when she saw his bandaged foot. "What on earth has happened to you?"

When Alec failed to respond, her eyes immediately darted in Mackenzie's direction as if Mackenzie had personally crippled her precious Alec.

"He cut his foot jogging on the beach," Mackenzie said as she unsnapped her own seat belt and left the car.

"Oh, you poor, poor baby," the redhead cooed as she smoothed her groggy darling's hair back from his forehead. "But everything's going to be okay now. Gail's here, and I'll take very good care of you, Alec."

Like hell you will, Mackenzie thought, but she said, "Then you can start by helping me get *baby's* wheelchair out of my trunk."

The redhead shot her a mean look, then followed Mackenzie to the back of the Mercedes. Mackenzie opened the trunk, but when she motioned for Alec's *new* nurse to pick up the opposite end of the wheelchair, the redhead's perfectly painted face took on a rather worried look.

Wiggling her three-inch fingernails in Mackenzie's direction she grimaced and said, "Gosh, I just had these done. I sure wouldn't want to break one."

"Oh, forget it," Mackenzie told her disgustedly, "just try to keep Alec from falling out of the car until I can get his butt in this wheelchair."

Alec's newest angel of mercy hurried back to her patient while Mackenzie wrestled with the steel contraption, breaking one of her own fingernails before she finally got the blasted thing out of the trunk. She could still hear the redhead murmuring soothing words of comfort in her phony Marilyn Monroe voice. And though Mackenzie knew full well that nurse Gail would be ready and willing to administer much more than Alec's stupid medication once he awoke from his drug-induced state, she couldn't very well ask her to leave, now could she? No, that would have to be Alec's job. That is, if Mr. If I Only Had You really did have the ability to finally say *no*.

"I think he's waking up," Gail called out.

Mackenzie jerked the wheelchair open with a pop, gripped the handles as if they were Gail's slender neck she was squeezing, and reached the passenger's side door in time to see Alec's eyelids flutter and finally open.

"Try to help him up so we can sit him in the chair," Mackenzie instructed.

Gail sent her another grimace. "Maybe you should do it," she suggested.

Mackenzie swallowed a smart remark, fastened the locks on the wheelchair to keep the chair from rolling backward, then waited until Gail stepped aside. "Do you think you can stand up if I help you, Alec?" Mackenzie asked when he tried to focus in her direction.

Alec nodded, but when Mackenzie bent down and put his arms around her neck to give him an upward boost, the last words she heard as Alec leaned his regal head over her shoulder were, "I think I'm going to be sick."

"Gross!" Gail squealed as she sprinted out of the way to safety.

By the time Mackenzie dropped Alec into the wheelchair and jerked off the T-shirt she had put on over her skimpy jogging top, Gail was standing at the far end of the parking lot where the dimwit should have been parked in the first place.

Way *over* being nice even one second longer, Mackenzie glared in her direction. ''What happened to your 'I'm going to take very good care of you, Alec?''' Mackenzie shouted. ''Now, get yourself back up here and help me get him inside so he can lie down!''

''I *am* going to take very good care of Alec,'' the redhead insisted as she prissed back in their direction. ''I just don't do *sick* very well.''

''Like *I* do,'' Mackenzie tossed over her shoulder, then wheeled a green-faced Alec decidedly across the parking lot.

To her surprise, Gail did have enough sense to open the door to the building without having to be told, but it was Mackenzie who pushed the wheelchair down the hallway until they reached Alec's front door.

''His keys are in his jacket pocket,'' Mackenzie volunteered, having now vetoed her big idea of letting Alec stay with her. Unless, of course, nurse nitwit decided to abandon her new career. And since the red-haired vulture was already drooling over her lifeless victim, Mackenzie decided the odds of Gail giving up and going home were as likely as her winning the Publishers Clearing House Sweepstakes.

''But his jacket is all messy,'' Gail whined, wrinkling her nose in disgust when she took a few steps closer to the wheelchair.

''Oh, for God's sake,'' Mackenzie complained and practically pushed Alec out of the wheelchair as she searched through his jacket pocket for his keys.

"Am I home yet?" a feeble voice asked as Mackenzie turned Alec's key in the lock.

"Yes, sweetie, you're home now," Gail said, hurrying inside ahead of them. "And we're going to get you all cleaned up and get you straight to bed."

"Who's 'we'?" Mackenzie wanted to know, but Gail ignored the question and motioned for Mackenzie to follow as she headed directly for the master bedroom.

"You seem to know your way around pretty well," Mackenzie told the flashy redhead when she wheeled Alec into his bedroom behind the witch.

Gail giggled. "Alec's such a peach. I stayed over a few weeks ago when my flights were too close together for me to go all the way home to Columbia."

Yeah, he's a real peach, that Alec, Mackenzie thought, slightly pleased when he groaned again.

Gail heard the groan too and rushed forward to squat down in front of Alec's wheelchair. "Alec," she cooed. "Alec, honey, look at me. Look at Gail."

Alec's head jerked up and Mackenzie felt like pulling him bald when he said in that sleepy, sexy voice of his, "Hey there, Gail."

"Hey, yourself, you little cutie," she said right back. "You've been hurt Alec, and I'm going to stay right here and take care of you. Would you like that?"

"Uh-huh," Alec said before his head dropped back to his chest again.

Sending Mackenzie a satisfied smirk when she stood up, Gail pointed to a door and said, "Alec's bathroom is right in there, hon. You go bathe him off and I'll get our— I mean—I'll get *his* bed ready."

Of course, had Alec been lucid enough to realize what was going on around him at that very moment, he might have noticed that Mackenzie's piercing laugh suddenly had a rather demonic ring to it. "Sorry, *hon*," Mackenzie said, purposely mimicking Gail's breathy voice. "You don't do *sick*, and I don't do *baths*. But I am going to tell you what I will do, Gail. I'm going to gather up everything you're going to need to take care of *baby* here. And then," Mackenzie said as her voice continued to rise to a level that matched her own rage, "I'm going to stay right here with your little *cutie* while you get yourself outside and move your car out of my *reserved* parking space! Got it?"

"Well," the redhead said with a huff. "There's no reason to be rude about it."

"Oh, yes there is," Mackenzie said as she stomped out of Alec's bedroom. "I earned the right to be *rude* when I was stupid enough to let loverboy throw up all over *my* back instead of *yours*."

AFTER RETURNING TO HER own side of the hallway, Mackenzie paced around her jungle of a living room like a caged tigress who had just been bested by a scroungy jackal. And in a way, she had been. When she stomped into her kitchen for a glass of water to down some medication for the migraine that was now threatening to blow her head off, Mackenzie got mad all over again.

Kicking at the shiny buttons from Alec's shirt that were littering her kitchen floor, all she accomplished was launching Marmalade off the kitchen counter to bat a few of the buttons around with her paw.

"Just don't mess with his hat," Mackenzie said when Marmalade lost interest in the buttons and strolled in the direction of her bowl where Alec's captain's hat had landed. "I want the satisfaction of taking care of that my-self."

Walking across the kitchen, Mackenzie stood with her Nike poised directly over the object that was causing her to frown. She envisioned herself flattening Alec's captain's hat like a pancake, but she just couldn't bring herself to do it. Besides, who was she kidding? It wasn't even Alec she was angry with.

No, Mackenzie was furious with herself.

It had been on the tip of her tongue to inform the ditzy redhead that *she* was there first. And didn't that sound familiar? And that's when Mackenzie's hopes for a relationship with Alec had popped like a soap bubble right before eyes.

She was her mother's daughter after all. And the episode with the redhead had given Mackenzie a quick glimpse of what a future with Alec would actually be like.

It wasn't a pretty picture.

Like her mother, Mackenzie knew her own insecurities would eventually destroy them both. She'd become needy and suspicious and push Alec farther and farther away, forcing him to finally act on her accusations, just like her mother had done with her father. So what if her parents *had* finally worked through their problems?

Hell, it had taken them almost twenty years to do it!

"Well, I don't intend to spend the next twenty years of my life in agony," Mackenzie told Marmalade, then bent down and picked up Alec's hat.

She then scooped up his jacket from the floor by her kitchen table and marched back through her condo. Folding his jacket neatly, she placed the hat on top and laid both items on her catchall table just inside her front door. She would return his things later, after his nursemaid left,

Mackenzie decided. She dusted her hands off in a good-riddance gesture the same way she mentally did to her slightly bruised heart.

She wasn't even going to spend another second being jealous of the dizzy redhead with the three-inch talons, though her guilt over serving up a practically unconscious man for Gail's amusement didn't make Mackenzie very proud of herself, either.

Not that Alec would mind, Mackenzie convinced herself. After all, this wasn't the first time Gail had *stayed over,* as she'd so candidly put it. *And you'd better believe it won't be the last time Gail or someone like her shows up to stay over,* the little voice inside her head spoke up, reminding Mackenzie why she'd gone into the kitchen in the first place.

After a trip back to the kitchen to swallow enough aspirin to soothe her throbbing head, Mackenzie reached down and pulled Marmalade into her arms. Carrying the cat with her she headed for her bedroom, trying not to dwell on her rumpled sheets, or the faint smell of Alec's aftershave that still lingered in the room.

"I'm glad I'm a cat person," Mackenzie told her furry friend. "Old maids are supposed to like cats."

Marmalade didn't object when Mackenzie placed her on the bed and curled up beside her.

"And I'm not going to spend another second worrying about what's going on across the hall," Mackenzie said, opening one eye to see if Marmalade was listening.

She propped herself up on her elbow then and reached out to stroke Marmalade's long, silky fur. "Besides, Alec told me on the way to the emergency room that he was already marked off the flight schedule for the next four days. Not that his co-worker wouldn't know the proper people at United to contact for him."

Marmalade smacked at her hand, then bent her head to lick her fur back in place.

"And it's not like I didn't leave everything he needs to care for himself right in plain view by the side of his bed," Mackenzie added. "Of course, I doubt his new *nurse* is smart enough to figure it out, but Alec is certainly intelligent enough to read the directions on his medication and follow that instruction sheet on how to take care of his foot."

Marmalade leveled one of her questioning catlike stares in Mackenzie's direction. "You're right," Mackenzie said. "I probably should have made sure he had something to eat before I left. Gail will probably let Alec starve to death before it crosses her mind that he might be hungry."

When Marmalade smacked at her hand again, Mackenzie said, "But it's not really *my* problem. Alec's a big boy, and if he gets hungry he can tell the witch to get some of her famous Chinese takeout. Okay?"

Marmalade's only reply was a slight swish of her tail.

"Besides, I've got problems of my own," Mackenzie told the cat as she eased her pounding head back onto her pillow. "And what I need to do right now is try and sleep off this headache."

Marmalade had already closed her eyes. Mackenzie sighed as she closed her own. Too bad getting over a *heartache* wouldn't be so easy.

THE FEEL OF SOMETHING cool on his forehead brought a smile to Alec's lips. Still unable to force his eyes open, he moaned, "Umm, that feels nice."

He moaned again when a pair of soft lips delivered a tantalizing kiss to the corner of his mouth. "That feels even better," he whispered, and caught his breath when a smooth hand slid across his chest, then moved lower following the trail of black hair that trickled into a thin line just above his navel.

"Do I dare go any lower, Alec?"

Alec tensed. *Wait a minute!* his fuzzy mind complained. *That voice doesn't match the mental picture you were just enjoying now.*

When Alec's eyes snapped open, he found himself staring into a pair of bright green color-enhanced contacts, instead of the soft brown eyes he'd envisioned in his mind.

"Gail?" Alec muttered pushing himself up on his elbows. "What are you doing here?"

"Why, I'm taking care of you, Alec," she said as if he'd just asked her the most ridiculous question in the world.

Alec shook his head to clear it and glanced around his bedroom. "Where is Mackenzie?"

"Who cares?" Gail said rolling her eyes. "I'm telling you, Alec, that neighbor of yours is a real psycho. She practically ran over me when she roared into the parking lot. I only parked in her stupid parking space for a second so I could run in and say 'hi' to you, but you'd have thought I'd committed a felony or something. And then when you threw up all over her, well…"

"I did what?" Alec bellowed, forcing himself to sit up.

"Well, I'm sure you didn't throw up on her on purpose, Alec," Gail said, trying to blot his forehead with the damp cloth again. "Of course, when I told her to bathe you off while I got our bed ready, she practically turned into a wild woman. She started ranting and raving about what she *was* and *wasn't* going to do, and then..."

Alec grabbed the cloth from Gail's hand, placed it on his forehead himself, then dropped back against his pillow with a loud groan. "Spare me the rest of the details, okay?" Alec interrupted. "And please go home now, Gail. I'm not exactly in the mood for any company."

"But Alec," she protested. "I've already called and had my flight schedule changed so I could take care of you tonight."

Alec forced one eye back open. "I'm sorry, Gail. I appreciate you wanting to help, but all I want to do right now is get a little sleep."

"I can be a really good snuggly snuggler, Alec," she said in her irritating baby-talk voice.

Alec pushed himself up on his elbows again and shook his head determinedly. "Look, Gail, I'm trying to be nice about this, but you're going to have to stop dropping in on me without calling me first."

"I see," she said, jumping up from the side of the bed.

"Well, excuse me for trying to be here when you need someone, Alec," she huffed. "Because if you think for one minute your bitchy neighbor is going to take care of you, then you're in for a rude awakening."

Alec didn't even bother to argue, but seconds later when Gail slammed his front door at the other end of the condo, the force actually caused the crutches propped against his bedside table to clatter to the floor.

Well, isn't this just great, Alec thought as he dropped back on the bed and stared at the ceiling. Just when things were coming together for them. Just when he and Mackenzie were on the verge of acting on their feelings for each other, this had to happen.

Letting out a long sigh, Alec thought back over Gail's words, deciding that his hopes of convincing Mackenzie he *wasn't* some womanizing playboy were now as far fetched as Alec ever asking the *snuggly snuggler* to share his bed. *But dammit,* Alec thought as he forced himself back into a sitting position. *I'm the one who should be pissed, not Mackenzie.*

So, what if Gail *had* shown up unexpectedly again? So what? What about the deal he and Mackenzie had made? Hadn't they both agreed there wouldn't be any more games between them? Yet, she'd walked out and left him with Gail while he was too drugged up to notice.

Glancing at his bedside table, Alec was relieved when he saw Mackenzie's business card still by his bed. Unfortunately, he also noted the prescription bottle and some other pieces of evidence from the hospital that proved he wasn't just having one hell of a bad dream. Reaching for the phone, he picked up the card and punched in the appropriate numbers.

And though Alec really didn't expect her to be home, Mackenzie answered on the third ring.

"I just wanted to thank you for everything you did for me today," Alec said as sincerely as possible.

"Don't mention it," she answered but the frost coming through the line left Alec's hand frozen to the phone.

Alec squeezed his eyes shut when he added, "And I'm sorry about…well, you know, getting sick and all."

"I'll send you my dry cleaning bill," she said, but there wasn't even a hint of humor in her voice.

"I think the medicine has worn off now, but I'm still a little fuzzy-headed," Alec said in a desperate attempt for even a sliver of sympathy. "Would you mind coming over and helping me sort out what I'm supposed to do with all of this medicine and stuff?''

"If you help Gail with the *big* words, I'm sure she can figure it out," Mackenzie was quick to point out.

"I've already sent Gail home, Mackenzie," Alec said, "and..."

"Look, Alec. I'm sure you have a dozen other little playmates who would love to come take care of you. Call one of them."

"Damn," Alec cursed when the loud *click* threatened to burst his eardrum.

He remained sitting in the middle of his bed for a second, then threw his phone across the room. His ear was still ringing, his foot was *definitely* throbbing, and now his blood was climbing steadily towards a point near boiling. And for a moment, Alec was tempted to hobble across the hall on his crutches and place Mackenzie directly over his knee.

Once again the game of cat and mouse they'd been playing for the last few weeks had resulted in him, the cat, being only one paw away from a definite catch. But he was going to catch that mouse whether she liked or not. And come hell or high water Alec intended to make Mackenzie listen to what he had to say.

"You can run, Mackenzie, but you can't hide from me forever," Alec yelled, hopefully loud enough for her to hear him all the way across the hallway.

MACKENZIE SWITCHED OFF the ringer on her telephone, then pulled the sheet back over her head. The only thing important to her at the moment was getting rid of the freight train that was roaring through her head. Everything else would just have to wait.

She wasn't in the mood to deal with Alec. She wasn't going to call the office and play twenty questions with Angie. And unless she could get over the migraine, she wasn't even going to keep her dinner date with John. Although she really did need to keep that date with John if possible.

The fact was, John was just too nice of a guy to string along. And that's exactly what she'd be doing if she kept dating John now. She was in love with Alec, plain and simple. And the fact that they probably didn't have a future together wasn't even the issue. Mackenzie simply wasn't the type of woman who could be in love with one man and date another.

When another sharp pain kicked in, Mackenzie decided what she needed to do was stop thinking about Alec *and* John and figure out a way to get her life back on track. No more Alec. No more John. She would simply throw herself back into her work. She wouldn't even mind her weekends filled with movies and popcorn again. In fact, just thinking of a nice, quiet weekend alone without the aggravation relationships seemed to cause gave her hope that she might survive after all.

But what I need to do first is get rid of this migraine, Mackenzie reminded herself.

She'd have a talk with John and with Alec later, and then surely everything would fall neatly back into place.

6

MACKENZIE APPLIED THE finishing touches to her makeup, then glanced at her watch, pleased to find it wasn't quite five o'clock. That meant she could still catch John at his office and tell him just to meet her at the restaurant, instead of coming all the way across town to pick her up.

"How does this sound?" she asked Marmalade who was sitting on her vanity playing with a tube of mascara. "John, you're one of the nicest men I've met in a long time, but I'm at a difficult stage in my life right now. I need some time to myself. I hope you can understand."

Marmalade yawned, then licked her paw and ran it over her face a few times.

"Too boring, huh? Okay, then how about this?" Mackenzie asked. "John, this may be hard for you to understand, but I've decided to enter the convent."

Marmalade swatted the mascara. It landed in the floor.

"Yeah, you're right, he'd never believe that."

"Well, let's see. How about…"

Mackenzie's sentence was cut short when someone rang her doorbell to the point the noise was one continuous long assault on her still slightly throbbing head. Leaving her bathroom, she walked into the living room and stood staring at the doorknob someone was now trying to turn. But when a fist started pounding on her door to the point the animal prints on her wall started doing the shimmy, Mackenzie stomped across the room and pulled her door open.

"Thank God. You're alive," Angie cried out and practically collapsed into Mackenzie's arms.

Mackenzie pushed Angie away from her, startled to see not only her best friend, but John standing in the hallway as well. "Of course, I'm alive. I've had a migraine, but…"

"Don't you realize how worried we've all been?" Angie scolded. "You call in early this morning and tell Karen to cancel your appointments. Then your mother calls the office and goes a little crazy to find you're not at work. And then she calls back, terrified because not only are you not at work, but you won't answer your phone. Then I call John, praying to God you're with him, and find out he's been trying to call you, too, and your mother keeps insisting she's afraid you've done something horrible to yourself because you were so upset about the reconciliation." Angie paused long enough to take one deep breath. "And why in the hell didn't you tell me your parents were getting back together, Mackie? I'm your best friend, and I know that had to upset you. And that's why what your mother was saying halfway made sense, and…"

"Stop it!" Mackenzie finally said, reaching up to rub her temple again. She looked at John and back at Angie before she said, "Look, I'm sorry if everyone was worried, but it was after midnight last night before I got home from taking Mother to dinner and then to the airport."

"So the only thing wrong is a migraine?"

"Yes, Angie, I got the migraine this morning and then I slept it off the way I usually have to do."

"And I'm sure you haven't eaten a bite all day, which

is why you always get those horrible headaches in the first place.''

Mackenzie rolled her eyes. ''Well, I was planning to go to dinner with John,'' she said, looking in John's direction. ''In fact, I was just getting ready to call you, John, and suggest…''

Mackenzie suddenly stopped talking when the *last* person she wanted to see opened his door and hobbled out into the hallway on his crutches. Her headache roared to life again when she saw the unmistakable gleam in his eye.

''I thought I heard voices out here,'' he said, looking directly at Mackenzie.

''What happened to you, old man?'' John asked when Alec maneuvered himself in their direction.

''Ask Mackenzie,'' Alec said with smile. ''The last thing I remember we were running down the beach together this morning side by side.''

Mackenzie felt like grabbing one of his crutches and whacking Alec over the head. Glancing back at John she said, ''Alec was crazy enough to jog barefoot on the beach. I just happened to be there to witness his idiocy.''

''Not a smart thing to do, old boy,'' John confirmed, prompting Mackenzie to send Alec a satisfied smile. *But, at least I can stop worrying about deserting him now,* Mackenzie thought as she looked him up and down. Not only was he managing fairly well on his crutches, but he had also managed to get dressed by himself. *Or had Gail performed that service before Alec asked her to leave?*

''I admit it was a stupid thing to do,'' Alec agreed, ''but I was hoping I could talk Mackenzie into helping me change my bandage.''

''Sorry, but we were just leaving,'' Mackenzie spoke up. ''John's taking me to dinner.''

"Then could I at least get my coat and hat before you leave?"

Mackenzie blushed. She stepped back inside the door and grabbed his things from the table, but when she started to hand them over, she realized Alec had no way to take them. "I'll just put these inside on your sofa," Mackenzie said, walking toward his open doorway, but when she walked back out into the hall, she heard the amusement in Angie's voice when she asked, "And you were jogging in your flight uniform and cap, Alec? How original."

Alec grinned. "No. I'm afraid I left my coat and hat at Mackenzie's last night when I stayed over."

If looks could inflict pain, Alec Southerland would have screamed like a girl at that very moment.

"You did what?" John spoke up, immediately turning to Mackenzie for an explanation.

Mackenzie glared at Alec again before she said, "Alec did stay over, but it was totally innocent."

When John frowned, Alec nodded, "She's right. Totally innocent. She was upset about her parents, and..."

"See, you *were* upset about your parents," Angie said with a pout. "I knew it."

"Okay," Mackenzie said, throwing her hands up in the air. "I admit it. I was upset about my parents. Alec stayed over. He cut his foot this morning and I took him to the emergency room. Then I got a migraine from hell, which is why I refused to answer my phone. Now! That should answer everyone's questions, and I'd really like to go to dinner. John?"

"Wait," Alec said, then turned and wobbled back across the hall. When he returned, he maneuvered past Mackenzie and laid a key on the table by her door. "That's a spare key to my front door," he said as if she were too stupid to figure that out. "When you get back, I'd sure appreciate it if you would look at my bandage, Mackenzie. Just let yourself in," he added with a wink. "I'm finding out these crutches aren't the easiest way to get around."

Mackenzie didn't even bother to answer. Instead she grabbed her purse from the table and pulled her door shut. "Ready?" Mackenzie asked John, prompting Angie to say, "And what about me? I was so upset thinking something had happened to you, John stopped by the office and picked me up. Do you mind if I tag along, too, Mackie? I'm a little hungry myself."

"Me, too," Alec chimed in. "My cupboard's so bare, Old Mother Hubbard would probably agree to adopt me herself."

"Then maybe you should call Gail," Mackenzie couldn't resist saying. "I'm sure she'd run back over with some of her famous Chinese takeout."

"Who's Gail?" Angie wanted to know and John, being the nice guy that John really *was,* said, "Look, since everybody's hungry, why don't we all just go out together and get something to eat?"

Alec's face lit up like a Christmas tree. "Hey, thanks, John. If your date doesn't object, I'll sure take you up on that offer."

"Count me in," Angie said, and everyone looked at Mackenzie, waiting for her answer.

Okay. She could either appear to be the Wicked Witch of the West? Or, Mackenzie decided, she could accept the fact that Alec obviously didn't intend to let her have the evening alone with John. Of course, that meant she'd also have to postpone her talk with John until she got rid of Alec and Angie and John brought her back home. And then, she'd have to wait until she got rid of John, before she could check Alec's stupid bandage and tell Alec face-to-face that things would never work out between them. And if she could possibly manage to keep all of that straight, then what damn difference did it make if they all went out to eat together?

"Whatever," Mackenzie finally said with a sigh, then started down the hallway with everyone else.

To her surprise, Alec managed to swing right along beside them, never breaking his stride.

"How long will you have to stay on those crutches?" John asked when they reached the back door leading out to the parking lot.

"Maybe you should answer that question, Mackenzie," Alec said, glancing in her direction. "I'm afraid I wasn't real clear on those details when we left the emergency room this morning."

You're going to be on crutches much longer than you think if you don't shut up, Mackenzie thought to herself, but she waited until John opened the door for everyone before she looked at John and said, "I guess how long he uses the crutches depends on Alec, John. Some men are big babies. Some men aren't."

John smiled at her comment but Mackenzie increased her step when Alec looked as if he might whack *her* with his crutch this time. She then headed for the lower end of the parking lot and John's SUV. Alec calling out her name, however, brought her to an abrupt halt.

"What now?" Mackenzie said when she wheeled back around to face him.

"Sorry, but I don't think I can get in and out of John's Suburban," Alec said holding up a crutch. "And since the Jag's too small for all of us, maybe you should drive."

"Alec's right. I don't think he could get in the Suburban even with all of us helping him," Angie said as she looked down at Alec's bandaged foot. "You don't really mind driving, do you Mackie?"

Mackenzie pulled out her keys and stomped back in the direction of her Mercedes. Though John didn't seem to mind crawling in the back seat with Angie, Mackenzie sent Alec a she-devil glare when he slid into the front passenger's seat beside her.

"Is the Crab Shack okay with you, Your Majesty, or would you like to pick another place to eat?" Mackenzie wanted to know.

"I love the Crab Shack," Alec told her with one of his famous smiles. "And dinner's on me. I insist."

"If that's supposed to cheer me up, it doesn't," Mackenzie let him know real quick.

"Hey, cut it out, you two," Angie spoke up from the back seat. "If I didn't know better I'd think you two were an old married couple."

"Not in this lifetime," Mackenzie declared, backing out of her parking space.

"Wanna bet?" she thought she heard Alec say, but when she looked over in his direction, he was staring out the passenger's side window with a totally innocent look on his movie-star quality face.

SURPRISINGLY, SHE AND Alec both kept quiet during the meal, leaving it up to John and Angie to carry on the conversation. But then one of John's clients beckoned to him from across the restaurant, and Angie picked that particular moment to excuse herself for the powder room. And that meant, of course, Mackenzie was left alone at the table with *him*.

"Enjoying your date?" Alec asked as he raised one eyebrow a bit.

"What do you think?" Mackenzie tossed back, but

Alec startled her when he suddenly reached across the table and covered her hand with his own.

"Listen, Mackenzie," Alec said so seriously Mackenzie froze in place. "I thought we made a deal. No more games, remember?"

"Alec," she began, but he quickly cut her off.

"You still don't get it, do you?" Alec demanded and squeezed her hand a little tighter. "I'm stark-raving mad about you, Mackenzie. Give me a chance to prove you can trust me."

Her heart flip-flopped as she tried to ease her hand from beneath Alec's searing touch, but he wouldn't let go. "I'm sorry, Alec, but I don't think I could survive it," she tried to explain. "I'd only end up making us both miserable. I would always be waiting for Gail or someone like her to show up. And your patience would grow thin, trying to deal with all of my crazy insecurities."

"Look, I already know all about your dear-old-mom complex," Alec said innocently. "We can work through it together. Just promise you won't lump me in with all those losers your mother always warned you about, Mackenzie. Give me a chance. Let me prove our relationship won't be anything like the relationship your parents had."

If Alec had reached out and slapped her, Mackenzie couldn't have been more shocked. *Dear-old-mom complex?* her stunned mind repeated. *Well, there was no doubt about who had originally coined that phrase!*

"What did you just say?" Mackenzie demanded, and she could tell from the alarmed look on Alec's face he realized he'd just made a huge mistake.

"Now, wait a minute, Mackenzie," Alec stuttered, but she quickly cut him off.

"How dare you go behind my back and pump my best

friend for information about me!'' Mackenzie fumed. ''And how dare Angie give it to you!''

''It wasn't like that,'' Alec tried to explain.

''Oh, really?'' Mackenzie seethed. ''That's a laugh. I can practically hear the two of you hashing over the twisted details now. Poor, pitiful Mackenzie, that bitter mother of hers has ruined her for all mankind.''

When Mackenzie stood up, Alec did his best to stand up with her. ''Now dammit, Mackenzie, you're blowing this whole thing out of proportion, and you know it.''

''Well, I'm sorry, Alec, but I don't see it that way,'' Mackenzie shouted right back. ''In one breath you give me that song and dance about trusting you, and in the next breath you let it slip that you were devious enough to go behind my back and question my best friend about me.''

''It was a harmless conversation, nothing more,'' Alec tried to tell her.

''And don't even get me started on that big belly laugh you must have been having when I bared my soul to you in the car. I can't imagine how you even kept a straight face! If you're really so damn trustworthy, Alec, why didn't you speak up then? Why did you let me make a complete fool of myself rambling on about my crazy parents when you already know all about them?''

''Don't do this, Mackenzie,'' Alec pleaded. ''I apologize. I'll get down on both knees, bandaged foot and all if that's what you want me to do. Just tell me what to do, and I'll do it.''

Alec reached out and grabbed her arm, but Mackenzie jerked it free. ''I'll tell you what you can do, Alec. You can do us both a big favor and forget about me. I think we're both smart enough to figure out that it never would have worked out between us anyhow.''

She expected him to argue, but Alec stared at Mackenzie so intently she shivered when the softness in his eyes disappeared. "If that's really the way you feel, Mackenzie, then you have my word. I'll never bother you again."

"That's really the way I feel," Mackenzie told him before her heart could reach out and snatch back those fatal words.

Alec shook his head sadly, then lowered himself back down in the chair. And when he refused to even look at her again, Mackenzie knew she couldn't spend another second standing in that restaurant.

"Hey, guys. What's going on now? I could hear you shouting at each other all the way across the restaurant," Angie said as she hurried back to their table.

Mackenzie sent Angie a frosty look that made her dark eyes widen with concern. "Nothing's going on out of the ordinary, Miss Sigmund Freud," Mackenzie said with a sarcastic little laugh. "As usual, I'm just suffering from my dear-old-mom complex that seems to be your favorite topic of conversation these days."

Mackenzie pushed past Angie and headed for the door.

"Mackie, wait," Angie called out and Mackenzie paused at the door for a second until she heard Alec say, "You'd better let her go, Angie. Thanks to me, she's not very happy with either of us right now."

Mackenzie pushed through the restaurant door and made it outside to the parking lot before she let herself cry. Unfortunately, she wasn't sure if her tears were from anger, or if they were tears of regret.

Alec's last words had sounded so final.

She should have felt nothing but relief that he'd never bother her again. Instead, a cold fist gripped her heart and made her shiver the same way she had when the expression in Alec's eyes turned to blue ice.

She had admitted to Alec that her biggest fear was not being able to survive their relationship.

But what frightened Mackenzie now was the possibility she wouldn't be able to survive without him, either.

7

MACKENZIE GOT UP early the next morning feeling like a totally new person. And why wouldn't she? She had finally made some concrete decisions about what she intended to do with the rest of her life.

She hated to admit it, but the thought of Alec never bothering her again was far more terrifying than an occasional blonde or redhead who might show up unexpectedly now and then. And she also hated to admit it, but Alec had been right about her blowing everything out of proportion.

She *had* overreacted.

But then, no one really liked hearing the truth about themselves, now did they? Especially if they weren't yet ready to admit some of those truths themselves.

And maybe that's why it had always infuriated her when Angie referred to her little idiosyncrasies as her dear-old-mom complex. Mackenzie *did* have a few issues she needed to work through. She'd even admitted them to Alec herself.

And ultimately, the truth had set her free.

Alec hadn't even blinked an eye when she'd blurted out her fears. In fact, he'd even said they could work through her insecurities together.

And so, Mackenzie now knew what she had to do.

First, she would apologize for acting like a spoiled brat at the restaurant. She would then fall on her knees and beg Alec's forgiveness. She would promise to love him at least one century beyond forever if he'd only give her one more chance. And then she'd tell him if he didn't make love to her at that very moment, she was going to tie him up, take him hostage and ravage *him* like he'd never been ravaged before.

Throwing back the covers, Mackenzie sat on the side of her bed for a moment, making a mental list of what she needed to do to put her new plan into action. After she'd left the restaurant the previous evening she'd headed straight for the office where she'd caught up on everything pressing on her desk. She had then purposely stayed at the office until after ten o'clock, certain by the time she arrived home Angie and John would have come and gone and Alec would have been tucked back under the covers of his sick bed.

She had been surprised to see John's big SUV still parked at the lower end of the parking lot when she got home, but assumed that Angie, party animal that she was, had used her persuasive powers to keep the boys out late.

And with that thought in mind, Mackenzie picked up her bedside phone and left a short message on the office answering machine saying that not only would she not be coming into the office that day, but that she also didn't intend to answer any calls or her doorbell. "I think trying to run the office alone with a hangover is a just punishment for your Auntie Angie spilling her guts to Alec, don't you?" Mackenzie asked Marmalade who didn't even bother to open her eyes.

Mackenzie left the big cat in her bed, and headed off to take a hot shower. After some heavy-duty primping, she dressed in a sexy pair of short-shorts and a tank top, then strolled into her kitchen to prepare a breakfast fit for a king. The type of breakfast the king, whom Mackenzie assumed was also still asleep directly across the hallway, was sure to be impressed by.

Her very own specialty. Eggs Benedict.

A short time later, and with breakfast tray in hand, Mackenzie grabbed the spare key Alec had given her on the night before and made a determined march across the hall. Slipping quietly inside his condo, she sneaked through his living room, down a small hallway and came to a stop at his closed bedroom door. She started to knock and announce that room service had arrived, but decided the element of surprise would be to her advantage. After all, it only stood to reason that Alec could still be as angry with her this morning as he'd been last night when she'd told him to just forget about her.

Yet, if she surprised him with breakfast in bed?

Slowly turning the doorknob, Mackenzie stepped into the darkened room and flipped on the overhead light. "Room service!" she announced softly, then almost dropped her breakfast tray when Angie's tousled blond head popped out from under the covers on Alec's big king-size bed.

"Mackie? What are you doing here?"

"What am *I* doing here?" Mackenzie yelled, and just as she was about to walk across the room and murder her ex-best friend, a severely hung-over John Stanley pulled the pillow off his head and saved Mackenzie from the electric chair.

John looked as surprised to see Mackenzie as Angie did, but neither of them were more surprised than Mackenzie. She briefly wondered if she shouldn't be embarrassed. After all, she was staring at the man she *had* been dating because she had sneaked into the bedroom of the man she *should* have been dating all along. But who was she kidding? The man she hadn't even had the chance to dump yet was stark naked and in bed with her own best friend!

"What on earth is going on here?" Mackenzie demanded. "Where's Alec?"

John, now flushed a bright red, sat up in the bed and pulled the covers practically up under his chin. Angie, however, leaned over and grabbed her sweater from the floor, and without the least bit of modesty pulled it over her head. They briefly traded looks before Angie said, "I'm sorry you found us like this, Mackie, but John's not stupid and neither am I. We both know something's been going on between you and Alec. It was late when John and I took a taxi back here last night to pick up his Suburban, and then we decided since we'd both had a little too much to drink that John probably shouldn't be driving, and..."

"But what about Alec," Mackenzie broke in, still holding the stupid tray out in front of her like an outdated carhop.

Angie looked at John. John looked back at Angie.

"Alec left the restaurant right after you did last night, Mackie. He said since he'd have to take medical leave until his foot healed, he was going to see his parents for a few days, and then said something about going out to Oregon to see his brother."

Mackenzie more or less stumbled in the direction of the bed, then sat down beside Angie, still holding the tray. She didn't even object when Angie picked up the fork and helped herself to the eggs Benedict. Mackenzie absently placed the tray in the middle of the bed between John and Angie, poured coffee from the carafe into the two cups that she'd meant for her and Alec, and motioned for the two new lovebirds to help themselves. They didn't hesitate to oblige her.

"Did Alec say when he was coming back?" Mackenzie asked, still stunned.

John cleared his throat and remained staring into his coffee cup when he said, "Alec gave us the impression that he might not come back, Mackenzie. His older brother in Oregon is a pilot too, and he's trying to get a struggling air freight business off the ground. Alec said Josh has been begging him to come and work for him for months, and..."

"And so he plans to stay in Oregon," Mackenzie said to no one in particular.

"That's a good possibility," John said. "He gave me the key to his condo and asked me if I would take care of things for him here if he needed me to sell the condo and ship his things out to Oregon."

Angie reached out and patted her hand, "But you can always call him, Mackie. John knows how to get in touch with his parents, and..."

"No," Mackenzie said, standing up. "It's better this way. Really. If Alec didn't even bother to tell me good-bye, then he's already made up his mind."

"Don't run off like this," Angie called out as Mackenzie started out of the room. "I'm worried about you, Mackie. Are you going to be okay?"

"Enjoy the breakfast," Mackenzie called back over her shoulder, but by the time she reached the safety of her own condo, Mackenzie was crying so hard that even Marmalade took pity on her and rubbed against her legs, offering what little comfort she could.

MACKENZIE THREW HERSELF into her work like a demon possessed after Alec left Charleston. Angie complained about Mackenzie reverting back to her old lifestyle, but Mackenzie didn't care. Her work was the only thing that helped keep her mind off Alec. Work had always been her solace but this time she hoped her work would somehow eventually heal her broken heart.

Angie, on the other hand, was practically walking on air. She and John had become inseparable over the last six weeks, and despite Mackenzie's own woes in the love department, she couldn't have been happier for both of them. They were actually the perfect couple when you thought about it. John had money, and Angie knew exactly what to do with it.

Of course, both John and Angie didn't help matters with the contradicting advice they kept giving her.

"I know Alec, Mackenzie," John kept insisting. "He's stubborn. And if he said he'd never bother you again, he'll stick by his word regardless of how badly he's hurting. Make the first move. Call him and tell him how you feel."

Unfortunately, Mackenzie had a stubborn streak of her own, and she was inclined to agree with Angie when she would always argue, "Don't be ridiculous, John. A man doesn't declare he's crazy about you one day and move across the country the next. Unless, of course, he didn't mean what he was saying in the first place."

"But don't you see?" John always protested. "Alec's running scared. He's always envisioned himself as this invincible bachelor. It had to throw him for a loop when he realized he'd fallen in love with Mackenzie."

"And what about Mackenzie?" Angie would wail in response. "Don't you think Mackenzie's going through her own emotional turmoil over this?"

And that's exactly how Mackenzie felt about the situation. She was in an emotional turmoil. Sadly, one of her own making. She'd given Alec mixed signals from the first moment she met him. She'd even tried to seduce him one night, only to tell him a day later that she wanted him to forget about her.

Who could blame the guy for throwing up his hands and moving as far away from Charleston as possible?

No, it was better if they left things status quo, Mackenzie told herself repeatedly. Her safe, predictable life was back to normal now. Her heart didn't stop every time she drove into her parking space for fear of running into Alec. She could even enjoy the peace and solitude of her movies and her popcorn. And it certainly didn't seem likely that Alec was going to return any time soon and send her life back into chaos again.

Not only had he not cared enough to say goodbye, but not once in the six weeks since Alec had left Charleston had he tried to contact her. And did that sound like a man who was stark-raving, crazy mad about her?

Of course, it didn't.

Which is exactly why Mackenzie was determined to put Alec behind her and stop pining away for what might have been.

MACKENZIE'S PARENTS WERE married in a ceremony to end all ceremonies on the fourth of June. Angie and John had been kind enough to fly to Indianapolis with her to attend the gala event. And if Mackenzie threw her share of birdseed a little too forcefully, especially at the effervescent bride, no one seemed to notice.

"I'm still surprised someone from the *Jerry Springer Show* hasn't jumped out from behind the bushes to offer you a deal for this story," Angie commented as she and Mackenzie waved a final goodbye to the gleaming white limousine that was whisking the happy couple away for their honeymoon in Hawaii.

"Yeah, I can see the caption now," Mackenzie agreed.

"Soon-to-be thirty-year-old spinster serves as maid of honor at her own parents' wedding."

Angie laughed as she linked her arm through Mackenzie's. They headed for the church's parking lot where John was already waiting in a rental car that would take them to the airport. "Well, at least you're able to joke about it now. For a while there, I was worried that you might go berserk and murder both of them."

"Mother was the only one in real danger," Mackenzie insisted. "Although I probably should have put poor Daddy out of his misery. Spending the rest of his life with Mother is going to be a long, hard death sentence."

Angie laughed again. "So, can I breathe a sigh of relief and cancel that private room I reserved for you in the mental ward?"

Mackenzie nodded. "Yes, I guess you can. If I can survive my parents' wedding, then the rest of my life should be an absolute breeze."

"Good," Angie said, then pulled Mackenzie to a stop. "Because I've been dying to show you this all week. I just wasn't sure you were mentally stable enough to handle it."

Mackenzie gasped as she looked at the huge diamond twinkling back at her from Angie's ring finger. "You've got to be kidding."

"Five carats. Perfect stone. Eighteen carat gold band with platinum prongs," Angie said proudly.

"Which you picked out, of course."

"Damn straight," Angie said. "I intend to wear this ring for the rest of my life. Why wouldn't I pick out exactly what I wanted?"

When Mackenzie didn't answer, Angie reached out and grabbed her hand. "You could have an engagement ring of your own, you know. And maybe I've been too harsh,

Mackie. Maybe John's right. Maybe you *should* give in and call Alec."

Mackenzie snorted. "Yeah, that's exactly what I need to do. I haven't heard from Alec since he left Charleston, but if I pick up the phone and call him, he'll rush back to Charleston and drop on his knees and ask me to marry him."

Angie let out a sigh, but Mackenzie took Angie by the shoulders and gave her best friend a gentle shake. "Now, stop this. Understand? I won't have you walking around on eggshells because you're getting married and I'm not. This is going to be the happiest time of your life."

Angie forced a smile. "And the busiest," she added. "And that's the other part I wasn't sure you could handle. John's idea of the perfect wedding would be for us to run off to Las Vegas tonight and get married in one of those tacky little wedding chapels. But you know that's as ridiculous as me purchasing my wedding gown off the rack."

"Las Vegas doesn't sound so bad to me," Mackenzie mentioned, trying not to show the dread she was already feeling now that another damn wedding was looming in her near future.

"The only problem is that John hates the idea of all the planning that goes into a big wedding."

"And who could blame him?"

"But we've finally reached a compromise," Angie said with a grin. "I promised John he wouldn't have to do a thing but show up at the altar."

"Smart move."

"Save that opinion until I tell you the date."

Mackenzie sent Angie a puzzled look.

"July fourth," Angie added before Mackenzie could ask.

"You mean next year, I hope," Mackenzie said.

Angie laughed. "Try this year. Four weeks from now. It's John's favorite holiday. And we plan to take the entire month off and sail his catamaran all the way to the Florida Keys."

"My God, Angie, why the rush?"

Angie glanced over her shoulder at John who waved at them from the driver's side of the rental car. "That was another point of contention between me and John. He's the type of man who's ready to act on the situation once he makes a decision. So, I assured John it would be no problem to arrange a wedding by next month."

"But that's impossible," Mackenzie argued. "Especially with the type of wedding I know you'll want to have."

"Don't worry, I can pull this off," Angie said. "I've been planning my wedding since the day I got my first period, Mackie. I promise you, I can do this."

Mackenzie frowned. "But are you really sure you love John, Angie? My God, it's only been a little over six weeks, and...."

"Time doesn't have anything to do with this," Angie interrupted. "I told you when we first met John that he was the perfect man. You accused me of saying that because he comes from old money. But he is perfect, Mackie. He's perfect for me. And his bank account has nothing to do with it. John doesn't even want children. And you, of all people, know I'm way too selfish to have kids of my own."

Would Alec have wanted kids? Mackenzie suddenly wondered. She'd never had the chance to ask him. But she did. She wanted a house full.

"Look," Angie added, "I just can't risk dragging

things out and have John get so frustrated with the whole mess that he ends up running out on me..."

"Like Alec did on me?" Mackenzie finished for her.

Angie sent Mackenzie an apologetic look. "I'm sorry, but I just can't take that chance. I know John loves me. And I do love him, Mackenzie. I really do."

After only a moment's hesitation, Mackenzie said, "Then if you're really determined to this, I guess we'd better get busy and plan the biggest wedding of the new millennium."

Angie hugged Mackenzie to her. "You're the greatest, Mackie. I knew I could depend on you."

Yeah, I'm the greatest, Mackenzie thought as she walked over to offer her congratulations to the new groom-to-be. *I'm probably the greatest fool in the world for not telling Alec I loved him when I had the chance.*

IT HAD BEEN ALMOST three months since Alec left Charleston. While Mackenzie was getting over the fifth wedding she had already attended that year and preparing for the *sixth*, Alec was burning up the skies with his daily trips back and forth from Portland to British Columbia. Unfortunately, Alec soon discovered that regardless of the vast distance he had put between himself and Mackenzie, all he had managed to change was the scenery.

The situation still remained the same.

Mackenzie still plagued Alec's thoughts as easily as if he'd remained in Charleston living right across the hall. And even the long line of lovelies his older brother, Josh, continued to steer in his direction only paled in comparison to the woman who had sliced, diced and pulverized Alec's aching heart.

As hard as he tried, Alec just couldn't seem to get Mackenzie out of his mind. Like now, he reminded himself on his return flight to Portland. The peace and solitude he'd hoped to find high above the clouds had only given him too much time alone. Time he usually spent agonizing over unwanted visions of Mackenzie and John Stanley, entwined in a steamy embrace behind the sexy netting surrounding Mackenzie's big bamboo bed.

Alec frowned, thinking how eager his old buddy, John, had been when Alec decided to leave town and asked John to handle his affairs. But thank God, in retrospect Alec had refused to give the jerk that satisfaction. Instead, Alec had enlisted the help of one of his fellow pilots to put his belongings in storage. And just as soon as his real estate agent closed the deal on his condo, Alec's final tie to Charleston would thankfully be severed.

Forever.

Or would it?

Alec was still pondering the answer to that burning question when a sudden grumble from his right engine jarred Alec from his troubled thoughts. He checked the instrument panel in the small Cessna. Everything looked perfectly normal. They'd been having trouble with this particular plane for a number of days now, but Josh had torn the engine apart several times and had yet to find anything wrong.

You're just being paranoid, Alec told himself, but when a second sputter shook the plane, Alec grew concerned. He tried to increase the gas flow, but the right engine only coughed and sputtered again. When the engine suddenly ground to a complete halt, Alec knew he was in serious trouble.

The plane made several dips. Alec pulled back on his control yoke trying to keep the nose of the plane up, but he couldn't compensate for the lost engine. When the plane took another dive, his only resort was to search the carpet of earth directly below him for a place to land the plane. As luck would have it, the Olympic National Forest stretched out before him as far as the eye could see. The only thing below him was a thick cover of trees.

Alec already knew there wasn't another airport for at least fifty miles, and in such a small aircraft there wasn't any such thing as a parachute jump. The altitude was much too low.

He kept searching for a break in the canopy, knowing he could set the plane down on a dime if he had a flat place to land. And then he saw it. A small meadow up ahead in the distance.

Leveling the plane, Alec took the Cessna down with a prayer on his lips. He thought he was home free until his remaining left engine failed and ground to a halt. In an instant, the nose of the plane took a dive forward and plummeted downward toward the earth below.

Alec fought the plane, holding tightly to the control yoke and trying to stay on course for the meadow and away from the trees. He'd almost made it when the plane's left wing suddenly crashed against a tall spruce, instantly throwing the plane sideways. Alec braced himself, watching in horror as the ground rose up to meet him.

The last thing that flashed through his mind before his head smashed against the instrument panel was the beautiful face of Mackenzie Malone.

ALEC'S PLANE CRASHED ON Thursday afternoon at around two o'clock Pacific Standard Time in Oregon, which was around five o'clock Eastern Standard Time in South Carolina. And as Mackenzie straightened her desk and slipped several folders into her briefcase, she felt a cold shiver run up her spine. Rubbing the gooseflesh on her arm, Mackenzie shook off the eerie feeling that something was wrong, and focused instead on the chaos that stretched ahead of her for the remainder of the week.

"Don't worry, Mackenzie, you and Angie can count on me," Karen said from the doorway as if she'd read Mackenzie's mind. "I promise, I have everything under control."

Mackenzie nodded, satisfied that she'd already given Karen such detailed instructions, she didn't see how Karen *couldn't* keep everything under control in their absence.

"Thanks Karen," Mackenzie offered. "I know you'll hold down the fort until I get back on Monday."

"Want me to lock up?" Karen asked as she looked down at her watch.

"No, you go ahead," Mackenzie told her. "I have a few things I need to finish here first. I'll lock everything up before I leave the office."

"Okay, then I guess I'll see you guys at the wedding rehearsal tomorrow night," Karen said.

Mackenzie nodded again. "Just remember, don't even think about calling me tomorrow unless it's an absolute emergency. I'll have my hands full trying to keep Angie cool and collected."

"Got it," Karen insisted. "As far as I'm concerned, it would take an act of Congress to make me interrupt you guys tomorrow."

After Karen left, Mackenzie finished up a few loose ends, then walked through her office suites straightening chairs and flipping off lights. After locking the front door to the office, she started to her car, stopping only when a group of teenagers on in-line skates sped across her path. Glancing at their youthful bodies, Mackenzie tried to remember if she'd ever been that young and that carefree.

And when she couldn't, Mackenzie suddenly felt as if she were a hundred years old.

Reminding herself that even a teenager would have been haggard after the schedule she'd been keeping the last few weeks, Mackenzie opened her car door and slid behind the wheel. Not only had she been running the business single-handedly, she had also been Angie's gofer on the side, while Angie pulled together the wedding of all weddings with a guest list that now tipped the scales somewhere between five and six hundred honored guests.

Mackenzie's parents were even flying in from California for the big event, though Mackenzie had tried to discourage their attendance. As usual, her mother had finally won the argument with the statement that "It would be positively rude of us not to attend Angie's wedding when she and John were sweet enough to be present for ours."

Mackenzie's only consolation was that during the two weeks her parents planned to stay in Charleston, maybe they could finally sit down and have a long heart-to-heart talk. Her parents had practically driven her crazy with the constant calling *just to chat* that had been going on since their celebrated wedding and their consequent move. Mackenzie knew they were just trying to make up for lost time, but the past was the past. What they all needed to do now was just move on.

Like her situation with Alec.

It had now been almost three months, and not once had he tried to contact her. She had hoped to glean some information from John once Alec called to have John settle his affairs, but to John's surprise one of Alec's fellow pilots called to say *he* would be handling Alec's affairs instead. And the fact that Alec *hadn't* called John only led Mackenzie to believe Alec was so determined not to see her again he wouldn't even risk the chance that John might leak information on how Mackenzie could find him.

But time was an excellent healer, Mackenzie reminded herself, and she was pleased that Alec was beginning to be nothing more than a faded memory for her. She'd even had the resolve to keep him out of her dreams.

Well, at least *most* of the time.

And on those occasions when Alec did manage to slip beyond her mosquito netting to interrupt her peaceful slumber, Mackenzie simply relaxed and enjoyed their imaginary time together, telling herself the next morning that the feelings she'd had for Alec had never been anything more than a pipe dream anyway.

THE FIRST THING Alec saw when he regained consciousness, was a pair of huge brown eyes staring back at him. Unfortunately, those particular brown eyes belonged to a white-faced cow who was methodically chewing a tuft of fresh grass she seemed to be enjoying despite Alec's presence.

He sat there for a moment staring at the bovine, but when his head slowly began to clear, Alec forced himself into action. Not only did he taste the blood in his mouth, but his left eye was already swelling to the point he could barely see through it. He winced when he took a brief look down at his bloody shirt, and the excruciating pain radiating up his left arm left no doubt that his arm was badly broken.

The smell of gasoline fumes, however, warned Alec that he couldn't stay inside the plane a second longer.

Taking a deep breath, Alec eased his injured shoulder against the dented door of his wrecked plane, and breathed a sigh of relief when the door popped open without much effort. He finally managed to pull himself from the wreckage, causing his inquisitive friend to let out a loud moo before bolting toward the center of the meadow. It was then that Alec heard the noisy motor of a tractor. When it topped a small rise in the distance he began to shout for help.

"Over here," Alec yelled, waving to get the farmer's attention, but his flurry of movement sent a pain up his left arm that literally brought Alec to his knees.

Slumping to the ground, Alec cradled his injured arm against his side, relieved when the farmer waved back and steered the big John Deere in his direction. And as he sat there in a field a thousand miles from nowhere, Alec said a silent prayer of thanks that his life had been spared.

Surviving the crash had been nothing short of a miracle, but Alec's near-death experience had left him with much more than a few aches and pains and a badly broken arm. When his life had flashed before his eyes, Alec had made himself a solemn promise. He promised if he did survive the crash, he wouldn't waste another minute of the life he had left.

And as soon as Alec got himself put back together, he was going back to Charleston.

Mackenzie was going to marry him. It was as simple as that. And someday when Mackenzie was happily bouncing their grandchildren on her knee, Alec just might tell her how close he'd come to dying before he finally came to his senses and asked her to be his wife.

8

THANKS TO HIS SAVIOR farmer, a medivac helicopter had been called to transport Alec out of the wilderness and back to Portland for medical treatment. It was late Thursday night, however, before Alec was finally released from the emergency room and settled into his own private room on the orthopedic floor.

He now had two pins in his left arm and a cast that completely covered his shoulder. He had sixteen stitches in the top of his head. And he had a swollen black eye as proof that his *mild* concussion could have been much worse than it was. The medical staff had even given him the nickname *The Miracle Man*. And in a way Alec guessed he was a miracle man.

Rather than being guest of honor at his own funeral, instead he was a recovering patient who would soon be making plans for his wedding day.

"You try and get some rest now," the pretty nurse told Alec as she checked his IV fluids and adjusted his covers. "And Josh said to tell you he'd be back first thing in the morning to check on you."

Alec groaned slightly as he turned his head so he could look at the nurse with the eye that *wasn't* swollen shut. "You know my brother, Josh?"

The nurse sent Alec a coy smile and said, "I certainly know Josh now."

"The jerk," Alec grumbled aloud to himself when the nurse left the room.

Here Alec had been, facing possible peril under the surgeon's knife. The Federal Aviation boys were having hissy fits trying to determine the cause of the plane crash. Disgruntled insurance agents were breathing down Josh's neck like Godzilla. And what had his brother been doing? Josh, the big oaf, had been romancing the pretty redhead as though his love life, not his brother and the plane crash, was his first damn priority.

But was he really any different from Josh? Alec suddenly wondered as his pain medication kicked in again. Only by the grace of God was he still alive, yet Alec's first thoughts hadn't been about the extensive investigation that would be conducted over the plane crash. Nor had his thoughts been about the potential hassle Josh could have reaching a settlement with his insurance company.

No, Alec's first thoughts had been of going back to Charleston to punch John Stanley squarely in the nose before he informed Mackenzie that she *was* going to marry him.

And Alec *would* be heading back to the sunny South just as soon as he was able to travel. Unless, that is, he could somehow convince Mackenzie that *she* should come to Portland instead. Of course, calling her up and playing on her sympathy because he'd just survived a life-threatening plane crash, was a little underhanded, and Alec knew it. But as Alec settled his head back against his pillow and closed his one good eye, he decided calling Mackenzie might be the perfect plan after all.

Besides, hadn't he always heard that all was fair in love and war?

Wincing when the smile tugging at the corner of his

mouth reminded him he also had several stitches in his lower lip, Alec kept smiling anyway, deciding he would have Josh call Mackenzie at her office the following morning and deliver the news that Alec had survived a near fatal plane crash. And if Mackenzie did rush to his bedside, as Alec prayed she would, Alec would then have her all to himself and safely out of John Stanley's clutches.

"Just give me a second chance, Mackenzie," Alec muttered aloud.

Because if Alec had anything to say in the matter, when and if the two of them did decide to return to Charleston, they would be returning together as husband and wife.

WHILE ALEC DRIFTED off to sleep that night pleased with his new plan, Mackenzie was trying to keep *her* eyes open. Angie, who was understandably plagued with a huge case of the prewedding jitters, had unfortunately decided to share her insomnia with a late-night call to her weary best friend.

"I know you think I'm being silly," Angie rambled on, "but I have this overwhelming feeling that something is going to go wrong and spoil all of my perfect planning."

Instead of answering immediately, Mackenzie glanced at her bedside clock, wondering how either of them were going to make it through Friday's busy schedule if they didn't get some sleep.

"We've gone over everything from start to finish, Angie," Mackenzie said, not even bothering to suppress a loud yawn, "and there isn't even one stone we've left unturned."

"I know, but...."

"Look," Mackenzie said, trying to be as supportive as she could be at one o'clock in the morning, "the only thing that's going to foul up your perfect planning is if you fall asleep during the wedding rehearsal or at the rehearsal dinner tomorrow night. Now please. Hang up the phone so we both won't be dead on our feet tomorrow.''

Angie breathed out a long sigh into the telephone. ''You're right. I know you are, but...''

''I just hope you won't have dark circles under your eyes tomorrow,'' Mackenzie threw in for good measure and actually heard Angie gasp at the thought. ''I know you're paying a fortune for that thief you call a photographer, but I doubt he can do a thing to touch up the pictures if you show up looking like last year's corpse.''

Mackenzie heard another gasp before Angie reminded her for the fiftieth time that they had to meet John's mother at nine o'clock sharp the next morning and go over the menu for the rehearsal dinner one last time.

''Thanks for being willing to chauffeur me around tomorrow, Mackie,'' Angie said before she finally hung up. ''I'll be so nervous, I'd be a threat to society if I got behind the wheel of a car.''

''Which is exactly why I offered to take you anywhere you need to go tomorrow,'' Mackenzie said with another yawn. ''Now get some sleep, okay? And I promise I'll be there to pick you up bright and early in the morning.''

Mackenzie felt like cheering when Angie finally broke their connection, but when she switched off her bedside light and snuggled back beneath the covers she found she was suddenly wide awake. Lying there, looking up at the moon shining through the skylight above her bed, Mackenzie cursed Angie for waking her up, then found herself mentally running back through the myriad upcoming events one last time.

She hadn't dared admit to Angie that she, too, had the feeling that some type of impending doom was lurking just beyond the shadows. The feeling had overtaken her shortly before she left the office that evening, and as hard as she'd tried to shake the feeling off, Mackenzie's sixth sense kept telling her that something was wrong.

But what?

They'd gone over the wedding plans to the point that everyone involved knew the details were carved in stone. That changing something even as trivial as a seating arrangement wouldn't be tolerated under any circumstances. And even though common sense told Mackenzie that with a guest list of six hundred people there were bound to be a few little glitches here and there, nothing in particular immediately sprang to mind.

Telling herself it was only having to play hostess to her newlywed parents that was making her nervous, Mackenzie turned on her side and purposely closed her eyes. She'd only been teasing Angie about the potential dark-circles-under-the-eyes problem, but Mackenzie didn't want to take that chance herself.

It was bad enough she would be under the scrutiny of six hundred people while she again played her ridiculous maid-of-honor role. But what she *wasn't* going to do, was have them add a haggard-looking, aged, pitiful maid of honor to their unkind thoughts about her. Because if she *were* destined to always be the bridesmaid and never the bride, then Mackenzie intended to be the best damn looking spinster to ever float down the aisle before the honored bride arrived.

And they can take that to the bank, Mackenzie told herself, then buried her head under the covers and promptly fell asleep.

JOSH SEEMED RATHER surprised when he walked into Alec's hospital room on Friday morning and found his bruised and battered brother totally alert and sitting up in bed.

"What took you so long?" Alec growled the minute Josh stepped inside the room. "That redhead you were romancing yesterday said you'd be here early."

Josh frowned. "Hell, Alec, you knew I had to meet with the FAA and the insurance company this morning. Besides, it's only noon."

"Yeah, but it's already three o'clock in Charleston and I'd hoped Mackenzie might make it here by tonight. Now, there's no way she can get here until tomorrow afternoon at the earliest."

"You mean she's really coming?" Josh wanted to know.

"Hopefully," Alec said, then motioned Josh closer and pointed to the phone beside his bed. "That is, as soon as you make the call and put the wheels in motion."

Josh sent Alec a troubled look. "Me? You're kidding. Right?"

"Ah, come on, Josh," Alec begged. "Even if Mackenzie didn't hang up on me the minute she heard my voice, me telling her I survived a plane crash wouldn't be near as dramatic as my brother calling to tell her about the tragic accident."

"Talk about desperate," Josh scoffed.

"You're right. I am desperate," Alec agreed, wincing when the stitches in his lip gave a little tug at his sudden outburst.

"Desperate enough to pull a rotten trick like that?"

Alec frowned. "Yeah. I guess I'm desperate enough to do just about anything right now, Josh. So are you going to help me out, or aren't you?"

Josh shook his head in disgust, but he reached for the

phone when Alec handed it over. "Okay, lover boy, exactly what do you want me to say to this woman?"

"Be brief," Alec coached. "Tell her you're my brother. Assure her I'm all right, but tell her I survived a plane crash yesterday and that I've been asking for her. Tell her you just thought she'd want to know."

"You're one real sick puppy. Do you know that, Alec?"

"Maybe. But it's a dog-eat-dog world out there, Josh," Alec said, with no visible signs of remorse. "Now stop trying to be my conscience and make the damn call."

When Josh finally nodded in agreement, Alec dialed the number. "I'm calling her office," Alec said. "Ask for Miss Malone."

Josh took a deep breath and did as Alec instructed, but Alec tensed when Josh frowned and put his hand over the receiver. "Miss Malone is out of the office today," Josh whispered.

"Tell the secretary it's an emergency," Alec whispered back.

Josh obeyed again, but his eyes grew wide with surprise when he looked at Alec and said, "The secretary says she's sorry, but Miss Malone won't be back in the office until after the wedding."

"The *wedding?*" Alec yelled. "To who?"

Josh put his mouth back to the receiver and asked the urgent question, but when Josh turned to Alec and said, "Some guy named John Stanley," Alec practically levitated off the bed.

"Hey? That's not the same John…" Josh began, but he stopped midsentence when Alec slugged him on the arm.

"Tell her you need information about the wedding," Alec ordered as his mind sped forward. "Find out when and where, Josh, and don't hang up until you do, dammit.''

When Josh hung up, he looked at Alec and said, "Sorry, Bro. The wedding's tomorrow at five o'clock. At the Stonehenge Cathedral on Meeting Street.''

Alec remained motionless for so long Josh reached for the pitcher on Alec's bedside table and poured his brother a glass of ice water. Alec absently took the glass, but after he swallowed several gulps, he tossed the plastic cup to the floor and threw back his bedcovers.

"Now where the hell do you think you're going?" Josh barked.

"I'm going to Charleston," Alec said as he eased himself slowly out of the bed. And the fact that every muscle in his body screamed the second his feet touched the cold tiles of the hospital floor, didn't deter Alec from his slow shuffle across the room.

"Are you nuts?" Josh demanded. "You're in no condition to travel. The doctor said he wasn't even going to release you for a couple more days. He wants to keep you here under observation."

"To hell with the doctor," Alec said as he wrestled with the IV pole he was pulling along beside him. "And do me a favor and go round up your girlfriend so she can unhook me from this tube I have in my arm.''

Josh stomped after Alec who had finally made it into the small bath that was only a few feet away from Alec's bed. "And what do you intend to do when you get to Charleston, you crazy numbskull?" Josh demanded.

Alec frowned, more at the ghastly reflection staring back at him from the tiny mirror above the sink, than he did at Josh's name calling. "There's no way I'm going to let Mackenzie marry John Stanley, Josh. I made up my mind when I lived through the crash that Mackenzie is going to marry me. And that's exactly what I'm going to do.''

"Marry you?'' Josh snorted. ''What happened to all that bull about pilots making lousy husbands and fathers? What about that, Alec?''

"You're right. It's bull,'' Alec answered as he pushed Josh out of his way. ''Pilots get married and have families every day of the week.''

"And do you really think Mackenzie is going to be overjoyed to see you? That she's going to give up her current groom so she can become the bride of Frankenstein?'' Josh argued. ''Face it, Alec, you look like hell warmed over right now. In fact, if I didn't know you were my brother, I wouldn't even recognize your stubborn ass.''

Even Alec had to admit that his appearance was frightening. Aside from the fact that his left arm was held out from his side in a grotesque position by his bulky cast, the entire left side of his face was purple and swollen beyond recognition. It also didn't help matters that the left side of his head had been shaved because the moron who put sixteen stitches in his scalp had been too lazy to work around his once thick hair. And the stitches at the right corner of his mouth didn't do much for his looks, either.

In fact, the stitches made Alec look as if he were wearing a permanent sneer. Which he would be wearing if he allowed Mackenzie to go through with the wedding and marry John Stanley.

"Listen, Alec. You need to be reasonable about this,'' Josh spoke up, jarring Alec's mind back into action. ''Call Mackenzie if you have to, but give up this nonsense about trying to get to Charleston before the wedding.''

Feeling somewhat like a mummy as he dragged his bandaged self out of the bathroom and back across the room, Alec waited until he reached the bed before he closed his eyes and jimmied the IV needle slowly out of his arm by himself.

"Now that was brilliant," Josh scolded.

Refusing to look at Josh, or at the blood that was oozing to the top of his hand, Alec grabbed a tissue from the nightstand and applied a few seconds of pressure, but as his mind flipped through the details of the journey he intended to make, it suddenly occurred to Alec that checking himself out of the hospital was totally pointless if he didn't have any clothes.

And he didn't.

Shoes he still had, they were right by the side of his bed, but the rescue team had cut his shirt off the second the helicopter arrived in the hayfield. And who knew what had happened to his pants?

Groaning just from the effort it took to merely pull out the drawer to his bedside table, Alec breathed a sigh of relief when he saw that his watch, his wallet and his keys had all thankfully been preserved and sent to his room. But even with his finances intact, there was still no way he could travel all the way across the country in a hospital gown who's open back left his bare butt exposed.

"Take off your clothes," Alec said when he whirled back around to face Josh.

"The hell you say," Josh boomed.

"I'm serious Josh, I'm going to need your clothes."

"I'm beginning to think your concussion is more serious than they thought, little brother," Josh insisted. "Because you're a crazy man if you think I'm going to strip off right here and hand over my clothes."

"Well I sure don't have time for you to make the trip all the way back to your apartment for mine," Alec argued as he strapped his watch on his arm. "In fact, I'll be lucky if I can even get a flight out this afternoon, Josh. It's the Fourth of July holiday weekend, remember? And even if I can get a flight out, who knows how many connections I'll have to make or how long it will take me to get back to Charleston?''

Despite Alec's urgent pleas, Josh still didn't budge.

''Don't you realize I'm fighting against the clock here? It's already almost four o'clock in Charleston. That gives me just a little over twenty-four hours to travel all the way across country and make it to the church in time to stop the wedding.''

''You're wasting your breath, Alec,'' Josh practically yelled. ''Because there's no way in hell I'm going to be a party to this ridiculous damn plan of yours.''

''Hey guys, what's all the fuss in here? We can hear you all the way at the nurses' station,'' the pretty redhead said as she poked her head around the door.

Josh barely acknowledged her arrival, but Alec looked at the woman as if the Virgin Mary herself had suddenly appeared to save him. ''Come inside and close the door,'' Alec urged, and though the redhead hesitated for a second, another look at Josh helped her make her decision.

''I'll give you one hundred dollars if you'll find me a pair of those scrubs they wear in the operating room,'' Alec said with a gleam in his one good eye.

The redhead looked at Josh, then back at Alec. But she frowned when she noticed the abandoned IV tube that was currently dripping a steady stream of life-saving fluid into the floor. ''Okay, what's really going on in here?'' she demanded, bringing her hands to her shapely hips. When neither of them had an immediate answer, she headed straight for Alec. ''Now get back in bed, Mr. Southerland, so I can fix your IV tube.''

Josh sent Alec a satisfied smile until Alec grabbed the

nurse's hand and said in a pleading voice, "Have you ever been in love?"

She flushed slightly. "Not really," she said, but she kept her eyes on Josh when she added, "At least, not yet."

"But do you believe that everyone has a true soul mate?"

She looked back at Alec, and this time she didn't even grimace at his horrible appearance. "Why, yes. I do believe everyone has a soul mate out there somewhere."

Alec's lopsided grin twisted his face into an even more hideous expression. "Well, so do I. And if I don't get to South Carolina by five o'clock tomorrow evening, my soul mate is going to marry someone else. So, please. In the name of love. Find me something I can wear so I can get to the airport before it's too late."

Without another word the redhead hurried from the room and before Alec even had time to collect his shoes and the rest of his belongings, the redhead returned and held out a pair of pale green surgical scrubs.

"I could lose my job if anyone found out I willingly helped a patient discharge himself from the hospital," she said when Alec grabbed the clothing.

"You have my solemn promise, I'll never say a word," Alec assured her.

"And we're going to have to cut the left sleeve so we can get it over your cast," she told Alec as she pulled a pair of surgical scissors from her lab coat pocket.

Alec reached up to yank off his hospital gown, but a frown from Josh stopped him before it was too late. "Guess I'd better start with the pants," Alec told the nurse with a sheepish grin, then shuffled back to the bathroom trying to hold the back of his hospital gown together with his one good arm.

"Damn, no underwear. No socks," Alec grumbled to himself as he finally got into the pants and slipped his bare feet into his loafers.

Tying the string that went around the waistband of the pants, however, was impossible. Shuffling back out of the bathroom with a half-bare chest, since his cast covered most of the left side of his body, he was still holding on to the strings when the nurse said, "Here, let me tie that for you."

Alec then waited until she cut the left sleeve of the scrub top and helped Alec ease it over his head. "Well?" Alec asked Josh the minute his head popped through the opening, "Are you going to take me to the airport, or do I have to call a taxi?" It wasn't until the redhead looked at Josh as if he were a traitor that Josh finally said, "Hell, why not, little brother? Far be it from me to stand in the way of true love."

WHILE ALEC WAS MAKING a mad dash to the airport, Mackenzie was standing at the back of the church with Karen and two other bridesmaids, getting ready to make their third attempt at walking down the aisle to Angie's satisfaction.

"Remember, pace yourself to the music," Angie called out from the front of the church. "It's important that you reach the altar at the exact time the music comes to a finish."

Karen groaned, but only loud enough for Mackenzie to hear. "How long do you think she'll keep this up?" Karen whispered to the back of Mackenzie's head.

"Until we get it perfect, of course," Mackenzie whispered back.

"But do you think we'll ever be perfect enough for Angie?" Karen mumbled.

"Sorry," Mackenzie said. "I'm afraid all brides become anal retentive when it comes to the most important day of their lives. And believe me, after the number of weddings I've already attended this year, I could write a book on the subject."

"Great. And since Angie's already a perfectionist, I guess that means we'll still be standing here when the guests start arriving tomorrow."

Mackenzie muffled a laugh with her hand. "Just keep reminding yourself that we love her in spite of this hell she's putting us through now," Mackenzie whispered back over her shoulder. "And if there's any justice in this world, her time will come."

Before Karen could comment, the organ came to life again and Mackenzie took a step forward with her hands clasped in front of her pretending to hold a bouquet like Angie insisted they all should do for optimum effect. Mackenzie was almost tempted to yell out a good old Southern "Yee-ha," pretend to toss her imaginary bouquet over her head, and then do a series of acrobatic cartwheels down the aisle, but her love and devotion for the anxious-looking blonde who was standing at the altar held Mackenzie to the precision pacing she was doing now.

After all, like she'd just told Karen, tomorrow would be the most important day of Angie's life to date. And like everything else in her carefully controlled life, Angie intended for her wedding ceremony to be absolutely perfect.

By the time the final bridesmaid made it to her designated spot, Angie sent them all a contrite little smile and said, "Well, that was much better girls, but…"

"I'm over it, Angie," Mackenzie finally spoke up in self-defense. "In fact, we all are. And if you continue to make us walk up and down this aisle for another hour, we're all going to be late for the rehearsal dinner."

Glancing at her fancy Lady Rolex watch, Angie let out a small sigh then looked around for John, who had become so bored with the entire ordeal that he was currently thumbing through a hymn book as if it were the latest edition of the *Sports Illustrated Swimsuit Issue.*

"Sweetie," Angie called out, snapping John to attention. "I think we're all wrapped up here. Could you go outside and ask the limo driver to bring the car around?"

Apparently delighted to have any chore that would put an end to the hours of endless rehearsing, John made a quick exit to summon his bride's chariot to the church's front steps. And Mackenzie quickly elbowed Karen, then nodded towards the front door of the church.

"If we hurry, we can at least ride to the restaurant in peace," Mackenzie said, but as they attempted their escape, Angie called out behind them.

"I think Mackenzie and the bridesmaids should all ride to the rehearsal dinner in the limo with me and John," she insisted, heading in their direction. "Because we still have a few things I think we need to work on, girls. Like the way I want you all to smile for the guests, for one thing. And especially you, Karen. You've had a perpetual frown on your face all evening."

Karen sent Mackenzie a pleading look, but Angie quickly summoned her two cousins who were also acting as bridesmaids and herded them all down the aisle.

"Remind me to elope if I ever decide to get married," Karen mumbled as Angie swept past them to lead the way.

"Don't worry, I will," Mackenzie assured her. "I'll even pay your plane fare to Las Vegas if you promise I won't have to attend the ceremony. In fact, I never want to hear the word *wedding* again as long as I live.''

''It's a deal,'' Karen said as the long white limousine pulled up to the curb.

''What's a deal?'' Angie wanted to know as she ushered her captive audience into her luxury carriage.

''I just made Karen a deal that I'd move out of the way so she could catch the bridal bouquet tomorrow,'' Mackenzie lied and winked at Karen.

''You shouldn't make deals you can't keep, Mackenzie,'' Angie said with authority. ''Because I intend for *you* to catch the bridal bouquet tomorrow, even if I have to walk up and personally stuff the bouquet firmly down the front of your dress.''

AS THE LIMOUSINE WHISKED Mackenzie off to John and Angie's rehearsal dinner, Alec was making his way toward the United ticket counter. He ignored the horrified looks people were sending his way, the same way he was ignoring Josh, who was still at Alec's elbow griping about what he called the stupidest stunt Alec had ever pulled.

''I told you all you had to do was drop me off,'' Alec complained when the ticket counter looming in the distance still didn't seem to be getting any closer.

''And I told you I wasn't going anywhere until I was sure you could actually book a flight that would get you to Charleston before the wedding,'' Josh argued.

''Don't worry. I'll get there before the wedding one way or the other,'' Alec said with conviction.

''But if you can't, be prepared for me to take your sweet ass right back to the hospital, bucko,'' Josh informed his brother with just as much conviction. ''Because there's no telling how much trouble we're already in with the FAA, the National Transportation Safety

Board, and the insurance company now that you've checked yourself out of the hospital against doctor's orders.''

''Don't worry. I'll plead insanity,'' Alec said.

''Like that would be a lie,'' Josh jeered. ''You're borderline certifiable right now, man, and that's the truth if I ever told it.''

When they finally reached the far end of the terminal, Alec took his place in line behind a zillion other anxious travelers, then glared at his watch that seemed to be devouring time in five minute increments. Thanks to their lovely guide, they had taken the back way out of the hospital, and as they made their long journey through the bowels of the hospital, the redhead had managed to extract a commitment from Josh to take her to dinner later that night for all of her trouble.

Unfortunately, once they'd said goodbye to the helpful nurse, the heavy downtown traffic had made a quick trip to the airport virtually impossible. And now that he was facing a long line ahead of him at the ticket counter, Alec was beginning to worry that he might end up right back in the hospital just as Josh threatened.

''Mommy, Mommy, there's a monster back there,'' a little girl who was standing only a few feet in front of Alec suddenly squealed.

Alec automatically turned around with everyone else to see what the child was talking about until it suddenly registered the little girl was referring to him.

''See,'' Josh said with satisfaction when the mother pulled the child to her hip and moved as far away from them as possible. ''Frankenstein ain't got nothing on you, buddy boy.''

''Very funny,'' Alec grumbled, almost relieved that his

face was currently too purple for anyone watching to detect his embarrassment.

After another torturous thirty minutes, it was finally Alec's turn at the ticket desk. And like the little girl, the preppy young ticket agent standing behind the counter looked as if he didn't know whether to ask how he could assist Alec with his travel plans, or leave his station and run through the airport terminal screaming for help.

"I don't have a ticket, but I need to get to Charleston, South Carolina as soon as possible. First class if you have it," Alec told the young agent who was making a concentrated effort not to openly gawk at Alec's mangled face.

The *first class* brought the lad's eyebrow up a bit, and after punching his computer keys for several minutes, the young man sighed and said, "Sorry, but the first thing I have available in first class would leave at seven in the morning, with connecting flights in Denver and Atlanta, and arriving in Charleston by seven tomorrow night."

"That's not good enough," Alec was quick to say. "Try coach, but book me two seats," he added. "I'll need the extra room with this arm in a cast."

The young agent sent another wary look at Alec before he returned to his computer. After another few minutes of continuous typing, he looked somewhere over Alec's head when he said, "I can get you out of Portland at eight tonight, but you'll have a several long layovers, both in Chicago tonight and again in Atlanta tomorrow...."

"That doesn't matter. What time will that put me in Charleston?" Alec interrupted.

"Two o'clock tomorrow afternoon," the young agent said. "Of course, I hope you realize this is going to be very expensive," he added as if he were talking to some derelict, which he probably thought he was from Alec's current appearance. "Not only will you have to pay the last minute rates, but if you insist on booking two passenger seats...."

"I'll take it," Alec growled.

The agent sent Alec a condescending smile. "Sir, I'm not sure you fully understand what I'm trying to tell you. Two seats for such a short notice flight will cost you nineteen-fifty plus tax. And I don't mean nineteen dollars and fifty cents."

Alec slammed his gold card down on the counter with a thud. "I said I'll take it. Satisfied?"

The young agent shot Alec a contemptuous look, then retrieved Alec's card and checked the information carefully. Looking back at Alec he smiled. "I'll need to see a photo ID," he said as if he clearly suspected Alec of credit card theft.

Reminding himself it was only standard airport procedure to ask passengers for photo identification these days, Alec reluctantly pulled his driver's license from his wallet, wondering if the fool actually expected him to look like the picture on his license in his current condition.

"Could I see another form of identification, please?" the snotty agent insisted.

Alec sent him a one-eyed glare, then fished through his wallet until he found his pilot's license. *Let him suck wind when he sees I'm a pilot,* Alec thought to himself, but the agent still didn't seem convinced.

Of course, when he thought about it, Alec really couldn't blame the poor kid for doubting his credentials. How many other pilots walked around the airport terminal wearing green surgical scrub clothes and looking like a reject from some Hollywood horror flick? None of the pilots Alec knew, and that was for sure.

But before Alec could try to explain his current predicament to the cautious young lad, the agent left without a word and quickly disappeared behind closed doors.

"Hey, what's the big hold up?" an angry passenger yelled from the crowd at about the same time Josh walked up beside him.

"Trouble?"

Alec shrugged. "We'll know if he comes back with the security police."

"Calling security sounds reasonable enough to me," Josh said with a grin. "Because I sure wouldn't want to sit next to your scary butt on the airplane."

Before Alec could come back with a smart reply, the agent returned and punched in a few more keys. "Has anyone given you any packages, or asked you to take a package of any description on board for them?"

When Alec assured the agent neither of those scenarios had taken place, the agent looked Alec up and down again before he asked with more than a hint of disdain, "You don't have any luggage to check?"

"Sorry, but I didn't have time to grab the poor guy's clothes before I helped him break out of the mental hospital," Josh spoke up, causing several people standing in line behind them to snicker.

The agent only snorted at Josh's comment, but he eventually handed Alec back his ID, and when he finally produced Alec's ticket, he said with an extremely strained smile, "Have a nice flight and thank you for flying the friendly skies of United."

When they walked away from the counter Alec said, "Shouldn't you be heading back to town for your big date tonight?"

"Nah, I've got plenty of time, and you have a couple of hours to kill, so I thought we'd stop off at the pilots' lounge and see who was there."

"Yeah, seeing me in this condition should really cheer everyone up before they head off for the cockpit."

"Don't you think you've earned a few bragging rights?" Josh argued.

Alec didn't answer, but he also didn't argue when Josh led the way down the terminal to the nearest pilots' lounge.

9

ALEC SPENT the few hours before he left Portland making the necessary arrangements for what he would need when he did land in Charleston. He had called his pilot friend who'd been handling his affairs and arranged for his buddy to leave him a change of clothing at the airport in Charleston.

"Nothing fancy," Alec had told the guy, knowing it was pointless to ask for the loan of a sports coat and tie with his arm in a cast. A simple pullover polo and a pair of dress slacks would have to suffice. And though Alec couldn't bring himself to ask the guy to loan him some underwear, he also hadn't bothered to tell the poor guy he'd have to slit the left sleeve of the shirt to accommodate his cast. Alec made a mental note to reimburse his friend for the damaged shirt later.

He'd spent the remainder of the torturous wait trying to decide exactly how he was going to convince Mackenzie that she shouldn't marry John Stanley. Because there was no possible way she could be in love with the guy, and Alec knew it.

Maybe John was the quiet, respectable, solid-as-a-rock kind of guy, but Alec had never seen Mackenzie look even once at John with the same excitement, intensity and passion she'd shown him. Not to mention their cautious but steamy adventures on the night he'd stayed over because she was so upset about her parents getting back together.

And if I hadn't picked that untimely moment to panic because I realized I was falling in love with her, then I probably wouldn't be sitting here in Portland now.

Maybe I should have made mad, passionate love to her that night, Alec decided with a frown. He could have shown her what it was like to be loved by a real man, not some namby-pamby rich guy like John Stanley. Not that Alec thought for a moment that John's money had anything to do with the situation. He did know Mackenzie well enough to know that much.

No, marrying John had to be nothing more than some twisted desire to please that overbearing mother Angie had warned him about. And even though common sense told Alec Mackenzie's mother would undoubtedly be present for the celebrated event, even *old mom* wasn't going to stand in Alec's way. Maybe he was winging it, but Alec loved Mackenzie more than he ever thought possible, and he intended to spend the rest of his life showering her with more love and affection than any woman could hope for.

If, Alec reminded himself, Mackenzie would only listen to reason and give him half a chance.

"I'm on my way, Mackenzie," Alec mumbled under his breath as he stared through the airport window at the big 747 taxing across the runway. "I'm on my way now, and nothing or no one is going to stop me."

NEITHER ALEC NOR Mackenzie had a clue that they were both sitting in an airport terminal on opposite sides of the country at exactly the same time. While Alec was waiting patiently for his flight to Chicago, Mackenzie was dreading the fact that her parents' plane would soon be landing in Charleston.

But not because she wouldn't be glad to see her parents. Mackenzie was actually looking forward to their short visit. She only dreaded the lengthy inquisition she would receive from her mother about what was currently going on in her life.

Unfortunately, since her parents' recent wedding, Barbara Malone had become almost fixated over the fact that Mackenzie's life didn't have that *couple*-connotation to it. Not that Angie hadn't been just as bad lately. In Mackenzie's best interest, of course, Angie had purposely arranged for John's cousin to be seated next to Mackenzie during the rehearsal dinner earlier that evening. The guy had been pleasant enough, and even though Angie insisted the successful entrepreneur was both wealthy and available, Mackenzie had barely said more than two words to the man during the entire evening.

Call her crazy, but Mackenzie knew she could look the whole world over and there still wouldn't be anyone for her but Alec.

And the fact that he didn't feel the same way about her broke her heart at least a dozen times a day.

But that's another story, Mackenzie reminded herself when the loudspeaker announced the timely arrival of Flight 603.

Leaving her seat in the waiting area, Mackenzie walked up to Gate B in time to see her mother and her father step into the terminal. After accepting hearty hugs first from her dad and then from her mom, Mackenzie had just pulled back from her mom's warm embrace when Barbara said, "Good heavens, Mackenzie, you look exhausted."

"It's been a busy day, Mother," Mackenzie reminded her with a sigh.

"Well, I'm sorry we had to take such a late flight, but your father had a business meeting first thing this morning."

"I couldn't have been here any sooner myself," Mackenzie assured them. "It was after eleven o'clock before I finally got away from the rehearsal dinner."

"And how is Angie holding up?" Barbara wanted to know as they headed for the baggage claim area.

"As well as can be expected, I guess."

"She isn't having second thoughts, I hope," Barbara said with a worried look on her face. "I mean this was a whirlwind romance, you know."

"She's not having second thoughts about John," Mackenzie said. "But you know Angie. She's frantic that something will go wrong and spoil her perfect ceremony."

"Well, if that's her only concern, then there shouldn't be a problem," Barbara insisted. "Angie's such a stickler for details, what could possibly go wrong?"

Dave Malone laughed at his wife's last statement. "I'll never understand you women in a million years," he said. "It's almost as if you attract disaster with all the fretting and worrying you do. But this isn't a perfect world, girls," he added. "And anyone who expects everything to be perfect all the time is only setting themselves up for a big disappointment."

"Well, *I* sure wouldn't want to be the poor soul responsible for fouling up Angie's perfect wedding," Mackenzie said with a laugh. "She'd have that person's head on a silver platter sitting right next to her five-tier wedding cake."

Dave laughed again, then reached out and removed two matching suitcases from the moving conveyor belt, but

Mackenzie didn't miss the collaborating look her mother was currently sending his way.

Clearing his throat, Dave said, "I know you invited us to stay with you while we're here in Charleston, princess, but your mother and I decided it might be better for you if we didn't impose."

Mackenzie started to protest, but Barbara quickly chimed in, "Your place is so small, dear, and even after the wedding you'll be working every day. Having us underfoot would only complicate matters."

"We made reservations at a bed-and-breakfast not far from your condo," Dave said.

"And you can have all day tomorrow without having to worry about entertaining us," Barbara pointed out.

"That really isn't necessary," Mackenzie said with a frown.

"Sure it is. You need your privacy, and we old married folks need ours," Barbara said, making Mackenzie blush slightly as they walked toward the parking garage.

And rather than risk having them change their minds, Mackenzie simply shrugged and said, "Whatever you say, guys, but you know you're perfectly welcome to stay with me."

However, as Mackenzie drove towards the quaint bed-and-breakfast her mother was rambling on about, she had to admit she was extremely grateful that her parents were being so considerate. She would have been happy to do it, but she certainly hadn't been looking forward to bedding down on her rather uncomfortable sofa during their stay. And as silly as she knew it was, just the thought of offering up her bed to her now reconciled parents had actually given her a mild case of the willies.

After all, Mackenzie had enough trouble sleeping in her own bed at night with intimate thoughts of Alec flying around the room. But thinking that her own parents would have possibly been doing God only knew what behind the mosquito netting on her big four-poster bed?

Well, for sanity's sake, Mackenzie wouldn't even allow her mind to wander in that direction.

MACKENZIE AWOKE ON Saturday morning to the terror-stricken shrieks of the soon-to-be bride. "You're not going to believe this," Angie wailed the second Mackenzie picked up her beside phone, "but the florist just called to say that the carnations and daisies turned out to be one shade *lighter* than the color I originally ordered."

"Sorry, but that's the price you pay for insisting on fresh flowers," Mackenzie made the mistake of saying with a yawn. "But believe me, Angie, no one else will notice."

"But I'll notice," Angie screamed in Mackenzie's ear. "Besides, I made it perfectly clear I wanted the carnations and the daisies to be the exact shade of purple as the bridesmaids' dresses. I even left a swatch of material so the idiot could make the perfect match. And what did the florist assure me? 'Why, that's no problem, Miss Crane, we'll be able to match your color exactly,' he said. And now he calls up on the day of the wedding to inform me that the color might be a full shade lighter? I just knew something would go wrong. I just knew it!"

Mackenzie let out a sigh, wondering why the florist had been stupid enough to even admit to such an oversight. But given Angie's reputation, Mackenzie also imagined the poor florist was literally shaking in his boots, wondering what on earth he was going to do with a shop full of purple daisies and carnations. In fact, Mackenzie suspected the only other flower-filled event that could even compete with Angie's order had to be the celebrated Rose

Bowl Parade that was held in Pasadena every New Year's Day.

"Didn't I tell you a crisis like this was going to happen?" Angie practically sobbed again. "And if I stop by the florist to see what can be done about *that* problem, I'll never make it to my salon appointment on time. If I'm not there early, there's no way I can have my manicure, my pedicure…"

"Don't worry. I'll handle it," Mackenzie broke in, though she had no idea what she could do short of taking a magic marker with her and personally coloring each bloom exactly one shade *darker*. "You go on to your salon appointment," Mackenzie added, "and I'll head to the florist."

"Thanks, Mackie," Angie said with a sigh of relief. "But you tell that shyster I'm not paying one cent for defective flowers. I want the shade I ordered. And I don't care if he has to send someone to outer Mongolia to get the right shade. Understand?"

"Got it," Mackenzie assured her best friend, but when she disconnected the call, Mackenzie briefly entertained the thought of volunteering for the trip to outer Mongolia herself. Especially if the early morning phone call from Angie was any indication of what the remainder of the day held in store for her.

With a loud sigh, Mackenzie pulled herself out of bed, then padded into her small kitchen to brew some coffee, hoping a jolt of caffeine would give her the energy she needed to come up with a solution to the current carnation crisis. Without the worry of having to entertain her parents for the day, Mackenzie had planned to take a long run on the beach and then get ready for the big event at her own leisure.

But now, of course, there were more pressing matters

to disrupt her peaceful morning. And a mad dash to the florist, which she doubted would produce any *acceptable* results, would have to be the first thing on her list.

"God, please just get us through this day," Mackenzie said aloud as she filled a cup with the dark liquid and swallowed a healthy gulp.

Her only saving grace was the knowledge that it was only ten hours away from countdown. And with that thought in mind, Mackenzie carried her coffee with her and headed for the shower, never once suspecting that the carnation crisis would be an infinitesimally small blip on the horizon compared to the full-force hurricane that planned to blow into Charleston later that afternoon.

ACCORDING TO THE itinerary the snotty ticket agent in Portland had printed out for Alec, he was scheduled to arrive in Atlanta, Georgia, at 11:15 Eastern Standard Time on Saturday morning. The problem was that at precisely 10:00 a.m. on that same sunny morning, the baggage handler and airplane mechanics' union had staged the largest strike to hit the airline industry since 1982.

And like a multitude of other bewildered holiday-bound passengers who were stranded at the giant hub of the South, Alec found himself in a total panic.

Rather than waste even a second standing in line when he already knew it could be hours before he found another flight to Charleston, Alec bolted as best he could in his condition through the terminal with a herd of other seasoned travelers in search of the nearest car rental agency. But even his good fortune at being one of the first people in line didn't mean Alec's problem had been immediately solved.

In fact, after one look at his compromised condition, the efficient rental agent informed Alec on the spot that renting a car to a man with one arm in a cast, and with only one eye left for visibility, was totally out of the question.

"But that's ridiculous," Alec argued. "I'm a pilot, dammit. I'm competent enough to carry passengers across the country coast to coast, and I'm definitely competent enough to drive a car."

Still unimpressed, the agent shook his head and said, "Look, we both know there's no way they'd let you in the cockpit of a plane in your condition any more than I'm going to look the other way and hand over the keys to one of our rental cars."

"Fine. Then I'll just take my business elsewhere," Alec said with a threatening look.

"Be my guest," the agent said. "But renting a car in your condition won't be any different at the next place, buddy. You can count on that."

Alec reluctantly dropped out of line and started back down the terminal glaring at his watch. The drive from Atlanta to Charleston would take a good five hours without any traffic problems, and it was already ll:30 a.m. And even if he left at that very moment, arriving in Charleston by five o'clock would be cutting it extremely close.

But what other choice did he have?

Hurrying through the terminal, Alec stopped at the first ATM he found. Minutes later he was standing outside, trying to hail a taxi from the long line of cabs that were slowly inching their way toward the main doors of the terminal.

Alec waved to the nearest taxi and limped in its direction, but the driver quickly shook his head and pointed to a nicely dressed couple standing only a short distance away from Alec on the sidewalk. Frowning, Alec walked toward the next taxi in line and received the same treatment when the driver took one look at his disheveled appearance before he revved the engine and eased the taxi forward to safety.

Tempted to throw himself on the next car hood and beg for mercy, Alec was surprised when an extremely battered green and white taxi suddenly came to a stop directly in front of him. A tall man with skin the color of midnight quickly pulled himself from the confines of the car, then hurried around to open the back passenger side door.

For a second, all Alec could do was stare at the man. He was dressed in the comfortable attire common to the Caribbean, wearing a wild print shirt and khaki shorts and sandals, and his dreadlocks sported a wide assortment of brightly colored beads. He smiled at Alec and his shiny ebony face disappeared behind a huge set of spectacular gleaming white teeth when he said in his thick Jamaican accent, "Rafe at your service, mon. Where are you going on dis fine Saturday morning?"

Rather than be concerned that Rafe's old wreck might not even make it out of the terminal parking area, Alec slid into the back seat of the taxi without a second thought, prompting another wide grin from his appreciative driver. Rafe closed his door, then ran back to the driver's side and quickly settled himself behind the wheel.

"I need you to take me to Charleston," Alec told his colorful rescuer as Rafe eased away from the curb.

"No problem, mon," Rafe assured him. "De plaza or de avenue?"

"The city," Alec told Rafe as if it were a perfectly reasonable request. "I want you to take me to Charleston, South Carolina."

Rafe's multicolored beads began tapping out a little tune as he quickly shook his head, but Alec didn't let his driver's first refusal deter him from his mission. Leaning forward, Alec fanned out five crisp one-hundred dollar bills under Rafe's nose like a professional card dealer.

"There's another five hundred in the deal if you get me to Charleston by five o'clock," Alec informed his now wide-eyed driver.

Rafe eagerly reached for the money, but Alec jerked the bills away. "Cash on delivery," Alec insisted.

Rafe hesitated for a second, then grinned his wide-toothed grin. "No problem, my friend. For dat type of money, Rafe will race you to de city of Charleston on de wings of de wind."

"That's the answer I wanted to hear," Alec told him, but when Rafe lurched forward and cut off several other taxis in order to take the lead out of the terminal, Alec realized Rafe's penchant for racing with *de* wind had probably caused most of *de* dents and *de* dings in *de* side of *de* cab.

But what the hell, Alec thought as Rafe slammed his foot down on the accelerator and zoomed away from the terminal. Wasn't a wild ride with the zealous Jamaican worth the gamble if it got him to the church on time?

And besides that, Alec reasoned, the odds that he would be involved in a plane crash *and* a car wreck all in the same week had to be pretty slim.

IT WAS TWO-THIRTY BEFORE Mackenzie finally got the flower situation firmly under control. Unable to console the hysterical florist, whom Angie had called repeatedly from the salon on her cell phone with threats of a lawsuit, it had finally been Mackenzie's decision to stop fretting over the daisies and carnations they couldn't change. Instead, Mackenzie decided to find some blasted bloom that *did* match the small swatch of purple material the poor man held in his trembling hand.

To Mackenzie's relief, the iris turned out to be the suitable flower of choice. And though it had taken both Mackenzie and the florist running all over Charleston to collect every available iris in the city, by adding a few iris blooms in with the sainted carnations and daisies the wedding arrangements had turned out to be absolutely breathtaking by anyone's standards.

Except the bride in question, of course.

Not that Angie wouldn't have to accept the choice Mackenzie had made, because Angie would. Just as Mackenzie had been forced to accept the fact that her perfect plan to spend a leisurely afternoon before the wedding had been tossed to the wayside once she took on the role of flower arranger extraordinaire. Now, Mackenzie would barely have time to jump in the shower and throw on her dress before she was expected to be at the chapel with a smile on her face.

Roaring into her parking space, the last thing Mackenzie needed was one of those disarming moments of sentimentality. But that's exactly what happened when Mackenzie glanced wistfully at the vacant space where Alec's Jaguar should have been. Without warning, a tidal wave of pent-up emotion washed over her the second she turned off the ignition. And all she could do was sit there and allow the quintessential downpour to run its course.

And why shouldn't she have a good cry? she kept asking herself.

Sure, she'd kept up a false bravado for Angie's sake, but there had been very few moments during the past weeks of hectic planning that Mackenzie hadn't felt it should have been her own wedding she was planning with such a fervor, and that she and Alec should have been the honeymooners who were sailing off for the Florida Keys for a full month of blissful lovemaking. But plans like those were as unlikely as Angie being satisfied with the substitute flower arrangements she would find waiting for her at the chapel. Telling herself it was only her frayed nerves that had caused her to give in to such hopeless romanticizing in the first place, Mackenzie wiped her eyes with her fingertips, then left the car and hurried toward her building.

Mackenzie knew Angie would only grumble over the modified flower arrangements, but she wouldn't forgive her maid of honor strolling nonchalantly into the church late, with puffy, swollen, red-rimmed eyes.

She'd have me killed right there on the spot, Mackenzie reminded herself, then turned her key in the lock and hurried into her bathroom to ready herself for the big event.

ALEC THOUGHT SURVIVING the plane crash had been a miracle, but he couldn't believe his good fortune when he found himself on the outskirts of Charleston that Saturday afternoon with almost forty-five minutes left to spare. And he owed his thanks for this miraculous occurrence to the grinning speed-demon with the braided hair, who had never slowed down under ninety miles an hour from the moment they hit the interstate in Atlanta.

Alec was even beginning to believe Rafe's claim that rubbing the shriveled rooster's foot hanging from the taxi's rearview mirror had brought them luck and helped speed them on their way.

In fact, he had just let himself relax when he happened to look behind them to see that what he thought was the light at the end of his tunnel was actually the South Carolina State Police.

"Damn," Alec swore, pounding his fist against the door panel as the ominous blue light continued to flash them a warning signal.

"Do you want Rafe to make a run through it?"

"I think you mean a run *for* it, Rafe," Alec corrected, "but no. You'd better pull over."

Rafe did as Alec instructed and seconds later two rather sullen policemen arrived at the side of the car. "What's the big hurry today, boys?" one of the officers asked as both men looked at Rafe, then through the back window at Alec, who could only guess what the long arm of the law had to be thinking.

They had stopped a speeding, broken-down taxi with Georgia license plates. They'd found some grinning dude with beads in his hair driving, and a shriveled rooster's foot hanging from the rearview mirror. And they'd found a passenger who resembled the hunchback Quasimodo with his arm held grotesquely out to his side in a cast and dressed in, of all things, stolen green surgical scrubs.

The possibilities were limitless, and Alec knew it. He and Rafe could be anything from drug dealers to circus performers. Alec only prayed Rafe didn't have any type of contraband inside the taxi if the officers did decide to search it.

"Driver's license and registration," Officer Grant, according to his name tag, demanded while the other officer moved back a bit further and spent his time giving Alec the once-over again through the back passenger's side window.

"What's an Atlanta cabbie doing all the way down here in Charleston?" Officer Grant wanted to know when Rafe produced the necessary papers.

"My flight out of Atlanta was canceled because of the airline strike," Alec spoke up from the back seat. "And I have to be at the Stonehenge Chapel on Meeting Street before five o'clock this evening."

"What for? To hear your last rites?" Officer Grant

asked with a chuckle. "Because you sure look like death warmed over to me."

After the two policemen shared a good laugh at Alec's expense, Alec said, "I have to be at the chapel for my wedding." The obvious lie prompted a frightened look from Rafe, but Alec ignored it and added, "My cabbie was just trying to get me to the church on time."

Officer Grant looked at Alec, then back at his partner. "I think this smart guy is trying to con us, Joe," Officer Grant said with a sneer. "He must think we're a couple of real morons if he expects us to believe he's getting married dressed like that."

Common sense told Alec to just drop it while he still had the chance, but the two obviously bored officers were quickly eating up what little time Alec had left. "My tux is at the church," Alec said as calmly as if be believed the second lie himself. "And we are running late. Could you please just write out the speeding ticket so we can be on our way? I sure don't want to keep my pretty bride waiting at the altar."

The two officers exchanged knowing looks before handing back Rafe's credentials. "You know, I think it might be a good idea if we gave this anxious groom a police escort to the wedding he doesn't want to be late for," Officer Grant said with a rather sadistic smile.

Alec paled. "Uh, I sure don't want to put you officers to any trouble. If you'll just let us be on our way, I'm sure we can make it on time."

"Did you hear that, Joe?" Officer Grant said, elbowing his partner in the ribs. "The groom doesn't want to put two idiots like us to any trouble."

Alec cringed when Officer Joe bent down and looked through the window at Alec again. "Yeah, isn't that real sweet of him? Wonder if he's smart enough to know the penalty for lying to a police officer?''

Alec wiped away a bead of sweat before it rolled into his one good eye. ''Of course, if you guys have the time to give us a police escort...''

''We'll *make* the time,'' Officer Grant assured Alec, and minutes later Rafe was racing with the wind again behind a black and white police cruiser with a wide-open siren.

''Mon, Rafe don't want no part of no jail, don't ya know,'' Rafe said as he sent Alec a nervous glance over his shoulder. ''And de jail will be a home for you and for me if you don't come back out of dat church with de bride.''

''She might be kicking and screaming, Rafe, but I promise you, I intend to come out of that church with the bride,'' Alec assured his driver with a confident pat on the shoulder.

Rafe nodded and mumbled something in his native patois, but Alec caught Rafe also reaching over and giving his rooster's foot another hearty rub. A short time later, the siren stopped blaring and the police cruiser came to a stop almost three full blocks away from the church.

Alec leaned forward in his seat, amazed at the long line of cars that were already parked on both sides of the street. In the distance he could even see a uniformed police officer standing in the middle of the street, trying to direct the bottleneck of traffic that was trying to park in the vicinity of the Stonehenge Church.

''Dis must be one big wedding, mon,'' Rafe said, reading Alec's thoughts.

When the cruiser finally came in line with the traffic officer, the fellow officers chatted for a second before the traffic officer waved them through and directed them to a vacant space directly in front of the church. A worried Rafe followed close behind, then pulled into a vacant space directly behind the cruiser. Alec was still trying to figure out the next plausible plan of action when Rafe suddenly turned around and held out his palm.

"Cash on delivery," Rafe said, sending a nervous glance back over his shoulder at the two officers who were now walking in their direction. "Just as we agreed."

Alec reached into the pocket of his scrubs for his money clip at the same time Officer Grant opened Alec's door and took him by his good arm. "Better hurry," Grant insisted as he helped Alec out of the taxi. "We sure wouldn't want the man of the hour to get married in those scrubs."

Alec managed to pull his arm free, then looked back through the open door at Rafe's forlorn face. "Wait for me," Alec said, deciding it probably wouldn't be wise under the circumstances to flash a thousand dollars under the surly officer's nose.

"Don't worry, your cabbie's going to wait right here," Officer Grant said with a laugh. "In fact, we're *all* going to wait right here and pay our respects to the happy bride and groom. Aren't we, Joe?"

"I wouldn't miss this for the world," Officer Joe agreed and laughed when Officer Grant gave Alec a little push in the direction of the stone steps that led up to the church.

Alec straightened his shoulders as best as he could with his arm in the ridiculous cast, tried to smooth his rumpled green surgical smock, then raked his fingers through what was left of his hair. He then marched up the steps with several other last-minute stragglers, who were all now gaping in his direction with open mouths. Holding his breath, Alec was only one step away from making it inside the church when an able-bodied usher suddenly stepped forward, blocking his path.

"The soup kitchen isn't open today, buster. You'll have to come back tomorrow," the goon in the tuxedo informed Alec as he crossed arms the size of tree trunks across his massive chest.

Alec sent an anxious glance over his shoulder, relieved to see that his captors were currently talking over old times with their traffic cop buddy. "Look, I'm not some homeless person looking for a free meal," Alec told the guy desperately. "I'm here for the wedding."

"Not dressed like that, you aren't," the bruiser informed Alec with a confident smirk.

"Listen, *buster*," Alec said, pronouncing the word with the exact inflection his adversary had used, "I'm a good friend of the groom. He expects me to be at this wedding."

"A good friend, hey?" Mr. Muscle-bound snorted. "Well, I just happen to be the groom's first cousin, and I know for a fact that John would have my hide if I let some beat-up reject like you inside to stink up the church."

Alec was tempted to just push his way past the idiot, but he quickly gave up that idea when Officer Grant suddenly called out from behind him, "Hey, what's the problem?"

Alec looked back at the scowling policeman and waved, then surprised John's cousin by reaching out and pumping his hand up and down several times. "Just finding out where I need to go, that's all," Alec called out as he headed back down the church steps, but when both officers started walking in his direction Alec made a mad dash around the side of the church and found a hiding place behind the heavy shrubbery that was planted along the side of the building.

"Where in the hell did he go?" Officer Grant wanted to know when he and his partner bounded around the side of the church after Alec.

"Damned if I know," Officer Joe said, "but it's not like he won't stand out in the crowd."

"Well, one of us needs to sit on that cabbie," Grant grumbled. "My guess is he'll try to get back to the car."

"I'm on my way, now," Officer Joe said. "Call me if you need any help when you find him."

"If I can't take down a man with his arm in a cast and only one eye open, then I'd better quit the police force," Grant snorted in his partner's direction, then lumbered down the sidewalk in search of his soon-to-be prisoner.

Alec waited several seconds, then parted the limbs of the thick spruce shrub he'd been hiding behind in time to see Officer Grant round the corner at the back of the building. Hurrying from his hiding place, Alec made a beeline for the side door of the church and when he was safely inside he headed for the stairs with a grimace. He had no idea exactly where the stairs would take him, but Alec knew the music filtering down from the upper floor of the church wouldn't be hard to follow.

Each step he climbed tortured every muscle in his still bruised body, but when the wedding march suddenly kicked into high gear, Alec fought back the pain and took the stairs two at a time. He had just opened the door at the top of the stairs and stepped into the main vestibule of the church when he caught a glimpse of a long white train disappearing through the doors that led into the main chapel.

Without a second thought, Alec lumbered forward.

If he lost his courage now, he would also end up losing the woman he loved.

And Alec hadn't spent the last twenty-four hours traveling across country under the most trying circumstances to get this close and back out now.

10

MACKENZIE FELT A TEAR roll down her cheek as she and six hundred guests watched the absolutely breathtaking bride float effortlessly down the aisle on her proud father's arm. As far as Mackenzie was concerned, there had never been a more beautiful bride. Nor had there ever been a more perfect wedding, Mackenzie decided at the same time some type of scuffle broke out in the back of the church.

Mackenzie's eyes darted from the panic-stricken look on Angie's face to the poor bandaged soul who was being dragged out of the church by a uniformed police officer. But when a blood-curdling *Mackenzie* echoed through the church in the same tortured way Stanley called out for Stella in *A Streetcar Named Desire,* Mackenzie actually dropped her bridal bouquet.

Alec! Mackenzie's mind screamed as the doors banged loudly behind the man she loved and the officer who was dragging him away. *I have to get to Alec,* her brain kept insisting, but there was standing room only in the chamber of the church.

Mackenzie ran forward, knowing her only option was to escape *up* the very aisle that the rattled bride was currently trying to walk *down.*

"I'm so sorry, Angie," Mackenzie mumbled as she brushed past her startled best friend, and she might have gotten away with a barely noticeable escape if the heel of

Mackenzie's pump hadn't tangled in the sheer netting of the twelve-foot train that was attached to Angie's tiny twenty-two-inch waist.

It was Angie who screamed Mackenzie in agony this time, but Angie's father thankfully reached out and caught his daughter before she fell backward in the floor. Mackenzie, on the other hand, never once slowed down. She simply kicked off the tangled shoe and bolted for the door in a hip-hop run that brought her outside the church in time to see a bruised and battered man who hardly resembled Alec at all being whisked away in a police cruiser that had been parked at the curb in front of the church.

"Where are they taking him?" Mackenzie yelled to an officer who was standing below the church steps talking to a tall black man with a head full of braids and beads.

"Downtown. To the police station," the traffic officer called back.

"You know dis mon called Alec?" the black man asked as he hurried up the steps in her direction.

"Yes, I know him," Mackenzie said, now completely confused. "Who are you?"

A beautiful set of white teeth immediately flashed back at her. "It is I, Rafe, who brought Alec to here from Atlanta."

"Atlanta?" Mackenzie echoed. "What on earth was Alec doing in Atlanta? And exactly what's happened to Alec, anyway? He looked like he'd been run through a meat grinder."

Rafe shook his head sadly. "De injuries, ah, yes. Dose happen during Alec's near-fatal plane crash," Rafe said, mimicking Alec word for word.

"Alec was in a plane crash?" Mackenzie gasped.

"Oh, yes," Rafe said, nodding his head up and down and setting his beads in motion.

Suddenly suspicious, Mackenzie asked, "Okay, mister. How do you know so much about Alec?"

Rafe grinned. "Riding five hours with a heartsick man gave Rafe plenty time to learn about Alec. Poor Alec, he survived de plane crash only to find dat de woman he loved was marrying dat no good snake, John Stanley. And since he could not stop de wedding, his poor heart will be broken. Right? Which is why his new best friend, Rafe, must find Alec very quick."

"Don't let him fool you, lady," the traffic officer who had obviously been listening to their conversation said when he walked up beside them. "This cabbie just finished telling me the guy you're talking about owed him a thousand dollars. And that's why he wants to find his new best friend *very quick.*"

Mackenzie's mind was reeling with so much information, she literally had to shake her head to clear it. "Okay," she said looking directly at Rafe again, "let me get this straight. Alec was involved in a plane crash, and after the crash…"

"Alec realized he could no longer live without de woman he loved," Rafe chimed in with a sad look on his face. "But when my poor friend call to tell her, dey say she would not be back until after de wedding."

Mackenzie laughed, causing Rafe to point a stern finger in her direction. "Dis is not funny," Rafe scolded. "In my country, to laugh at someone's misfortune can bring you very bad karma."

"Believe me, this is much funnier than you think it is," Mackenzie said and laughed again. "And if you'll go get your taxi, I'll tell you why it's so funny on the way to the police station."

"Police station?" a shrill voice echoed from behind her and Mackenzie turned around to find her scowling mother coming down the church steps with Mackenzie's shoe in her hand. "I demand to know what's going on, Mackenzie, and I demand to know it now," Barbara Malone said when she stopped on the step above Mackenzie.

Mackenzie opened her mouth to speak, but never got the chance.

"And who was that horrible creature who stormed into the church screaming your name? Why, the very idea of you running out of the church like that. Not to mention the fact that you practically dragged poor Angie out with you. Thank God, her father caught her when he did. Angie could have broken a leg or something. And wouldn't that have been wonderful for her and John on their honeymoon?"

"Mother...."

"Of course, I'm sure everyone in the entire church is so bumfuzzled right now, I doubt anyone will even notice when the ceremony takes place. And poor little Angie. Why, I don't know how the child has the fortitude to stand there in front of all those people long enough to exchange her vows. If Angie decides she never wants to speak to you again, I personally wouldn't blame her. But right now I want you to put on your shoe and march back in there and apologize to your best friend and all of her guests who just watched you make a complete fool of yourself."

Knowing it was pointless to argue with the queen of verbal debate, Mackenzie sent an anxious glance at the battered green and white taxi waiting at the curb, then she reached out and quickly plucked her shoe from her angry mother's hand. "I'll apologize to Angie later, Mother," Mackenzie said as she hurried down the steps. "But right now I'm going to the police station and post bail for that horrible creature who was screaming my name."

"Post bail?" Barbara called after her. "You'll do no

such thing, Mackenzie Malone. You get back here this very minute! Do you hear me?''

Mackenzie hurried to the waiting taxi and slid into the back seat, and when she gave the signal Rafe wasted no time pulling away from the curb. ''Mon, dat is one very mad lady, don't ya know,'' Rafe said, setting his beads in motion again as he shook his braided head.

''Unfortunately, I do know, Rafe. She's my mother,'' Mackenzie said, then let out a long sigh and never looked back.

ALEC SAT ON HIS SIDE OF the jail cell trying to ignore his new cell mate who stank of cheap whiskey and was trying to light an old cigarette butt with a badly shaking hand.

''Man, you look like hell,'' the old geezer had the nerve to say.

''Yeah, you should see the other guy,'' Alec mumbled back, knowing it was pointless trying to explain his current predicament.

Besides, who would believe him?

He had survived a plane crash that left him with a mild concussion, his arm broken in three places, sixteen stitches in the top of his head and a swollen black eye, only to find that the woman he loved intended to marry his old high school rival. He'd then escaped from the hospital in stolen scrubs so he could make a mad dash from one end of the country to the other in order to stop the wedding, only to find that the last portion of his flight had been canceled because of an airline strike. And then, he had hooked up with a Jamaican cabbie who thought he was a race car driver, got arrested by two cops who were having such a slow day they decided to torture him for amusement, and when he was only two steps away from grabbing the woman he loved and carrying her out of the church over the shoulder that wasn't encompassed in a cast, he'd been dragged off to jail for disturbing the peace.

The whole thing sounded like a poorly written plot for a bad movie. And that's exactly how Alec felt at the moment. He felt like a helpless victim trapped in a horror flick with nothing left in his future but a long stint in prison for disturbing the peace. And maybe prison was exactly what he did deserve for being so stupid, Alec told himself as he lay on his bunk and stared at the concrete ceiling.

Because he *had* been stupid.

He had been stupid to declare his love for Mackenzie one minute, then skip town the next. Hell, he'd even been too stupid to call her during all these months and apologize. First for snooping behind her back. And second for leaving town instead of staying so they could work things out.

Yes, he'd been stupid, stupid, stupid. He'd allowed his bruised ego to take control, and he'd run for cover like the coward that he was. And the fact that Mackenzie was now being spirited away for a sex-filled honeymoon only gave another sharp twist to the knife that was buried in the center of Alec's stupid heart.

"So? What are you in for, partner?" his cell mate asked when Alec let out an agonized sigh.

"Stupidity," Alec tossed back without thinking.

"Your smart mouth got you in trouble, did it?" the old guy quizzed, but before Alec could answer, a uniformed officer appeared at the cell door.

"Come on, Southerland. Someone's made your bail."

Alec jerked himself to a sitting position, wincing slightly at his sudden movement. "My bail?" Alec asked in disbelief.

But who could have posted his bail? He hadn't even

been allowed to make his *one* phone call yet. Not that Alec had been particularly eager to call Josh with news that his escapade had landed him in jail just like Josh predicted it would.

"Big black guy with beads in his hair," the officer provided to clear up the mystery.

"Thank God for Rafe," Alec said, then wasted no time being let out of his cage.

MACKENZIE WAS STILL standing in the police captain's office when she glanced through the glass partition and saw Alec enter the next room from behind the barred door. And Dear God, he did look awful. So horrible, in fact, Mackenzie was amazed that her mangled beloved was able to stand on his own two feet without any assistance.

He was still pumping Rafe's hand furiously when she strolled into the room, and for a moment Mackenzie feared Rafe really *would* have to help Alec keep standing.

"Mackenzie?" he stuttered as if *she* were the one who was unrecognizable.

"Hi, Alec," she said casually as she propped herself against the doorjamb.

"But…but what are *you* doing here?" came his next shocked question.

Mackenzie put her finger thoughtfully to her cheek and shook her head as if she were thoroughly confused herself. "You know, it was the strangest thing. I was standing at the front of the church, watching my best friend walk down the aisle so she could marry the man of her dreams, and…"

"Your *best friend?*" Alec interrupted, but Mackenzie ignored his question completely and continued her story.

"And then this crazy person ran into the church. He

started screaming my name when the police officer tried to remove him from the sanctuary.''

"A crazy person, huh?" Alec wanted to know, and though Mackenzie thought Alec was smiling, she couldn't be sure with the twisted way Alec's lip was curved up in a snarl.

"Oh, yes," Mackenzie assured him. "I'm sure the poor man was crazy. And he looked absolutely dreadful. Like he'd been run over by a train or something."

"Maybe he'd been in a plane crash," Alec volunteered, playing along with her little game now.

"Hmm, I guess it could have been a plane crash," Mackenzie agreed.

"And maybe this crazy person thought *you* were the one who was walking down the aisle to marry the man of your dreams."

"Me?" Mackenzie gasped, feigning surprise. "But that's impossible, Alec. You see, I'm madly in love with this guy who ran off to Oregon and left me behind."

Though Mackenzie had no idea Alec could move that fast in his current condition, he closed the distance between them in the blink of an eye.

"Alec, be careful! Your arm," Mackenzie protested when he pulled her soundly against him, but Alec ignored her warning and gave her a half-lipped kiss that was so passionate, Rafe and every other officer in their vicinity whistled on cue.

"Say you'll marry me," Alec whispered when their lips broke apart.

"Do you want kids?" Mackenzie was quick to ask.

"At least a dozen," Alec assured her.

"Then I'll marry you under one condition," Mackenzie told him with a grin. "We have to elope. Right now. This very minute."

Alec frowned. "Before you change your mind?"

"No, before Angie hires a hit man to kill both of us for ruining her perfect wedding."

Alec grabbed Mackenzie and kissed her again so forcefully, Rafe clapped his hands with glee. "Rafe loves dese happy beginnings," he beamed, making both Alec and Mackenzie laugh.

"I think you mean happy endings," Alec said, but Rafe shook his head and said, "Oh, no, mon. For de two of you, it will be happy beginnings. Rafe, he is certain."

"Then how about giving us the name of a good wedding chapel in Jamaica?" Alec said, pulling Mackenzie close.

"For you, my friend, Rafe will do much better," Rafe declared, holding up the fist of bills Alec had just paid him. "Rafe will go with you himself to his homeland and be your own personal wedding guide."

"MACKENZIE? WHERE ON earth are you?" Barbara Malone demanded, prompting Mackenzie to hold the phone away from her ear until the voice on the other end of the line calmed down. "You ruin your best friend's wedding, then you disappear. Then your father and I return to the bed-and-breakfast and find your house key with a note that only says 'take care of your grandcat. I'll call you later.' Do you have any idea how worried your father and I have been about you? I swear, if I didn't know better I'd think you were on drugs!"

"I'm not on drugs, Mother, I'm in Jamaica."

"Jamaica?" Barbara yelled.

"And I'm getting married. To that demented creature who stormed into the church screaming my name," Mackenzie said, then placed the phone on the bedside table in her hotel room and busied herself slipping on the colorful pink and green island sarong she had chosen for her wedding dress.

"Have you completely lost your mind? I thought I'd raised you better than that, Mackenzie. But obviously I haven't. Why, the very idea that you would run off...."

Mackenzie put the phone down again and pulled a comb through her dark hair, then tucked the gorgeous island orchid Alec had bought for her gently behind one ear.

"You know I've always counted on giving you a huge wedding with all the trimmings and..."

Down went the phone again, but after applying a touch of lipstick and assessing her appearance in the mirror one last time, Mackenzie snapped her compact shut and picked up the phone.

"Listen, Mother," Mackenzie said, interrupting Barbara's noisy outburst. "I love you and Daddy to death, but Alec and I want a *private* ceremony."

"Well, you'd better hope it's a *private* ceremony," Barbara scoffed. "I doubt even you would have the guts to stand before a crowd of people with a groom who looks like he's a candidate for a handicapped poster."

"Why, Mother," Mackenzie said, pretending to be shocked. "I thought you'd be pleased."

"Pleased? Pleased about what?" Barbara demanded.

"Pleased that the man I'm marrying today won't be *too* handsome," Mackenzie said and laughed.

Barbara was still ranting and raving, but Mackenzie calmly placed the receiver back on the hook, knowing that her mother would eventually calm down. She always did. And especially when she found out later that Mackenzie and Alec had decided to throw a big reception when they returned from their honeymoon so that both sets of parents and the rest of their friends and family wouldn't feel left out.

Thankfully, Mackenzie didn't even have to worry about a hit man possibly following them to Jamaica. Angie, who was never too far away from her cell phone, had been tracked down earlier in the day and Mackenzie had promised her everything short of her first born child if she would only forgive her for ruining her perfect wedding. Surprisingly, Angie had been so excited about Mackenzie and Alec eloping she had made Mackenzie promise she and Alec would join them in the Keys in a few weeks for some heavy-duty double-honeymooning partying.

And so, with a wonderful new life with Alec stretching out before her and a smile on her face, the lovely bride left her hotel room and went in search of her patiently waiting groom.

She found him a few minutes later, standing on the beach with Rafe and a white-collared minister who was one of Rafe's distant cousins. Mackenzie smiled and waved as she padded barefoot across the sand in their direction.

Alec waved back.

He was barefoot himself and clad in a simple pair of khaki shorts and a brightly printed topical shirt that helped camouflage his bulky cast. His sunglasses and an old Panama hat Rafe had loaned him hid Alec's swollen eye and his partly shaved head.

I think he's beautiful, Mackenzie decided with a grin, then took her place beside the man she would promise to love at least a century past forever.

The backdrop for their ceremony was a spectacular tropical sunset while the gentle rush of the ocean, with its white-tipped waves foaming around their ankles served as the music. Even their guest list was limited. Only Rafe, the minister and a few graceful seagulls soaring above them in a ceremonial flight witnessed the joyous occasion.

"Happy beginnings, my love," Alec said as he took her hand in his. When the beauty and her beastly looking groom turned to face each other, their sacred vows were filled with the same miraculous love that had guided them together from the first moment they met.

Much later that evening, long after they'd reached the thatch-roofed honeymoon hut Rafe had reserved for them on a secluded part of the island, Mackenzie's satisfied sigh filtered through the thin bamboo shades covering their bedroom window and out into the peaceful tropical night air.

"Oooh, Alec," she said with a giggle. "It really *is* worth mentioning, after all.

Princes...Princesses...
London Castles...New York Mansions...
To live the life of a royal!

In 2002, Harlequin Books lets you escape to a
world of royalty with these royally themed titles:

Temptation:
January 2002—*A Prince of a Guy* (#861)
February 2002—*A Noble Pursuit* (#865)

American Romance:
The Carradignes: American Royalty (Editorially linked series)
March 2002—*The Improperly Pregnant Princess* (#913)
April 2002—*The Unlawfully Wedded Princess* (#917)
May 2002—*The Simply Scandalous Princess* (#921)
November 2002—*The Inconveniently Engaged Prince* (#945)

Intrigue:
The Carradignes: A Royal Mystery (Editorially linked series)
June 2002—*The Duke's Covert Mission* (#666)

Chicago Confidential
September 2002—*Prince Under Cover* (#678)

The Crown Affair
October 2002—*Royal Target* (#682)
November 2002—*Royal Ransom* (#686)
December 2002—*Royal Pursuit* (#690)

Harlequin Romance:
June 2002—*His Majesty's Marriage* (#3703)
July 2002—*The Prince's Proposal* (#3709)

Harlequin Presents:
August 2002—*Society Weddings* (#2268)
September 2002—*The Prince's Pleasure* (#2274)

Duets:
September 2002—*Once Upon a Tiara/Henry Ever After* (#83)
October 2002—*Natalia's Story/Andrea's Story* (#85)

 Celebrate a year of royalty with
Harlequin Books!
Available at your favorite retail outlet.

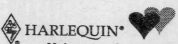

COOPER'S CORNER

The newest continuity from Harlequin
Books continues in September 2002 with

AFTER DARKE
by *USA Today* bestselling author
Heather MacAllister

Check-in: A blind date goes from bad to worse for
small-town plumber Bonnie Cooper and city-bred columnist
Jaron Darke. When they witness a mob hit outside a
restaurant, they are forced to hide out at Twin Oaks.
Their cover: they're engaged!

Checkout: While forced to live together in close
quarters, these two opposites soon find one thing
in common: *passion!*

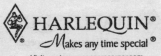

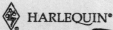

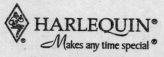